THIRD WISH

A NOVEL IN FIVE PARTS

PARTS
3, 4 & 5

by Robert Fulghum

Willow Bader's Book

2·11·14

Third Wish, Volume Two
Part Three: If You Love Me Still, Will You Love Me Moving?
Part Four: Waltzing the Bull
Part Five: Third Wish Granted

FIRST EDITION (English Language), 2009
Previously published in The Czech Republic by Argo Publishers, 2005, 2006

Library of Congress Control Number: 2008937176

ISBN-13 (2-vol. set): 978-1-60830-043-3

Manufactured in China

Slipcase and Book Jacket Illustration: Digital composite by Barbara Witt of work by Karen Lewis, Margaret Allen Dougherty, and Gretchen Batcheller

Book and Package Design: Barbara Witt

Copyediting: Kathy Bradley

10 9 8 7 6 5 4 3 2 1

becker&mayer! Books
11120 NE 33rd Place, Ste. 101
Bellevue, Washington 98004
www.beckermayer.com

Parts Three & Four - Tracks 6-12

Written and Performed by Barbara Lamb

(with the exception of Track 12, co-written by E. Scott Esbeck and Barbara Lamb)

6 - The Really, Really Green Waltz 3:06

7 - Wonko's Waltz 2:44

8 - White Rabbit Suit 2:21

9 - Ariadne's Air 3:20

10 - Waltzing the Bull 2:58

11 - The Saddest Waltz 3:29

12 - The Waltz of Strangers 5:04

Part Five - Tracks 13-21

Written and Performed by Cosy Sheridan

13 - Eros & Psyche 3:42

14 - Three Wishes 2:47

15 - Night Train to Barcelona 2:40

16 - Jumwillies 5:03

17 - The Queen of Queen Anne Hill 2:49

18 - Sweet Sunday Morning 2:08

19 - Left/Right/Surprise *a cappella* 2:21

20 - Left/Right/Surprise 3:36

21 - Walk On 2:57

PART THREE

IF YOU LOVE ME STILL, WILL YOU LOVE ME MOVING?

Including

The Illustrations of Margaret Allen Dougherty

The Music of Barbara Lamb

SNAPSHOTS

IN SEATTLE, ALLYSON OCTAVIA RILEY - Alice - is in a salon having her white hair dyed black. She would not stay long in Seattle. No matter how the "spy story" might unfold, she would go on to Japan as soon as possible, then to Athens, and then be in Crete by October.

But first, her hair: Black. And short.

Her encounters with Alex and Max-Pol opened a door she had been keeping shut. The Man/Woman door. Today she has been considering new names to use when she walks through that door: Padua, Aalis, Maady, Andalucia, and Cid-Artha are on the list.

But why no male names? Her Kabuki actor friend, Zenkichi, has no problem using female names or playing women's roles onstage. Why not male names for herself?

As long as she was having her white hair dyed black, she might as well have it cut very, very short. Mannish. And when the hair grows out, it will be half black and half white. Unique.

IN CRETE, KOSTAS LIAPAKIS is playing backgammon with fierce concentration, shouting "Nai, Nai (Yes, Yes)," at the tumbling dice. He felt abandoned by fortune when his mother died and his "cousins," Max-Pol and Alex, went away. But today fortune has returned - he cannot seem to lose. He owns the board and the dice and the luck. He kisses the dice, laughs, and rolls again. Yes! Yes!

IN ATHENS, MARIA MICHAELIDIS, the companion of Polydora Vlachou, has found a photograph of Max-Pol Millay on Polydora's desk. She looks at the picture in the spirit of the evil eye: with jealousy and envy.

She says aloud, "May you have bad luck."

She turns the picture over, spits on her finger, draws an X, and returns the photograph to its place on the desk.

"There," she says. "Stay far away, or there will be trouble for you."

1

IN TOKYO, THE EMPEROR OF JAPAN grieves over the discontent of the crown prince, his beloved son and heir. The crown princess has not produced a son. True, she has given birth to a daughter. But a woman cannot succeed to the throne. Can she? The emperor and his son mourn their common dilemma, all caught, like the nation, between tradition and the future. How can destiny be rearranged?

IN KYOTO, the emperor's subjects, Morioka and Iwai Hanshiro XI, ask the same questions, on a much smaller scale. Morioka ponders how the ancient art of Japanese tattoo can adjust to the modern mania for trivial body decoration. And Matsui Zenkichi, the actor, puzzles daily on how classical Kabuki theater can accommodate the tastes of modern Japan.

WAITING OFFSTAGE for their cue to play their parts in the unfolding of destiny are Jackson "Baba" O'Rourke, Nelson Bellingham, and India-What Millay. The spirit of the English writer of nonsense, Edward Lear, will be called back for an encore.

MEANWHILE, ELLIOT BROWNELL, "Wonko," is sitting in his pub-office, The Boat, in Thrupp, pondering an invitation to dinner with Max-Pol and Alex. Why is he invited? What do they want from him? Shall he go as Wonko the Weird or Wonko the Sane or just as Elliot? Or all three?

Whose company do they want?

MAX-POL MILLAY AND ALEX XENOPOULOUDAKIS are on The Oxford Canal aboard the *Ariadne*, about to begin the inevitable conversation they have both been anticipating and avoiding.

THE REALLY, REALLY GREEN WALTZ

TWO MEN AFLOAT

Alice makes men want to break rules. For her, you consider changing plans, committing indiscretions, and acting recklessly.

She makes you think back with pleasure on experiences with her that never took place, but might have been . . .

Alex did not say these words aloud. He had written them in the journal of his mind, and repeatedly polished them to say to someone sometime. But not now. And certainly not to Max-Pol.

There are truths that cannot be told.

Besides, when Max-Pol had said, Tell me about your two weeks with Alice, it was a vague enquiry - an invitation offered by one gentleman to another. An opportunity, not an investigation.

*

Max-Pol and Alex are sitting in dappled shade in the stern of the canal boat *Ariadne* in the late afternoon light of a fine day in May, thoughtfully drinking their way through Alex's last bottle of Greek wine made from the black Aghiorghitiko grapes of Nemea.

They passed through the lock at Duke's Cut, and will walk back to The Trout Inn for dinner. The first day afloat has gone well. Max-Pol has quickly learned the ways of the canal, the boat, and its captain. Showered and changed into clean clothes, the two men sit, contented, ready for conversation but reluctant to be the first to speak.

The humid calm is punctuated with rumblings of thunder in the clouds slowly floating down from the far-off Cotswolds. From time to time, three mallard drakes shatter the peacefulness of the canal with squawking assaults on a small hen and her scattered, peeping brood of ducklings. Avian love is not tender.

When the water became a mirror again, the landscape repeated itself upside-down, with Max-Pol and Alex and *Ariadne* in the picture. The power of the stillness siphoned thoughts and conversation into it.

Silence prevails.

Alice is foremost in the minds of the two men. Each one knows her in unique ways under unique circumstances. But each is missing long chapters of the Book of Alice.

She had left that morning. Now the two men would spend a week together on the Oxford Canal. Of course, the subject of Alice must inevitably be addressed.

"How was your time with Alice?" asked Max-Pol.

"Well, then," began Alex. As always, this opening signaled both that he could speak at length on a subject and that he wished to respect the patience of the listener. And he truly wished to respect the feelings of Max-Pol. He could not tell Max-Pol the whole truth and nothing but the truth. Alex was grateful not to be asked a specific question, especially one that might raise suspicions about what might have occurred between him and Alice.

There are truths that cannot be told.

Alex had slept with Alice.

They had made love.

But both phrases were opaque euphemisms that did not apply to the truth of the situation. Yes, they had been asleep in the same bed. And yes, they had constructed something like love. Yes. But there had been no sexual contact, even though they had been naked in bed. They were not lovers in that way. And would not ever be. But there was this nameless interweaving of their deepest knowing - this singularity of bonding. How could Alex explain that to anyone? Who would believe it?

"Well, then," repeated Alex, and stopped. Fearful of what a long silence might imply, or of saying too much, he quickly sidestepped: "*You* tell *me* about Alice, Max-Pol. You have had an ongoing relationship with her, albeit at a distance - this Witness thing - but I could not help but notice when she was here a certain *convergence*. How shall I put it simply? Falling into something serious - perhaps - love, yes?"

"Oh, no," said Max-Pol. "No, it's not like that."

"But . . ."

"You spent two weeks with her, Alex. You must know that nothing normal applies to any relationship with Alice. After seeing her at Waterloo, I went away realizing how strongly I was drawn to her. I didn't want to be or expect to be, but I was. The Witness arrangement was in total disarray. And that troubled me - disappointed me."

"Why?"

"Before Waterloo, our paths seemed parallel. After Waterloo, we seemed to be on a collision course. Your word is apt - convergence. No longer just Witnesses. *Participants*. And I went off to Seattle expecting I would come back to whatever might happen next with Alice. I admit I was very conflicted in my feelings, but . . ."

"And today?"

"Today I am derailed, blindsided, blown off course. Pick one. But not only by Alice."

"Who else? Not by me, I hope."

"Of course not. By someone you don't know. Before I talk about Alice, I need to tell you about my cousin."

"Cousin?"

"My cousin. Her name is India-What."

COUSIN

"What? Cousin? India-What?" Alex raised his eyebrows.

"My aunt - her mother - named her India, and when family and friends were told, they responded the same way you did: 'What?' So, ever after she has been known in the family as India-What. Her full name is India Iris Millay."

"Ah," said Alex. "Iris is a Greek name, you know. The goddess of the rainbow, and a messenger of the Gods. Homer mentions her in the *Iliad*."

"Well, for me, she was a messenger of the devil. You must have seen little girls like her - the ones who chase boys by the time they can walk. And the boys responded because she was also red-haired, blue-eyed, freckled, brash, and cute.

"Our families shared a beach cottage in Oregon, and we spent every summer together when we were growing up. She was my only cousin. We were inseparable. She was two years older than I, and always way ahead of me in the games little boys and girls play. India-What introduced me to 'Show Me Yours and I'll Show You Mine,' 'Doctor And Nurse,' and 'Kiss Me.' She passed through puberty early and made me fondle her when we slept out in a tent on the beach. And when I finally hit puberty, she fondled me and taught me how to masturbate."

"Did you. . .?"

"No. We never had intercourse, but it was always a close thing. And the older we got the more attracted we became, which was a little strange because, when she grew up, most people would not call her attractive. They thought of her as *funny-looking*."

"You mean deformed?" asked Alex.

"No. I mean that literally. She has a round face, red cheeks, a red nose, freckles, and a wild mop of naturally orange-red hair. When her face is relaxed, she looks like a clown - her eyebrows arch high, her eyes are large, and the corners of her mouth turn up into a natural smile. Most people's faces look solemn or unhappy when no emotion is being expressed. But India-What looks *funny* - as if she's amused by some private joke, even when she's not in a good mood. Most people – men especially – are put off by her clowny looks.

"Too bad they only see the façade of India-What. She has one of the most beautiful bodies I've ever seen – and I've seen quite a few as a physician. Inside that body is a beautiful human being.

"There's no way around it, she's the most sensual woman I've ever met. The kind of woman who always touches you when she talks to you. Who always takes your arm when you are walking together. The kind of woman who wears perfume you don't notice when she's with you but remember after she's gone. The kind of woman who looks you straight in the eye and laughs softly, as if she takes delight at something only she sees in you."

"Lovely," said Alex.

"There's more. She always wears fresh flowers in her hair, which she piles loosely on her head. And she has a way of shaking her hair loose that seems like she's about to take off her clothes. When she asks you to zip up the back of her dress, you can't miss the fact that she's not wearing a bra. That kind of woman."

"Well, well," said Alex. "I have known only one such woman, but that is a long story for another time. Go on."

"Still, India-What and I are *first cousins*. That's part of the attraction, I suppose – the temptation of taboo. If we hadn't been cousins, well, who knows what would have happened? Most young people are entangled by carnal desire – sheer chemistry. If India and I had met for the first time in college, we might have married, had kids, a house – all that. The acceptable repeat of our parents' lives. And it would have been a serious mistake, because now we have little in common besides our childhood memories and sexual attraction."

"What became of her?"

"She went to art school in San Francisco and moved to New York, where she works in the fashion industry and lives an arty New York life, but I really don't know much about it."

"Do you ever see her?"

"We agreed *not* to see each other because the older we got, the more open-minded we became about what can happen between people. Risky. Even so, when we did meet once ten years ago at a family reunion, the temptation to go to bed with her was just as strong as ever. The chemistry has never faded. But. As I say again, we were cousins, dammit, and since we both care about our families, and, well . . . No. No. And then I saw her in Seattle last week."

Leaving Alex hanging on the thread of the unfinished story, Max-Pol refilled his wine glass, looked far off down the canal, stared down at his reflection in the water, and grinned.

"And, and . . .?"

"India-What was already in Seattle when I got there, but not because of me. Big family trauma. Her father - my father's brother - needs a kidney transplant. India volunteered. She was so persistent that our uncle finally had to explain to her why she might not be eligible. Why? Because she's adopted. *Adopted.* And guess who she called first with the news? And why?"

"And so?"

"Yes. And so. Unchained lust. Three days and three nights in a hotel, making love every time our libidos recharged. Followed by the kind of sadness that comes when you know that's likely all there's ever going to be."

(Silence.)

"Sure, we're both single, and both free to travel or live a long way from Seattle. But living any kind of life together is just not possible. Of course it's not really incest now, not biologically, not technically. But, the world would see it that way. Our families would never understand or forgive us. We simply will not do anything to hurt our parents. We care too much about them.

"But, the cousin problem aside, we don't share much of the rest of what makes a longtime companionship. We don't want the same kind of life. We grew up together in many ways, but then we grew apart."

"Does she feel the same way about you? Are you the sexiest man she has ever known - and all the rest?"

Max-Pol blushed, grinned, and looked away. "No comment.

"I can't imagine she hasn't threshed through a whole field of men by now, but I didn't ask and she didn't say. We talked only about each other, and since we're adults now, we could speak very rationally about our situation and our feelings. We put our cards on the table. We laughed at the absurdity of it. And after laughing, we went back to bed again. And again."

"And you will see her again?"

"How can I? And . . . And . . . How can I not?"

"And that means that, whatever may come between you and Alice, if sex is included, then there is a problem?"

"That's it in a nutshell, Aleko. Derailed. Blindsided. Blown off course. The Great Bird of Fate has laid a great big egg in my nest."

"If you sit on it long enough, it will hatch," said Alex. "We Greeks say, *Kathi thokimahsiah yenah ya efkeriah*. Every difficult situation contains opportunity."

INCOMING

YOUR SPY WILL COME IN TO BE DEBRIEFED TUES 10:00.

Nelson Bellingham considered the terse E-mail message on his computer screen. He frowned and sighed.

"Alice," he said. "Who else?"

The message was not unexpected. Nor was the fact that her appointment was declared, not requested.

Up front and in your face, as always, he thought.

Bellingham stared at the E-mail, thinking hard. Knowing that it might be a testy encounter, he wanted Jacks O'Rourke to be there. O'Rourke still had a consulting contract with the company, and he was the only one who could match wits with Alice. And despite their intellectual clashes, Bellingham had always suspected an unfulfilled attraction between Alice and Jacks. But that was when they had worked together. Maybe the surprise of seeing Jacks again would throw her off balance - and keep the flak level down.

She would at least be surprised by Jacks's appearance. Since he left the company he had gone from flabby to lean, from pale to tan, and from shaved to bearded. He had made the classic dropout's Far East pilgrimage - Bali, India, Nepal, and Bhutan. Friends called him "Baba Now" - partly as a joke, but also out of respect for a new depth of personality.

Clearly, Jacks had changed. Quiet and self-contained. No sign of the old arrogant, hard-driving egomaniac. What would Alice make of that?

Bellingham called his assistant on his intercom.

"Ellen, get in touch with Jacks O'Rourke and ask him to call me ASAP. Tell him I need him to come to my office. Tell him it's an official priority and a personal favor. "

"Do you think Baba Now will come?"

"If you tell him Alice Riley is back, he will."

11

CHEMISTRY

Alex knows about Jacks O'Rourke - it happened when Alex once asked Alice about love. It was on that afternoon when Alice had stripped off and gone swimming in the river. She had sat naked in the sun and explained about the port-wine birthmark on her breast.

"Love me, love my wound," she'd said.

Alex turned her words over in his mind. Whatever else he thought about love, it was like that: if you love me, then love my wounds - and my flaws, and my contradictions, and my excesses.

Later, after they had moored on the shady side of the canal and sat under a willow tree on the bank, Alex dropped the bait into the pond of Alice's mind.

"Have you ever been in love?"

"No, I don't think so. Not fairy-tale love - the all-consuming This Is It! form. And I've never had the heavy No-Matter-What, Until-Death-Us-Do-Part inclination either. Infatuations, yes. Short-term romances, yes. Erotic friendships, yes. Though, to be candid, sex has never been very satisfactory for me because men always seem to want only something for themselves and as quickly as possible. But then, they were all young men. What did they know?"

Perhaps an older, more experienced man . . ., thought Alex.

Alice went on. "The young ones confuse lust with love. And the older ones think love is a substitute for lust. But there was one exception. It wasn't love. It should have become love but it didn't, and I've never figured out why. I think it was because we were so busy competing with each other intellectually that we never got around to love. Or even sex."

"Tell me," said Alex.

"When I was in high school I sat next to the same guy in physics, chemistry, biology, and calculus. His name came after mine in the alphabet, so we not only sat next to each other, we ended up doing lab work on the same team. We were not close friends – never dated – never went to the same parties. No big deal.

"But. We were *very* aware of each other. We were the smartest kids in our class, and what bound us together was competition. Test score for test score, lab report for lab report, grade for grade. When one of us took extra-credit work, the other did, too. And it was always a tie between us, right up to the end. Same perfect SAT scores, 4.0 grade average, and shared valedictory honors. And both of us were accepted at Stanford University.

"I thought he hated me for competing for the spotlight. I thought he was one more guy who couldn't handle a woman being as smart as he was. I was more than willing to take him on, no holds barred.

"Mind you, he wasn't really a nerd. He played the violin rather well and was captain of the soccer team. Good-looking, too, in a standard sort of way. Nobody understood why we weren't a couple. But the only chemistry we shared was a class, not a feeling. I couldn't imagine kissing him or going to bed with him. Now, looking back, I realize that romance never entered my mind. I was too busy trying to whip his butt with grades.

"I rarely saw him at Stanford, and even then only at a distance. He was pre-med, and ran in rather elite company. He had two things I didn't have: money – and by that I mean big money – and the charming confidence of a born salesman.

"At the end of his third year, he left Stanford. He'd made important contacts in Silicon Valley. Using family money, he bankrolled a start-up tech company focused on undeveloped areas of electronic security. Everyone thought he was on his way to fame and fortune.

"A year later I found him waiting for me in the hall outside my neuro-science class. He was standing in the hall like someone waiting at an airport, with a sign: Message for Alice Riley."

"What did he want?"

"Are you sure you want this whole story? It's not about how I fell in love. It's about how I didn't."

"That makes it interesting," said Alex. "Go on."

"So, then. Where was I? Did I tell you his name? Jackson O'Rourke. But he was always called 'Jacks.' He told me he needed me in his new company. It was going to take off like a rocket, have a huge affect on science and culture. Make piles of money. He wanted me to help him set up a research lab. He said it would be the most exciting adventure of my life."

"Why you?"

"Well, for one thing he didn't want experience. He wanted somebody who *didn't* already know all the answers. Experienced people weren't bold enough for him. But it was his other reason that hooked me. He said he wanted me to work with him because I was the second smartest person he had ever known. Before I could ask him just who was the smartest, he said he was, but if I didn't think so, I could come work for him and prove him wrong."

"And that did it?"

"Of course. He knew it would. As I said, he was a gifted salesman. And nothing else he could have said would have convinced me to leave Stanford. I could always finish my degree and go to graduate school later. But set up and run a lab? Starting next week? With unlimited funds? Who wouldn't have jumped at the chance?

"I thought I could do anything. So. I did it. And he was right about intellectual excitement. What a ride! Oh my God, what a ride! And you know the rest of the story. Microsoft buyout, the big payoff."

"What about Jacks?"

"When people heard we were back working side by side, they assumed that *now* we would finally become a couple. And I admit I considered the possibility because we became like Siamese twins - but joined at the mind, not at the heart or the crotch. It was like being in combat. No time for romance or love or sex. Work hard! Think big! Do the Impossible! Win!"

"Did you?"

"We did. When the company was sold for millions, I stayed with it for a while. But not Jacks. Big surprise. He put his share of the money to work as venture capital and went off to spend a year traveling. He didn't say where he was going or why. Didn't even say goodbye. And I haven't seen him since. But somewhere in the back of my mind, I know we're not finished with each other."

"Why?"

Alice laughed. "Because I still don't know which of us is smartest. And maybe even what 'smart' means has changed for both of us."

"You are deeply connected with this man, Alice," said Alex.

"It always puzzled me that we seemed so perfect for one another, and yet the spark never jumped between us. Now there's a major chemistry project for you: What special force draws two people together or drives them apart?"

"There is no answer," said Alex. "We will never figure it out. But that is what makes the great conundrum of Men-and-Women so exciting. It is always a matter of mysterious chance – a random throw of the dice onto the infinite table of fate.

"You may never get what you want. But you are free to want what you get. And if not him, someone, somewhere, sometime. Never easy, always troublesome."

"I'm not looking for that kind of trouble, Alex."
"But that kind of trouble is always looking for you, Alice."

OSHIGUMA

The afternoon before her appointment with Nelson Bellingham, a gift arrived for Alice by air express from Japan. She knew it was a gift because the sender was Matsui Zenkichi, who once told her he never wrote letters. He only sent gifts, but his gifts always contained messages.

A plain wooden box, about 3x3x18 inches. Inside, a scroll with the following note wrapped around it:

> Read first.

> On this scroll is loosely mounted an *oshiguma* (a face pressing) - a pressing of my stage makeup onto a piece of ivory silk, done immediately after the end of a performance. While I was dressing for the play, Morioka told me you were returning, and you were on my mind at all the pauses in the performance. I have altered the print to reflect the feelings expressed by my true face at the thought of seeing you again.

Alice unrolled the scroll to find the image of a white mask marked with strong red and black lines. She could not read the Japanese calligraphy on the scroll, but she could read the extra lines drawn on the face - glasses like those worn in real life by Zenkichi, a Charlie Chaplin mustache, and a large grin. Gravity over-drawn with delight.

When Alice looked up oshiguma in a dictionary of Kabuki terms, she learned that an actor makes one face print per performance - signed, dated, and marked with the actor's personal seal. These are considered valuable gifts - often the sign of a special relationship between actor and patron. Red makeup indicates righteousness, strength, and passion in the character being played.

Onstage, Zenkichi was the actor, Iwai Hanshiro XI, playing a famous role in a great drama. To draw a cartoon over the face pressing was a deliberate breach of protocol. It was Zenkichi's way of saying, For you, I am also a man - with a light heart.

Alice - she of many names and roles of her own - understood.

The gift resolved any doubts she had about going back to Japan. Not that Zenkichi was her heart's desire. Not at all. But he intrigued her, and he could provide access to aspects of Japanese culture usually denied to a foreigner.

Furthermore, going to Japan meant she would not be in Seattle when Max-Pol returned after his week with Alex. Her attraction to him almost defeated her resolve not to give up her claim on herself. She liked being his Witness, and he was an attractive man, but beyond that . . .?

No. She didn't want to be anywhere near the temptation to move toward conventionality. Seeing Max-Pol again had been a close call. "Out of sight, out of mind," made sense.

Pressing the oshiguma to her own face, she said aloud, "I'm coming soon."

I, Spy?

The office of Nelson Bellingham, CEO of Security Laboratories.

Bellingham: Second-generation leader of a successful high-tech company - more manager than innovator - more a conservator of his company's assets than an entrepreneur. Serious and smart - a PhD in neuro-anatomy and an MBA. Wearing a tie and a white shirt, but with sleeves rolled up, collar unbuttoned and tie loose. Hard-driving, open-minded, and shrewd. Agitated, he walks back and forth in front of his desk.

Sitting at ease on a couch, Jacks O'Rourke: Founder and former CEO of Security Laboratories; calm, quiet, finely fit, tan, and balding - with a neat, short, gray beard. Wearing faded indigo drawstring pants, a collarless, faded-blue chambray shirt, brown leather sandals - no socks. Unadorned - no watch, no rings, nor other personal jewelry.

He has come early to meet with Bellingham, who has explained the "Alice situation." Bellingham expects an explosive encounter with her as a reaction to her having been considered a security risk.

"We put her under moderate surveillance as a precaution. Frankly, she's acted suspiciously enough to concern us. We thought we ought to let her know. And now she's pissed off enough to come charging in here to give me a hard time. She thinks we think she's a spy or a double agent or who-knows-what."

Jacks O'Rourke smiled, but said nothing.

Bellingham continued. "We both know she's a wily poker player. And we've both seen her mad. I need your help with this one, Jacks. You used to say she was the second smartest person you ever knew. I hope you're still smarter than she is."

Again Jacks O'Rourke smiled, and again said nothing.

*

18

Twirling her security-badge necklace in one hand, Alice walked unannounced past Bellingham's secretary, swung open the office door, and stopped in the doorway. Enter the spy.

*

Both Bellingham and Jacks were too surprised to speak. Alice? They hardly recognized her. Tailored black pantsuit, white blouse, no makeup, tortoiseshell glasses. More astonishing was her very short, very black hair. Her sensible, black walking shoes even matched.

Was this really Alice Riley?

She established the mood of the meeting with the boldness of her sudden appearance and the all-business way she walked directly to a chair, sat down, and locked eyes with Jacks.

(Silence.)

No words of greeting. Bellingham was at a loss for words.
Jacks was at ease without words.
And Alice had nothing to say. Not yet.

Bellingham had expected steely coolness, tension, confrontation, and anger. Even shouting. Now the room felt as if invisible snow had suddenly fallen, stifling sound and motion. Bellingham had expected a grenade, but he wasn't sure if the pin was pulled out or not.

*

In the silence between Jacks and Alice, long-standing conflict was instantly reconsidered and settled between them. Two people who had once competed for a prize stepped out of the race, suddenly knowing that winning the laurel had become meaningless.

No competition now. They were simply keepers of one another's history, and the tie between them was not a dead heat at the tape, but a soft ribbon that binds up the past into a keepsake to be put away.

Alice had been told Jacks had changed, but she hadn't expected to feel it from across the room. She felt herself relax.

And the chemistry? That had not changed. The two of them still formed an inert compound. Alice had potent active ingredients in her life now - Alex and Max-Pol and Zenkichi - even Wonko stirred something in her. But not Jackson O'Rourke.

Alice would never know why.

Jacks did. But he would never say.

*

Jacks had come to grips with a confused identity that had tormented him since puberty. Women did not attract him. Never had. Never would. But men did not attract him, either. Never had. Never would. What, then, was his category? Certainly not bisexual. But what? In a society that required labels for sexual preference, nobody believed one could have *no* sexual preference or desire. Monks, priests, nuns, bishops, and popes and eunuchs are celibate.

But celibacy is a choice and a commitment, not a condition.

O'Rourke had cut his ties with Security Laboratories not because, as everyone thought, he had made his pile and was off to bigger things. He wanted to know if he was developmentally disabled or crazy. He had spent most of a year researching his sexuality, and finally decided he was one of those rare human beings whose libidinal energy was virtually nil. What had bothered him was not being different but not knowing why.

He had never consulted an expert. He had never told anyone. As had always been his style, he had worked it out for himself. And when clarity came to him, he had found the calm that had eluded him. He would say he was simply a man finally content with who and what he was.

At peace with himself, he found it easy to pay attention to other people, and his friends were many. They were drawn to his intelligence, his humor, and most of all to his serenity. His selfless commitment to social causes inspired them. The beauty of the oriental garden he was creating enchanted them. It was as if he were a priest without a church or dogma. They thought him wise and good and kind - even noble. Wherever Jackson O'Rourke went, fine things happened.

*

Alice sensed this - the presence of something deep. She had come expecting him to be here - expecting an intellectual tournament - even verbal combat. She had come ready to tear a piece off both Bellingham and Jacks and say goodbye, this time for good.

Now she reconsidered.

Never taking her eyes off Jacks, she spoke to Bellingham.

"I understand about the spy thing, Nelson. I do. And I can't fault you for keeping track of me. I know you care about the company. I accept that you also cared about me. You probably kept me safe in ways I didn't even know about. I should be grateful. And I am."

Bellingham sat back in his chair.

"I also know that by now your research and development must have gone way beyond what I know about the science. Implantable microchips scannable by satellite, or DNA that's read without drawing blood - who knows? Already I'm far behind and out of date and of no real threat to the company. You must know that."

"Yes," Bellingham said.

Alice maintained eye contact with Jacks as she spoke to Bellingham.

"Still, I admit the thought of being a spy intrigued me. And it brought me a connection with at least one astonishing character, Wonko. It also gave me reason to look up colleagues from the good old days. I would hate to give up being a spy, especially if it's a little dangerous.

"I know you can't be too careful, but by now you must know that I haven't compromised any proprietary information. And I won't. On the other hand, if it would be useful to you, I'll continue to connect with old friends in the world of biometric security science. I miss being around brilliant people. You may have some suggestions. I'll keep my eyes and ears open."

Bellingham leaned forward on his desk.

Still looking only at Jacks, she went on.

"And now you will ask me what I want in return. I'm not naïve and I know the world becomes more dangerous every day. The Koreans and Chinese play hardball, and I *am* on my way to Japan. Alert me if I am in harm's way and I don't realize it. That's all I ask."

(Silence.)

And more silence, as if the snowfall had increased.

Finally, Jacks spoke, as if replying to a conversation not taking place in the room - as if his agenda was unfinished business of a transcendent nature. He said what Alice least expected.

"Alice . . . Alice . . . We never fell in love, Alice. We never will. I won't explain. But you are the most attractive woman I know. And I've often thought of you these last two years, and can say something to you I haven't ever said because *you* are the smartest person I've ever known."
He smiled.

"So you will figure out what I mean when I say that, in my way, I love you, and, in my way, always have. Forgive me for not knowing how to tell you for so long. It's so simple, after all. I love you."

Tears welled up in Alice's eyes.

Bellingham started to speak, "Alice, I . . ."
She held up her hand and said, "Not now - later - E-mail me."

(Silence.)

Disarmed by Jacks' generosity, Alice couldn't reply to him.
Slowly, she stood up to go.
Jacks stood at the same time.

Alice walked over to him, took both his hands in hers and, looking at his tranquil face, she said,
"Oh, Jacks, dear Jacks. Being with you now has been like being in the same room with a prince of the realm. They said you were different. I didn't believe it. Now I do. Maybe . . . maybe . . . you've always been the way you are now and nobody got it, least of all me. Someday . . . Someday I want you to tell me. Fare you well, Jacks O'Rourke . . . I love you too."

Alice dropped his hands, kissed him lightly on each cheek, touched her lips and touched his.

She turned and walked slowly out of the room.

Without looking back, she closed the door of the room and the door of the past - closed them softly, gently, behind her.

CONSIDERATIONS

Why cut anything you can untie?
For that which is untied may be refastened.
Why break anything you can disconnect?
For that which is separated may be reunited.
Why pour out that which may be distilled
into something stronger?

> —Fabuliste Curnonsky

In other words, if you screw up your goodbyes, saying hello
again may be a problem. Why slam doors when you could
walk through walls?

> —Alice

An Other…Who?

Alice preferred beginning a long journey slowly. Not for her a mad dash in traffic for an airport - the tense lines and impatient waiting rooms full of anxious travelers pacing around the gates, pushing into the plane - their noise silenced only by the jet's screaming assault on the sky. No. That was like being in a mob launched by a catapult.

The morning train for Portland, Oregon, leaves Union Station in Seattle at eight o'clock, scheduled to arrive at noon. As her car began moving almost imperceptibly, Alice took a deep breath, leaned back in her seat, closed her eyes, and smiled. If "they" were keeping track of her, they would be confused again, wondering, Why is she leaving by train for Portland if she said she was going to Japan?

Alice laughed aloud. Tomorrow she would be on a plane to Japan from Portland. Meanwhile, she has time to collect her mind and gather her thoughts. This afternoon, she wants to see a certain painting. Monet is on her mind. And Alex.

*

A photograph of Claude Monet taken July 8, 1915, shows him sitting outside under a large umbrella, working on one of his *Nymphaea* series. Standing beside him, leaning forward as if as engaged in the painting as Monet, is a woman in a long white dress and sun hat. Blanche Hoschede-Monet. His stepdaughter and daughter-in-law.

*

That very painting - the one in the photograph - hung for many years on the dining room wall of Monet's son, Michel. In 1959 it was acquired by the Portland Art Museum. It is this painting Alice has come to see.

*

She climbed the marble stairs to the second floor, turned right, and there it was. In the center of a grand atrium, hung by itself on a free-standing wall. About six feet wide and a little over five feet high.

High clerestory windows provided varying light from a day of sun and showers. The changing light and the brush strokes combined to give the painting the feel of rippled water. Shimmering blues and greens, water lilies blooming - pale blues and bright pinks and yellows.

Unmistakably Monet.

Alice sat down on a bench at some distance from the painting.

She knew exactly where Monet had set up his easel on that day. More than once she had stood at that very spot. Alone, and later with Alex. She had made drawings and watercolor sketches right there, and later burned her work and scattered the ashes in tribute on Monet's grave in the village cemetery.

Memories flooded her mind. May, sun, green, lilies, dragonflies, willows, blue. As if in a trance, she rose, walked slowly toward the painting, feeling she was falling into it, as if nothing else existed but her and the flowers and the pond. But as she moved forward, the lilies and the water disappeared. From a foot away, there was nothing on the canvas but smears and daubs of layered paint.

She realized she was as close to the canvas as Monet had been when he painted it. What he said was true. He painted the space between himself and his impressions. There was no picture on the canvas - only airy, colored light. Ephemeral.

Without looking to see if anyone else was close by, and against all the rules of museums, Alice touched her lips and then touched the painting at the lower, right-hand corner where Monet had signed his name, and touched her lips again.

Backing away slowly until the splashes of color became water lilies once more, she opened the museum catalog to the page where the painting and the photograph appeared side by side.

Only then did she realize it was not only the painting itself that commanded her attention. She had, in fact, seen several of the *Nympheas* series. No, not just the painting. It was the photograph. She was drawn to the man and the woman and their intense engagement with the third part of the picture - the creation of art.

Monet and Blanche had each other. The Third Thing - the beauty on canvas - was a product of that relationship. He began painting again because of her. Because of him, she went on living.

Each had An Other.
And Alice?
Would there ever be An Other?
Or just an ever-changing shift of actors playing the parts necessary for the action of the time being? The memory of the photograph was so strong, so vivid. And memory is preserved desire - a revision of the past into a wish.
Alex was on her mind.

Slowly she walked down the stairs and out into the light rain of a sudden shower, carrying reverie as an umbrella, and wondering, *How can I be so good at being solitary and yet be so needy of being . . . of having . . . what? . . . what? . . . what?*

She realized she was homesick.
For a home she did not have.
Yet.

HOME

From her mother's mother – her Japanese grandmother – Alice learned these words, a lullaby sung to a child afraid of being lost:

Inoru. Inoru.
Inagasaki ni oni ga iru.
Ato miriya ja ga iru.

Wants to go home. Wants to go home.
On the way home a demon is waiting;
If you look back, you will see a dragon.

Why do adults think such scary songs will lull little children to sleep? "Rockabye Baby," for example, has a tiny child up in a tree. And when the bough breaks, the cradle will fall. And down will come baby, cradle, and all.

What?

Why? Because adults know things about the world a child does not. Such songs bear contradictory truth: peace and trouble, joy and sorrow, calm and chaos – are always companions. A child might as well know as early as possible. Welcome to the world!

As good as we imagine that leaving home and going back home might be, demons and dragons wait along the way in either direction. Still, *"Inoru, Inoru"* – wants to go home. And just where is that? Back there? Out there?

Where?

Alice wrote "home" words in her journal:

Homework, homemade, homely,
Homesick, Anybody home? Homeless,
Come home. You can't go home again.
Home is where the heart is. Home away from home.
Home, sweet home. Home, home on the range.

A house is not a home. Home is anywhere you are.

She drew a house in the way she had always drawn it as a child.
She had never seen such a house.
But it was the invisible house she lived in now – she carried it with her – built on a meadow in her mind. She had always wondered why there were no people in her house picture.
Maybe she could draw them in.

WONKO

Elliot Brownell knew he had blown his cover.

By telling Alex about his surveillance of Alice, he had let it be known that he worked for a security agency. And few people could keep a secret, not even Alex. Deliberate leaks were always for a reason – he knew that.

What was Elliot's?

He supposed it was because he was tired of the duplicity his job entailed. True, it was only a part-time occupation. He was called on as needed, and they seldom needed him now. Just as well. He always liked the people he spied on better than the people he worked for.

Alice and Alex for example. The world had nothing to fear from them. But it did have something to fear from his employer's paranoia that could not distinguish between intrigue and those who were intriguing.

Playing Wonko wasn't actually a cover. Being an entertainer and an eccentric canal character was real enough. And everyone knew a clown had an offstage life. But if people discovered that he was also an under-cover agent for a security agency, what would they think?

End of the show – end of Wonko.

*

Being young and strong and smart and courageous and self-disciplined had qualified him for service as a U.S. Navy SEAL. And that experience qualified him for private security work when he retired from the navy. But he was no longer young or strong, and maybe not so smart, either.

And courage? What was that now? He would never again be called on to kill silently, or assault a beach, or parachute behind enemy lines, or even carry a weapon.

As for discipline, learning to juggle flaming torches and to play a fiddle while walking a slack rope on stilts were the skills that engaged him now. He would rather inspire laughter than fear.

And there was another thing. All his life he had been a man's man, beginning with Boy Scouts and on into hunting, fishing, and team sports - football, hockey, and rugby. He wrestled in college, and took up rock climbing, sea kayaking, and skydiving. Joining the SEALs was a natural for him - it pushed him as far mentally and physically as he ever wanted to go.

Except when it came to women.

Not that he was afraid of women. And not that he had no experience with women - far from it. He was not particularly good-looking, but his muscular physique and his athleticism attracted women. But not his type of women. Dates, yes. Affairs, yes. Even romance. But never a deeper connection. Nothing that called for the courage that love demanded. That his public persona, Wonko, had a mythical wife amused him. But Elliot Brownell had never married. Marriage was not in his plan. And yet, somehow . . .

At age 45, in a moment of profound personal insight, he realized that the skills of observation he had mastered for unobtrusive surveillance probably veiled his search for someone to love. His curiosity about women was a disguise for his yearning for at least a companion.

Watching Alex with Alice, and then watching Alice with Max-Pol, he began to understand that he would have to take off that disguise. There was room in his canal boat for two.

The spy must come in out of the cold, he said to himself, smiling.

Wonko's wider audience had seen his show and liked it. Applause. Applause. But the back flip onto a wet sponge while wearing a Viking helmet was an easy trick now. Finding someone to share poetry by the fire on a late winter's night - well, *that* would be harder.

But that's what he wanted.

Even more, he wanted someone to dance with. Though an accomplished and confident dancer, he had never found a partner whose skills and flair matched his on the dance floor. A dancer. He wanted a dancer in his life.

In this mood, Elliot Brownell left behind his Wonko disguise, took a cab into Oxford as far as the Jericho Bridge, and strolled at ease across the great, green open space of Port Meadow, toward Godstow and dinner with Alex and Max-Pol at The Trout.

As he walked, he whistled.

WONKO'S WALTZ

Rosamund and The Trout and Alice

A Benedictine nunnery dedicated to Saint Mary and Saint John the Baptist was founded in 1133 on the west bank of the river Thames. Built on the far end of Port Meadow, an hour's walk from Oxford, the site was called Godstow (God's Place).

Fair Rosamund, daughter of Walter de Clifford, died and was buried in the cemetery of Godstow nunnery in 1175. She was the young, beautiful, and much-beloved mistress of King Henry II. Many are the tales and songs about the ill-fated love of Henry and his Rosamund.

It is said that the king kept his mistress as a virtual prisoner in a secret garden reached only by a complicated labyrinth - the way through found only with a silver thread. The king's knight, Sir Thomas, guarded Rosamund and was the keeper of the thread.

While the king was away at war, his queen, Eleanor of Aquitaine, had Sir Thomas murdered. She had found the silver thread, followed it through the labyrinth, and poisoned Rosamund. The bereaved Henry had a church built at the nunnery to honor his true love, and the archbishop of Canterbury dedicated the church in Henry's presence in 1179.

Eleanor packed up and went back to France.

The Trout Inn began as a hospice built on the opposite bank of the Thames around the same time as the founding of the nunnery. When King Henry VIII dissolved the monasteries in 1538, Godstow passed into the hands of George Owen, fellow of Merton College and royal physician to Henry VIII. Over the ensuing centuries, wars, a hurricane, floods, fire, and pillage destroyed most of the nunnery, leaving only the shell of walls visible today.

The ruins of the nunnery were quarried to enlarge the former hospice into an inn. The Trout came into existence around 1625, where it served travelers crossing one of the key bridges over the Thames.

The Trout looks today much as it did when it was reconstructed in 1787: long low buildings, slate roofs, leaded windows, oak beams, flagstone floors, open fireplaces, and a terrace overlooking the river and the ruins of the nunnery beyond.

Long a haven of tranquility for the university community, it is said that enough ale has been drunk here by Oxonians over three hundred years to fill the river all the way to the sea.

Though many are the names of the great and famous associated with The Trout, the five people in a small boat who had tea on the river's bank nearby on Friday afternoon, July 4, 1862, are best remembered.

On a rowing expedition, which began at Folly Bridge in Oxford, came The Reverend Robinson Duckworth, three little girls - the Liddell sisters, Lorina, Edith, and Alice - and Charles Lutwidge Dodgson, a mathematician.

Dodgson later wrote, "I told them the fairy tale of Alice's adventures underground." Writing as Lewis Carroll, Dodgson published the fairy tale as *Alice's Adventures in Wonderland*.

THE CATERPILLAR'S QUESTION

"Who are *you*?" said the Caterpillar.

…Alice replied, rather shyly, "I - I hardly know, Sir, just at present - at least I know who I *was* when I got up this morning, but I think I must have been changed several times since then."

"What do you mean by that?" said the Caterpillar, sternly. "Explain yourself."

"I can't explain *myself*, I'm afraid, Sir," said Alice.

From *Alice in Wonderland*

*

Consider the three men sitting on the terrace of The Trout Inn as the fading summer evening light softens the landscape of the Oxfordshire countryside. Alex. Max-Pol. Elliot. And Alice Riley is also there, unseen but very much present in spirit.

For the moment they are in the first stage of Hello. All three seem to be at ease, as if they are already well acquainted. However, as is often the case in human affairs, that is a false assumption. What they know of one another is inconsistent and incomplete and oblique. Consider:

Alex knows Max-Pol largely through their Cretan companionship.
Alex has experienced Elliot mostly in the guise of Wonko.
Alex knows Alice from a week in Giverny and a week on the canal.

Max-Pol knows Alex from their Cretan experiences.
Max-Pol's knowledge of Alice is a collage of letters and moments.
Max-Pol has never met Elliot or Wonko.

And Wonko knows Alex and Alice and Max-Pol from a distance - from what has been passed on to him from his agency and by looking at them through a peculiar lens. As Elliot Brownell, he is largely a stranger to all three.

Yet if they were asked if they *know* one another, they would say, Of course, and believe that they do. And they would be mostly wrong.

*

The knowledge of others is always partial and never consistent. Even what we know about the person appearing before us in the mirror in the bathroom each morning varies from day to day, constantly reframed by remembering and forgetting – unpredictably edited and rewritten.

Life is more fiction than fact – mostly invention, an imaginative consensus, and a Wonderland adventure.

Even the Caterpillar knows only the questions.

ALICE AND ALICE AND ALICE

After some discussion of the merits of the ales in the bar, the three men ordered their pints and adjourned to the terrace to watch the sunset.

"Well, then," said Alex, and, opening his mental encyclopedia to the sections on the history of Godstow, The Trout, and the adventures of *Alice in Wonderland*, he launched his lecture.

As fascinating as the history might be, and as well-informed and entertaining as Alex was, Elliot could not keep from speculating about Max-Pol. Elliot knew of his correspondence with Alice Riley, and that Alice and Max-Pol had recently met briefly in Waterloo Station. What was their relationship? Elliot entertained one wild surmise after another. His training taught him to keep an open mind and assume the widest range of possibilities.

For his part, Max-Pol was glad not to have to participate in active conversation. He felt ill. Symptoms: A general malaise, a slight fever, the beginning of a headache, and not much appetite. Self-diagnosis: Onset of a cold or even a case of flu. Without enthusiasm, he drank his ale and nodded politely as Alex rambled on.

Both men became alert when Alex suddenly said, "Alice was here. Did you know that? The original Alice. On a summer afternoon. A long time ago. If we had been sitting here on that afternoon in 1862, we might have observed the two men and three little girls having tea on the bank nearby, and, as they floated away home down the river, we might have overhead parts of that remarkable tale told to please one little girl in particular.

"What was the relationship between Alice and Dodgson? Much speculation. Despite the most scholarly and most twisted conjecture, the exact nature of the relationship between Alice Liddell, age ten, and Charles Lutwidge Dodgson, age thirty, has *never* been established. And likely never will be."

Alex drank his ale. His companions looked interested. Onward.

"Still, we wonder. Was he in love with her? Did he make inappropriate advances? Her mother certainly broke off the family's connection and burned his letters to the child. A page concerning the episode was torn out of his diary. And Alice remained aloof from him the rest of her life, enduring in distant, uncomfortable silence the fame Lewis Carroll brought her."

Alex reined in this line of thinking. He wondered if Elliot thought much about love or sex or fairy tales. And Max-Pol seemed too far affected by alcohol now to discuss sensitive matters.

"Well, then. Did you know, by the way, that a long-lost section of the original manuscript of *Alice Through the Looking Glass* has been found? It is a short piece about Alice's encounter with an aged wasp, who has a yellow kerchief tied around his head, which is crowned with a wig of bright yellow curls."

Looking steadily at Elliot, Alex remarked, "Some of our more eccentric friends on the canal might appreciate such a wig."

"They might, indeed," said Elliot.

At that moment the rest of the evening's conversation became a three-dimensional game. The subject was "Alice." Ostensibly the imaginary one, but between Alex and Elliot the subtext was the Alice Riley Wonko knew about. And Max-Pol vaguely understood the conversation to be a veiled reference to the Alice Riley he knew.

And Alex? He would have said Alice and Alice and Alice had much in common. Moreover, there was one more version of Alice - his own - as real and as imaginary as all the rest.

*

Fragments from a most confusing game:

"Are you familiar with Alice?" asked Alex.

"Not from childhood. But I've studied her as an adult," said Elliot.

And Max-Pol chimed in, speaking through a wine-colored haze, "Not as familiar as I would like to be."

"If you could be one of Alice's acquaintances, which one would you be?" asked Alex.

"That's easy," said Elliot. "The Caterpillar or the Cheshire Cat."

"Why am I not surprised," said Alex. "And you, Max-Pol?"

"Humpty Dumpty," said Max-Pol. "Humpty Dumpty."

"And I would be the White Rabbit," declared Alex.

"That could be arranged," said Max-Pol.

"Whatever became of Alice?"

"She disappeared."

"She grew old and ugly and died. They all do."

"She's on her way to Seattle."

If any of the Alices had been present in person, she would have said that she was not *real* in this company, but a pawn on a chessboard, and it would soon be time for her to move.

It was also time for the three men to go. Max-Pol had made a valiant effort to recite the entire *"Jabberwocky"* poem, but he kept getting stuck at "Beware the Jubjub bird," and when he began again for the fourth time, he abruptly fell asleep, muttering, "Alice, Alice, Alice . . ."

*

Alex and Elliot managed to get the silent and barely functional Max-Pol into a cab, to the moorage, across the gangplank of the *Ariadne*, and into bed. They placed a mop bucket beside his bunk, just in case.

"I did not think he had that much to drink," said Alex.

"He didn't," said Elliot. "Maybe there's something else wrong. Call me at Thrupp if you need help during the night. In any case, call me tomorrow. Wonko's troupe is performing at a grand jumble sale, and as long as you are stuck here, you might like to come along. It might be interesting to know what Max-Pol thinks of Wonko. He does, after all, own a rabbit suit, if my memory serves me, and he brought it with him. Perhaps he knows a few tricks. We can always use new talent."

DIFFICULTIES AND OPPORTUNITIES

Max-Pol's hangover was like sheet lightning in his head. The slightest sound or movement made him wince. His body felt like a baked apple looks. When Alex came banging back onto the *Ariadne* from an excursion ashore, Max-Pol pulled his pillow over his head and pretended not to exist.

"Max-Pol! Bad news and good news! Where are you?"

Max-Pol, staggered out into the galley, holding his pillow over his head and a finger to his lips. "Shh . . ."

More amused than surprised by Max-Pol's condition, Alex lowered his voice. "Word has come down the canal that a drunken young fool trying to move a client's canal boat to a repair yard rammed it into a gate at Roundham Lock. Stupid lout! He was trying to go it alone and at night."

"Shhh . . .," pleaded Max-Pol.

Whispering now, Alex continued. "To make things even worse, the idiot called a friend of his who had a small tow truck to pull him out of the gate in the middle of the night. The boat rolled over, pulling the truck into the lock on top of it. Bloody hell! Now there is a mess to be cleared up, the lock to be repaired, and twenty boats are stuck stem-to-stern in the canal above us. We are stranded here for days."

"Good," muttered Max-Pol. "I'm going back to bed."

"You will feel better by noon. But we must not sit idly by and twiddle our thumbs. You must rally yourself. Opportunity knocks, but it does not nag. Carpe diem! We shall hire a car and visit Blenheim Palace, Churchill's grave, and Hampton Gay."

Max-Pol shook his head.

"Then I will take you to the Ashmolean to see a new exhibit of Lear's drawings and some of the pots from Knossos I restored. As a special surprise, I will introduce you to the legendary Wonko. And, as chance allows, we shall sample the wares of the historic pubs of Oxford."

At the word "pub," Max-Pol slowly shook his head again and shuffled back to his berth.

He does look hungover, thought Alex. He expected Max-Pol to hold his liquor better than this. They had not really had all that much to drink the night before.

*

By afternoon, Max-Pol was ambulatory and willing to go along with Alex. But he was dull company. He sat crumpled on a bench by Churchill's grave in the parish church cemetery in the village of Bladon. Loyally, he tried paying attention to Alex's rambling monologue about his love/hate feelings for Churchill.

Staring at the plain white marble slab, Alex concluded, "He was a brilliant megalomaniac, capable of making monumental decisions, which proved either terribly wrong or terribly right. He was a distant shaper of my fate during the war. Because of him, I lost many friends. Because of him, many of my friends survived. Bloody awful, wonderful man!"

Max-Pol had become as still and as silent as the gravestones.
Alex walked over and considered him thoughtfully.
"Max-Pol? Are you all right?"
"No. To be honest, I feel ill. More than hungover."
"Your eyes are not bloodshot. They are more . . . yellowish, actually."
"I was afraid of that. I'm sick. Maybe flu. But maybe worse. I don't want to alarm you, but if I accept the obvious facts, I've got all the symptoms of infectious hepatitis - fever, nausea, weakness, and no appetite. If I'm jaundiced, that's not a good sign. I don't know if my liver is enlarged or not, but it feels sore when I palpate it. Drinking too much booze last night didn't help."
"What is to be done?"
"Just take me back to the boat and let me sleep. Maybe tomorrow I'll have a clearer idea of what ails me."

THE BODY

By morning Max-Pol's hangover was gone. The symptoms of hepatitis remained. Though he did not completely trust his self-diagnosis, the rise of the bilirubin level that yellowed his eyes was an unmistakable sign of hepatitis. Knowing he could be quite ill, Max-Pol had decided he should return to Seattle for medical care. Even if his case was mild, hepatitis was not to be taken lightly. And despite his optimistic view, he might have one of the more serious forms of the illness - one leading to permanent liver damage and a long recovery. Or worse. He wanted to be in the care of physicians he knew and trusted. The sooner, the better. Max-Pol was going.

While sitting in the sun on the deck of the *Ariadne* waiting for the car to take him to the airport, he reassured a much-distressed Alex. He carefully explained that he felt well enough to travel, but not well enough to delay diagnosis and treatment.

"Besides, if I stay here you will kill me with kindness."

"Well, you are the doctor."

"Yes, but even though I'm a physician, I'm still mystified by the human body," said Max-Pol, edging the conversation away from his malady.

"We know far less than people give us credit for. And the more we know, the bigger the mystery. When I dissected a corpse as a first-year medical student, I often had tears in my eyes out of awe, fear, and humility.

"I'll never forget opening the skull and holding a brain in my hands the first time. Three pounds of rippled, gray meat - 80 percent water. And somewhere in there had been . . . what? All the words we have are metaphors: personality, mind, spirit, soul, conscience, and so on. But we can't point to any place in the meat and say, That's the center of it all. When I say 'I,' where am 'I?' Nobody knows.

"The feelings persisted when I assisted in a morgue, in an emergency room, and in intensive care wards. Delivering babies always left me stunned. I knew the science and had the skills, but, still, I was always dumbfounded by seeing a child being born."

"When you talk like that, Max-Pol, it is hard for me to understand why you are not practicing medicine," said Alex.

"Over time the daily busy-ness of being a doctor overcomes the wonder and awe. Routine smothers excitement. So many unhappy people. So many naked bodies. It's hard for me to look at anyone and not imagine what their body must look like and what flaws and diseases they may have."

Max-Pol smiled.

"Talking about bodies makes me think of my cousin, India-What. Having to go back to Seattle is not all bad news, you know. She may still be there."

Alex laughed. "And Alice too."

Now Max-Pol laughed. "Well, why should life be simple? I wonder what *her* body looks like?"

Alex smiled. He knew.

Not that he would ever tell Max-Pol how he knew or what he had seen. But he wondered if Max-Pol would find out for himself, and what he would think of what he found.

*

The driver of the airport car arrived at the gangplank of the *Ariadne*.

Max-Pol handed his suitcase to the driver, and held out a large black plastic bag to Alex.

"There wasn't time to wrap this, but have no doubt, this is a serious gift. You may put it to good use. In fact, you must."

He embraced Alex warmly, and he was off.

Alex watched the car until it was out of sight, and then turned to the gift. Tearing open the top of the bag, he saw something fuzzy. Reaching down, he pulled out a large white rabbit suit, complete with feet, a hood with ears, and a plastic carrot. The same bunny disguise Max-Pol had worn that day he first appeared in Alex's poppy patch.

"What am I supposed to do with this?" he asked aloud.
Wonko the Weird came to mind.
Wonko would have some ideas.

WHITE RABBIT SUIT

ALEX ALONE

(Alice is on her way to Japan, where a new episode of her life will unfold. And Max-Pol is on his way to Seattle to heal his body and mind. Wonko will spend the summer going from fair to fair with his troop of performers. But what of Alex? He will be offstage for some time.

Will he be OK in the meanwhile? Yes, though behind the curtain of our ongoing story a curious set of circumstances will lead to contradictory conclusions. How Alex seemed to other people and how Alex seemed to himself would be at great odds that summer. And what is the truth? Trust Alex.)

*

"The old man is losing it."

"All of a sudden he's old and frail. A real Methuselah."

"I heard he had a hard fall outside The Old Bookbinders Ale House."

"And he'll fall on his boat, break a hip, and that's it."

"It's the beginning of senility. He's going bonkers."

So said the friends and acquaintances of Alex when they gossiped in pubs and shops around Oxford that summer. The evidence for their judgments:

> 1. Alex, always shaved and trimmed, had let his beard and hair grow, adding years to his appearance. Elderly.
>
> 2. Always dressed as a man of his generation, he was often seen now in blue jeans and sandals, with a shawl thrown around his shoulders instead of wearing a jacket. Gone to seed.
>
> 3. He seemed to walk gingerly, slowly, with an undisguised limp, using his cane for support instead of style. Getting feeble.
>
> 4. He fell just after going out the door of The Old Bookbinders Ale House - so hard he cracked the large pane of glass he fell against. And it was true that he had also been found sprawled on the grass alongside the path to Sheep

Meadow, though he denied falling and insisted on getting up by himself without help. Mentally confused.

5. For the first time anybody could remember, Alex seemed absentminded - forgetful - allowing long pauses in his conversation as if he was uncertain about words and events. His voice seemed scratchy and hoarse. No doubt - mind and body were failing.

6. Then there was the business of the bunny suit. He had been seen with that wild fool, Wonko the Weird, dressed as a white rabbit, carrying a basket full of red rubber noses. Mad as a hatter.

There was little doubt in anyone's mind. Alex Evans was over the hill, headed down and out. His last days had come. They said, Poor man. And, How sad. And, We ought to check in on him any day we don't see him.

*

Alex himself was not aware of any of these symptoms of aging. He did notice a new warmth of affection among his friends, a pleasant willingness to sit with him and listen to his stories and pay for his ale. But he attributed this cordiality to his own enhanced perception of them. His view of his friends and his world that summer was a product of his own generous state of mind.

For the first time in a long while, there was juice in his life. Like a re-activated power plant, there was a resurgence of energy, fueled by his experiences with Max-Pol and Alice and Kostas and Wonko and the German general and Crete and Giverny. The fates had handed him a fresh deck of cards, and, by God, he would play them well.

Simply said, Alex was happy. Carelessly happy.

And all the troubling signs observed by his friends had other explanations. The evidence for the defense:

First. As to the beard, it was Max-Pol's doing. He was clean-shaven when he arrived, but, feeling lethargic, he had not shaved since coming to Oxford. Alex, who had never had a full beard, challenged Max-Pol to a contest to be decided in Crete in October. Best beard wins. Alex had never had long hair, either, but he decided to let his hair grow as well.

It amused him to try a new look at his age. He called it his "sagacious Socratic style."

Second. Alex was limping because he had a blister on his heel from wearing new summer sandals. He had admired Max-Pol's sandals and ordered a pair for himself, but, with the necessary orthopedic adjustments, it was always hit or miss when it came to a good fit right away. So he walked a little carefully to break in the sandals and not break the blister.

Third. He wore blue jeans for the summer both on and off the *Ariadne* because Alice had admired them. She said they were the color the Cretan skies must be in summer. The shawl he wore was Alice's. Woven blue silk and linen. He had traded her his black Cretan wool shawl.

Fourth. When Alex came out of The Old Bookbinders Ale House one day, a kid riding a motorbike on the sidewalk instead of the street caught him by surprise, and Alex jumped backwards to keep from being hit. He was impressed by his own agile reaction and grateful he had not broken through the glass into the pub. He could still move at speed when he had to.

Fifth. He had been lying on the grass in Sheep Meadow watching clouds and enjoying the blissful summer afternoon when a friend found him and became relentlessly determined to help him up. It had not occurred to Alex that someone would think he had fallen. Of course he got up by himself. He had got down by himself in the first place.

Sixth. His scratchy voice came from continuing to smoke too many cigars as a result of Max-Pol having left behind too many Havanas.

And, finally. Alex's slowness of speech and seeming absentmindedness were simply products of his contented state. The time with Alice and the time with Max-Pol had filled him with delight. The memories of those days kept interrupting the present moment. He preferred daydreaming.

In sum, he did not see himself as others saw him.
And others did not see him as he saw himself.

*

He had done one serious thing.

On a trip into London, he had gone to a Greek Orthodox Church. In the vestibule he bought an expensive beeswax candle as tall as himself, and placed it beside an icon in a small side chapel. Such a candle is lit to ask for an exceptional dispensation from God. And another may be lit in thanks for prayers answered.

The candle was for Max-Pol.

On second thought, he bought another candle to light.

For Alice.

JAPAN

TOYKO

KYOTO

UJI

SANAA'S SCRAPBOOK

Seven hours into the flight to Japan. The first-class cabin of the plane is dark. Most passengers have taken advantage of seats that make down into beds. With eyeshades and earplugs in place, covered in dark blue blankets, and their heads pressed into soft pillows, they have settled into sleep. The cabin crew works quietly behind the drawn curtains of the galley.

One reading light is on. One passenger is still awake, still upright in her seat. Alice is about to consult a small, black notebook trimmed in red leather. Closing her eyes, she first opens her memory to the last time she was in Japan. She called herself "Sanaa" then. The notebook in her hands is "Sanaa's Scrapbook."

Will she be Sanaa this time? Or choose a new name? Some Japanese take many names. Notably those in the arts - poets, painters, actors, potters, calligraphers, and singers. Her favorite Japanese artist, Hokusai, used more than fifty names over seventy years, each new one signifying some change in his life or art. Sometimes his pseudonyms seemed playfully chosen - mere reflections of a whimsical mood. Only Hokusai knew why. And Hokusai never explained.

Alice's friend, Matsui Zenkichi, has also had many names. Kabuki actors change names as they progress through their careers.

Why not me? she thought.
My life is my art. And I feel change coming.

*

She opened Sanaa's Scrapbook to a page entitled "Things to Remember the Next Time I Am in Japan."

1. *Uchi* and *soto* - big difference. Being on the inside as opposed to being on the outside. To Japanese, foreigners are mostly soto.

2. *Gaijin* - foreigners - all non-Japanese are the same. And

they call me a *henna gaijin* - weird foreigner - because I'm part Japanese, speak some Japanese, and know about Japanese history and culture.

3. *Yoroshiku* - part of a first greeting - "*Dozo, yoroshiku.*" Meaning: "Please, I am completely in your hands." Statement of trust. Understanding that comes from the Japanese assumption that they are of one mind about social obligations. Wordless accord. Also implies they know each other's minds. Not said to henna gaijin.

4. *Enryo* - respectful distance - always maintained between people.

5. *On* - obligations - debts - what one owes to another.

6. *Shirankao* - an "I-don't-know" face - revealing no thoughts or feelings - poker face - the face Japanese offer to foreigners - easily misunderstood.

*

Zenkichi had explained to Alice that Japanese were politely patient and forgiving of outsiders. But the closer a foreigner moved toward the inside of the culture, the more suspicious and threatened the Japanese became. "Don't try to be too Japanese," he admonished.

"Remain soto - outside."

He had also explained that someone like Alice - a single, confident, self-reliant young American woman who spoke passable Japanese - posed a unique social challenge to the Japanese Way. The extremes of Japanese politeness were a defense against her stepping over what they perceived as cultural boundaries.

"What seems like, Yes, of course, to you may in fact really mean that what you ask is impossible.

"We are, I regret to say, racist, sexist, and xenophobic in the extreme. But we hide it well. It's easy to overlook this because of our elaborate attention to formality and social grace. Our manners are our mask. And you must wear your mask - *yasashii* (polite, gentle) and *hazukashi* (modest, self-effacing, humble)."

Before she could object, he tempered his suggestion with a compliment. "It's only because you are smart and self-disciplined that you can play the part expected of you in the theater of Japanese life."

Zenkichi did not say, as is the Japanese Way, what he really thought. He did not say that what fascinated him and drew him to Alice were precisely her non-Japanese traits of personality and style and appearance. A fascination with gaijin women is characteristic of Japanese men.

*

For many of these same reasons, the tattoo master, Morioka, was conflicted about his relationship with Alice. With great civility and elaborate politeness, he had tried to explain to her that he would not be willing to do a classical Japanese, full-body tattoo on her.

She was not Japanese. No. Impossible.

But Alice heard "Perhaps" inside his refusal, and was only encouraged by the ruse of his offer to draw the invisible tattoo on her with flesh-colored ink.

However, when Alice modestly showed him the port-wine stain clutching her breast, he fathomed her need, and softened his attitude. To combine the ugly with the beautiful was a different order of opportunity, and very Japanese. An honorable task. He promised to consider the matter, though, in truth, he did not expect to see her again.

*

Alice turned to the page in Sanaa's Scrapbook where she had attached Morioka's business card. Never mind the invisible tattoo. She would ask him to tattoo her chest - at least that. To make art of her birthmark. She knew he would be doing her a great favor. Her *on* - her obligation - to him would be large and hard to reciprocate. She also knew that debts could be repaid in oblique ways - through other members of his family - to someone like his nephew, Matsui Zenkichi, for example.

Alice shut her notebook, turned out her reading light, and closed her eyes. *This could get complicated,* she thought, *but I like complicated.*

She fell asleep.

When she awoke, it would be morning in the Land of the Rising Sun.

KYOTO

Heeding Zenkichi's admonition to remain soto – to stay outside as a paradoxical way of gaining access to the inside of Japan, Alice had reserved a room in the ultra-modern Kyoto Station Hotel. Previously she had stayed in a 300-year-old *ryokan* – a classic Japanese-style inn near the heart of the oldest part of the city.

That had been awkward. Sleeping on the floor on a futon, being served her meals on the floor in her room, sharing the bath with other guests, and accommodating the schedules and customs of the inn were all as trying for her as they were for the innkeeper's staff. She and they knew she was only playing at being Japanese. Her situation reminded her of a Japanese couple trying to be cowboys at the dude ranch in Montana where she worked one summer as a teenager.

Moreover, when the staff of the ryokan realized that she knew enough Japanese to understand the comments they made about her, the awkwardness increased. Gentle politeness became cool formality.

The Western-style Kyoto Station Hotel catered to both Japanese and international travelers. The staff spoke English, and was proud to offer Western amenities with a Japanese touch of restrained elegance: well-designed beds and chairs and tables, and a private bath with shower – complemented by Japanese textiles and prints, and fresh flowers daily. The almost-instant service was smoothly efficient.

Though many foreign Japanophiles avoided the hotel and its location as not being the "real" Kyoto, they were romantics imagining an ancient, two-story city that no longer exists. Fire, flood, earthquake, and war have destroyed the wooden past, again and again. All that remains are a few historic districts, Amida temples, Zen monasteries, Shinto shrines, gardens and palaces – all maintained mostly in support of cultural nostalgia and the financial rewards of tourism. "Old Kyoto" has become a Japanese form of Disneyland.

Kyoto Station is the reality of modern Japan. In addition to the hotel, it houses shopping centers, bookstores, restaurants, and fast everything

- food, laundry, shoe-repair, florists, and almost every consumer service for the traveler imaginable. It is a city within a city - the hub of the wheeling life of contemporary Kyoto - built of steel and stone and glass and plastic - not wood, plaster, and bamboo.

Alice liked looking down from her high window and seeing hundreds of trains and buses and taxis taking thousands and thousands of people anywhere and everywhere at all hours of the day and night. She liked knowing she could come and go at high speed on short notice simply by asking the hotel staff to arrange the reservations and tickets. And unlike her feelings of alienation in the ryokan, she felt completely anonymous and comfortable in the Kyoto Station Hotel, part of the frenetic but well-oiled machinery of the modern city.

*

From her window Alice could look out over the street grid of the city, still laid out as it was when Kyoto was founded in 794. The pattern made it easy to find specific locations. She tried to pinpoint Morioka's tattoo studio. *Close by Yasaka Shrine at the end of Shijo-dori*, she thought. *There.*

Further down the same street she could see the roof of the Minami-za - the Kabuki theater on the east side of the Kamagawa River. Just beyond the Shijo Bridge. She recalled seeing the plaque on the west wall of the theater honoring the beginnings of Kabuki in the dry bed of the river in 1596. Though Kabuki is strictly limited to male actors now, Alice knew Kabuki's founder was a renegade temple dancer named Izumo-no-Okuni - a woman with unconventional ideas.

Though summer is not the season for Kabuki performances in Kyoto, Alice was certain that the actor Iwai Hanshiro XI - Matsui Zenkichi - would have come down from Tokyo to meet her. She came a day earlier than she told him she would arrive. A Shinto priest had once told her that jet lag was caused by the body moving faster than the soul. She wanted a day to let her soul catch up with her. Tomorrow she would meet Zenkichi at noon in front of the Minami-za.

Alice had seen Zenkichi in his Kabuki roles and costumes. She was particularly intrigued when he played *onnagata* parts, dressed as a woman. She wondered how he would feel about her new look - short black hair, mannish clothes, and glasses. Now she needed a new name for this new episode in her life. A man's name. Zenkichi, of all people, would understand. The name was there, waiting for her in the back room of her mind. At the right time she will be certain.

The Possibles Bag

Turning away from the window, Alice picked up the shoulder bag she used for traveling, unzipped an inner compartment, and withdrew a small, drawstring purse. Made from antique silk kimono fabric, a multi-colored flower print on the outside, crimson red silk on the inside. She bought it the last time she was in Japan. Carefully, slowly, she poured out the contents into the palm of one hand.

"Possibles" - a nine-letter word.
Nine tiny objects. Talismans. Keepsakes. Provocations.

Each one energized with the power of memory. Each one infused with the power of provoking creativity. She never carried more than nine at one time. There had been others, but her rule was that if she found something more immediately meaningful, she must give one of the original objects away. Even though she only carried nine objects with her, the others always remained in her possession at a distance. She knew where they were and why they were there. A shared caretaking.

Alice called the purse her Possibles Bag because each object reminded her of the myriad possibilities contained in momentary experiences. Any object and any moment could be a window on the world, if close attention was paid. It was all a matter of awareness.

Alice placed the nine talismans in a row on the bare, wooden top of the desk. She sat down in a chair and considered them:

Half of a walnut shell.

A yellow leaf from a ginkgo tree - protected in clear plastic.

A silver bell - smaller than the end of her little finger.

A white snail shell as small as the bell.

One of a pair of dice - black ebony with red and white spots.

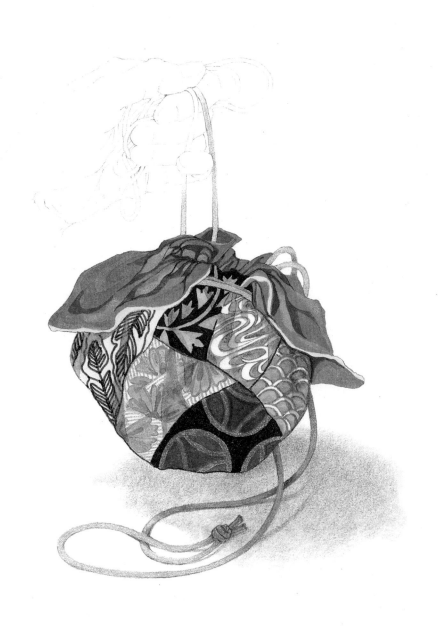

An inch-long statue of a Buddha - lying down asleep.

A wisdom tooth - her own.

A broken piece of mirror.

Three tiny wishbones - tied together with a strand of her white hair.

All worthless, as the world counts value.
All priceless in their value to Alice.
The visible forms epiphanies may take.

LADY FUJITA AYA

In Sanaa's Scrapbook, Alice accumulated words describing characteristic qualities of Japanese literature:

> Evanescent, temporary, transitory, elusive, momentary, contradictory, enigmatic, nostalgic, transient, bittersweet, poignant.

The best Japanese literature combines the tragic and the beautiful. Alice called it, the "it-hurts-so-fine" tradition.

Notable in most famous love stories - unrequited, unconsummated, and impossible love, as well as illicit, bizarre, and deadly love. In Japanese stories, lovers rarely live happily ever after. The suicide of star-crossed lovers is much favored by Japanese readers and theatergoers.

Beauty is found in the moment. And the moment does not last.

Love is not chosen. It chooses you.

You must take the consequences.

So say the Japanese.

*

Alice had a collection of small, handmade pieces of heavy, ivory-colored paper, much like a deck of cards. On these she had begun recording the thoughts of Lady Fujita Aya. One said the following:

> *Nothing lasts. Everything quickly becomes something else. The cherry becomes the cherry tree becomes the cherry blossoms becomes the cherry. The Way is flowing.*

Another said:

> *Love will always lead you over the cliff. Fall carefully or fall carelessly, landing involves pain and sorrow. And even death.*
> *The pleasure is in the falling.*

*

Lady Fujita Aya is another alternative personality of Alice Riley: an Asian version of Fabuliste Curnonsky. Instead of collecting thoughts from the diaries and pillow books of women of the imperial court of bygone days, Alice wanted to think and write as if she *was* one of those women.

The Pillow Book of Sei Shonagon is one influence. Written a thousand years ago by a woman of the court, it is a collection of observations and anecdotes and 164 lists of things Sei Shonagon liked or disliked - things, people, and behavior.

Alice also liked *The Poetic Memoirs of Lady Daibu*, a collection of alternating poetry and prose, written by a member of the court in the early thirteenth century.

Finally, and above all, Alice was inspired by Murasaki Shikibu, the author of the greatest work of Japanese fiction, *Genji Monogatari - The Tale of Genji*. This long account of court life in Heian Japan across the end of the tenth century and into the beginning of the eleventh contains the essence of the intrinsic tone of Japanese literature: evanescence - the temporary and transient nature of life.

It is the first novel, written five hundred years before Cervantes' *Don Quixote*. Though twice as long as *War and Peace*, there is no ongoing plot and no thesis. It is character-driven. The author only declares: "This is the way it was and is, moment by moment."

The author was an unconventional woman who lived in a time and place ruled by convention. Alice wondered what it would be like to live and think and write like she did. To tell stories that might be remembered for a long, long time.

THE WALNUT SHELL

Alice picked up the walnut shell half from her Possibles Bag collection, held it in the palm of her hand, and began telling a story she had been constructing in her mind.

"One fine day," Alice began, "there may or may not have been a fair young maiden, who walked barefooted along the sandy beach of Amanohashidate, where she had walked many times before. Her shapely bare legs were showing because she had tucked the hem of her pale blue kimono up under the scarlet sash at her waist.

"A fisherman had beached his boat on the sand, and was pulling his net onto the beach. She had seen him several times before, but she had looked closely at him only once, and ever after looked away when she passed him. Because the fisherman's face had been disfigured by fire - charred on one side, and that side of his mouth had been scarred into a permanent grin, exposing some of his teeth - she could not tell if he was young or old.

"On this day, the fisherman picked up something from the sand and approached her. In one hand he held what appeared to be a small wooden ball. In his other hand he held a knife.

"The fair young maiden stepped back in fear.

"The fisherman said 'walnut' - showing her that the sea and sand had worn it smooth. With the point of his knife he split the shell, picked out the nut, and ate one half to assure her it was safe and good. He offered the other half to her. She ate it, finding it salted by the sea. Then he placed half of the empty shell in her hand. He closed her fingers over the shell to say that she should keep it. She turned away and walked on.

"Only when she had gone a long way down the beach did she open her hand to look at the shell. There was a perfect heart shape on the inside. When she looked back, the fisherman was out on the sea, rowing away towards the harbor.

"She would never know that the fisherman had often watched her as she came and went in the village. He had fallen in love with her. She would never know that there were no fish near that beach. Nor would she know that he was not even a fisherman, only a love-struck young man who had borrowed the boat and the net, and had rowed out each day he saw her walking on the beach.

"Because he was disfigured, because he was not her social equal, and because he was poor - for these unchangeable reasons - the young man would never approach her again. She would forever be out of his reach.

"Impossible love.

"And so. He gave her his heart in the shell of the walnut.
"Worthless and priceless.
"The young woman threw the shell away.
"I found it on the beach. Only I know the story.
"And now you know.
"If I give you the walnut shell, will you understand why?"

Alice walked to the window of her room, her fingers closed around the walnut shell with the heart inside. She looked out over Kyoto and beyond. She wondered if she would ever tell this story and give the shell away - and to whom - and what she might be given in return.

"So ends the *Tale of the Walnut Shell* from the Possibles Bag of Lady Fujita Aya," she said, as if someone else were in the room.

Tsuyu

In early summer, being on the same latitude as California and Crete, Japan is hot and humid. June marks the onset of *tsuyu*, the plum rain season. Set as it is in a bowl of hills inland from the sea, Kyoto has the atmosphere of a city built in a hot-spring bath. Rain falls almost every day, washing away the memory of the flowering trees of spring.

Sadness.

In compensation, every growing thing that can be green is green and even greener than that. It is the season of the rain-loving hydrangeas in their range of hues from strong lavender through timid blue into bleached-bone white. The tiny flowers are pressed into keepsake books because, when dry, they hold their color, and preserve the memories of another passing of tsuyu.

Nostalgia.

At the beginning of the month, *Kaminari-yoke Taisai* - a festival to honor the god of thunder - is held at Kitano Tenman-gu shrine. And at the end of the month, *Nagoshi-no-harai* is observed. This ritual is meant to purify people of the sins they have committed during the first six months of the year, in order that they might face the test of the hot summer months with pure hearts and restrained tempers, remembering that the heat will pass, as it always has.

Acceptance.

*

Alice wished she could walk out into the rain carrying a traditional Japanese umbrella, made of pale yellow oiled paper, the struts and handle of bamboo. There was still one maker in the Gion district. She had ordered an umbrella there the last time she was in Japan, requesting the plainer, larger version carried by men. The maker hesitated until she explained it was a gift for a Japanese friend. When she picked it up from the workshop, she carried it with her all day, even though it was not raining. She carried the umbrella as a symbol of delight – an example of something simple, functional, and lovely that could not be improved upon. Sturdy. Lightweight. Beautiful.

The color of the paper reminded her of ginkgo leaves in autumn – a pale, translucent, butter yellow that stained the gray light of a rainy day with a hint of the sunshine above the clouds.

She often used this umbrella when walking in Seattle. Strangers would stop her to appreciate it and ask to hold it themselves. They wanted to know its story. They wished they had one.

But she would not carry such an umbrella open in Japan. The Japanese would not approve. The umbrella could not belong to her. The umbrella was uchi – inside – and Alice was not.

Therefore, when she walked out into the light rain of Kyoto, Alice carried the epitome of modern Japanese umbrella technology. Black nylon, steel ribs, plastic handle – small, strong, lightweight – collapsible into a tiny package no larger than a rolled newspaper, and easily tucked into her shoulder bag. Efficient. International. The same umbrella carried by every Japanese she passed on her way to the Minami-za to meet Zenkichi.

Umbrellas do not change the influence of the rain. However it may be constructed, an umbrella does not alter the slightly melancholy feeling of loneliness one gets while walking alone under one in the rain. Umbrellas distance people from one another. Umbrellas are portable privacy, turning thoughts inward.

Umbrellas intensify fundamental solitude.

*

Crossing the Shijo Bridge, Alice remembered the first time she saw Matsui Zenkichi. There were three black-and-white photographs on the foyer wall of Morioka's tattoo studio. In one, Zenkichi was the Kabuki actor Iwai Hanshiro XI in the elaborate costume and makeup of a young woman, striking a time-stopping *mi-e* – a pose meant to stamp an image of perfect beauty on the imagination of the audience.

In the second photograph, he was a fierce demon, momentarily frozen in the middle of a roaring, whirling dance of terror, smashing a fearful hole in the atmosphere of the drama.

And in the final photograph, he was a strong-featured young Japanese man in Western suit and tie. Solemn, confident, unmistakably masculine.

She wondered what form his character would take today.

The shower stopped as Alice neared the end of the bridge. And Alice stopped briefly to pay her respects to the statue memorializing the woman who began Kabuki, Izumo-no-Okuni.

Concentrating on shaking the water off her umbrella, and then folding and stowing it neatly, she was not aware of the motorcycle cruising slowly along behind her.

SEX

Noon. Where is Zenkichi? It's not like him to be late.

Experienced actors time their entrances precisely. Alice stood on the granite stones of the forecourt of the Kabuki theater, facing the elaborate doors, expecting him to come striding out at any moment.

Slowly, the motorcycle rolled up over the curb behind her, and stopped on the edge of the sidewalk. It was a heavy Kawasaki - Vulcan 1600 cc - stock black frame with an understated amount of chrome. Black leather seat. No frills. A machine designed for speed. Standing still, it seemed to be moving at a hundred miles an hour. The low, deep throb of its idling engine implied muscular authority.

In cycle parlance, "a serious ride."

The rider was likewise serious in appearance. He wore an unadorned black leather jacket, blue jeans tucked into plain black leather boots, black leather gloves, and a plain black utilitarian helmet. He sat looking one way and then another, waiting for an American woman with long white hair.

At that moment, Alice turned around, and noticed the motorcycle. The rider raised the plastic face shield of his helmet and stared at her. Alice stared back. A bold, face-to-face, eye-to-eye confrontation.

Zenkichi.

Alice.

Contact.

From the first time they met, their encounters had felt like a finely polished script, played out as if by actors who knew their cues and lines well. Regardless of how long the pauses might be - seconds, months, years -they would continue where they left off without any formalities of greeting.

They never spoke of it - they just *did* it.

Moreover, there was a feeling of enigmatic connecting: thoughts without words, sentences without verbs, songs without music. Haiku conversation, with meaning between lines and behind words. Alice called it "Talking in Zen telegrams."

"Ah, so. Kabuki actor on motorcycle," she said. "Bushido samurai."

Taking off his helmet, and minimally bowing a greeting with a nod, Zenkichi said, "*Hai.* Always costumes and disguises," he said. "Still you?"

"Never sure," she said.

He laughed.

"The new Saana. Short black hair, glasses, black pants and jacket. Nice. Motorcycle perfect. Helmet in saddlebag. Ride?"

Alice nodded her consent.

With the expertise of one already familiar with motorcycle helmets, Alice quickly had hers adjusted, with the strap tightened under her chin. Without further conversation, she mounted the cycle behind Zenkichi, set her feet firmly on the pegs, and hooked her thumbs into the pockets on either side of his leather jacket. She touched her helmet to his back. Ready.

Slowly, Zenkichi steered out into traffic, and then moved off swiftly up Shijo-dori. No harsh muffler blasts - no engine revving - no macho showing off. If you know who you are, you don't need to impress strangers on the street. If you are doing exactly what you most want to be doing with the person you most want to be doing it with, the world around becomes a soft blur in the background of your existence.

As the motorcycle began its turn at the next intersection, Alice tightened her grip around Zenkichi's waist and snuggled up against his back as they leaned together into the turn. This moment of connection - intimate synchronicity - is one reason why men and women ride in tandem, not in sidecars. Two riders merge into one. Ready! Go!

Now the Kawasaki picked up speed, weaving through traffic, now leaning left, now leaning right, binding the riders closer. The pulse of the throbbing four-stroke engine thrust them impatiently forward, on to the winding roads of the foothills of the mountains north of the city. Free of traffic. Faster. Faster! Spine-tingling speed, screaming power, imminent danger, gearing down, gearing up, sudden slowdowns, sudden speedups.

Lean left. Faster. Lean right. Faster! Electric shocks of adrenalin; heart pounding *DON-don, DON-don, DON-don* - knees and arms and hands and neck muscles clinched.

Pedestrians might be dismayed as the motorcycle soared by. They would hardly believe or understand that the motorcyclists were having sex. Being in tight tandem astride a motorcycle at full speed provides a power rush to the crotch. Sex with velocity. Sex with your clothes on. Sex on the edge. Sex!

Alice and Zenkichi would never come any closer to sexual intimacy than this. But it would happen as often as they rode. The most orgasmic moments of all would come at night, at three in the morning, roaring down the Osaka Expressway at one hundred miles an hour in the rain.

VROOOOOM! "YYAAAAHH . . .!"

*

At the end of the ride, when the beast was parked and switched off, they dismounted, removed their helmets and stood side by side, leaning on the motorcycle in silence. They never spoke about their feelings.

Zenkichi would light a cigarette and pass it to Alice. Neither one of them was a regular smoker. This sharing of one cigarette was an unspoken ritual. The pensive pause after sex. Stillness after explosive action.

Kabuki!

KABUKI

Understanding and appreciating Kabuki theater is not easy for a gaijin. The last time Alice was in Japan, she had asked Zenkichi to explain aspects of Kabuki to her on several occasions. When she was alone she would summarize his explanations in Sanaa's Scrapbook.

From Sanaa's notes, typed and folded and pasted into her scrapbook:

1. SHAKESPEARE AND ELIZABETHAN DRAMA have much in common with Kabuki. Late sixteenth century. A golden age in England and Japan. Plays performed outdoors - audience standing. Risky themes of aristocratic corruption, revenge, greed, incest, death, war, confusion. Actors and playwrights were lowborn - supported by the wealthy and powerful. Elaborate costumes, dance, and music played big part. Contradictions in themes abound - tragedy/comedy, love/hate, joy/sorrow, stupidity/wisdom, evil/good. Actors have always been both social outcasts and social lions. Kabuki is actor driven. Playwrights and directors not so important.

2. KABUKI - word comes from Chinese characters - ka, bu, ki - song, dance, skill. Came to mean offbeat, avant-garde, unconventional.

3. KABUKI BEGAN WITH IZUMO-NO-OKUNI - renegade temple dancer set up small stage in dry bed of Kamagawa River below Shijo Bridge. Troupe of entertainers sang and danced and told ribald stories of common people - made vulgar fun of aristocracy. Three innovations: Women acting. No masks. Folk-style dancing lifting feet off the floor. Elaborate costumes both on and off stage.

4. LICENTIOUS LIFE STYLE of Kabuki troupes soon led government to ban women actors from performing. Too vigorous - too lusty. Maybe prostitution. Kabuki survived with

popular support and unofficial aristocratic interest - stylized conventions - influenced by Noh plays and Bunraku puppetry - tradition of male actors playing all roles. Became a high art form, frozen in time. Like Western grand opera.

5. RENEGADE SPIRIT REVIVED NOW - New Kabuki - Super-Kabuki - rock and electronic music, high-tech lighting and stagecraft, adaptation of Western plays - Shakespeare in Kabuki style. Western interest in traditional Kabuki through international performances.

6. BANDO TAMASABURO V - contemporary Kabuki superstar. Beautiful, young - plays traditional onnagata roles, also acts in Western theater - Shakespeare, as Lady Macbeth - experimental drama, playing both male and female lovers - dances in Western ballet - directs and acts in film - TV. Wildly popular with both women and men, young and old. Most versatile and talented contemporary Japanese artistic personality. Though he inherited great name in Kabuki, he is an outsider, the seventh child of a restaurant owner. No peer and no successor. But because Kabuki has always been actor driven, he represents the future of Kabuki.

NOTE: All this is folded into the personality of Matsui Zenkichi.

7. TO BE A KABUKI ACTOR, one must be a chameleon. Depending on the role, Zenkichi must be able to seem to be tall or short, wide or thin, old or young, terrifying or beautiful, male or female, peasant or prince, warrior or priest, good or evil. A living personality who controls the changes. This is why I'm drawn to him and why I'm also afraid of him. He can be anybody.

Besides, as Lady Fujita Aya observed:
Everyone is normal until you get to know them.

GINKGO LEAF

After they had shared their cigarette, they went into the Perugia, a Japanese/Italian restaurant, where Zenkichi had reserved a table on the sheltered terrace. They were not offered menus. Zenkichi was a pampered regular customer, and, without asking, the staff served him and his guest dishes chosen by the chef.

Rain began falling once more, veiling the view of distant Kyoto. Continuing the conversation, Zenkichi began:
"Play your game. Answer a question I have not asked."

(Pause.)

"Vincenzo," said Alice. "That is my name for this episode of my life. It's a man's name. Your turn."

(Alice surprised herself. Out of the archive of her mind came this name. Of course - she was in the Perugia. Vincenzo Peruggia was the name of the Italian man who stole the Mona Lisa *from the Louvre in 1911.)*

"Vincenzo. Sounds Japanese. Vin-cen-zo," Zenkichi said.

"Vincenzo, my answer to your unasked question is Wednesday. Morioka will see you to discuss your tattoo. Perhaps begin. Design is decided."

"Wonderful! I know he sometimes works at night. I like doing important things at night. Could I come at three o'clock in the morning?"

"I will ask. I like that. May I watch? He has allowed me to watch before."

"Yes." *You will be a Witness,* she thought.

"Vin-cen-zo," said Zenkichi. "*Daijobu* - OK. We turn life upside down, inside out. Sleep all day. Live all night. It is quiet. Suits Kabuki life. In season I sleep until six. Go to theater. Rehearse, perform. Go out. Eat, drink. And go to all those places empty of crowds and tourists. Old streets, the riverside, gardens. Even an *onsen* is open - the hot springs outside at night - perfect. In bed before dawn. Live the life of night, Vin-cen-zo. I have so done for long periods of time. Do you think?"

71

"Yes," said Alice.

Just then a waiter brought small, clear glass cups of chilled sake.
"To the night," said Alice, lifting her glass.
Zenkichi touched his glass to hers. "To the night."

"Do you know sake, Alice-chan?"
"No. Educate me."
"This is *junmai-daiginjo*, super-premium, pure rice sake, made from Yamadanishiki rice, and brewed with deep spring water by Sudo Honke, established in 1141 and continued by fifty-five generations of the same family.

Alice considered her glass.

Zenkichi continued, "Sake is the distilled essence of Japan, not just a drink. Rice cultivation is traditionally regarded as a religious act, invoking the *inadama*, the fertile spirit of the plant. This sake is the best of the best, and I would drink it only on auspicious occasions. Like this."

Alice reached out and took Zenkichi's glass, handed her glass to him, and said, "To rice."
They drank, each from the other's glass.

"Vin-cen-zo - tell me one of your stories," said Zenkichi.

Alice drank her sake in small sips while looking out into the steamy landscape, more water than air - rain, mist, clouds.
She sat still - in her Mona Lisa pose - hands crossed in front of her on the table - a slight smile. Melancholy swirled around her like invisible fog. She recalled one of Basho's haiku:

> *"Even in Kyoto -*
> *Hearing the cuckoo's cry -*
> *I long for Kyoto."*

Reaching into her purse, she retrieved her Possibles Bag. Loosening the drawstring, she picked out the yellow ginkgo leaf in its clear plastic envelope. Carefully, she eased the fragile, fan-shaped leaf onto the palm of her hand. "This is a leaf from one of your own bonsai. Remember?"
They both knew that the ginkgo tree - *Ginkgo biloba* - also called the

maidenhair tree - is ancient. There are fossils from the Mesozoic era - 220 million years ago. The tree is perhaps the oldest living seed plant. In China there are trees a thousand years old. It is a sacred tree, planted in temple grounds. Ginkgo trees are dioecious: Their female and male parts are produced on separate trees. The male tree must exist nearby for the female to produce seeds.

Alice need not remind Zenkichi of what she knew about ginkgos. Nor would she tell him about the bonsai ginkgo in Alex Evan's greenhouse on the Oxford Canal. As he asked, she would only tell him a story.

*

"It is said," Alice began, "that once upon a time, there may or may not have been a young maiden, the daughter of a powerful daimyo, who was captured by bandits while traveling from her father's castle to the castle of her grandfather. She was taken to the high mountains, to the monastery of rebel warrior monks, to await ransom.

"Though her clan searched high and low, and though many of the bandits were captured, tortured, and finally killed, the whereabouts of the young woman remained unknown. As winter approached, she was still a prisoner. The monastery was cut off from the rest of the world by the deep snow that came very early that year.

"One of her guards, a young monk, brought food every day. Slowly, as guards and prisoners will, they became bound together by strands of strange affection. But his vows and her highborn position made it impossible for them to express their feelings. When she began suffering from the cold, the young monk would make tiny fires in a brazier in her room. He would untie her hands and let her warm them over the fire.

"The wood the priest used was slow-burning and fragrant. The fire kept her warm, and the aroma of the wood made her forget she was a prisoner. Each night, after he made a fire, the young monk would tell her stories of long ago and far away.

"The young woman did not know that the monk was cutting down ancient bonsai trees from the monastery's collection. He was building the fire from trees more than five hundred years old, but no more than three feet tall. If he were caught, he would be put to death. But love had captured his mind. The fires he made each night expressed the fire in his heart.

"One night he brought in the broken limbs of a rare old ginkgo tree to feed the fire. One small leaf clung to one branch of the tree. The young woman rescued the leaf before the branch went into the fire. Moments later, senior monks came to drag the young man away. They had discovered his crime.

"The young monk went calmly, without resisting. From the first fire he had known the fate that awaited him. He was immediately put to death.

"The young woman heard his last gurgling cry as his throat was cut. She heard the crash of his body when it was thrown into the trees in the ravine below the monastery.

"Knowing her situation was hopeless without him, the young woman overturned the brazier, setting a smoky fire that the night wind raked through the monastery, asphyxiating the young woman in her cell.

"The fire attracted the attention of the young woman's clan, who were still looking for her. They found her scorched body, and carried it back to her father's castle. When her body was being cleaned and prepared for cremation, the attendants noticed a peculiar thing. Her right hand was inside her kimono, clutched to her breast over her heart. When they pulled her hand away, they found beneath it a single yellow ginkgo leaf, perfectly preserved.

"So ends the story," said Alice.

(Pause.)

Zenkichi stared out into the falling rain. He wanted to know more about the young monk. He wondered what became of the ginkgo leaf. But he did not ask.

The Japanese refer to moments like this as *aun no kokyu* – the act of breathing or thinking or feeling in unison with others. At the end of the story of the ginkgo leaf, Zenkichi was breathing deeply. As was Alice.

TATTOO

Three weeks later. Half past three in the morning. Morioka's studio.

The clatter of fat rain falling in drumrolls across the roof is the only sound. On the traditional tatami-mat floor, on a firm futon covered with clear plastic, Alice - Vin-cen-zo - lies as still as death. Over her eyes is a white cloth. Between her teeth is a white towel. She is wearing plain white panties covered with another white towel, which is stained with blood. Sweat shines on her skin.

The smell of sandalwood incense tints the air.

Alice's left arm is raised to rest beyond her head, allowing Morioka to kneel close to her. Holding her left breast, gently stretching it flat, he methodically works black ink into his delicate design around the nipple. He works quickly, for this is the most painful part. But Alice does not wince or clench her teeth or cry out. Morioka is not surprised.

Last year, when he had drawn the part of the invisible tattoo that went down her back, he had finished the work by putting tiny Japanese characters for Change at the bottom of her spine. This he did with needles. Testing her. She knew what he was doing and why. She had not flinched.

Morioka had grave doubts about tattooing Alice from the beginning. She was not Japanese. And he was not sure if she understood about the tradition, the time, the cost, or the pain. Moreover, she was a woman. Morioka had few women clients, and their tattoos were always done on the back. Even for men, the chest, and especially the area around the nipple, were hard to tattoo because the skin there is exquisitely sensitive. Even the bravest men often winced from the needles. And there was one more problem: Because a woman's breast is soft and pliable, it would be hard to keep the design concise and clear.

Alice's determination made her hard to dismiss. Morioka had tried, but she took his polite, self-abasing refusal as Japanese modesty. She would not understand or accept *No*.

Alice had insisted that he see her chest. When she unbuttoned and

opened her blouse, and Morioka saw the breast deformed by the port-wine stain, he understood the challenge to his art. If he could turn this into something beautiful . . .

A traditional Japanese tattoo would not do. No gods or demons or warriors. For almost a year he had thought about it. When Zenkichi told him Alice's story about the ginkgo leaf, Morioka's design took shape in his mind.

Morioko had not anticipated two things: that the skin marked by the port-wine stain was far less sensitive than normal, and that Alice was capable of bearing pain better than any client he had ever had.

Alice had not anticipated one thing: that the pain from the tattoo needles quickly became a rush of near-masochistic pleasure. Her body seemed to defend her with an ecstatic euphoria while Morioka worked.

Only afterward, when she soaked in a hot bath to set the ink, did the accumulated pain strike her like lightning. In the first moments a scalding scream rose from her throat, contained only by clenching her teeth and clutching her mouth hard with her hand. *Oh, mygod, mygod, mygod . . .*

*

Each week, while Alice lay unmoving and Morioka rhythmically pushed dye under her skin with the needles, Zenkichi sat in the shadows of the room watching, nervously drinking tea. He was surprised that she had agreed so readily to have him watch. She had never told him about being a Witness.

Her courage impressed him. He had not been tattooed and never would be. Just watching the bloody work made him light headed. And at the same time he felt a sensual pulse in his own blood. Each time he watched, he felt the beginnings of arousal. He wondered if Morioka experienced the same feelings.

No. An idle question. For Morioka, tattooing - *irezumi* - is a fine art. What he does is not a job or even a craft. It is a Way. A life whose path is in the spirit of transient beauty. Sex has nothing to do with it. His skills and feelings are those of a physician. He would only laugh at the insistence of Freudian psychotherapists that if there is a man and there is a woman, then sexuality must be a dimension of their relationship. No. For Morioka, Alice's skin was only a living canvas for his art. Male or female had nothing to do with it.

He worked on, as if in a trance. The concentrated energy required of him and the endurance required of his client meant no more than an hour's work was feasible at any one time. He glanced at the incense stick burning time in the tokonoma. Already half gone.

When he had shown Alice his design on paper, she had said only, "Please begin, sensei." In that first session he had drawn the design on her body with indelible black ink. She had not even asked to see herself in a mirror. Her trust encouraged him about the rightness of his decision. The emphasis she placed on sensei - master - told him what he needed to know. They were in accord - of one mind.

In the second session, he had tattooed the main outlines in the black ink that would appear dark blue under the skin. When Alice returned for the third session he found that she healed quickly. Very little scabbing remained. No sign of infection or reaction to the dye. He could press on with details in black, and begin filling in broader areas with color. Perhaps eight more weeks to finish. Perhaps less, if all went well.

The Floating World

In Sanaa's Scrapbook there is this folded information sheet she picked up in a museum when she went to an exhibition of Japanese prints:

Ukiyo-e In a Nutshell

Ukiyo-e (you-kee-yo-eh) is a word made from three Chinese characters: *uki* (float), *yo* (world), and the suffix *e* (indicating "picture"). In modern usage, ukiyo-e usually refers to the woodblock prints of ordinary Japanese life and the life of the pleasure world from the mid-seventeenth century until the Meiji Restoration. Both Westerners and Japanese prize the prints, especially those of Hiroshige, Hokusai, and Sharaku. The latter's depiction of Kabuki actors are the most commonly recognized and reproduced today.

Endless, disputatious volumes have been written by scholars of art, culture, and history trying to define and codify the larger meaning of the term. Ukiyo-e—the Floating World—also refers to a demimonde—a subworld of artists, musicians, courtesans, writers, and dancers.

Toulouse-Lautrec's Bohemian life exemplifies a Western version of the Floating World. He lived out his life and produced his art in Parisian cabarets, brothels, circuses, and theaters—fueled by absinthe and debauchery. Furthermore, the artistic style of Toulouse-Lautrec owes much to the art of ukiyo-e; he was deeply affected by the examples of the art available in the Paris of his day.

Much of ukiyo-e depicts an amoral world in which rules are suspended, values turned upside down and inside out. It is the world of night, imagination, and evanescence.

In its broadest sense, the idea of the Floating World refers to the sad transience of a world in which one can live intensely only in the moment; one should eat and drink and sing and dance now, for tomorrow you may die. Life is an art—and only through the art of beauty and pleasure can one fling defiance at the inevitable.

*

Alice felt like an insect on a Mobius strip. Her topology had changed. She had been moving around the outside surface of Japan, always coming back to where she began. Soto.

Now it seemed that the hands of Fortune had cut across her path, given it a twist, and reconnected the ends. Without conscious effort, she found herself moving around both the outside and the inside of Japanese culture. Reversing day and night was the twist in her path.

*

Zenkichi was an insider to the nightlife of Kyoto, and, as a respected Kabuki actor, he was an honored guest where gaijin were usually not welcome. That he brought with him an attractive, androgynous, American woman was acceptable so long as she remained hazukashi - demure, modest, and unassertive. Alice became his silent companion, Vin-cen-zo.

*

The area of Kyoto called Gion Shinbashi is a small, triangular block of *o-chaya* - teahouses - on either side of the Shirakawa Canal. This historic preservation district appears much as it has for hundreds of years. By day the lanes are filled with camera-wielding tourists hoping to see an apprentice geisha - *maiko* - or to glimpse inside the teahouses.

These o-chaya are quasi-private clubs, and do not welcome visitors or strangers, especially gaijin. No *ichigen* - "first look" - customers allowed. The o-chaya are open only at night, devoted to the pleasures of eating and drinking. Their dauntingly expensive services involve elaborate protocols, and are provided only for valued clients and their guests.

Within the wooden walls of an o-chaya, history lives on in the traditional architecture and furnishings, the rituals of drinking tea and sake, the presentation of the elaborate *Kyo-ryori kaiseki* cuisine, and the classical dance and music of geisha.

By bringing Alice with him, Zenkichi stretched the rules of the house. However . . . Because he was a respected customer, because he was an established Kabuki actor, and because he was yasashii (a generous and courteous man), Alice was accepted. A man who respected tradition and who did not drink to the point of foolishness and misbehavior - such an honorable man was always welcome - even with a henna gaijin at his side. The contrast was appreciated: a traditional Japanese man with an exotic foreigner who knew her place.

*

On Tuesday nights, Zenkichi would come for Alice in a chauffeured car, knowing that after the tattoo session later on, she would not be able to ride behind him on his motorcycle.

In Gion Shinbashi they would spend the evening in an o-chaya with a few of Zenkichi's friends, who had been thoughtfully selected and prepared for Alice's presence in advance. They were to call her "Vin-cen-zo," and speak as much English as possible.

The guests would include writers, poets, actors, painters, and artisans. Though such gatherings of Japanese men are often an excuse for rowdy, ribald, and childish behavior, Zenkichi's friends were gentlemen. They drank slowly, and only to the point of lightheartedness. Usually they discussed literature or film. Sometimes a guest would read poetry.

And often they played verbal games. Zenkichi introduced them to "Give me an answer to a question I have not asked." He did not tell them he learned the game from Vin-cen-zo.

Several times Zenkichi retold the stories Alice had told him, bringing his acting skills to bear on the tales. The stories were enthusiastically applauded. He did not tell them the name of the author or that the applause was for her.

Some truths must not be told.

The geisha prized such occasions. Zenkichi and his guests paid respectful and knowledgeable attention to their talents: playing samisen, singing, reciting poetry of the Heian court, and performing the slow, complicated, and delicate dances of a Japan long past.

Though these occasions in the o-chaya went on for hours, they were not tedious. Leaving behind the mad rush of the modern world, the guests drifted in the stream of nostalgia. Eased in their journey by just enough sake, their senses satiated by the beauty of the food and the entertainment, they experienced the timelessness of the Floating World. Ukiyo-e.

The sadness that came when the pleasure of the evening ended was anticipated. Parting - sweet sorrow. Suitable, because the feeling balanced the equation; appropriate, because the guests and staff knew that "Vin-cen-zo" would be going to Morioka-sensei's studio to continue her tattoo. She would be going from pleasure to pain.

Zenkichi had explained the situation to both the staff of the o-chaya and his guests. Such matters would not be mentioned or even acknowledged during the evening. While the tattoo might stimulate private speculation and gossip, it was also grounds for respect. The Way of the Floating World.

*

The events of Tuesday-night-into-Wednesday-morning became ritual.

Leaving the o-chaya around half past two, Alice and Zenkichi arrived at Morioka's studio just before three o'clock. Few words were exchanged. Zenkichi honored the state of mind Alice needed for the tattoo session. When they reached the studio, Alice went with Morioka into the workroom, while Zenkichi stayed in the kitchen to prepare tea.

Alice disrobed behind a folding screen, lay down on the futon, put the rolled white cloth between her teeth, and closed her eyes. After Morioka covered her eyes with a white towel, he moved his inks and tools into place, lit a stick of hour-lasting incense, and knelt beside her. He waited before beginning. In silent stillness, Morioka and Alice summoned the courage required for the task ahead.

*

When Zenkichi smelled the incense, he would come in and sit down in a dark corner of the room. Alice had asked him to watch carefully. She wanted him to remember for her what she could not see.

When the incense had burned out, Morioka would stop and sit still again. Zenkichi would leave the room and return to the kitchen while Alice dressed. One night Morioka showed Zenkichi the white cloth Alice had clenched between her teeth. The center was marked by the crimson stain of blood. "She bit her lip," said Morioka. "But not a sound."

The evening ritual continued when Alice appeared in the kitchen. Morioka would pour three small cups of sake. They drank in silence.

Then Alice would bow slightly to Morioka, saying only "Sensei." And meaning, "Master, you honor me with your art."

Morioka would bow deeply in return, saying only "Dozo" as a sign of modesty, meaning, "Please. It is you who honor me."

*

The evening ritual concluded with the silent ride back to Alice's hotel. Then came the ordeal of her bath, the screaming pain from the hot water, and exhausted sleep by dawn.

Alice had explained about the tattoo to the manager of the hotel in unexpurgated detail. She offered to pay extra for the bloodstained towels and sheets, and for the revision of the schedules of the maids and room-cleaning service. She offered to pay extra not to be disturbed in any way during the day. Perhaps a large tip in advance to the maids would be appropriate?

Her candor impressed the manager.

This challenge to the hotel's service would be met.

To demonstrate his understanding, he saw to it that the usual white towels were replaced with black ones, and the white sheets were re-placed with flowered linen - woven in the purple and green shades of summer iris.

Parinirvana of the Buddha

And so the days passed into weeks. Each Wednesday the same.

Before dawn came, just before collapsing into bed, Alice would stand before the mirror in the bathroom and consider her chest: vivid red welts, puffy, swollen skin, and bloody scabs - as if someone had used a cheese-grater and a wire brush on her skin. The sight made her a little nauseated.

It hurt even when she lightly daubed petroleum jelly over the damaged areas. It hurt when she covered her chest with a large square of sterile gauze. It hurt when she taped down the edges of the gauze. Pain, pain, pain - like one long, deep splinter being shoved further under a fingernail.

Gingerly, she would pull a fresh white T-shirt over her head and down over the gauze. Having to lift her arms up over her head for the T-shirt made her light headed.

Fever flushed her skin. Ever since the first night of the needles she had felt hot and sweaty - her body's reaction to the invasion of the needles and dyes. A nonstop, low-level headache pounded in the front of her head. She felt sick all over. Every Wednesday she feared she could not go through with it again.

*

Tonight the pain was so sharp that she had increased her medication - two codeine tablets, an antacid, an antihistamine, and two strong sleeping pills. She sat on the toilet seat, sipping a glass of water, holding it with both hands to steady her trembling.

Barely able to rise, she moved to the bathroom door, and paused to glance back at herself before turning out the light. She asked the flushed face in the mirror, "Are you crazy?" She would have sworn the face in the mirror smiled and replied, "Cuckoo."

I'm hallucinating, she thought, as she closed the double curtains of the windows. With effort she hung the special Do Not Disturb During the Day sign on the outside of her door. Finally, at the limits of her energy,

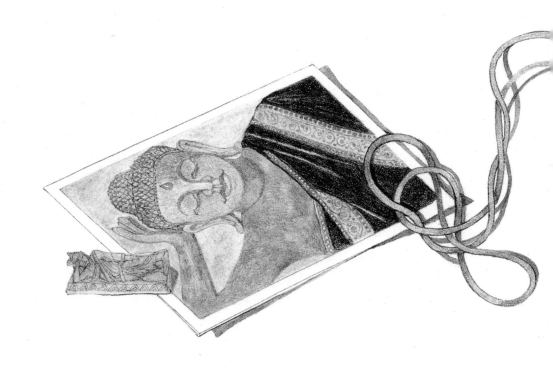

she slowly lay down on her back in the bed. She pushed earplugs into place, and positioned her sleep mask on her forehead. As a last detail of her bedtime ritual, she considered the tiny, gold image of the reclining Buddha - the one she carried in her Possibles Bag. She kept it on the bedside table.

On a trip to Thailand, she had seen many images of the reclining Buddha. He lay on his right side, head resting on his right hand, eyes closed, feet crossed, with a contented look on his face. In her ignorance of Thai Buddhism, she thought he was taking a nap. Such a human thing to do. Such a casual denial of his deity. Taking a nap. And such a contradiction to what Alice thought was the essence of his doctrine: Be awake.

Only later did she learn how wrong she was. The image did not portray him napping, but dying. The traditional account says that, feeling ill, he reclined in this position between two trees, closed his eyes, and passed from this life into another. Alice laughed when she learned the truth. Not napping - dying.

Still, going to sleep was a lot like dying - like passing into a parallel world. In that world Alice had never felt pain or fear. It was always a comfortable place to be for a while, if not forever. She touched the image of the Parinirvana Buddha, said, "Sweet dreams," pulled the sleep mask down over her eyes, and turned out the light.

As she began drifting down into sleep, she started telling herself a story she had told so many times she knew it by heart. It always seemed to be the gateway to dreams.

More than once upon a time, there may or may not have been a man who was so wise people thought he was a god. The man insisted this was not so. To prove it, the man would ask, "Do you think a god would eat, or go to the toilet, or bleed, or get sick, or cry, or sleep? Of course not. These are the acts of humans, not gods." He did those things. He was not a god.

One day he lay down to sleep and never woke up again. But his followers needed him to be a god, and their desire was enough to prove he was divine. They never understood that it was they who were asleep. They never understood that it was they who did not wake up. They never understood what he meant when he said that the source of all grief is unfulfilled desire. Sorrow comes from wanting to be a god or to have a god. That is what he said. And so . . . and so . . . and so . . .

MIND OVER MATTER

Alice spent the days after each tattoo session recovering in her hotel room. Waking, she would have tea and fruit brought by room service. Next came the dreaded ordeal of removing the dressing from her chest, taking another hot bath, replacing the dressing, and sleeping again to escape pain.

As she recovered, she would sit at the desk by the window while the silent and efficient maids quickly tidied her room and changed the bed linen.

Anticipating this stage of convalescence, she had made a list of things to occupy her mind while her body healed itself:

Five Diversions While Waiting

1. Reread *Genji Monogatari* (*The Tale of Genji*).

2. Watch classic Japanese sword-and-kimono films on TV.

3. Make lists in the style of Sei Shonagon's Pillow Book.

4. Continue the thoughts of Lady Fujita Aya:

> *Love is a stream, not a pond - waves, not a shore -*
> *Tide, not a lake. Still, you may drown in any water.*
>
> *Love creates as many problems as it solves.*
> *Love solves as many problems as it creates.*
>
> *Love makes the time pass.*
> *Time makes the love pass.*

5. Write poetry - not haiku - invent a form - Alice-ku:

> One-man woman.
> One-man band.
>   One-trick pony
>   One-way street
> One-night stand.

One eye open
One-track mind
   One for the money
   Two for the show
Three days at a time.

*

Alice wrote long letters to Alex and Max-Pol. But she tore them up, and instead sent each of them an envelope containing only a single sheet of blank music composition paper - lines without notes. She meant this to say that she had no words, but when she thought about Alex and Max-Pol, she thought in music.

By the third day after a tattooing session, she would be clearheaded and restless. And by the third day, Zenkichi longed for her company. He sent fresh flowers to her room on Saturdays, as a way of asking if she felt up to going about in the world again. Today, the note accompanying the flowers asked if she would like to go to Uji.

Yes. Perfect. Uji. She had long wanted to go.

Uji and the Floating Bridge of Dreams

Simply said, the hub of the wheel around which *The Tale of Genji* turns is the complexity of socially unacceptable love between highborn men and the women they desire. Such a summation vastly oversimplifies a novel that contains a thousand pages, relates events of seventy-five years, and involves three generations and more than five hundred characters.

But Lady Fujita Aya would say, "It is a love story. Everybody wins for a while. Everybody loses in the end." The author of the novel, Lady Murasaki Shikibu, might agree.

The last thirteen chapters of *The Tale of Genji* are set in the green valley of the Ujigawa River at the village of Uji, ten miles southeast of Kyoto, on the road to the ancient capital of Nara. Among other things, Uji is famous for its tea, fireflies, and evanescent atmosphere.

The main characters of the novel's final chapters are Genji's son and grandson, and three daughters of Prince Hachi. To royally complicate matters, Genji's "son" is actually the illegitimate child of Genji's wife and his best friend's son. A complex verbal banquet is served up: passion and betrayal - love and sorrow - intrigue and tea - pain, beauty, and pleasure.

When Alice reread the last chapters of the tale, she had imagined herself at Uji. At night. In the rain. On the Yume no Ukihashi, the Floating Bridge of Dreams, over the Ujigawa River. Standing under a Japanese umbrella with a prince, with whom ordinary love was desirable but impossible.

*

She asked Zenkichi to bring the right umbrella - a traditional Japanese one from Gion. They traveled by train from Kyoto Station on the JR Nara Line to Uji Station, on a rainy summer Sunday night, when the fewest tourists would be abroad.

*

90

Fujiwara Michinaga (966-1027) made his summer residence at Uji. The most powerful man during the golden age of the Heian Court, he was also famed as a poet, musician, and the builder of the magnificent villa called Byodo-in. At his death, the villa became a monastery, still in use after nine hundred years. It is the only example of Heian period architecture still standing intact, having somehow survived fires, wars, typhoons, and earthquakes.

Many literary scholars think Michinaga was the model for Prince Genji, and that Uji and Byodo-in are the setting for the final, melancholy chapters of the novel.

If you stand on the modern bridge in the rain at midnight on a summer night, *The Tale of Genji* seems more present than past, as if the characters are asleep in their chambers in the villas half-hidden in the trees along the river bank. In such a time and place, life seems a fragile dream between one state of existence and another, a bittersweet mix of beauty and sadness, punctuated by the sudden flashing of mating fireflies.

So it seemed to Alice and Zenkichi. They walked from the station in the humid mist, to stand alone together in the middle of the bridge. There was no other sign of life - no pedestrians, cars, trains, or even lights in the village houses. The night was so silent that the river could be heard sluicing past, through the bridge pilings beneath them, as if it was the stream of history itself passing through this valley.

Gently, the light, thin rain began again. Zenkichi opened the large umbrella. Gently, Alice pressed against his side, putting her arm around his waist, leaning her head against his shoulder. Gently, Zenkichi put his arm around her shoulder, and leaned his head against hers.

They were alone. And also lonely - for what each knew the other could not provide in the long term. The worlds of a Kabuki actor and a nomadic female henna gaijin could never merge. Meanwhile, they were as close as they would ever be. Content. If their feelings were a color: a deep, persimmon orange.

Alice remembered her night aboard the *Ariadne*, cuddled skin-to-skin with Alex. Perhaps these tender moments of subtle erotic companionship were the best that love ever had to offer. Beyond sex. Even beyond sensuality. Wordless, tranquil states beyond naming, with no other agenda than being *there, just there,* together.

She hugged Zenkichi closer. He squeezed her shoulder with his hand, and kissed the top of her head. Alice felt her skin flush - passion? Or just tattoo fever?

*

And in this blissful, intimate, romantic moment, Zenkichi suddenly hiccupped. *Heek-unh.* And again. *Heek-unh.* And then again. His struggles to repress the involuntary jolts from his esophagus produced squeaks and barks: *Heek-unh.*

Alice giggled. Alice laughed out loud. Zenkichi alternately laughed and hiccupped, and then sneezed, which only made Alice laugh harder. And when she hiccupped herself, she lost control.

Hysteria. Sobbing laughter. Alternating hiccups, and then hiccups in sync. They had to grasp the bridge railing, lest they be rolled overboard by waves of that purgative, cathartic laughing that knows no bounds or reason or end. *Heek-unh . . . heek unh . . .*

*

In times to come, when Alice called up Japan in her mind, the most vivid visual image of all would be this scene on the bridge at Uji. "My God! My God! I never laughed so hard in my life," she would say.

*

She had arrived in a solemn mental mood, prepared to shed tears and immerse herself in the lovely sadness of the world of Genji. Bring on the sweet sorrow.

Instead, she had laughed until she hurt, and in that visceral, giddy encounter with the Great Joke of Existence, she overpowered Zenkichi's embarrassment by covering his laughing, hiccupping face with kisses, there on the Bridge of Dreams.

Finally, she tossed their umbrella high into the air, watched it rise in eccentric loops and fall lightly into the river, floating slowly away downstream and out of sight. No regrets. Not an act of sorrow. An act of invincible joy.

(She didn't realize it at the time, but that memory would become a hinge on which the door to the next part of her life swung, leading from a state of solemn uncertainty to one of jubilant conviction.)

"Come on, Zenkichi," she said, "let's go see it all." And still laughing and hiccupping, they marched off the bridge with their raincoats pulled over their heads. Like cowled monks, hands tucked into their sleeves, they sloshed through the warm night, up into the silent hills by the gate of the Ujigami Jinja, the oldest Shinto shrine in Japan. Then down to the Asagiri Bridge, crossing to the island in the middle of the river, where they could faintly see the outline of Byodo-in on the opposite shore.

They saw nobody. Nobody saw them. Only the spirits of *The Tale of Genji* were about. Were it not for the streetlights and night-lights of the parks and shrines and temples, they could be back a thousand years.

"Did anybody wander around in those days, late at night, laughing and hiccupping? Did the prince ever have any fun?" Alice wondered aloud.

"Probably not. Too bad for them," said Zenkichi.

Exhausted and sopping wet, they sat across from one another in the station, waiting for an early morning train back to Kyoto.

Heek-unh . . . Ha!

*

This is the Floating World.

For the time being, as sweet as life gets. A short, ecstatic episode of joy, that passes indelibly into memory. A glance under the plain covering of existence, seeing the furnace of fate that finally consumes all.

Alice had never connected hiccups with enlightenment. Yet had not the great Zen masters said the Absurd and the Sublime were twins? And was she not with a man named Zen-kichi?

They were still laughing when they boarded the train for Kyoto, which was already occupied by early morning commuters.

Alice briefly considered inviting Zenkichi to her room when they reached Kyoto Station. She was reluctant to part with him. After such a night, it was tempting to push on down the path of intimate possibility.

Tempting. But. No. There was the matter of the tattoo, which was still scabbed and healing. And one other thing: confusing a Witness with a sexual partner would be unworkable. Impossible love. There are times to leave well enough alone. This was one.

THE TALE OF THE SILVER BELL

The next night.

Zenkichi and Alice had been walking for hours through the dimly lit streets and paths of the Sagano Toriimoto, the historic district on the western edge of Kyoto. They had been playing Left/Right/Surprise - turning in alternate directions at intersections, wandering aimlessly and deliberately at the same time. More than once they found themselves back where they began, having walked in a squared circle.

They had set out to see the thatched-roof country houses that were preserved in the upper valley of the district. On the way down, they passed the Rakushi-sha, the simple cottage where the poet, Basho, wrote many of his finest haiku. And they walked the path through one of the last extensive groves of timber bamboo in Japan, feeling like guests in a cathedral.

Despite the tranquility of the district, they talked nonstop, answering questions not asked. In a freewheeling mood ever since what Alice called "The Great Uji Bridge Hiccup and Laughing Festival," their answers stayed in the realm of information, avoiding feelings. Zenkichi told Alice more about Kabuki than she could ever remember. And Alice told Zenkichi more about Monet and his garden than Zenkichi could absorb.

*

In time they came to rest in a small boat on a pond in a large garden owned by a wealthy patron of Zenkichi's. A surprise prepared for Alice.

It had begun with their entering through a hidden gate left unlocked in anticipation of their arrival after midnight. They found that an oil-burning lantern had been left lit for them just inside the gate. When they came to the pond, they walked out on stepping-stones to where the boat was moored under a thatched pavilion.

Another low-burning oil lantern had been placed on the deck-boards of the boat. Two cushioned seats faced one another, and between

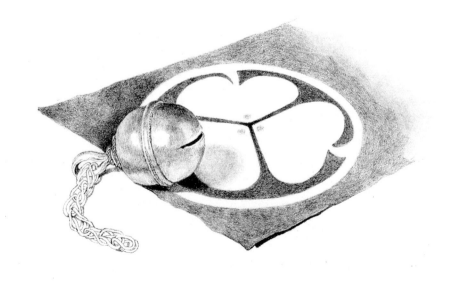

them, on a tiny table, was a three tiered, orange-lacquered *bento* box, containing strawberries, powdered sugar, and salted pumpkin seeds. A small round wooden bucket held a stoneware bottle of sake and two matching, thimble-size cups.

The only sound was the clamorous, burpy crank of the love songs of frogs, and the rhythmic dripping of rain from the edges of the white wisteria overhanging the water. From time to time giant carp - mottled in black, white, orange, and gold - surfaced through the mirror of the pond, attracted to the boat by the lamplight. The fish blew bubbly kisses at Alice and Zenkichi and sank back behind the mirror, leaving on the water only the upside-down duplicate of the boat and the faces of the man and woman in it.

A Floating World - as real as imagined.

The moment reminded Alice of the chapter in *The Tale of Genji that* she had read only that morning. *Ukifune* (drifting boat) is the character Ukifune's simile for herself in her poetic reply to Niou as they cross the Uji River together:

> *"The enduring hue of the Isle of Orange Trees may well never change, yet there is no knowing now where this drifting boat is bound."*

*

They ate the strawberries dipped in sugar, leaving white mustaches above their lips. The salty pumpkin seeds balanced the sweetness, and the cool sake loosened their tongues and minds.

"Vin-cen-zo."

"Hai, Zen-chan," replied Alice.

"Story, dozo."

"Hai, Zen-Chan."

Anticipating the opportunity, Alice had brought her Possibles Bag with her in her coat pocket. From the bag she took the tiny silver bell - the size of the end of her little finger. Holding it by the loop at its top, she shook it to show it was a functional bell: *Chinkle, chinkle, chinkle.*

"Hold out your hand," she said.

Placing the tiny silver bell in the palm of Zenkichi's hand, Alice leaned back in her seat, closed her eyes, and breathed deeply. She would not explain where the bell came from or that she wore it around her neck at times when she lost touch with herself. The bell's *chinkle* helped find her way home.

But I'm not lost. I'm here, she thought, and began the story.

*

"Once upon a time there may or may not have been a girl who was of the People of the Sea, and a boy who was of the People of the Mountains.

"She lived on a small island just offshore of the mainland.

"He lived in a village high up on a ridge.

"Between them was a narrow channel of water. Sometimes the tide would go out far enough to expose the mud flats between the island and the shore. The People of the Sea and the People of the Mountains would meet when they came to harvest clams and mussels. When the sea returned, the people returned to their separate homes.

"On such a day of meeting and leaving, the boy and the girl fell in love. They did not talk or touch. But they knew how they felt. As the years went by, they saw each other only at harvest times, when the sea withdrew at low tides. They began to dream their life together.

"Though they did not know it, their dreams were identical. They dreamed of finally touching, embracing, marrying, having a child, and living somewhere else far away.

"When their first dream-child was born, they named her 'Someday's Child.' They hung a tiny silver bell around her neck so that if she got lost, they would be able to find her. All of this in their dreams. The same dreams.

"And then one day, the earth shook, the island disappeared beneath the sea, and the villages fell from the mountains. A tsunami washed all away. No record was left of the People of the Sea or the People of the Mountains.

"But forever after, those who visited that place would swear that at night when the wind died and the sea was calm, they could hear the *chinkling* sound of a small bell, as if something was lost and wanted to be found."

(Silence.)

Zenkichi's gaze was fixed on the silver bell in his hand.
"Keep the bell, Zen-chan," said Alice.
"No. It must find its Way on. Watch."

He tapped the surface of the water with one finger. When he saw a huge orange-and-red carp rising, he tossed the silver bell into the air. As it splashed into the water, the carp was there to meet it. And to swallow it.

Zenkichi explained. "Someday the carp will die or be caught and cut up. Someone will find the bell. They will wonder how the bell came to be there. They will have to tell their own story to find out."

THE FOLLOWING

June became July became August – summer flowed on – and the weather followed its usual course as well: warm-and-wet became hot-and-dry became wet-and-mild. Alice continued her upside-down life, which had become an emotional roller-coaster ride, driven by the ongoing tattoo ordeal.

The calm of the Tuesday evenings at the o-chaya was followed by the pause at the peak of stillness just before the first needle was plunged into her skin. Then came the gut-clenching fall into pain that plunged her whole being down and down and down, until the next slow climb of days of healing until the next summit and the next plunge.

Kyoto celebrates summer with grand and prodigious festivals. Thousands and thousands and thousands of people crowd the streets for Gion Matsuri, featuring the display of monumental decorated carts, pulled by teams of hundreds of men through the streets.

And more: *Obon* dancing, ceremonies honoring the spirits of ancestors, processions of priests, re-enactments of samurai contests, and the lighting of fires on the five hills surrounding Kyoto. Every temple and shrine and neighborhood holds celebrations of a lesser scale. All in respect of the *kami* (the spirits that dwell in all things) and to honor the spirits of all ancestors, who arrive in August, as relatives will.

Alice observed at a distance. She was afraid of being jostled in a tightly packed crowd and not being able to protect her scabby chest. She watched from her hotel window, never going out until the throngs went home and the streets were quiet again. Not that she disliked celebrations. But she would celebrate when the tattoo was finished.

Zenkichi regularly returned to Tokyo on business for several days at a time, leaving Alice on her own. As she healed and felt better, she went out in the evenings to attend films, exhibitions of art, and music recitals. Whole evenings were devoted solely to working her way through the shelves of art books and crafts magazines at Maruzen and other bookstores. Once she came home with all the books on Kabuki she could carry.

Remembering her promise to Nelson Bellingham and Jacks O'Rourke to reconnect with the world of security research, she called Toshiba in Osaka, hoping to contact colleagues from the days when she had made visits to their research laboratories. Though she left messages with her cell phone and hotel numbers, she got no response.

*

On Sundays and Mondays she stayed up until dawn, walked to one of the famous shrines or temples, and remained until the first waves of visitors came, before returning to her hotel and bed.

It was during one of these early morning temple visits that she realized she was being followed. Moreover, she realized that her follower was himself being followed. She was reminded of Oxford, and Wonko warning her to be careful.

*

The Man - she was certain it was always the same one - had turned up several times recently. Though he was not always dressed the same way, she noticed and remembered his face. Japanese. He was sitting in the lobby reading a book when she came down this morning. He followed two blocks behind as she walked. And as she wandered through the grounds of the Buddhist temple of Kiyomizu-dera, she glimpsed him several times at a distance. When she moved, he moved.

And when *he* moved, a *woman* moved in tandem with him. Japanese.

Alice went up to the *hondo* or main hall of the temple, built over-hanging the edge of a cliff. Walking along its open veranda, she could look down on the grounds below and see both her follower and his shadow. Both of them had glanced up at her. Odd. It seemed obvious. Did they want her to see them?

Boldly, she walked down the long steps leading to the base of the Otowa no Taki, the Sound of Feathers Waterfall, below the hondo, rinsed her hands in the spray in the customary act of purification, and then strolled out into the park, well beyond the temple buildings. Sitting exposed and available on a bench, she waited.

You know I know, she thought. *Come and get me.*

Suddenly, her cell phone rang.

"*Moshi moshi*," whispered a female voice. "Hello. I am friend. You understand?"

"Hai. I've seen you this morning."

"So-so. It is my honor to speak to you. But you are safe. Have you seen the man who follows you?"

"Hai. I've seen him this morning."

"So-so. Not to worry. He is only a man writing a novel. There is an American woman in his novel. He follows American women."

"How do you know? That may be a cover."

"Ask him. He will say."

"Just walk up to him and ask?"

"Hai."

Alice stood up and looked around. No sign of the Man. She walked toward the entrance gate. Stopped. Looked around again. No. And no woman either. She walked back to the temple area, paid to draw a wooden stick from a container, and exchanged it for a paper fortune.

If the fortune was unfavorable, a pilgrim would tie it to a nearby tree, leaving the matter in the hands of the gods, in hopes it would not come true. Not knowing if the fortune was good or bad, she tied it to the nearest tree.

Let them figure it out, she thought.

She also bought a small wooden plaque used for appeals to the gods. On one side was the image of a green dragon riding a golden bell. On the blank back side she wrote:

"The eye looks. The mind sees." She signed it, Lady Fujita Aya.

And hung it on a wall covered with hundreds of similar plaques.

Quickly, she walked around a small adjacent shrine and came back to stand out of sight by a stone staircase, and waited.

Five minutes later, the Man bought a wooden plaque, wrote something on it, removed hers from the wall and replaced it with his. Alice waited. Soon the Woman did the same thing - removed the Man's offering and replaced it with her own.

Just as Alice was about to walk over to the wall of entreaties, her cell phone rang again. The Woman's voice, sharp and urgent: "Go back to your hotel. Now!"

"Hello? Hello?" The caller had hung up.

Intimidated enough by the intensity of the voice to follow the no-nonsense instructions, Alice obeyed. But though she looked around and behind her often, her followers were not to be seen. Not in the park. Not on the walk back to the hotel. Not in the lobby. Whose side were they on? What did the messages on the replacement plaques say?

She never saw them in Kyoto again.

But they saw her.

THE REVEALING

September.

Morioka finished Alice's tattoo a week earlier than expected. Zenkichi was in Tokyo that night. Alice came alone. Morioka inspected his work as she lay on the mat before him. Tenderly smoothing a healing salve onto her skin, he softened and removed the last little pieces of scab. With a very fine needle he lightly touched up one small detail. Sitting back on his heels, deep in thought, Morioka murmured as he ran his eyes over the tattoo, still surprised at what he had done.

"*Saaaaa . . . ummmm . . . so . . . so . . .*"

Morioka lifted the cloth from Alice's eyes. Placing one hand lightly on her chest, and breaking his usual mask-like expression, he smiled.

"Vin-cen-zo - finished," he said.

He went on to explain that she must come once more - at the same time next week - with Zenkichi. "No more painful irezumi - only ceremony." She was reminded to take many hot baths in the meantime - to enhance the colors. Morioka wanted to have one last look.

A ritual look.

*

A week later. The last night with Morioka.

When they arrived, Morioka was not in his usual working clothes of blue jeans and black T-shirt. Wearing a chocolate brown, linen kimono, he greeted them as honored guests, not clients. Zenkichi wore a similar kimono, but he had instructed Alice not to dress up - to wear only her raincoat, with only panties under that.

"Trust me," he said, "You like surprises."

Kinky, thought Alice, as she got into the car, knowing Zenkichi knew she was almost naked under her raincoat. She felt her skin flush as she sat next to him. *So, surprise me,* she thought.

Morioka's studio had been tidied and cleared of tools and inks and towels. Instead of the usual working futon, the faded-yellow reeds of the bare tatami displayed only a large, rectangular box, wrapped in silver paper and tied with red silk ribbon.

"Dozo, please," said Morioka, pointing to the box and the folding screen behind which Alice usually undressed. Morioka and Zenkichi bowed, and left the room.

Zenkichi had sent ahead a plain white silk under-kimono, and a plain black silk outer kimono, marked in the center of the back with a plain white circle where a family crest would usually be. Also a narrow, lightweight silk sash, dyed scarlet with the distillation of safflowers. No traditional obi - too tight, too wide, too formal, and too Japanese.

Alice opened the box, admired the creamy silk under-kimono, and, on impulse, not only took off her raincoat, but removed her panties as well.

If they are up for surprises, I won't let them down, she thought.

When Morioka and Zenkichi returned to the studio, they found Alice standing in the center of the tatami wearing the black kimono, with the edges of the white silk under-kimono modestly displayed around the neckline in proper Japanese fashion.

As if not really seeing her, Zenkichi said, "Kneel, please."

He put two boxes down beside her. From one he took hairpins and a can of spray lacquer. He pinned and patted and sprayed her hair tight against her head, working impersonally as if she were a mannequin.

Out of the larger box, he lifted a black wig used in Kabuki. The Wig of a Beautiful Young Courtesan - one he himself used in onnagata roles. He had gone all the way to Tokyo to fetch it for this occasion.

Opening a box of ceramic pots of stage makeup, he consulted with Morioka in Japanese too rapid for Alice to understand. Morioka kept shaking his head, until finally he himself picked up a pot, touched his forefinger to the paint, and with great delicacy put a single spot of crimson red in the middle of her lower lip.

"Hai. Finished," he said.

Standing, the two men removed the boxes, and stood well back from the tatami in silence. "Stand, please," said Zenkichi, softly.

Slowly, Alice rose.

"Reveal, please," whispered Zenkichi.

Slowly, Alice opened the black kimono.

Slowly, she opened the white under-kimono to her waist, pulling both garments far enough apart to display most of the tattoo.

The two men stopped breathing.

And in that silent, infinite moment, Alice let both kimonos slide off her shoulders and down around her feet. She stood before them naked, slightly turned in a Kabuki pose - a mi-e - like the night she stood before the mirror at the onsen to see the invisible tattoo become visible.

Eyes wide open - standing strong - in a Kabuki actor's stance that says, Observe! Remember! This is the moment of truth.

Even though they had seen the tattoo as it developed, the two men had not seen it this way. It was like the moment an artist and patron see a painting framed and hung in a gallery for the first time. And in their most vivid imaginings, they had not anticipated seeing Alice naked. The "frame" and the "work" combined to create a sense of *yoin!* - like the sudden striking of a temple bell that continues ringing even as it fades away.

Where once there had been the ugly, maroon birthmark of the port-wine stain, now bloomed a magnificent poppy - magenta petals with flame-red edges. Her nipple had become the black center of the poppy. The dark green stem seemed to rise out of her navel, but the leaves were not poppy leaves. Instead, Morioka had used ginkgo leaves - as green as summer grapes before they ripened.

What seemed at first glance like a vine entwined around the poppy's stem was in fact a long, slender, black snake. It disappeared behind the poppy. Its head reappeared at the upper edge of a petal. Its eyes were two tiny patches of port-wine stain just below Alice's shoulder. Its delicate forked tongue seemed to have just flicked out.

The design was alive, moving as Alice breathed.

Her white skin set off the intense colors - and the strange beauty of the design was enhanced by the loveliness of Alice's right breast and the rest of her body.

Slowly, both men sank to their knees, closed their eyes, placed their hands on the floor in front of them, and bowed deeply in respect.

When they sat up and looked again, Alice had slipped back into her kimonos, and was tying the scarlet sash around her waist. The men had seen something they had never seen before and would never see again.

Morioka's wife appeared with ceremonial tea. The finest, pale green powder ground from selected leaves of the earliest picking at Uji was whisked into a jade froth in white porcelain bowls. They made polite conversation about the season while eating sweets and sipping tea.

The revealing was over.

*

While Alice avoided goodbyes if she could, this was Japan, and all the formalities must be respectfully observed. Much bowing. Many polite phrases. Morioka apologized for his inadequate skills, for his lack of talent, and for his inability to completely finish the tattoo. He said, "*Yuki to doki masen,*" again and again, asking her forgiveness.

Only a true sensei would say these things. The tattoo was indeed unfinished. All traditional craftsmen leave a tiny place in their work incomplete, lest they offend the gods by aspiring to perfection. Only Morioka and the gods would know where the tattoo was incomplete.

Alice felt inadequate to these ceremonial formalities. Saying "Thank you" over and over in English and Japanese was not enough. As she was going down the steps to the taxi, she looked back at Morioka, still bowed at the waist, hands on his thighs. She might never see him again. But he was part of her now.

She knew what to do.

She went back to him, took his hands in hers, turned them palms up, and kissed them. Then she placed both of her hands on his face, looked long into his astonished eyes so that he might see her tears of gratitude. Finally, she made a most un-Japanese gesture. She winked. And turned away - down the stairs, and into the taxi.

As it moved away into the night she looked back and waved, laughing because she was thinking, *If only I had remembered to bring my red rubber nose.*

Morioka shook his head. He would never, ever understand the ways of henna gaijin. When colleagues quizzed him later about his experiences with Vin-cen-zo, he would only shake his head and smile.

He would never forget the moment of revealing. He could not find the words to speak of it. But Alice's pose reminded him of his favorite Kabuki mi-e in the play, *Benten Kozo,* when the main character, disguised as a woman, pulls his kimono off his shoulder and arm, revealing his tattoo. Though you knew the moment was coming, if it was well done it was always as if you were seeing it for the first time. Yet even that memorable scene could not match The Revealing of Vin-cen-zo as a woman.

*

Later, at the o-chaya, where Zenkichi had arranged a dinner for two, Alice drank too much sake. She lay down on the tatami, head on her arm, lightly sleeping. How beautiful she looked. Like a child.

The mistress of the establishment, who knew about the tattoo, begged to have a look when she saw just the edge of it showing. She was in awe of a female gaijin who could undertake such a thing.

Zenkichi was firm. No. Not even after the lady made it clear the cost of the evening was a gift of the house. The tattoo belonged to Vin-cen-zo.

Zenkichi never expected to see it again.

But he could not help wondering who would.

THE ACTOR

Matsui Zenkichi.

His biography suggests more promise than fulfillment. Superior education. Superior marks. Broad interests - literature, science, history, and art. In fact, everything he studied commanded his attention. For a while. But inner restlessness would lead him to the next attraction. "One who begins well, but does not finish," was his father's judgment.

Zenkichi's mind, like the body of a decathlon athlete, qualified him for several events. He was good at almost anything he tried, but without excellence in any one endeavor. Hence, his life direction was likely to be decided by external happenstance - family tradition, a great teacher, friends, luck, something unpredictable.

However, there was one element of his life that affected everything else he did or would do: Kabuki. His family had a long association with theater, including a line of famous and not-so-famous actors, beginning with Iwai Hanshiro I in the seventeenth century. A weakening of the line in recent generations left Zenkichi in a side eddy of the mainstream of Kabuki. But the family tradition remained strong enough and important enough that he was placed in training for the stage at an early age, and played minor parts as a young man. His talent, while not perceived as great, was nevertheless seen as promising enough that, if he had the desire and commitment, he could be successful. So thought his family.

Zenkichi did not think so. To pursue Kabuki as a way of life demands inner fire, not embers. He did not feel the fire. He could not commit himself to the art. It felt too much like entering a cloistered world as a monk. No.

As it happened, Zenkichi visited New York City after university graduation. He invited an American friend to attend a performance of Japanese Super Kabuki - the blend of classic conventions and modern technology as presented by a famous Japanese theater company on tour. They also performed Shakespeare's *Macbeth* in Kabuki style, in Japanese.

The enthusiastic response of the audience clearly went beyond appreciation for an exotic Japanese art form. The universal elements of Kabuki were as moving as ancient Greek drama or grand opera.

Zenkichi suddenly saw his country's theatrical traditions in a new light. In a flash of comprehension, he knew what he wanted to do: Kabuki. Not only as a conservator of the past, but as an advancer of new possibilities for an old art form.

Actually, Kabuki had always been malleable. It would become codified and rigid for a time, and then change again, always bearing the germinating seed of innovation first planted in the dry bed of the Kamagama River by the temple dancer, Izumo-no-Okuni.

Zenkichi knew his decision would be treated with suspicion and skepticism. The odds were overwhelming against his achieving significant roles because he had waited so long to fully commit himself to the discipline. Questions would be raised about the depth of his dedication to the art. He would be tested. Would he have the strength of character to endure the unrelentingly rigorous training?

In a word, yes. Finally, in his own backyard, he had found something to challenge every fiber of his being and absorb every ounce of his mental and physical energy. Kabuki is equivalent to a martial art in its demands.

What drove him on in the most stressful times was the discovery that he was a natural-born actor. Being an actor was not a job. It was a calling - the profound self-realization of his nature. It was as if he had entered the priesthood after all, but on his own terms.

From the day he returned to training seriously, his talent was quietly acknowledged, as if he might well be the reincarnation of a former great actor. In time his talent was publicly recognized when he was given the name Iwai Hanshiro XI by his aging uncle, with the blessing of his family.

Would he become truly great and famous? Only time would tell. But he would grow in his craft, and, thanks to the new openness of Japanese culture, he was cast in non-Kabuki roles in television and film. As his confidence and reputation grew, he moved further afield into experimental theater and Western drama, and consequently enriched his traditional skills.

If he had settled on a few roles in traditional Kabuki plays, Zenkichi might have achieved ranking status. But the challenge he found in playing a wide range of roles was what gave his life excitement. Playing female characters pushed his talent to the limit. Even the harshest critics acknowledged his range of success while bemoaning his lack of focused concentration. He responded to them by saying, "I am an actor, not a priest."

To be an actor one had to be able to put one's self inside the mind and soul of a character. And it was this capacity for empathy that most attracted Alice to Zenkichi. He wanted to know and understand, though he never seemed to pry or judge. She thought of him as she thought of Alex and Max-Pol. He was a Witness.

Once, in a store selling international arts and crafts, he had held up two of the famous Russian nesting dolls. Each doll came apart to reveal a smaller doll inside, which, in turn, contained an even smaller doll, and so on.

"I bought two of these dolls on a trip to Moscow. They seem to be identical in every way. But the last dolls in the center are different. In one set, the last doll is very tiny, but solid. In the other, the last doll is hollow. I wish to give you one of these sets as a present. Which do you want? Solid or hollow?"

"You decide," said Alice.

Shaking his head, he put both dolls back on the shelf. It was very much in keeping with his feelings for her to not force an opinion that might touch on deep issues. Was she empty at the center? Or solid? It was not for Zenkichi to judge. But at his center, he was solid. Of that, he was certain.

*

Knowing his shirankao - the capacity to always wear one face without revealing what was going on behind it - and knowing he seldom talked about himself, Alice was surprised when Zenkichi announced he had important personal things to say to her before she left. It would not take long. He would take her to a special place to speak his mind.

HERDING THE OX

Sanjusangendo.

This Buddhist temple was first built in 1164. Destroyed by fire in 1264 and immediately rebuilt. The hondo - main hall - of this astonishing wooden building is unique. Almost 400 feet long, though only 55 feet deep - like a huge display case for its one thousand small golden images of *Juichimen Senju Kannon* - plus one large image.

These 1,001 representations of the Goddess of Mercy symbolize the 33,033 ways this deity can help mankind. (1,001 images multiplied by 33 incarnations.) There is nothing like this presentation of the size and power of Mercy anywhere else in Japan.

Zenkichi brought Alice to the temple early - when it opened at 8:00 a.m. - giving them time to stand alone in silence in front of this representation of this most generous avatar of the gods. No explanation is necessary - or even possible. One senses the meaning in a wordless knowing. *Yugen* is the Japanese term - an experience that triggers feelings not completely grasped by the rational intellect.

When the hondo became crowded, Zenkichi led Alice outside and around to the long wooden veranda running the length of the building. It is here, on New Year's Day, that archers have come for centuries to shoot arrows at targets almost two hundred feet away.

They sat on the edge of the veranda. After first explaining the history of the event, called *toshiya*, Zenkichi continued.

"As you probably know, in Japanese archery the purpose is *not* to try and hit the target. The purpose is for the archer to be so prepared *within* that all he must do is pull the bow and release the arrow. If the contestant is centered within himself, the arrow will take care of finding the center of the target.

"This is a metaphor for enlightenment - satori. It is said that some archers are so prepared that they close their eyes before they shoot. And it is also said that one archer-priest achieved satori sufficient to hit a bull's-eye every time. And he had been blind since birth.

"The question raised in this place is, What is the aim? The self? Or some target out there? As for me, I am not an archer. Neither monk nor priest. I am only an actor who spends time Herding the Ox."

Alice sat silently still.

Somewhere far off in the hills a temple bell sounded.

Eventually, Zenkichi bent forward, and with his finger, drew an *enso* - an almost-complete, almost-perfect circle - in the damp, rust-colored earth.

"Enlightenment - satori," he said. "Never quite finished. Never closed."

Sitting back, he contemplated the enso for a time, then turned to Alice and continued, "There is a Zen parable about an ox herder. It is often illustrated with nine pictures, drawn inside a circle. The story is based on an encounter between a monk and a disciple. The novice wanted to know how he could search for the Buddha if he doesn't know the way.

"The master said, 'It is like looking for an ox left in one's care. You think the ox has strayed - without realizing you have been riding on it.'

"These are the nine illustrations:

One - searching for the ox, as if it were lost.

Two - seeing the footprints of the ox.

Three - seeing the ox.

Four - catching the ox.

Five - leading the ox.

Six - riding the ox.

Seven - forgetting about the ox.

Eight - forgetting the self.

Nine - entering the marketplace with an open mind and heart."

Zenkichi bent down and placed his finger in the center of the enso, then drew a line through the opening in the circle, out into the dirt of the open courtyard.

Looking back at Alice, he said, "Of course, this story and these illustrations have been discussed for centuries. They have many meanings, depending on who considers them. I have often thought about where I am in the stages of Herding the Ox. Kabuki is an example of an ox I was looking for without knowing I was already riding on it. The idea of the ox is always on my mind."

Alice sat still, thinking Zenkichi had finished.

He had not.

He moved closer to her.

"And you, Alice. I think you are an archer, thinking about the target out there. Thinking about hitting a bull's-eye with many arrows. Perhaps what you want is not about bows or arrows or bull's eyes."

(Pause.)

Alice smiled and reached into her purse. Pulling out a small, black leather case, she took out her business card and gave it to Zenkichi.

As she pointed to the parts of the design, she explained.

"The capital letter Q with the arrow through it means to keep asking the next question. The triangle and the circle and the square stand for the basic shapes with which an artist conjures up the world - the fundamentals. The arrow continues through them, sometimes in a spiral - repeating, but always going on. The three arrows coming out the end of the square are like the line you drew going beyond the enso - beyond the apparent boundaries. The exclamation mark emphasizes the final mark - an *ongoing arrow*."

Zenkichi considered the card. "Surprise and continuation," he said, as he placed Alice's card on the ground in the middle of the enso.

Alice said, "The card illustrates intention. Sometimes I think I'm still back at the Q. Sometimes I think these symbols represent a pattern I've completed and repeated over and over again. Sometimes I'm the arrow.

"I know that my 'business' is not expressed by the name and numbers and address printed on the other side of the card. My 'business' is on this side. Questions. Movement. Arrows."

Zenkichi studied Alice's drawing for several minutes. Turning to Alice, he smiled, and said, "We swim in the same river."

Suddenly laughing, he said, "I just thought about The Great Uji Bridge Hiccup and Laughing Festival."

Alice laughed, and leaned her head on his shoulder as she had that night in Uji.

"Enough wisdom," she said. "Let's ride your ox. How about a motorcycle trip and lunch? At the Perugia?"

THE EYES OF THE DARUMA

Alice is leaving Kyoto tomorrow, but she does not talk about leaving.

She and Zenkichi have almost come full circle, the world turned right side up. Day has become day again.

After another wild, erotic motorcycle ride across the foothills, they are eating lunch on the terrace at the Perugia, the Italian restaurant where they first ate in early June. A September breeze has blown the air clean. In the distance, Kyoto stands out like a picture postcard.

*

"For you, I have this gift," said Zenkichi, holding out a small, plain wooden box - about three inches on each side - tied with a red silk cord.

"Open, dozo."

Inside was the smallest *Daruma* Alice had ever seen. A lumpish, red, round-shouldered, armless figure, mostly face. About the size and shape of a small red plum. Two round, white circles for eyes.

Alice held the Daruma in the palm of her hand.

"I know a little, but it's what a gaijin knows - probably all wrong. Tell me," she said.

"Daruma is the Japanese name for Bodhidharma, the founder of the Ch'an sect of Chinese Buddhism. In other words, Zen. He is said to have spent nine years sitting in meditation, facing a cave wall, seeking enlightenment. He represents perseverance.

"As an aside, you might like to know that in the slang of Osaka, a tattoo is also called perseverance - *gaman*.

"This image, which comes in many sizes, is weighted to be self-righting. If you push it over, it sits up again. There is a Japanese proverb, *'Nanakorobi yaoki,'* - 'seven falls, eight rises' - meaning no matter how often you fail - like Daruma - get back up.

"What's its story?" asked Alice.

"In the late seventeenth century, the Shorinzan Daruma, a temple near the city of Takasaki, instructed famine-stricken farmers to make

papier-mâché images of Daruma to bring them a change of fortune. Now these dolls are found all over Japan. People buy them when they are undertaking some important task, or desire success in personal affairs - love, marriage, employment. They are given as gifts at weddings, at the opening of a new business, at the beginning of an election campaign, and at the beginning of the New Year. Some of them are huge. Students often buy them before taking important exams.

"Strange-looking, isn't it? Fierce and funny. The black eyebrows are in the shape of cranes, and the black beard is shaped like a turtle - both considered auspicious creatures. And it seems to be grimly grinning.

"When you get one, you write your hopes and prayers on the doll's shoulders, and then you make your wish by filling in the left eye with black ink. When your desire is achieved, you fill in the right eye.

"Those who take this most seriously will return the doll to the Shorinzan Daruma. The monks will recite a sutra over the doll, and burn it in a sacred fire. On your own, you can burn the doll on a bed of earth purified with salt, and then bury the ashes in an auspicious place."

Zenkichi considered Alice, sitting very still beside him.

"The highest goal attached to a Daruma is enlightenment. Satori. If you think of enlightenment as some ultimate state of being - perfection - then you will likely not ever fill in the right eye. If you understand enlightenment to mean rare moments when you get a glimpse of the true meaning of things, then you may fill in the right eye, burn the doll, and get another one.

"I bought this little Daruma to give you the night before you began getting your tattoo. For your Possibles Bag. I thought you would fill in one eye at that time, and fill in the other when the tattoo was complete."

"Why didn't you?"

"Something kept me from giving it to you. It seemed to me you didn't need luck or courage. I never doubted you would go through with the tattoo. However, there seems to be something else you want - larger, deeper, harder. I don't know. I think you cannot name it or write it yet on the shoulders of the Daruma. So. I give this to you now. When you can name your desire, you can fill in the left eye and begin."

Alice held the Daruma carefully, running her fingers over its eyes.

"*Domo arigato gozaimasu, Zenkichi-san.* I am in your debt. But not for long. There is something for you in my Possibles Bag." She showed him the three small wishbones, tied together with a strand of her white hair.

"These are from wild quail. Each one represents a wish. Many fairy tales are based on three wishes given to someone as a reward, but also as a challenge to their own character and imagination. A Daruma doll is very much like a wishbone.

"Why I have these three is, as a dear friend would say, a 'long story for another time.' I give you one, not as a way of relinquishing one of my wishes, but in exchange for the Daruma. You have my kind of wish. I have yours. It is a transformation, neither gain nor loss. Just another way of seeking one's desire, yes?"

"I have a wish," replied Zenkichi.

"You must never tell, or it won't come true."

"What if it is coming true now?"

Alice put a finger to her lips. "*Sshhh.* I still don't want to know."

They sat in silence for a long while.

"You are leaving Japan. Will you still be Vin-cen-zo?"

Alice unpinned her hair, and let it fall along the sides of her face. She had not cut it or had it re-dyed. Now, as its true color grew out, it looked as if she had a loose white cap over black hair. She folded her hands before her on the table, and smiled her Mona Lisa smile.

"No. Vin-cen-zo was too serious, too sad, too dark - a person of the night." She laughed. "I needed to be a little bushido for the tattoo. Manly. I did that. But now . . . now . . ? No. Vincenzo stays here."

(Pause.)

"Would you like it if I gave you a name, Zen-san?"

"Yes."

"Tomorrow. In parting I'll give you a name. And will you give me one in return - a name for a name?"

120

"*Sasuga*," said Zenkichi. "As might have been expected."

"*Sasuga*. Come on, take me for one last ride on your black dragon."

"Would you like to drive?" asked Zenkichi. "I think you know how."

"Only if you want to die," said Alice.

"It would make a romantic ending to our time together. Very Japanese."

"Ah, but I am not Japanese," said Alice.

"Sometimes I forget. Or wish to."

Alice placed a finger across his lips. "*Sshhh* . . . Be careful. Don't waste a wish by accident, Zenkichi. That's what happens in fairy tales. A badly made first wish creates a need for one more wish to undo the trouble it caused. Save the wish for a Japanese woman."

"Hai. Come. I promise we will not die. Not today."

*

When Alice returned to her hotel room, a gift box was waiting for her. There was a note on the box:

> *Inside you will find* shinobu *(grasses of remembering), a fern that grows on thatched roofs; and* wasuregusa *(grasses of forgetting), an orange daylily. Gifts given in* The Tale of Genji. *Worthless and priceless. You will understand.*

SCARLETT'S FAREWELL

A day of leaving and staying.

When Zenkichi called Alice's room from the hotel lobby, there was no answer. When he inquired at the desk, he was told she had checked out very early that morning. Disappointed, but not surprised, he started to walk away. The desk clerk called him back. "Wait. She said you would come. She left something for you with the concierge."

Zenkichi had considered not coming. He knew Alice did not like saying goodbye and would likely be gone when he came. But he also knew she would not leave without making some parting gesture. She had promised him a name.

And besides, though he had not told her, he would see her in Athens. Soon. His Kabuki theater was going there in a cultural exchange program. Why did he not tell her? Alice likes surprises. And talking about Athens would have affected their being together in Kyoto.

The concierge gave him a large red envelope made of heavy, handmade paper. Inside was folded the life-size drawing Morioka had made for Alice's tattoo. And a note:

> I give you my name – Vin-cen-zo – a well-used name that belonged to Vincenzo Peruggia, the man who once stole the *Mona Lisa*. He was in love with the painting, but could not keep it. You will find a way to give me a name.

The note was signed: "Someday's Child."

Along with the drawing and the note, was a small, lumpy envelope. Inside was a compressed red rubber nose, and a note: "Wear this."

Puzzled by the signature of "Someday's Child," but pleased to keep Vin-cen-zo, Zenkichi wandered around the hotel lobby. What to do next? Finally, he laughed aloud, and went down the escalator to the train station below. He would take a train to Uji, and stand once again on the Bridge of Dreams. There, he would put on the red rubber nose.

As his train pulled out of the station, he addressed Alice in his mind.

I would have called you Scarlett. Sometimes I think you are like the woman in my favorite American movie. Strong. Beautiful. Strange. And now, you are truly gone with the wind.

Someday's Child

Once again launched into the air in a jet bound for far away, Alice closed her eyes. Unexpectedly, she thought of her mother. *Poor woman. I must have driven her crazy.*

Unlike her sisters, the sour-spirited ones who were always arguing and whining and complaining, Alice was the "good child." Her agreeable compliance was rewarded by the privilege of doing whatever she wanted to do when she was alone.

What vexed her mother most were the questions Alice would ask unexpectedly:

"If there is a God and he is all-powerful and can do anything, then why doesn't he make everyone happy? If I was God, I would; wouldn't you?"

And before her mother could cope with that, Alice would go on: "Why is there anything?" and "Why don't people come in all kinds of shapes and colors, like animals - with spotted skins and horns and tails and all that?"

And "If Daddy loves us so much, why isn't he ever home?"

And "I don't think the world is round; I think it is a cube, don't you?"

Surrendering under Alice's relentless bombardment of unanswerable questions, her mother would look over her glasses, sigh, lay a hand on Alice's shoulder, and say, "Someday . . . you will understand."

For a long time in her growing up, that answer had been Alice's mantra. "Someday, I will understand." She finally stopped asking those kinds of questions. Her mother didn't know the answers. Her father wasn't around to ask. Her sisters were stupid. And her friends thought she was weird for asking them. But she kept promising herself,

Someday, I will understand.

Now, as the plane hurtled on through the sky, she wondered if episodes in her life like the one in Kyoto were signs of sanity, or mental instability? Craziness, or creativity? A reflection of understanding, or further questioning? What was she looking for? What would become of her? What was waiting for her in Athens and Crete? What does it all mean? What shall I do with the Daruma?"

Easy does it, Alice, she thought.
She put her fingers under her blouse and touched her tattoo.
Someday, I will understand.
Not yet. But I'm still Someday's Child.

PART FOUR

WALTZING THE BULL

Including

The Illustrations of Margaret Allen Dougherty

The Music of Barbara Lamb

An Author's Dedication

This book is for you, the one I missed;
You, whose path I never crossed;
You, who never arrived in my life;
Still, this book is for you,
Because you *must* be there.

Many times have I altered my Way
To be where you might be:
On a great ship, crossing to England;
On the night train to Barcelona;
On the pilgrim route around Shikoku.

In Monet's garden in Giverny,
In Oxford at Blackwell's Books,
In the art museums of Vienna,
In Amsterdam at the Golden Tulip,
In Rouen in the cathedral.

Were you in Santa Fe last Christmas?
I looked for you there.
On the island of Crete last spring?
I looked for you there.
Where are you?

Will I ever find you?
Have you looked for me?
Come to me. Find me.
This book will tell you where I am.
This book is for you.

> – D.Y. Trabet –
> (The White Rabbit)

CANNONBALL

In Seattle, Max-Pol is alone, lying inert as a corpse.

He is a stranger in a strange house lent by a friend who is away for the summer. The friend has collected demon masks from his world travels and mounted them on the living room walls. Max-Pol hates being in this room, but the bedroom is dark and dreary and he is tired of bed. This demon-filled room is the only other place he can lie down.

Eyes closed, awash in the relentless sound of a five-day July rain thrumming against the windows, he curls himself into a fetal position and pulls a woolly brown blanket over his head.

Tests and examinations confirmed his hepatitis, though he has the mildest and least damaging form. Still, six to eight weeks' rest was prescribed. And complete inactivity.

Exhausted, enfeebled, Max-Pol has lived in his pajamas and bathrobe, moving with effort from bed to bathroom to kitchen to couch and back to bed. Losing weight, losing contact with the outside world, and losing his grip on his mind. Not even the energy to watch television, read, or listen to music. The telephone is turned off. Few, if any, friends know he is in Seattle. Even family visits have been discouraged.

A self-imposed, solitary confinement. Do nothing. Wait. Let the body repair itself. Meanwhile, the dreams of day and the dreams of night merge seamlessly into a state of semi-conscious limbo.

*

It seemed like such a short time ago that he had set off with great expectations for what he called "affirmative exile." Truly open to the unexpected, he invited the Fates to provide the next episode of his life.

In due course, the Fates complied: France, Spain, Greece, Crete; Alice, Alex, Polydora, Kostas; Delphi, Knossos. A great first act for this new play on the stage of his life. A drama critic would have warned him that second acts are always problematical.

The Fates turned perverse. The accident and near-death experience at Easter. Alice at Waterloo. Return to the States. The India-What sex fest. Then Alice and Alex again, but complicated by the likely loss of his Witness. And now this. Sick - an invalid - back in Seattle because of circumstances not of his choosing.

And now what? Alice had gone to Japan. His long-anticipated cruise with Alex was postponed. There was no sign of what the next stage of his life might be.

The only positive note was the unexpected re-attraction he felt for the practice of medicine - first when he came back to have his injuries attended, and then when he returned to confirm his disease.

Being back inside the medical environment resurrected his need to be useful. It also roused guilty feelings for not using his considerable training and skills. What to do? But any decision in that direction conflicted with his promise to join Alex and Alice in Crete in October. To add to his worries, his bank balance was falling toward the red zone.

Glorious me, he thought. *Despondent and weak and broke.* At times during his delusional days he found himself wishing he did not exist. Not that he was suicidal - there just was not enough juice in him to want to go on. *Well, it's just the hepatitis,* he thought. *Wait.*

*

"Max-Pol. Max-Pol, honey."

A soft, sweet, faraway voice. The voice of India-What.

A daydream. She's in New York, thought Max-Pol.

"Max-Pol!" An insistent, nearby voice. A rap on the window.

Opening his eyes, Max-Pol saw the funny face of India-What smushed up against the wet windowpane, distorted into a grinning, comic mask.

"Hey! Hey! Hey!" she shouted.

Before he could get up off the couch to greet her, she burst through the door and pranced into the living room. Sopping wet in a white cotton summer dress that revealed a lack of underwear, she knelt by the couch, took his hand in hers and kissed his palm, tickling it with her tongue. "Let's play, Max-Pol."

132

Max-Pol sat up laughing, "No. No. No! India. I'm sick. It won't do me any good," he said.

"Oh yes it will. I'll take your mind off being sick and make your body happy too. I've got to dry off first. Where's the bathroom?"

When she returned she was wearing a white towel wrapped around her head turban style, a white kitchen apron - and nothing else.

"I'll race you to the swing," she said.

When Max-Pol and India-What were children spending the summers with their families at the beach, they would run together to a rope swing tied to the limb of a madrona tree. The limb hung out over the sea. Timing their swings with an incoming wave, they would launch out and let go, flinging themselves high in the air. At the last moment they would tuck their legs up and cannonball into the water. *Kafoom!*

And there was that summer of adolescence, when India-What talked Max-Pol into swinging naked on the rope together - with kissing and groping in the water before being rolled ashore by the waves.

*

Now India-What turned her back on Max-Pol, slowly untied the apron, and let it fall. Unwinding the turban, she tossed it aside. Slowly she turned to stand naked in front of him, hands held high over her head. Shaking her red hair loose, she said,

"Here I come, ready or not."

"This could kill me," protested Max-Pol.

"Prepare to die then," she shouted, and cannonballed into the pool of Max-Pol's libido.

Kafooom!

*

Afterward, when they lay wrapped together in the blanket on the couch, Max-Poll unfolded the story of his affirmative exile in detail for India-What, emphasizing the concept of Witness.

"Now, I understand there are many Witnesses. You, for example, are one, because you were there at times in my life when nobody else was. You are the solitary archivist of that part of my history. Alice is another Witness . . . and . . ."

Before he could finish, he fell asleep.

India–What rose without waking Max-Pol, dressed, and stood looking down at him for a long time before she left. She was not smiling when she drove away in her car.

The Court of No Appeal

India-What did not return the next morning. Max-Pol had thought she might come early and fix him breakfast, but it was just as well that she did not. Though he had not been destroyed by her cannonball, he was exhausted. A day to recover his strength was welcome.

But at ten she was back after all, dressed for traveling, not for fun.

"I came to say goodbye. I've got a noon plane for New York."
"But I thought . . . I thought . . ."
She sat in a chair across the room from where he lay on the couch and spoke to him slowly and solemnly, as if she were explaining a serious and difficult matter to a child.
"I know what you thought. That I came back to Seattle just to be with you. To nurse you back to health, while at the same time trying to kill you with sex. *Wrong*, Max-Pol. So wrong."
"Wrong?"

Agitated, India-What moved forward to sit on the edge of her chair.
"I came to Seattle to see my father, because I'm moving to Milan in a week and I don't know how long it'll be before I have to get back here. You know about the odds of Dad surviving with a kidney transplant."
"Milan?"
"Yes. Sergio and I are opening a fashion house there."
"Sergio? Who's Sergio?"

India-What stood up, her voice rising in anger.

"How would *you* know? You never, ever, *ever*, ask me about my life, Max-Pol. You always talk about yourself or about us and the past. Yesterday you rambled on and on about *your* life, but you never asked me about *mine*, or even gave me a chance to bring it up. If you *had* bothered to ask, I would have told you that Sergio and I have been together since design school. Years and years. We have an incredibly symbiotic relationship - full of caring and collaboration."

"Is he . . .?"

"My lover? My fiancé? Gay? That's what you want to ask? None of those categories apply. Just what *is* my relationship with Sergio? I wouldn't even try to tell you because you wouldn't even *try* to understand. My life is merged with his in many marvelous ways, and will be for a long time."

She sat down, sat back in her chair, took a calming breath and went on.

"I will tell you this: Behind the public runway fashion show is a serious business based on intense creativity and hard work. Sergio is part of that."

"But . . ."

"But what, Max-Pol? Does he know about us? It's none of his business. It doesn't have anything to do with him. Sex between you and me answered the question of the cousin taboo, What would it be like? Now we know. Maybe the question would have been sweeter in the long run without the answer.

"To put it simply, you were fun in bed, but that's it. As far as I'm concerned, now we're just relatives again. Sex is sex. Love is love. One is about getting - the other about giving. Don't you know that?"

"Well, I . . ."

India-What stood up, pacing back and forth in front of Max-Pol, her rising anger tangling her thoughts. "What good . . .? What *good* . . .?" She planted her feet, faced him and raised her voice to a shout.

"What *good* does all your knowledge *do* you? All that physiology and psychology and chemistry and anatomy? I'll bet there's no course on *love* required in medical school. I'll bet the *word* isn't even *mentioned*. You're like a man who knows *everything* about a boat except why people go sailing.

"And this *Witness* thing of yours! My God! That's an intellectual avoidance of any *real* relationship. You only want people to see *you*, watch *you*, remember *you*! Don't you get it? Your *Witness* thing is a way of keeping people at a distance, not a way of holding them close. It's all about *you*. You don't give a *damn* about *them*."

Max-Pol tried to speak, but she again held up her hand to silence him. Trembling, she lashed him with words:

"I'm *angry* with you. I've been angry for a *long* time, Max-Pol. Everybody in the family always talked about *you* and *your* accomplishments – all about your grades and test scores and getting into Yale and medical school. The family Golden Boy. The Great Max-Pol!

"Well, not *everybody* was impressed. Most of what it took for you was a great memory, and your genes provided that. Do you want to know what you always wanted most? *Approval.* And you know why? Because you are so *insecure.* Nobody ever had doubts about you but *you.*"

"But, India . . ."
"Let me finish. I've wanted to get this out of my system for years."
She paced again, like a prosecuting attorney before a jury.

"I always was just a funny-looking girl with a great body and a screwball name. What I hated most was that nobody ever gave me any credit for artistic talent or for creativity or hard work. Who knew I had a *mind*? Who cared about *art*? 'Design school is for *losers.* Fashion is for *fruitcakes.*' My own mother said that. Nobody in the family ever came to New York to see *my* work or *my* world. You could have. But you never did. Why would you? You only cared about *you* and where *you* were and what *you* did!"

Fighting back tears, trying not to lose control, she whispered,
"And you have no idea how cruel you can be, Max-Pol."

(Silence.)

"I'm sorry that . . ."
Holding up her hand again, she snarled at him:
"*Don't . . . even . . . try,* Max-Pol! The truth is the truth. You are what you are. But I'm also what I am. And we don't have *anything* in common now except memories of childhood, and a rowdy roll in the hay. We're still family. I'll settle for that. And as for you, *I feel sorry for you.*"
"Because?"
"Because you're right back where you started. *Highly qualified.* That's you. Mr. Highly Qualified. For what? You don't *want* what you *have* and

you don't *have* what you *want*. And, worse, you feel sorry for yourself.

"Self-pity doesn't become you, Max-Pol. Nobody will *approve of you* for that. If that's the best you can do, then you can lie here and rot, for all I or anybody else cares."

Shaking with fury, tears falling from her face, India-What turned to leave. She had tried Max-Pol in his own court, judged him harshly, and left no room for appeal.

She took a deep breath. Then another. Letting it out, she turned and walked back to him and stood for a moment. She bent down, put both hands on his face, and pronounced sentence, in the gentlest but firmest way:

"Get over it, dear Max-Pol. Grow up. Get a life."

And with that, she left, slamming the door behind her.

THE DEFENSE RESTS

There are rare times when you are given a view of yourself that is so hard and clean and true that you cannot reply.

For Max-Pol, this was one of those times.

Everything India-What had said seemed incontestably true.

Waves of despair washed over Max-Pol – loneliness, shame, anguish. Worse even than having nothing to say, he did not know what to do. All he had was a longing for his life to be otherwise.

India-What was right. He had fallen into the slimy pit of self-pity. Anything he could say in his own defense would be quibbling.

Like a man who has been cast ashore after swimming through an undertow, he lay still. He had not drowned, but he had no strength or will to get up. Hepatitis is an endurable disease of the body only.

India-What had indicted his soul, and that might not be endurable. Standing outside his cage of misery, he said aloud what he would say to a patient, "Rest, wait, heal. Until then, suspend decisions."

October, he thought. *Everything will straighten out by then.*

Max-Pol pulled the blanket over his head, closed his eyes and slept.

(He did not know that India-What was pregnant.
Neither did she.
It was only a matter of hours.)

TRUTHS THAT CAN BE TOLD

Dr. Marcus Levine came to visit Max-Pol. Psychiatrists don't usually make house calls, but he came as a friend. The two men had been fellow students in medical school, and had become colleagues in medical practice. Max-Pol had treated Marcus's children. And while Marcus was not Max-Pol's therapist, he had become a caring confidant after the death of Max-Pol's wife.

On that last night before Max-Pol had left Seattle on his quest, Marcus Levine had patiently listened while Max-Pol worked through his plans to leave medicine and pursue affirmative exile, and had given the name "Witness" to what he thought Max-Pol wanted in the way of another person in his life. But he had cautioned Max-Pol to think of a Witness as an interim stage in his need for companionship.

He did not think Max-Pol had heard that part of his advice.

When Max-Pol first returned briefly to Seattle from Crete, Marcus had lunch with him. Max-Pol's comments about his Witness were enigmatic. Yes, he had found one. And now he was anxious that he might lose her.

Marcus kept his thoughts to himself.

Psychiatrists never say, "I told you so."

*

Now, when Max-Pol answered the door, Marcus was startled. A thin, unkempt man in rumpled pajamas greeted him with a limp handshake. Max-Pol had let his beard and hair grow. He was almost unrecognizable.

In the living room, Marcus sat in a chair while Max-Pol retreated to his nest of blankets on the couch.

"Max-Pol, I won't mince words. You look awful."

"I am awful," whispered Max-Pol.

"Hepatitis worse than you thought?"

"No. It's a mild case. I'm not jaundiced, as you can see. And I'm sure all the liver function tests will confirm recovery. No, hepatitis is not the problem."

140

"Tell me," said Marcus.

*

Without further prompting from Marcus, Max-Pol related the narrative of his life over the last year. Only when he finished relating the entire litany of judgments pronounced by India-What did he stumble, choking up with tears as he concluded.

"She nailed me, Marcus. I'm damned, and dead in the water. I feel like Job and Oedipus rolled up into one."

Marcus laughed.

"You think it's funny?" said Max-Pol.

"You're not in their league. Job was trapped by God into ultimate despair, and Oedipus was trapped by the gods into killing his father and marrying his mother. Sure, you've come to a difficult passage, but the gods are not involved, and you can do something about the situation. There's a name for this. One you know."

"What?"

"Catharsis. A time of purging and cleansing. You don't realize it yet, but not only are you over the hump of hepatitis, you are on the way out of your existential dilemma."

"It doesn't feel that way to me."

"Think about it. You've gone through a crisis brought about by conflict between what you think yourself to be and what you are. India-What called out the truth - as she saw it. To be frank, her assessment has merit.

"And you heard it. *You heard it*, Max-Pol, and you accepted it. Most people don't. That acceptance throws open the door to the rest of your life. Opportunities arise. You don't have to go back the way you came."

"Or blind myself, like Oedipus."

"Don't over-dramatize. Things are not as bad as they seem. Oedipus was at the end of his tether. *You* are *not*. Self-pity doesn't become you."

"That's exactly what India-What said."

"She was right."

Max-Pol sat up, the blankets and his sense of feebleness slipping from his shoulders at the same time.

"Let me give it to you hard and straight, Max-Pol. You're a doctor. And you don't think you want to be one. You're like a carpenter with all the necessary tools and skills and experiences, who has been building ordinary houses. You're ready to give it up because the work doesn't challenge you. Blah, blah, blah and so on. You know what I'm talking about.

"Old Freud emphasized only one aspect of the Oedipus tale, and it's kept analysts in business ever since. The story of Oedipus is a myth. There is no authorized version. It contains both the human yearning for self-knowledge and the anguish that knowledge must bring.

"Most of us want to understand ourselves because we want to be in control of our life stories. When we come to grief over our misapprehension of our actions, it's easy to blame the gods. Mostly we have ourselves to blame, because we get confused about the difference between those things we control and those we do not."

Marcus paused, wondering if he was saying too much or too little.

"Go on," said Max-Pol. "I'm following you."

"Disease, the acts of nature, other people, aging - we can't control these. But we *can* control how we *think* about these things and what we *do* in response. There's no ultimate point of stability. Life is always a changing, dynamic affair. That's not psychiatry, it's philosophy. As Epictetus said, 'Because things are the way they are, they will not remain the way they are.'

"You already know all this. I repeat: You *know* all this. But you can't focus on it from where you are at the moment. You *can* and *will* recover from hepatitis. You *can* and *will* figure out how to play the cards you've been dealt by changing your expectation of the game. You're down, but not out, Max-Pol.

"India-What was right. She kicked your butt and did you a favor. Self-pity really doesn't become you. You *can* give that up. You are indeed highly qualified - to make the decisions that will lead you on to something better."

"You make it sound so easy," said Max-Pol.

"Easy to say, hard to do. Sure. But I know you well enough to say that you have the strength to persevere in difficult tasks. You've done it before. India-What put it best: Get a life, Max-Pol. Get the next part of your life. You can give yourself permission to do that."

(Silence.)

Max-Pol got up from the couch, walked into the kitchen for a drink of water, and came back into the living room. He opened the front door, walked out onto the porch, and stood for a time considering the blooming green of summer in the garden and yard. He recalled Alex's notion about working hypotheses. He was not as sure as Marcus and India-What were about his circumstances, but they each had a working hypothesis and he did not. And he trusted the integrity and good will of these two Witnesses.

He returned to the living room, but not to the couch.

"Yes . . . OK. You're right."

"Believe me," said Marcus, "when you look back someday on this part of your life, you will see that you were already on the road ahead when I showed up."

"So, now what?" asked Max-Pol.

"Take advantage of what you *don't* have - no obligations, no job to quit, no debts to settle, no family to leave. You're a licensed, board-certified physician, and you're free to do almost anything.

"Make a *big* move - out of yourself - out of ordinary medicine. Consider working for Doctors Without Borders, or Physicians for Social Responsibility - organizations like that - ways of doing something challenging and useful - medicine that lets you make more of a difference than what you've been doing. Take a *chance*. Think *big*, think *far*."

Marcus had struck home. The wheels in Max-Pol's mind were turning smoothly for the first time in a long time.

He smiled.

Marcus continued, "But first, do what needs to be done now. I mean *right* now. Take a shower, *now*. Put on some clean clothes, and let me take you out for something to eat and then to a barbershop. You haven't been out of this house for a long time, have you?"

"No. And it's time," said Max-Pol. "But no barbershop. The beard and the hair are part of a bet. And may be part of the next phase of my life."

Fast Forward

In Seattle, Max-Pol is sitting across the desk from his travel agent, Elizabeth, working out an itinerary for Crete via Athens.

"Round trip or one way?" she asks.

"Round trip," he replies.

In Tokyo, Matsui Zenkichi is meeting with a committee, making final arrangements for performances of Kabuki plays in the Odeon of Herodes Atticus in Athens in October - part of a cultural exchange program that will bring Sophocles' *Oedipus, the King*, to Japan.

In Oxford, Wonko is speaking on the phone to his employer, explaining that he will be going to Crete by way of Athens - for a vacation, at the invitation of Alex Evans.

"No," he says, "I *will not* keep my eyes and ears open or give you a report. This is strictly personal."

In Athens, Polydora Vlachou is in her car, on her way to the airport to pick up Alice O'Riley, who has asked for Polly's services at Max-Pol's suggestion. Polly knows Alice only through the description Max-Pol gave her on their trip to Delphi. Interesting.

But she would rather be picking up Max-Pol again.

In Oxford, Alex is walking across Port Meadow on his way home from The Trout and a round of gin and tonics with friends. He is turning over in his mind an unexpected visit from Hans Dieter von Galen, the German general whom he had met on the train on his way back from France.

The General and the Lady

Alex had stayed put that summer. Too much traffic on the canals. Contented, but also bored with contentment, he was glad to have received a phone call from Hans. Alex had wondered what became of the romantic collision at Waterloo Station between the general and his fair English lady. He envied them their late-life ecstasy.

*

Hans's phone call was brief and agitated. "I must see you at your earliest convenience," he said.

"Of course, come tomorrow. Is there anything wrong?" asked Alex.

"I don't know," replied the general.

*

Hans Dieter von Galen and Winifred Lightfoot MacLeod had been quietly married in a quaint old parish church in the Cotswolds in June, in the company of a priest and two witnesses.

A honeymoon week in Scotland was followed by a grand celebration in Munich - a full-dress military event - marking the general's retirement and marriage. His regimental officers had turned out in amiable force, along with guests from NATO - men representing armies that had bitterly fought in two world wars, now fraternizing under the languid banners of Love and Leisure.

After a brief continuation of their honeymoon in the Bavarian Alps, the General and his Lady returned to the Cotswolds - to a cottage they had leased for a year, having wisely agreed to begin their new life together in a new place while they planned for the future.

Thus they lived happily ever after. For awhile. The first month was euphoric. They floated along on the current created by ceremonies and celebrations, buoyed by the frothy unreality of requited love and an unexpectedly fine sexual compatibility. Red-ribbon, chocolate-covered romance. Hearts and flowers and Whoopee!

And then. And then. Subtly, like a change in the seasons, the atmosphere between them cooled. Tension. Not entirely unanticipated, because Hans and Winifred were intelligent, mature adults who knew the settled ways of a lifetime would not be merged without stress. They knew they brought with them the baggage of the past and the impatience with compromises that accompany age. Their broad expectations were tested by specific conflicts. For example, each brought separate plans for the future, made after they were widowed.

Hans planned to hike for several summers with male friends until they had crossed Europe in stages, from the tip of Norway to the south coast of Crete. In winter, he anticipated hunting and skiing in the Alps from a base in a Bavarian mountain village. Perhaps a couple of months in North Africa in early spring. The mountains of Morocco. The Libyan Desert. Ethiopia.

Winnie's plans included sojourns in the cultural capitals of Europe - London, Vienna, Paris - art, music, museums, cathedrals. Winter in Mexico or in the American southwest - Santa Fe, Taos. Yoga. And finally, a cottage in the Cotswolds with a garden - and bird-watching.

When Hans described the situation, Alex did not think the plans all that incompatible. There was room for compromise, perhaps? But were there other, more vexing difficulties?

Yes. Precisely. Hans had come to talk with Alex because the couple's love boat had run aground on the invisible rocks of personal idiosyncrasies - those integrated habits of a lifetime that seem small, grow large, and become destructive. An accumulation of small leaks was threatening to sink the love boat.

*

Winifred was a Picker. She picked bits of lint from her clothes and those of other people. During a conversation her eyes would focus on what the person in front of her was wearing, and she would pick off a stray hair or a flake of dandruff. No loose thread evaded her eye.

At first, when Hans dressed up for formal occasions, he accepted Winifred's careful inspection as affectionate attention. But gradually he began to regard her picking habits as a neurotic obsession.

She picked food particles off clothing after a meal and collected crumbs off tablecloths, one crumb at a time. She noticed tiny bugs on flowers and plants and fruit wherever she might be – in a garden, at a vegetable stand or as a guest at a dinner party. It was as if Winnie had a license to tidy the world – with the best of intentions, of course.

Her obsessive habit did have its useful aspects. Nobody was better skilled than Winifred at removing splinters in fingers. Threading needles was child's play. She was adept at finding and prying up the ends of any kind of tape, and clever at untying difficult knots in string. The removal of price tags and labels drew her competent attention. In fact, anything stuck down that might be picked loose was fair game. She seemed to rejoice in this employment of her fine motor skills.

But her tendency knew no bounds. She picked at scabs on small wounds, at moles, warts, liver spots, and any other skin blemishes she found on herself and now, on Hans. On their honeymoon he got a blistering sunburn on his back and shoulders, and for days afterward Winifred scavenged his dead skin as one in a trance – taking glassy-eyed pleasure in seeing how long a strip of Han's exfoliating epidermis she could remove in one piece.

At first Hans considered her proclivity a charming eccentricity. He called her his *zupfliesl* – little picker-person – as a mildly barbed term of endearment. But eventually her habit became an irritation. Whenever they were in bed together naked after making love, Hans would be awakened from his drowsing bliss by Winifred's scavenging fingers lightly picking at something on his body.

Her delicate hands began to seem to him like small pink crabs that came at him waving pincers. Her well-kept, pink-polished fingernails appeared more predatory than affectionate.

Pick, pick, pick.

It drove him mad.

Finally, one morning when he saw her inspecting him after his shower, he barked at her, "Winifred, my zupfliesl, scratch me, claw me, pinch me, bite me, pet me, paw me, lick me – *anything* – but for God's sake, stop picking at me!"

But Winifred's picking was the unconscious predilection of a lifetime. And she was nonplussed by Hans's objections. Nobody else had ever mentioned the matter – neither her friends nor her family. Her late husband, George, had never complained. Surely Hans was over–reacting to a trivial activity. She sighed. Sighing was another one of her habits. Every time she sighed, Hans cringed. He began to sigh in response.

*

Winifred, on the other hand, had reasons of her own to be annoyed. She began to think of Hans as "General Sandbag." His lifetime of military service had trained him to sleep as quickly and deeply as possible whenever there was a chance. Day or night, if he could get into a prone position, he took advantage of the opportunity. He could sleep almost instantly - even for very short periods. A brief nap before or after a meal. A quick snooze while waiting for Winifred to get dressed to go out. And an hour of sound sleep moments after making love.

Hans never slept long. He could set his mind like an alarm clock. As a soldier, he had always slept with part of his mind awake - easily becoming fully alert at the slightest provocation.

He was a silent sleeper, as well. Unlike many men his age, he did not snore. His training had taught him that snoring could get a soldier shot. Winifred found his silence troubling. She was always afraid he might have developed apnea - or even died.

Ah, but Winifred snored. As Hans described it, she made the sound of the stroke of a knife cutting through celery, followed by the soft *put-put-put* of a distant outboard motor.

Worse, occasionally, unpredictably, Winifred had nightmares. Once she shouted, "Everybody out! Everybody out!" and another time screamed "Here they come! Here they come!" And she once gripped Hans tightly by the shoulder and whispered, "Don't move - they're in the room and they mean business." Even Hans found it hard to sleep after one of these air raid episodes.

He liked to roll up in a duvet, sleeping bag style.
She liked piles of shared covers.
He liked to sleep with the windows open.
She liked sleeping with the windows closed.
And then there were the indignities of aging - trips to the bathroom in the middle of the night to visit the toilet, flushing, and banging the lid down.

And there was the collection of pills and potions and ointments and lotions cluttering the bathroom cabinet and sometimes being spilled onto the floor to be stepped on in the darkness by the next user of the toilet.

They were getting on each other's nerves.

The iron plow of reality gouged deep furrows in the soft loam of love.

*

Alex listened, feeling sympathy for the general and anxiety for himself. Here was the tattered edge of the end of romance. He recalled the days of his own marriage, and the disorderly habits of his late wife. He remembered her subtle cynicism about all things great and small, and how that had soured their companionship and tarnished his view of the world.

Too much togetherness was deadly.

They had become what Alex called "The Three-legged Beast."

*

Alex concluded that the General and his Lady needed space between them – more room – some chance to be apart – something to occupy their energy besides the minutia of their intimate life together.

Alex had a brilliant suggestion.

"Remain two people. Keep the cottage, encourage her gardening, and lease my canal boat from me for six months. You learn all about the boat and the canal. Use it as your personal office. And take Winifred for trips from time to time."

Hans's broad grin told Alex that his idea had struck home.

"But what about you? What will you do?" Hans asked.

"Me? I have some plans of my own in mind. Too long to tell now. But it would please me to have you in charge of my boat while I am away. And Winnie could putter around my greenhouse and garden.

"And speaking of adventures, I hereby invite you and Winifred to join me in Crete – two weeks from now. Your father is buried there, if I remember correctly, but have you ever really vacationed there? With a Cretan for a guide? October is perfect, and I have friends you will like. You must come. I insist. Do not take time to think about it. Drop everything and come. Spontaneity should be one of the pleasures of retirement."

Another broad grin from Hans. Another hit right on target from Alex.

"One final thought. My boat and Crete will not solve your picker problems, but they will get your mind off these little things for a time. She will always be a picker, you know. But you, General Sandbag, will get used to it."

WONKO

September. The Oxford Canal. Still summer.

"Come to Crete in October, Elliot. Be my guest," said Alex.

The two men faced each other across the gangplank of the *Ariadne* - Wonko on shore, Alex on his boat. They had spent another fine evening together - supper on deck, wine, cigars, and the rich conversation both had come to cherish.

When they were alone together, as had often been the case during the summer, Alex had begun addressing the man behind the Wonko façade by his real name, Elliot. Wonko had not objected. This use of his name implied the acceptance of a more intimate friendship.

Wonko had drawn out Alex's playful nature by including him in his traveling entertainment troupe. Alex was a hit in his full bunny suit, handing out red rubber noses and even doing an awkward bunny dance when moved by the music. Wonko admired men whose sense of dignity included the wisdom to be playful.

By unspoken agreement they had become a two-man classroom, each holding forth on broad areas of knowledge unfamiliar to the other. Last week Wonko had described the canyon country of the American southwest, and the history of the Pueblo people of the Four Corners region. He had first gone to the area for survival training when he was in Special Forces, and had returned to backpack the canyons and canoe the rivers. The vast, quiet solitude of that remote landscape remained vivid in his mind.

Tonight, at Wonko's request, Alex had been describing the discovery and elaboration of the Minoan civilization in Crete - including his part in it.

Wonko sensed that his friend was prepared to unpack a great many archival trunks. While he wanted to see all the contents, it was after midnight and he began to yawn in a contagious way, which brought the evening's conversation to an end.

When Alex invited him to Crete, Wonko hesitated.

"I am quite serious, Elliot. This is not just a polite invitation. I truly want you to come. Several other friends will be joining me. People you would find interesting. But more important, I could show you the ruins of Minoan Crete, first hand. Please."

(Silence.)

"Please? It would mean much to me."
"Right," said Wonko. "Yes. I'll come."

His yes meant more than Alex understood. Yes, he would come, but he also knew about Alex's other guests. Alice, for one, would be there.

Though they had not discussed the subject of Alice and espionage, it had been a powerful subtext to their conversations. And Alex assumed Wonko would be interested in Crete in part because Alice would be there.

True. Wonko did want a closer look at Alice.

*

Even though she was no longer in his jurisdiction, Wonko had received a report on Alice's meeting with Bellingham in Seattle and her activities in Japan. Of course she was no spy, but she still might be in danger from those who were. He knew she was going to Athens. Not a safe place for an American with her knowledge. Too close to the Middle East.

He had walked a fine line with Alice. He'd had a job to do when she was in his territory. Observe her - keep her under surveillance while she was in Oxford. But while trying to retain his professional distance, he had none the less been drawn to her, fascinated by her. He wanted to know more. Not for his employers' sake, but out of his own personal sense of curiosity.

"I'll come to Crete," he said.

And went away humming a fiddle tune he was composing.

152

ARIADNE'S AIR

UNEXPECTED TRAVEL

On Athos, a man on a ledge
Made bets that came with a hedge.
Between sea and sky
He decided to fly
And calmly stepped out on the edge.

—An Alex limerick

*

There was no reason for Alex to visit Mount Athos. But reason had nothing to do with it. It was sufficient that he was a Greek, a Cretan, and a man baptized in the Greek Orthodox Church. And therefore, somewhere in the soil of his soul was planted the seed of aspiration: Make a pilgrimage to the Holy Mountain - the monastic community of Mount Athos.

This is a commanding conviction, not unlike that which calls men to Jerusalem or Mecca or Santiago de Compostela or Benares. A man may never actually go - most do not - but that seed of possibility remains planted in a corner of a Greek man's soul. And if the opportunity arises . . .

*

Unexpected travel plans are made by the travel agents of the gods.

The awareness of their arrangements is triggered by minor incidents.

There was an exhibition at the Ashmolean Museum of the watercolors and drawings done by Edward Lear when he had toured Mount Athos for two months in 1856. Alex saw the announcement of the exhibition. He did not realize it at the time, but he was already on his way to Athos.

On that same day, his friend, the Orthodox bishop of Oxford, remarked that Alex's long hair and beard reminded him of the hermit monks of Athos. And that very same afternoon, Alex passed a display of travel books about Greece in the window of a shop. Behind the stack of books was a poster showing monks in a procession on Athos. Alex saw his own reflection in the glass, superimposed on the poster, as if he had already joined the procession.

When he went from the shop window to the exhibition of Lear's drawings and paintings, the seed of an Athos pilgrimage sprouted. He imagined himself as a companion to Lear. Inclination turned into conviction. Yes. He *should* go to Athos. Soon. On the way to Crete. Now or never.

He spoke to the bishop. Though access to Mount Athos is limited, Alex's visa was swiftly arranged. As a classmate in seminary of the patriarch of Constantinople, the bishop had connections in high places. Done.

Leaving England a week earlier than expected, Alex flew to Thessaloniki, hired a car to Ouranopoli, passed through customs and immigration, and went aboard a modern version of a World War II landing craft filled with trucks and supplies and 250 other men, all bound for Dafni, the port of entry for the Holy Mountain.

Sitting on the upper deck in the shade of canvas rigged against the hot September sun, Alex opened an envelope given to him by the bishop of Oxford with the admonition that he was to open it *only* after the boat was underway - when his mind was fully concentrated on the experience to come.

Inside was a personal letter of greetings to Alex, a map, and a printed information sheet prepared by the bishop for English pilgrims making their first visit to the mountain, with special concern for the understanding of the non-Orthodox.

1. Athos is the easternmost of the three promontories of Chalkidiki - a peninsula stretching into the Aegean Sea between the Thermaic and Strimonic gulfs of north Greece. Sixty kilometers long, 8 to 12 kilometers wide; low and flat at the landward end; sloping to a great ridge, which ends in the bare rock slopes of Mount Athos, rising in a sheer pyramid from the sea to more than 2,000 meters. The physical setting has always been a defining condition of the spiritual atmosphere.

2. Since as early as the fourth century, those wishing to practice the rigors of an ascetic and contemplative life have sought refuge from the corruption and belligerence of civilization by coming here, to what the Greeks call Agion Oros - the Holy Mountain - the heart and soul of the monastic tradition of the Orthodox Church.

3. Monasticism is defined as the individual's renunciation of the world and his retreat into a solitary life to achieve the salvation of his soul through contemplation and closer communion with God. The keystones of monastic life are the virtues of chastity, poverty, and obedience.

4. The Holy Mountain has been closed to the world for centuries. Today there are more than 2,000 monks and 2,000 laymen workers living there, in twenty major monasteries and in uncountable smaller retreats and hermitages. Under the Greek constitution, Agion Oros is an independent state with its own government, police force, navy, and borders. In mid-peninsula is a town, Karyes, with stores, shops, a restaurant, and offices. Athos is its own discrete world, accessible only by boat. The numbers of visitors and pilgrims are strictly limited. A passport and visa are required for entry. Athos does not welcome the casual tourist.

5. Remember that Mount Athos is an entirely male society. That does not mean it is misogynistic. The Mother of God is the focus of veneration. No matter what the pilgrim may find in the way of aspects of the modern world, the traditions of the spiritual life remain primary. In the monasteries, the morning liturgy begins at 4:00 a.m. and continues until 7:00 a.m., followed by rest, a little food, and work. The liturgy begins again at 5:00 p.m. and finishes at 7:00 p.m., followed by a simple meal in silence while scripture is read. After personal devotions, the monks retire, until time to rise again the following morning at 3:30 and repeat the day. The pilgrim should participate in this routine, which has been followed for centuries.

6. Cell phones, laptops, radios, alcohol (except wine with meals), and all recreational drugs are forbidden. Possession or use of such items or inappropriate behavior can lead to expulsion.

*

Standing in line at the coffee bar on the ship, a priest eyed Alex with mild disdain. Alex, with his usual delight in appropriate costumes for special occasions, was dressed entirely in black and carrying a black shoulder bag. His dress, along with his black cane and long gray hair and beard, marked him as one more of the elderly pilgrims with monkish fantasies who so often turn up at the Holy Mountain in the last years of their lives.

While waiting for his coffee, Alex eyed the priest behind him, returning the same mild disdain. The man's clothes were well-tailored, fine-quality liturgical black. Polished, black city-dweller's shoes. Well-trimmed, short gray beard. Carrying an expensive black leather attaché case.

Sleek as a seal. An elite minion of some prince of the church, thought Alex.

Suddenly, the barman spilled a cup of coffee across the counter, splashing both Alex and the priest. When both uttered oaths in English, the barrier between the two men came down. And in no time they had settled down on the deck of the ship and begun opening the pages of the invisible account books travelers carry containing their lifetime journeys.

Father John was Canadian, brought up in the Rockies as the son of a civil engineer who built dams and power plants. Following in his father's footsteps, he had gone to university to become an engineer. But one thing led to another, and he discovered he had a vocation for the priesthood. Anglican. He married, had children, and served in parishes in British Columbia.

Widowed early, his children grown up and gone away, he left the priesthood and traveled in search of spiritual enlightenment. In Japan and India and Nepal, he studied the varieties of Buddhism and lived in monastic communities. Still unsatisfied, he came to Mount Athos.

And stayed. Converting to Orthodoxy, he not only found the religious community that suited him, but discovered that his education, technical training, and language abilities qualified him for special tasks on Mount Athos.

"I come and go," he explained. "As you will see, the monasteries are in a great phase of reconstruction. Someone must negotiate with construction companies, and someone must supervise the work of engineers who come to Athos from the outside. My abbot has assigned me this work. I'm just returning from Munich and meetings with contractors.

"If you see me while you are here, I'll be wearing a hard hat, supervising a construction site. This mixing of the spiritual life and practical work suits me. I'm happy. I have found my vocation."

In turn, Alex told the story of his life. Both men smiled with unspoken delight that their first impressions of one another had proved wrong.

Father John cleared his throat and gave Alex his most somber look.

"I would not insult your considerable intelligence, but since you will not be here long, may I share some thoughts with you? Short-term visitors are often confused and disappointed," he said.

"I would be in your debt if you would," said Alex.

"First of all, Athos is a world of men. With all that entails. There are old, fanatical, poorly educated monks, some of whom have been here all their lives. A few live as hermits in almost-inaccessible caves on the cliffs of the far south. Some of them seem quite mad. The Fools of God.

"At the other end of the spectrum, there are young men with university degrees in graduate studies, conversant with modern technology and science. They are fully computer competent, and quite experienced in the outside world.

"In between are the pious and impious, the talented and the inept, the scholars and the gardeners, the plumbers and the icon painters, the wise and the foolish, the lost and found, the competent and incompetent. While chastity is always a vexing issue, the monastic community is not, as too many people suppose, a hotbed of sexual perversion.

158

"There is a different sense of time on Mount Athos. For one thing, the community operates on the Julian calendar, which is thirteen days behind the rest of the world. But that's only symbolic of the deeper sense of timelessness. The activities of Athos have continued unchanged for more than a thousand years. Don't overlook that.

"You'll be there only a week. You'll probably feel overwhelmed. Go ahead and be overwhelmed. Don't give it too much thought – just *be* there. You will see what you look for, and you will understand what you are willing to understand."

ALEX ON THE HOLY MOUNTAIN

The bishop of Oxford had urged Alex to buy a small, handheld digital recorder. He knew Alex did not like writing, but because he did like talking, the bishop thought he should make at least an oral record of his reflections. The bishop did not say it, but he was concerned about Alex's short-term memory. He, too, perceived what he thought were increased signs of Alex's aging.

Heeding the bishop's advice, Alex bought the recorder. Most afternoons, while alone, he spoke to the device as if he was talking to Alice or Max-Pol:

> Two mornings ago I stood in the four o'clock darkness in a great church alongside the marble tomb of the founder of the monastery of Iviron. Over this burial chamber hangs a simple oil lamp, which has been carefully tended and kept burning for more than 800 years. Carried away by the hypnotizing liturgical chant mixed with the smoke of incense, and the tapestry of colors of the walls and the reflections of gold thrown by the flickering candles, I began wondering to myself - me of many words - "How can I possibly describe this?"

> I will try. Though I empathize with Edward Lear, who wrote in 1856 after his Mount Athos experience that it was "pomskizillious and gromphibberous, being as no words can describe it."

> The same Edward Lear, he of nonsense vocabulary, spent two months traveling the length and breadth of the Holy Mountain, drawing and painting all twenty of the monasteries. While he appreciated the awesome beauty he experienced, he was less impressed with the inhabitants, ". . . these muttering, miserable, mutton-hating, man-avoiding, misogynic, morose and merriment-marring, monotoning,

many-mule-making, mocking, mournful, minced-fish and marmalade masticating Monx. Poor old pigs!" I quote from his biography, which I brought along with me. Not exactly a book of scriptures, but his life inspires me more than Holy Writ.

There is truth in Lear's remarks. It does sometimes seem a solemn, joyless, and painful life. Especially for those who live in hermitages pasted on cliffs hundreds of feet above the sea. I thought of feelings I had last year when watching the high-trapeze performers at a circus as they flew through the air on the edge of death. I would not want to do that or devote my life to it. But there is no denying the single-minded discipline required of the acrobats. The monks are spiritual acrobats. It is a seriously scary way to live, requiring courage I do not have.

There are contradictions and astonishments on Holy Mount Athos:

The liturgy is performed exactly as St. John Chrysostom wrote it in Byzantine Greek in the fourth century. His head is preserved in a silver box kept on the high altar of the monastery of Vatopaidi. I saw it and touched the crown of the skull through a little opening in the top of the box.

In the same monastery there is kept what is claimed to be the forefinger of John the Baptist. And the girdle of the Mother of Jesus. Along with pieces of wood from the True Cross. And the feet, hands, arms and heads of too many martyred saints to name.

Very close by, in the library, is a state-of-the-art computer system - gigazillion megabytes of data storage - connected to huge scanners and color printers - so explained the bright, young monk in charge.

The oldest buildings (ninth century) in the oldest and most remote monastery, the Great Lavra, are under reconstruction. Alongside the monastery is a new helicopter pad for the convenience of visiting dignitaries and patrons, such as the Prince of Wales and his father, the Duke of Edinburgh. At the most isolated landings, the boat is met by strings of donkeys; it is the only way supplies can be carried up thousands of feet of switchback trails. At the main port, however, the boat is met by late-model four-wheel-drive Toyota pick-ups, Land Rovers, and Mercedes buses. Their drivers are cell-phone-carrying monks, who cowboy their vehicles at high speed on the rocky roads in typical young Greek male style.

The Internet already comes to Mount Athos, but only to the offices of the abbots, who rule like minor princes over Byzantine-style kingdoms. The use of the World Wide Web is carefully monitored. Several monks have been caught watching pornography, so I am told. I wonder what happened to them?

The monks are devoted to God and His Beauty. Yet their plastic-bagged garbage is shoved over the cliffs, into ravines, or into the sea. The monks are devoted to the Mother of God, the Virgin Mary. But everything female is rejected on the mountain.

The monks are focused on heaven. But I saw the latest copy of *Astronomy Magazine* in a monastery library. The magazine contained the Hubble photographs of the oldest galaxy yet discovered, thirteen billion light-years away. And it seems now there is evidence of enough water on Mars to have supported life. I wonder what the monks make of such things.

And so it goes. Contradictions and peculiarities and wonders abound. It is a human society after all, albeit a lopsided one. I suppose the other end of the spectrum of civilization – Las Vegas, for example – is just as lopsided.

Despite the unwelcoming attitude and fierce, raven-like appearance of black-cloaked men with long hair and beards, there were those who treated me, a secret heretic, with grace and kindness. And generosity - there is no charge for their hospitality. And I would reply to their tolerance of my way of life with tolerance of theirs.

We all say, "I need to get away from it all." And I do find being away from the news of the outside world to seek the news of my inner world is calming. It does give me perspective. The monk's world is no more mad than my own. Harder, I think, than the monastic way, is to stay out in the wider world as it is and maintain a spiritual life at the same time.

I think I am more of an ancient Greek than a Greek Orthodox. Like those philosophers of old, I care more for questions, speculations, and metaphors than creeds, doctrines, and liturgies. All these icons and services and gold and treasures impress me but do not speak to me. And I am not ever going to commit myself to poverty, obedience, or chastity. Never.

My Canadian acquaintance's prediction has come true.
I am overwhelmed.
Too much to digest - too few words to express it.

I shall put this little machine away and just be here.

ALEX AT THE END

On his last night on the Holy Mountain, Alex stayed in a remote *skete* - a semi-hermitage occupied by three icon painters. The monks carried out their tasks in cells where generations of monks before them had painted the same icons for hundreds of years. They accepted Alex's presence as an act of hospitality, but, except for meals, he was left to his own solitude.

The skete clung to a ledge high up on the steep cliffs at the end of the peninsula, where the south side of the mountain drops straight down to the sea. With little else to occupy his mind, Alex spent most of the afternoon sitting and staring out at the vast spaces before him - the calm sea and cloudless sky.

The only living thing in Alex's sight was a solitary hawk, which soared out and back from the cliffs above him. Alex watched the hawk with envy. One of the few complaints Alex had about being human was his inability to fly.

After the evening meal, eaten in meditative silence with the monks, Alex walked back out to the edge of the abyss. A rope hung there, tied to a ring embedded in the stone. He had been told that the monks held on to the rope and leaned out over the sea as an act of spiritual discipline - exposing themselves to the mercy of God.

Holding tightly to the rope, and crouching, Alex cautiously leaned out into the emptiness. It was as if he had reached the end of the earth. Slowly, he straightened his legs and thrust himself out as far as possible, to the very end of the rope. He was not sure if he had the strength to pull himself back to safety even if he wanted to.

More than once in recent years he had said that when it was time to die, he hoped he would be in charge of that moment. If he had his wish, he would suddenly disappear into thin air. Here was his chance. Let go. Fall through the air, and sink into the deep sea without a trace. The monks would not miss him anytime soon - if they missed him at all.

164

Or maybe the gods would decide.

This might be the moment when the old rope frayed and broke.

Or when the rusted ring gave way and pulled free from the rock.

Or when his strength failed and he could neither get back nor hold on.

I am not tempting the gods, he thought. *I am tempting myself.*

Alex recalled times when he had been afraid as a child - especially at night. But now, in this precarious situation, hanging out over the cliff with only darkness around him, he felt no fear.

I could let go, he thought. *I could turn loose of the rope and fling myself out into darkness. But I do not want to fall. I want to fly.*

And in that moment an image of the table at the Meltemi in Crete came to him. Alice and Max-Pol and Kostas and Wonko and the General and his Lady would all be waiting for him. He had invited guests for lunch. Letting go would have to wait.

Drawing on all of his remaining strength, moved more by an act of will than the power of muscle, Alex pulled himself back to safety and released the rope. His fingers were swollen and grooved from holding on so tightly. He was shaking and sweating.

"I am still here!" he shouted into the darkness. "Still here!"

When he went to bed in his cell, he thought of those companions he would soon see at the table at the Meltemi. They would like his limerick:

On Athos, a man on a ledge
Made bets that came with a hedge.
Between sea and sky
He decided to fly
And calmly stepped back from the edge.

"Onward," he said aloud. And fell into sound sleep.

THE ATHENIAN ORACLE

Hot. Hellishly hot. The smoggy, yellow, humid heat of the summer seemed to be piled up above Athens in unwashed layers - like dirty laundry accumulating during a windless September - behind an invisible atmospheric barrier that would surely break with furious storms when the first system of cool weather shoved its way down out of northern Europe. Meanwhile, the ominous heat relentlessly pressed its weight down upon the city, driving Athenians inside by afternoon - to hide, to sleep, and to wait for evening.

Polydora Vlachou was neither hot nor hiding. Spending her days driving around in her comfortable, air-conditioned office - her new, silver Mercedes sedan - was a sensual pleasure. The pungent scent of soft black leather was the smell of success.

She was moving up in the world quickly. Her companion and partner, Maria, drove their other car, which was also new - a BMW sedan. Neither car was used to cruise the streets or hotels looking for customers. Their clientele was upscale now, and their services were available by appointment only.

Athens was more than ever a diplomatic and economic crossroads connecting India, East Africa, and the Middle East with Paris, London, and the New Europe. Polydora's clients were from Bombay, Goa, Zanzibar, Dubai, Beirut, and Switzerland. Most were well educated Indians, Syrians and Arabs from families with long histories of trade. In past generations they had dealt in gold, diamonds, currency, and antiquities. And information, the most valuable commodity of all: what was available from whom, and when, and at what price.

Now, the younger generation bought and sold electronic technology, and security systems, and insider knowledge from their connections in banks and governments. And central to this flowing stream of money and luxuries and secrets were the Greeks - middlemen - connectors - arrangers - as ever.

All of her clients were men, though many of her passengers were the women who kept company with those men - models, dancers, singers, airline stewardesses - young and beautiful women with time on their hands. Like the men, the women were always in transit, passing through on the way to somewhere else, always looking for the next big opportunity while making themselves available for the pleasures of the moment.

Patrice had opened this world to Polydora. He was a half-Greek, half- French dealer in rare antiquities - jewelry, archeological artifacts, and coins. One of his brothers was a banker and the other was a diplomat. All three were multi-cultural, multi-lingual, and multi-talented. They had grown up in Bombay and been educated in France and England. Between them, they had extraordinary connections in Athens' international community.

Polydora and Patrice met when one of Patrice's Indian associates had hired her to take him to Delphi. He invited Patrice to come along and talk business in the privacy of the car. When they returned to Athens, Patrice asked Polydora to pick him up again that evening. He had paid more attention to her than to his client, and what he had in mind was not a destination, but a proposal.

Patrice needed the services of a car and driver - as a priority client. Maintaining a car and chauffeur of his own was too much trouble. He was prepared to offer her a substantial retainer, plus premium payment for each time he used her services. When he did not need her, she would be free to serve other clients.

"Why me?" she asked.

Patrice had been straightforward. The concierge at his client's hotel confirmed what he had observed. Polydora was attractive, intelligent, and clever. She was cultured, spoke three languages, and from her years as a flight attendant in the first-class cabin for Olympic Airlines, she was comfortable among rich and important people. She seemed to anticipate a client's needs the first time and remember them thereafter. She was much more than a chauffer.

And there was one more reason. Patrice expressed it bluntly.

"You are, I perceive, what the Americans call a 'lipstick lesbian,' yes?

Most people don't know, am I correct? Before you answer, I will tell you that I am gay, though not overtly so. I need a driver who is both broad-minded and discreet, who is not inclined to become involved with my male clients. Do you understand?"

Polydora parked her taxi. She considered Patrice: Charming, shrewd, wealthy, and well-connected. And surprisingly forthright. His proposal offered her financial security and a better clientele.

"Yes, you are correct. And yes, I understand. And yes, I'll accept. First for a month to see how it goes for both of us. But there are some things I will not do."

"Name them."

"Most people who want private cars are concerned about security, but I'm not a bodyguard and I won't carry any kind of weapon, except the mace I have in my purse for my own protection. I won't be involved in anything illegal, especially drugs. And I won't socialize with any of your clients. My companion, Maria, also drives. We're partners. Companions. You understand? You'll meet her and decide if she meets your standards."

"Agreed," he said.

By the end of a month, the arrangement had worked well for both Patrice and Polydora. He began thinking of her as The Athenian Oracle, because her comments about clients, while carefully veiled, seemed astutely perceptive. More than once one of her observations had given Patrice a substantial financial advantage in a business deal.

He made a new proposal: Polydora should have a better car; two in fact. Both would have their uses for his clients.

"I will make the arrangements," he said. "And whenever I am away, you can use the cars however you see fit."

*

This September, Patrice was in Switzerland.

And that is how it came to be that Polydora Vlachou was driving a new Mercedes the afternoon she picked up Max-Pol at the airport. He was not surprised by the car as much as he was surprised by Polydora's appearance. He had expected trim, all-black, all-business - as she had appeared on their trip to Delphi a year ago.

She greeted him wearing a white linen summer dress. Ignoring the offer of a handshake, she lightly kissed him on both cheeks. He was at a loss for words.

"Come on," she said. "There's a lot of traffic in town."

As they cruised in air-conditioned comfort through the heat-hazed streets of Athens, Max-Pol thought the traffic was light, and said so.

"That's not the kind of traffic I mean," she said. "Your friend, Alice, has arrived. And her friend, Zenkichi, from Japan. A man Alice calls Wonko is around. And some Japanese tourists who seem to want to go everywhere Zenkichi and Alice go. And now you, Max-Pol. Heavy traffic."

Honk! Honk! Honk!

Polydora suddenly braked and swerved to avoid an oncoming bus passing a truck in her lane. Skillfully swerving again to keep from running into a pack of young men on motor scooters, she adroitly guided her car into an opening and resumed speed up the avenue. No panic or swearing, just consummate driving skill.

"You're very good in heavy traffic," said Max-Pol.

"It is my profession - my specialty - with cars and . . . people." She turned and looked at Max-Pol as they waited at a red light.

Not wanting to accept the unspoken invitation to talk about himself, he thought, *Change the subject.* "How's your companion, Maria?" he asked.

"Maria . . . is . . .," she sighed. "Maria is . . . It's hard to say."

Wrong subject, thought Max-Pol.

CROWDS OF THREE

Maria Michaelidis had been sullenly silent for days. Her silence concealed her anger at her companion, Polydora. She feared what might happen if she said what she felt. Passive aggression is not the Greek style, but Maria is not a typical Greek woman.

She drives a taxi and dresses mannishly, consciously avoiding feminine traits and styles. She is most pleased when male taxi drivers treat her like one of them, even to the point of not bothering to censor their rough language and crude stories when she is around.

Nonetheless, she is a handsome woman. Like her companion, Polydora, she is intelligent, and competent. But, unlike Polydora, she signals to the world that she is a lesbian; she has increasingly declared and emphasized her identity: Pantsuits, and a mannish haircut; no makeup or perfume, no jewelry.

She has regarded her relationship with Polydora as a spiritual marriage with a lifetime commitment. They have worked well together, lived well, with an open affection between them in private and often in public. If asked, Maria would have said she was happier than she ever expected to be.

But during the summer she had sensed trouble coming. There was some change in Polydora. She seemed distant and distracted. And for the first time in their companionship, Polly wouldn't or couldn't talk to Maria about her feelings.

The tension between the two women rose to a crisis level in late September, when Polly took a day off to go shopping. When she came home in the evening, she was wearing makeup, her hair had been styled loose and curly, and she was carrying shopping bags and boxes from high-fashion boutiques.

"I just felt like a change," said Polly.

But her new clothes suggested more than a wardrobe upgrade. Dresses. Skirts. Frilly underwear. Flimsy shoes with high heels. And nothing black. Only whites, and flowery prints in lively colors. Even her new undergarments were colorful.

And there was a little white box with the label, Chanel No. 5.

"What do you think?" asked Polly.

That was the moment when Maria began to withdraw into herself. She could not speak her mind. She was afraid of what she thought. Rationally, she had always known that women moved more easily than men along a spectrum of sexual identity. She recognized her own movement toward unambiguous homosexuality. But Polydora was moving in the opposite direction. Maria felt the truth, but she could not bring it out in the open.

She was afraid she would lose Polly.

"Nice. Pretty," was all Maria could manage to say.

Later that week Polly added news that drove Maria further into fearful silence.

"Patrice is away and I don't feel like working. A former client of mine is coming to town, with friends. I'm going to show them Athens - as a personal favor. Do you remember the American doctor I took to Delphi? Max-Pol Millay."

Maria nodded, mute.

"I know you think three's a crowd, Maria, but I always say you can have a good time in crowds. I'm not forgetting that we've agreed not to socialize with clients. But I'm tired of being hired help, and I need a break from being all-business all the time.

"Indulge me. I want to play, and from what I know about these people, they're fun to play with. Don't worry. You don't have to be involved, unless you want to be. The woman I told you about, Alice, is also coming, but not *with* him - just coming at the same time."

Maria remained fearfully silent.

What troubled her was not so much what Polly said - or even the clothes and makeup and perfume. What hurt was the casual way Polly explained this new state of affairs, as if she was not aware of what was happening.

Maria felt her world falling apart.

She did not cry, ever. She thought she was too strong to cry.

But the afternoon when Polly left to pick up Max-Pol at the airport, the moment the door closed behind Polly, Maria collapsed on a chair, put her head down in her hands on the kitchen table. She cried.

And cried. And cried.

In Transit

They had ridden several blocks in silence while Polydora continued her expert slalom through the unrelenting unpredictability of Athens traffic, when she turned onto a one-way road leading into a park and stopped the car at a small parking lot in the shade of a grove of fine old pine trees. Switching off the ignition, she said, "I need a break - come."

As they had done once before on the way to Delphi, they got out of the car and walked a short way. Max-Pol waited for Polydora to speak first, sensing that she had something on her mind.

Sitting on a marble bench near a small fountain, she patted the place beside her. "Sit for a minute," she said. "There are other visitors in town - other friends sent by Kirios Alex."

"Who?"

"First came the German general and his wife," said Polly to Max-Pol.

"They don't know you, but they got my number from your mysterious friend Alex, who got it from you. The general rented a car and is off alone to see the ancient battlefields - Marathon, Thermopylae, Platea, and the Macedonian tombs near Thessaloniki.

"His wife is in Athens, being driven by Maria to art museums, exhibitions of folk costumes, and fabric stores. Nice people. Did you know Alex has invited them to Crete?"

"Chanel No. 5," said Max-Pol, sniffing. The signal from his nose was stronger than the information in his ears. Polydora's perfume was a clear, fragrant note on top of the pungent smell of the pine grove.

"I don't remember your wearing perfume. Chanel No. 5 is my favorite."

Polydora smiled, and continued her account.

"Next came Mr. Brownell. Said he knows you, but not well. Another friend of Alex's, who gave him my number. Mr. Brownell said to tell you that Wonko is in town, on his way to Crete."

Still distracted, Max-Pol glanced at Polydora beside him, considered her nail polish, toenail polish, and lipstick - all the same shade of scarlet red. Dangly gold earrings. Nice tan. All so very *feminine*.

"Forgive me for saying so, Polly, but you seem to be out of uniform. Lovely. But so different from last time I saw you. Has something changed?"

Turning her face to his, Polly pulled her sunglasses down and looked at him over the top them.

"Yes."

"That's all? Just yes? - You're going to leave it there?"

"Yes. Later. Not now. I'm telling you about your friends."

"OK, so who else then?"

"Alice. Your Witness."

"Really? What about Alex?"

"He was coming, but apparently he went to Mount Athos instead, and then directly on to Crete."

"That's a surprise. Anybody else?"

"A Japanese Kabuki actor."

"What?"

"That's all I know. He got my number from Alice, who got it from Alex, who got it from you. What's going on? Everybody seems to be connected somehow."

"Beats me," said Max-Pol. "Alex collects and connects people. And he likes surprises. It seems he's invited quite a crowd to Crete. Has he invited you?"

"No . . . Not yet."

"I don't usually comment on a client's appearance, Dr. Millay, but you aren't really my client today. Be my guest instead, if you don't mind. And I must say you're very thin, for one thing, and the long hair and beard are new."

"A bout with hepatitis. But I've recovered. And the hair and beard are to win a bet with Alex. I'll see a barber as soon as the contest is over."

Polydora reached over and lightly stroked Max-Pol's beard.

"Just a trim - the beard becomes you. I like it."

"Polydora, you're giving me very confusing signals. May I be blunt? I thought you were a lesbian."

"So did I."

"And?"

"You're a doctor, Max-Pol. Guess."

"Hormones - your female hormones have asserted themselves."

"Yes. And so?"

"You're thinking of having a child."

"Yes. And . . . so?" Polydora placed her hand gently on his.

Max-Pol froze. *Oh, dear God,* he thought. *By me.*

He cleared his throat, looked away, looked at his shoes, looked at the fountain, looked anywhere except at the face of Polydora and the next question she might ask.

Polydora gently withdrew her hand. *Not now,* she thought. *But he didn't say no. The time will come.*

Standing, she stretched, and said, "Let's go, Max-Pol - you need to check into your hotel and get acquainted with Alex's friends.

Relieved, Max-Pol stood and stretched and, accepting the change of subject, said, "Tell me more about these traveling friends of Alex's - where they're staying and what they're doing and do they know I'm here?"

While she answered his questions, Polydora and Max-Pol walked back to the car. He was tempted to reach out and hold her hand as a way of saying her implied invitation was being positively considered. But he did not. A reply had not yet settled in his mind. *Maybe,* he thought, *maybe not.*

WHO'S WHO?

Alex had urged his guests to spend two days in Athens on the way to Crete. "At least visit the Benaki Museum, The National Archeological Museum, the Acropolis, and the Agora."

He further insisted that they browse the Central Municipal Market – given five stars on his list of sites. He called it the "Food Museum – the greatest display imaginable of the finest ingredients of Mediterranean cuisine."

Polydora helped Alex's guests figure out plans to see the sights, but she could not quite figure out their relationships with one another.

Who is who? she wondered. And what's their connection?

She didn't know if this was a reunion or a collision.

What did they do when they met?

This man, Alex, was the catalyst, but where and *who* was he?

By the second morning, the members of the group had made plans of their own. Wonko and Alice were going with Zenkichi to watch his rehearsal at the Herodes Atticus theater, and Max-Pol asked Polydora to drive him to Epidaurus.

*

Wonko was not on duty; but the habits of a lifetime are hard to break. Walking through the busy Plaka district with Alice and Zenkichi, he sensed that they were being followed. Moving between Alice and Zenkichi, he put an arm around their shoulders, pulled them closer and spoke softly.

"Don't pay any attention to what I do. Just keep walking and don't look back. Stop and look in shops and then keep going. I'll explain later. Trust me."

Alice and Zenkichi walked on. Alice took Zenkichi's arm, and quietly explained, "We're probably being followed. Keep looking ahead and don't act surprised or respond to what I'm going to tell you. Wear your most enigmatic Japanese face and just listen. It's a long story."

Wonko turned away into a small shop to buy a *Herald Tribune*. An Asian couple passed by - the same couple Wonko had noticed outside the Cafe Chroma during breakfast, and in the Benaki Museum yesterday, and in the lobby of Alice's hotel at least once.

Wonko fell in behind them. The couple moved in sync with Alice and Zenkichi - stopping when they stopped, walking when they walked - all the way to the theater.

Wonko found Alice watching the rehearsal.

"I'm sorry to tell you, but you *are* being followed."

"I thought all that was over, or else you or I would have been told."

"So did I, but there's an Asian couple shadowing you. Probably Japanese. What concerns me is that I don't know anything about them. And I don't see them now."

Alice told him about the encounter with the man and woman in the temple grounds in Kyoto.

"Strange. I'll check it out," said Wonko. "This could be serious, but I don't want to jump to conclusions. I'm going to leave now. You leave in a little while and walk back to your hotel. Let's see what they do."

Wonko was nonplussed when he caught up with Alice. "For one thing, they didn't follow *you* - they followed *Zenkichi*. I checked with our friends in Seattle and drew a blank. Talking to Zenkichi would be a good idea, but he's tied up doing publicity for his performance."

"Should I be worried?" asked Alice.

"I'm not sure. There's a screwball quality to all this that I can't compute. I hate it when I miss something obvious. There's probably an explanation, however cockeyed."

"I'm going to the Kabuki performance this evening," said Alice. "Maybe they'll show up there. And I'm seeing Zenkichi afterward. Maybe they'll be around. Would you be willing to confront them? I don't want to go to Crete still watching over my shoulder."

"Neither do I," said Wonko. "I'll figure this out."

SNAKES ENTWINED

Max-Pol and Polydora are at Epidaurus, standing in the ruins of the Temple of Asklepios, the god of medicine.

"Polly, have you ever seen the symbol of two snakes coiled around a rod - associated with medicine?" asked Max-Pol.

"Yes. The caduceus."

"It's a reference to the cult of Asklepios. The healing arts began here, in Epidaurus."

"And you are here because . . .?"

"I wanted to touch base with the beginnings of medicine. A ritual gesture of starting over. I'm going back to being a physician - back to the States to find work that's meaningful and useful."

Polydora stepped closer to Max-Pol, slipped her hand in his.

"Do something meaningful and useful for me before you go away."

"I know what you want, Polly. I'm just not sure I feel comfortable doing it. You've become a very desirable woman - making love to you would be a pleasure, if you want to know the truth."

"All I want is a child, Max-Pol. Not a lover, not a husband. To be crude: a sperm donor. But someone I know and respect, and someone who will be a long way away and not part of my life here in Greece. Maria will be here for me and the child."

"But, Polly, I would always know. You would always know. And what about the child? Don't you think the child might come to find me some day?"

"There may be other men, Max-Pol. You'll never know if you or someone else is the father. No DNA testing either. I'll make sure of that."

"I can't say yes. I won't say no. Let me think about it."

"Could you take time off and come to Crete for a few days?" he asked. "Alex wanted to meet you anyway, and you like his friends. And. I'd like to talk more about being 'useful' to you."

"Yes," she said. And coiling her arms around his neck, she gave him a long, passionate, lingering kiss.

Kafoom!

THE PARTY

"Polydora, are you available?" Patrice's voice on Polydora's phone.

"I thought you were in the Swiss Alps."

"I've returned early."

"Is something wrong?"

"Yes, Switzerland."

"I thought you liked Switzerland."

"The cities, yes. Zurich, Geneva. But the mountain villages drove me crazy. So neat, so clean, so cute! And everybody is hiking, hiking, hiking. And the singing and dancing, my God! Yodeling and one-two-three, one-two-three. And *cows*. Everywhere, cows and cows and more cows. I *hate* cows. I couldn't stand it another day."

"What can I do for you? If you need my car, I'm already busy. I have friends in town."

"No, no. I need your company. I invite you to a party. Tonight. I know it's short notice, but three fabulous Indian musicians are in town - friends of mine - and they will come to play. Sitar, tabla, sarod. Wonderful music!"

"Patrice, you know I don't socialize with clients."

"No clients will be there. Only friends. Musicians, artists, poets. So why not bring *your* friends, as well. My cook will produce his usual miracles, and there will be a smashing end to the evening."

"Smashing?"

"Yes, I've brought back with me a Swiss Army cuckoo clock. Absurd. It is built like a border guardhouse, and on the hour a little soldier comes out of the door with a cow. He yodels. The cow moos. And at that moment I will jump up and down on top of the goddamned clock and kill it. You won't want to miss this. Performance Art, yes?"

*

Patrice's apartment was on the top floor of a building above the posh Kolonaki area, on the lower slopes of the hill of Lycabettus. From the apartment balcony there was a splendid view across Athens to the Acropolis on the other side of the city.

178

The party began at midnight, a normal hour for Greeks. A storm of Olympian proportions had ravaged the city earlier in the evening - lightning, thunder, rain, wind. The electricity was off, then on, then off again.

No problem for Patrice, who had lit the rooms of his apartment with candles and antique oil lamps. The food was being cooked on a charcoal grill on the balcony. The music was acoustic.

The guests will provide all the electricity we need, thought Patrice.

He always offered his guests only fruit juice to drink - mango, papaya, and tangerine. Not because he opposed alcohol. He just did not think alcohol mixed well with hashish, which was available to be smoked in large narghiles - Turkish water pipes - placed conveniently around the apartment.

To insure the mellowness of guests who might be timid about smoking, the cook had prepared a sauté of marijuana buds in butter, and blended it in with his meat sauce. This was standard practice for Patrice's parties, and the cook had a sensitive feel for what amount of "seasoning" worked well and what went too far. Not too much. Just enough. Guests should feel loose and light, not crazed.

At midnight Patrice asked the Indian musicians to begin playing. He lit sticks of jasmine-scented incense in the main room and hallway, and placed a bowl of gardenias beside the door. He wanted his guests to walk into an atmosphere that was already up and running.

"I'm exorcising the cow demons," he explained to his cook. "That's why I asked you to prepare beef kebabs. Tonight we are *demon eaters.*"

*

Polydora and Max-Pol were the first to arrive.

Patrice was seldom thrown off balance by human behavior, but when he opened the apartment door to find Polydora dressed like a fashion model, there was a three-beat pause before his welcome. Her appearance was part of his hesitation. But to see that she was holding hands with a thin, bearded, ponytailed, man . . .

Well, well, well . . . well, well, well . . ., he thought, not wanting to say anything that would reveal the level of his surprise. He almost said, "Looks like a great night for exorcising many kinds of demons."

But he did not.

He was saved from continued awkwardness when three people came down the hall from the elevator, laughing. People he did not know. "Friends of mine," said Polydora.

Wonko, Zenkichi, and Alice were laughing at the sudden, comic unraveling of what Alice called "The Mystery of the Mystery People." The evening performance of Kabuki had first been delayed by the storm and then canceled. When Wonko and Alice finally located Zenkichi outside the entrance to the dressing rooms, he was engaged in a tense conversation with a group of Japanese, led by a woman. The same woman who had followed Alice in Kyoto and here in Athens.

"Alice," Zenkichi called out, "please save me." Bowing his way out of the Japanese group, he said, "Come, you must take me away. Quickly."

Between the theater and the party, Zenkichi explained that the group was a fan club - Kabuki fanatics. Every actor who inherited a name from a line of famous actors also inherited a fan club. The members felt they owned the spirit of the actor, and assumed the right to protect the spirit by monitoring the private life of the current holder of the name.

"They are Kabuki cannibals. They think I belong to them. They come to every performance, shout comments on my performance, and follow me wherever I go. Tonight they wish me to take them to dinner in appreciation for their having come all the way from Tokyo to be here, and because they think I spend too much time with foreigners."

"So *that* explains . . .," said Alice, looking at Wonko and laughing.

"That *would* explain . . .," replied Wonko.

"You mean you thought . . .?" And Zenkichi joined the laughter.

"This is a plot for a Kabuki play," he said. "Misdirection is essential to Kabuki."

*

Sometime later, Wonko and Zenkichi were outside on the balcony of Patrice's apartment. "Do you ever feel any danger from these crazy fans?"

"A little. There are stories from the old days about fans kidnapping actors, and there have been acts of violence between fans - even suicide - out of jealousy and unrequited love. The woman who is the president

180

of my fan club - the one who often follows me - claims that her grand-mother was a concubine of my grandfather, and that her mother was my father's lover. And she, of course, aspires to a personal relationship with me. She even claims a secret affair between us."

"In America we call these people stalkers and we take them very seriously," said Wonko.

"Maybe," said Zenkichi. "But would she cause me any real harm? Hard to say. I can understand how my relationship with Alice would upset her though. She's jealous. And . . . people like her are capable of anything."

*

By four in the morning, the music and the food and the drugs had the guests floating in a warm pool of euphoria. Meaningful conversation had become muddled nonsense.

A Greek poet was standing in front of the hall mirror, softly reciting romantic poetry to his own image.

Two artists - an Italian woman and a Lebanese man - were drawing erotic pictures in chocolate sauce on the kitchen counter.

And Zenkichi was gracefully dancing near an oil lantern, casting his moving shadow onto the wall behind him.

The musicians, who had been playing for four hours, let their music fade away like a last dream, and stopped.

The cook appeared with a tray of small cups of Greek coffee.

In the sudden silence, Patrice said, "Polydora is a reincarnation of the oracle of Athens. Did you all know that?"

The guests nodded. In the state they were in, anything might be true.

"Polydora," said Patrice. "It's been an auspicious evening. The gods have announced their presence in the storm. Will you . . .?"

"If you wish," said Polydora, from where she lay with her head in Max-Pol's lap. She had not left his side all evening. Sitting up, she addressed the guests.

"Drink your coffee to the dregs. Turn your cup upside down on its saucer and leave it. I'll lift the cup and tell you the omens I see in the grounds."

As the Greeks in the room enthusiastically presented their muddy saucers, the Athenian oracle spoke in Greek - both mystifying and pleasing them, as is expected of oracles.

When Wonko offered his saucer, the oracle studied the pattern in the dregs, saw the shape of a crown and said, first in Greek, and then in English, "Seek the future in royalty."

Invited by Polydora, the general and his lady had arrived late but blended easily into the flow of the party, even though Patrice thought them the most exotic creatures in his evening's menagerie. By now, Winifred was asleep on cushions in a corner. Hans handed his saucer to Polydora, saying, "An oracle for two, if you please."

Looking at the two separate streams of coffee grounds flowing away from the center of the saucer, the oracle said, "Two will not become one."

"The future is in the past," was the oracle's divination for Zenkichi.

When Alice's turn came, Polydora took a long time. She closed her eyes, hummed to herself, looked again, and ran her finger along the grounds as if following a complicated design. Closing her eyes again, she spoke.

"Beware the labyrinth."

Max-Pol placed his saucer in the oracle's hands. Seeing her hesitate, he leaned very close and said, "You must at least grant me a wish."

She looked at him intently; then suddenly, as if in a trance, she said, "Two shall become one. One shall become three. If you wish."

Polydora did not have coffee. Oracles cannot divine their own futures, though sometimes they stack the deck in their favor.

The party came to a dramatic conclusion when Patrice smashed his Swiss cuckoo clock on the floor, jumped up and down on it, and threw the remains into the flames in the fireplace. "To hell with cows!" he cried.

After that grand finale, the guests left for home or hotel, and went straight to bed - as straight as possible in their dazed conditions.

Except Alice.

The Contessa Macaroni

Alice wanted to be the first of Alex's guests to arrive in Crete. As usual, she had not announced her precise travel schedule. Still, she was a little uneasy because she had not heard from Alex directly in two weeks. Polydora said only that she heard he had gone to Mount Athos. Nevertheless, Alice went straight to the airport from the party and caught the first flight to Crete.

After checking in at her hotel, the Casa Delfino, Alice wandered down through the maze of small streets to the old port. Spotting the Meltemi at the far end of the quay, she walked toward it, wondering if Alex would be there. In her hand she carried the amber komboloi he had entrusted to her the last time they were alone together on the Oxford Canal.

But no Alex.

Only a curious woman, sitting at a table at the cafe.

*

"Salutations, my dear. Sit with me. I know who you are."

"Really? What's my name?"

"Oh, I wouldn't know that. It would tell me nothing, really. The nametag on your luggage doesn't reveal the contents. I mean *I know who you are.*"

"You mean you see right through me?"

"Oh, no. What good would that do? I would only see a chair. No, I mean what I say. *I know who you are.* I see *into* you. Sit down, my dear, we must talk."

"This is a little mad," said Alice.

"Of course. I'm mad. You're mad. We're all mad here."

"How do you know I'm mad?" asked Alice.

"You must be," said the woman, "or you wouldn't have come here."

"You sound like the Cheshire Cat," said Alice.

"Cheshire Cats turn up anywhere at all, you know," said the woman. "Now won't you please sit down so we can talk?"

"They call me Contessa Macaroni," she said. "But you may call me Bouboulina. Please, *do* sit down."

Thinking this could be some welcoming joke played on her by Alex, Alice sat, willing to go along with it.

*

The contessa was once married to an Italian count. *So she claimed.* And lived for a time on his grand estate in Tuscany. *So she said.* She partied with the Riviera set, and once met Mussolini's daughter and Elizabeth Taylor. *So she said.* Now, she pawns the count's extravagant gifts of jewelry to maintain her style of life. *So the rumor goes.*

Her muddled accent suggests Spanish, French, or English. "She is not Greek, that is for sure." *So they said.* But her use of "Bouboulina" confused them. Bouboulina was the name of a Greek heroine of the War of Independence.

Like some exotic migratory bird blown off course, she has turned up in Crete every summer for several years, stayed until the end of October, and returned to who-knows-where?

Usually she wears a red dress, a leopard-print shawl, and leopard-skin high-heeled shoes. Her bulky purse is also leopard skin, leading one to suspect that not only is her underwear leopard-print silk, but she might cast a leopard-print shadow.

She always wears a white silk rose in the bun of her carefully coiffed, orange hair. Her makeup is more mask-like than cosmetic - pale pancake, eyes heavily accented with black kohl, and bright red lipstick emphasized with a black beauty mark that seems to migrate around her mouth from one day to the next. She smokes tiny cigars in an ivory holder. Too many little cigars have made her voice husky; her laugh has become a growl.

She has cultivated the image of a Gypsy flamenco dancer - retired or "between engagements." She seems to enjoy being the object of gossip, surmise, and rumor - the more, the better.

"It's all true," she says, throwing her head back, growling her laugh.

In fact, she is an American woman - a university professor from Madison, Wisconsin, fleeing from a bad marriage and a boring life, writing a novel by living out the role of its protagonist.

The contessa's main occupation in Crete seems to consist of spending afternoons and evenings at the Meltemi, luring people who interest her into conversation. She is not looking for companions or friends. She simply wishes to entertain and be entertained. And to populate her novel.

To that end she has cultivated an alternate personality that most people find charmingly eccentric. Some think she is functionally mad, though harmless. Some believe she is maddeningly functional, and dangerous. Some say she is a butterfly collector. Others say she is an exotic lizard catching flies.

But everyone agrees that she is an attraction at the Meltemi, appreciated by the owner for the amount of food and drink her impromptu guests consume. No doubt she will be mentioned eventually in some insider's guidebook to Crete. "Local color. A must-see."

*

"Do you read palms?" asked Alice.

"Oh no, my dear, that's been done to death, don't you think? Really! But I do read the lines on people's faces - those that come from living. The scars, the pits and pockmarks, the wrinkles. And all the attempts to alter reality - paints, pluckings, shaving. The past and the future are so evident in the masks people prepare for the world to see.

"I also read people's hair. Not many seers do that, you know. People arrange their hair to address other people, proclaiming themselves."

"Really? How do you read my hair?"

"Hmmm. It would be obvious to say that someone whose roots are white and the rest dyed black is a *contrarian*. It's usually the other way around, isn't it? Straight dark roots and dyed blond curls. In your case you've let it be half and half, when you could easily cut off the black or re-dye the white.

"*Defiant*, I would say. It's not that you don't care what other people think, though you like to pretend that is the case. You're announcing that you *are* different, and wish to attract those who are interested in your uniqueness."

The contessa growled her laugh at Alice's surprised silence.

"What do we have here?" she said, pointing at Alice's hands. "I see you display a fine komboloi, the kind only a Cretan man might carry. Unique. And your mismatched sandals add credibility to my perception, don't you think? You wished to be noticed - by the right people. You carry an invisible flag that says, 'I'm really different. Are you?' And my answer is obvious, isn't it? That's why you are sitting here now. We are a two-woman Committee of the Different - the meeting is called to order."

Alice gave the contessa a probing look. This woman was not the nut case Alice first thought her to be.

The woman returned Alice's look. "Have a cigar?" she asked, offering Alice a silver case.

"Thanks," said Alice. "I think I will."

Accepting the offer of a light, Alice puffed once on her little cigar, and said, "I'm looking for a man, Bouboulina."

"Oh, I can see that," said the contessa. "But not just *any* man. A very special man. There was one of those here last evening. I looked inside him. *I know who he is.*"

"Tell me," said Alice.

"Well, he was young, strong - a dancer, I'm sure. Lovely man. Wise, intelligent, and creative. Many scars, though, from conflicts I could not fathom. I had a most interesting conversation with him. Just before we parted, I asked him if there were things he would have been successful at doing, but had never done."

"And?"

The contessa thoughtfully drew on her cigar. "Should I tell you?"

"I'm looking for a man, remember?" said Alice, smiling.

"So you are. Well, he said he would have liked to find a note in a bottle floating in the sea. He could have come up with a good reply. He said he would have delivered a good oration for a certain friend, long dead. He said he would have been good at accepting a prize rewarding some great achievement. None of these opportunities had come or ever would."

"Interesting. What else?" asked Alice.

"And he said he would have been good at a grand and reckless love affair - the kind that comes from going back to find someone you wanted to love but couldn't love at the time because you were too young or whatever. And he said he would have been good at dancing because inside he felt the music, even though he was disabled in some way now and couldn't dance.

"Let me see. What else? He said he would be good at building a labyrinth. Oh, and there was one more thing. More than anything he wished he could fly."

Alex came to Alice's mind.

"I know a man like that, but he's not young and strong. He's old and crippled."

"I did not say how he appeared on the *outside*, but only what I saw when I looked *inside*," said the contessa.

"What was his name? Do you know?" asked Alice.

"Greek, I think. Xeno . . . something."

"Xenopouloudakis?"

"Yes, that's it."

"Then Alex is already here!" cried Alice.

"Nai, nai, is be here," said a voice from two tables away. "And you are the Alice, yes?" A Greek man rose from his chair and walked over to Alice's table.

"Yes, and you must be . . ."

"Kostas Liapakis. I am he. O Kirios Aleko is be expecting you."

REUNION

Alex had been sitting in the cool, musty cave of Kostas's shop, temporarily in charge while Kostas went to the Meltemi for cigarettes and coffee. Alex nervously whirled his komboloi beads back and forth around his fingers, while watching the door. His intuition was cocked with a hair-trigger – he *knew* Alice would come today.

And just as he got up to unfold a dowry carpet for two English customers, she suddenly appeared, standing in the bright sunlight outside the open door of the shop.

"Alice! *Katapliktiko!* Wonderful!"

Dropping the carpet on the feet of the customers, Alex pulled his red rubber nose out of his pocket, stuck it on his nose, and spoke the first line of Learical nonsense from the time he met Alice at Waterloo Station in the waiting room of the Chunnel train:

> "Surprising to find a Jumwillie here."
> "Jumwillies come at the call of a tear," Alice replied.
> "So Jumwillies must be nothing to fear?" said Alex.
> "They belong to the lodge of our friend, Mr. Lear."

Laughing, they continued, tossing the lines back and forth:

> "Jumwillies, Jumwillies, all in a row."
> "Jumwillies rain. Jumwillies snow."
> "Jumwillies come and Jumwillies go."
> "And nobody knows what the Jumwillies know."

*

Later that afternoon, the two English customers who were in the shop at the time of this encounter described the scene to friends, while drinking iced coffee at an outdoor cafe on the waterfront.

"We were in this nice carpet store, being helped by this nice old man with long, white hair and beard."

"Right. And all of a sudden he drops the rug on our feet, stares out the door transfixed, puts a red rubber ball on his nose, and starts spouting nonsense."

"There's this woman in the doorway - hair half black and half white - and she puts on her own red nose and recites nonsense back at him."

"Quite strange, really."

"Must be members of a cult."

"Then she charged into the shop, threw her arms around the old man's neck, and there they stood hugging each other - for far too long. Really!"

"Oh yes, *far* too long. Two feet away from us. As if we didn't exist. So embarrassing. She kissed him all over his face and kept holding on."

"And then - you won't believe this - this Greek man comes in and says sorry, but the shop is closed now, and he ushered us outside and closed the door behind us."

"I shudder to think what went on after that!"

KOLYMBARI

That evening, after their reunion, Alice rented a car while Alex went shopping for provisions for a picnic. Early the next morning the two of them set off.

"Take the National Road west as far as the Kolymbari exit," said Alex. For half an hour they rode in silence, not because they had little to say, but because there was too much. Where to begin?

*

There is a long stretch of almost deserted beach between the Tavronitis River and the fishing village of Kolymbari. The beach is not sandy, but stony and pebbly. It is a junky beach - usually littered with trash washed down the river from the inland villages in winter. Uncomfortable for walking and unpleasant for sunbathing. The water of the bay is often cloudy from the mud the river carries down when it floods. Unattractive to swimmers. So there are no hotels or tavernas nearby. Few people come here.

But by October the trash has blown away or been removed. The shallow water off the beach is clear and warm. There are patches of clean sand under isolated groves of tamarisk trees, and small dunes are piled up by the wind against stands of cane separating the beach from the inland agricultural fields.

The tourist season is over, children are in school, and the grape harvest draws the local population to the vineyards. The beach at Kolymbari is deserted in the very month when it is most beautiful.

*

With Alex navigating, Alice drove the car slowly along a dirt track through the cane fields. Their way was blocked by a large, black-and-white billy goat lying in the middle of the road. His immovable disdain proclaimed him lord of the landscape.

"Stop," said Alex. "Do not honk. He is not intimidated. When it suits him, he will get up and move." They waited.

"Do you know how to tell a goat from a sheep?" asked Alex.

"Tell me."

"Goats' tails are carried upright - sheep's are carried hanging down. Goats up. Sheep down. A mark of their personalities, when you think of it."

With the dignity of a bishop, the billy goat finally rose, paused, and processed toward the car, walked around it ignoring its occupants, and continued on its solemn way.

"When I die, I wish to return as a goat," said Alex. "And if not that, I shall return as a fine old cello. Would you play me, Alice?"

She laughed. "Well. I've heard you sing, you know. You would need voicing, I think."

"In the right hands, even an old and irritable cello can be made to sing, is that not so?"

"In the right hands," said Alice, as she parked in the shade of the tamarisk trees.

When she switched off the car's engine, the sudden silence and un-expected beauty of the beach held them still in their seats. The day was already hot, the sea was a mirror, the air windless, and the crayon-blue sky cloudless. The only sounds were the distant squawks of seabirds arguing over fishing rights at the mouth of the river.

*

LATER, ALEX WOULD SAY that after they unloaded their gear and provisions and arranged them in the shade, they took off their shoes and walked toward the sea; and that Alice took his hand to steady him while crossing the shoals of loose pebbles to the water's edge.

ALICE WOULD SAY that as soon as she had the chance she took Alex's hand because she wanted to touch him and be touched by him - a small-scale version of her desire to be as close to him again as she was the night they slept skin-to-skin together on the *Ariadne*.

ALEX WOULD REMEMBER Alice wading ahead of him, pulling him into the water with his clothes on, and plunging in alongside him. At the time it seemed one more example of her free spirit at play. Spontaneous mischief, Alice style.

ALICE WOULD REMEMBER a more serious plan. She wanted to get them both wet enough to require stripping naked to dry off in the sun. More than that, she wanted an excuse to show Alex her tattoo.

*

"Come on Aleko, don't be a chicken. Strip. We've seen each other naked before. I won't take off my clothes until you take off yours."

"I will *not* remove my undershorts. Nudity on the beach is against the law in Crete, and I do not wish to be arrested."

"But I want to see the frog tattoo on your butt in the light of day. And you *do* want to see *my* tattoo, don't you?"

"Well, then. If you are so determined. But you must show me your tattoo first."

Removing his shirt and trousers in a gesture of good faith in the bargain, Alex stood in tight, black cotton shorts reaching to his knees.

"Surprise! These are a souvenir of Mount Athos. The monks wear them."

Alice laughed.

Alex sat down on the blanket. "Your turn," he said.

She unbuttoned her dress, and let it fall around her feet. No underwear. Striking the same pose she made when revealing the tattoo for Zenkichi and Morioka, she asked, "What do you think?"

*

ALEX WOULD REMEMBER little else as vividly as that moment in what turned out to be a long and full day. Seeing Alice naked with her tattoo had not been the erotic experience he had feared. That was the real reason he had refused to remove his shorts.

And Alice's tattoo. He had expected to be surprised. Like Zenkichi and Morioka, he was speechless. Such beauty out of her deformity. Such brave shyness in her display. Such trust. Alice reached out, took Alex's hand, and placed it over the tattoo as if to say this belonged in part to him. Tears came to his eyes. Alex could only smile and nod his head in understanding.

He would remember not only what he saw and touched, but he would remember the complexities of his feelings. Bliss, delight, joy, and the odd sadness that accompanies the fulfillment of anticipation.

What made him happy was being so comfortably close to Alice - so at ease - the way he'd felt during the week they spent on the *Ariadne*. Once again he felt as if he had come home to a safe and invincible place outside the bounds of convention.

Though he *would not* because he *could not* describe this day to anyone, even if forced to recall details he would be hard-pressed to provide many. He knew that Alice had dropped beside him on her knees, commanded him to roll over, and pulled his shorts down far enough to examine his blue frog tattoo. And he knew that she wrapped a towel around herself, lay down beside him, and snuggled close to him with her arm around him and her hand clasped in his.

He knew he had said something so funny he thought Alice would never stop laughing, but he could not remember what. When she finally regained her composure, he knew that she had once again kissed him lightly all over his face, like a flock of butterflies landing all at once. Beyond that, he could only remember that they talked and ate and napped and walked - as if the day and life and the landscape were infinite.

ALICE WOULD REMEMBER spending the day by the flooding spring of Alex's knowledge and experience. Like a one-man bucket brigade he dipped into his reservoir and poured out gallons of information for her at the least provocation.

"It is my weakness to tell more than anybody ever wants to know. Even you must be impatient with me. I do try to reign in my tendencies to go on and on."

"But you have something you want to tell me, don't you?" said Alice.

"Very well. But stop me when you are bored. There is much more to this beach than meets the eye. I trust you notice the stones."

Alex picked up a small, striped rock. "Black basalt thrust up from the molten inner earth, white quartz thrust through the cracked basalt, cooled, ground down and rolled and polished smooth. A metaphor for Crete - an island and a people that have been through fire and chaos of every kind, and polished by time and the sea.

"There is one pebble on this beach for every story the Cretans have told from the beginning of time until now," said Alex. "And most of the stones have had blood spilled on them at one time or another."

"Keep going," said Alice.

"The Grand Fleet of the Ottoman Turks landed in this very place on June 23, 1645, with 100 warships, 350 troop transports, 50,000 men including 7,000 Janissaries - the elite fighting force of the Sultan. The Cretans who fought them were cut to pieces. Right here.

"And, if you had been here on May 20, 1941, you would have seen German paratroopers floating down out of the sky. Over the next ten days this beach would become littered with the wreckage of gliders and boats and men. And stained with the blood of Germans and the Cretans and the Allied forces that fought them."

(Silence.)

"There is more. I could go on. But I do not wish to spoil the day or the mood. Now you know why the beach is abandoned. The Cretans cannot see its beauty. It is too much an awful part of their past. But when we, *you and I,* look back on this beach and on this day, we will not recall sorrow and blood."

"No. Just as it is now."

Alice picked up another striped pebble, almost identical to the one Alex held.

"Kiss it, and throw it into the sea," he said. "Wish to return here."

"But I like this rock," she protested.

"Here. Take mine. Throw yours."

THE STORY STONE

As they wandered on, Alice rolled the remaining stone around the palm of her hand with her fingers, as if conjuring something from it.

"Aleko, would you like to hear this stone's story?"

"Tell me."

"'Well, then,' as you say when you begin your stories . . ."

Alex smiled and lay back on the blanket.

"Yes, well then. Does it begin Once upon a time?"

"No, it begins the day after Once upon a time," said Alice. "Be still and listen. Here's my story."

*

The day after once upon a time, not so long ago and not so far away, there may have been an island in the sea much like this one. So people say.

One day a small sailing boat landed on a beach much like this one. A young woman got out. People went to meet her. "Where do you come from?" they asked.

"The Coast of Tennessee," she replied.

"But Tennessee has no coast."

"Really? I could have sworn it did. I was misinformed."

"How did you come here?"

"From out there. Through three doors: The Door of Desire, The Door of Confusion, and the Door of Possibility."

"But there are no doors on the sea," they said.

"Really? Well, I must be confused."

"What can we do for you?"

"Take me to your king."

"We do not have a king. Never have."

"Really? Is this not the Island of AnywhereButHere?"

"No."

"Oh dear, not again," she said. And she began to cry.

"Why have you come?"

"I was given three wishes. I wished for a boat. I wished for a journey. And I wished to see the king. I'm not where I wanted to be. And I've used up my wishes."

"Ah, well, you have been deceived. Or you deceived yourself. But all is not lost. Actually, you are only misguided about the nature of wishing."

"What do you mean?"

"Long ago we stopped making normal wishes. We found they only led to trouble and disappointment. Especially when employed in threes. Now we trust only in *retroactive* wishes, one wish at a time."

"Retroactive wishes?"

"Yes. When you find yourself in a fine place having a fine time, you might remember a time when your life was awful, and how back then you would have wished you were here. But, you *are* here now. Look around you. It's a wonderful place to be. Where you are is exactly what you would have wished for, had you known. A *retroactive wish* come true. Choose a pebble from this beach to remind you of what you found."

*

"And she lived happily ever after?" asked Alex.

"No, just for the time being. But that was enough," replied Alice.

Alice brought out her Possibles Bag, opened it, and placed Alex's stone inside. Taking out the two remaining tiny wish bones still tied together, she undid the bow, and offered one to Alex.

"This is for you," she said, hoping he would want to know all about the wishbone and the bag it came from.

Alex accepted the bone, studied it for a moment, and put it back into the bag. He pulled the drawstrings to close it. Setting the Possibles Bag aside, he said, "No. Not now."

(Silence.)

"Alice, being with you is like being around an expert performer of close-up magic. At any moment you may say, Take a card, any card. It is hard to decline because you are so clever and creative. Then comes the magic trick. Always charming, always faultlessly performed. Surprise and delight are your stock in trade. But your cleverness is a move in a game of hide-and-seek."

Like a guilty child who does not wish to acknowledge what is coming next, Alice closed her eyes and bowed her head.

Alex continued. "You tell me important things only by evasion. You seem so afraid of committing yourself openly that you hide in ambiguity. I do not ask you to show me *how* you do your magic. I *do* want to know what simple truth you disguise with another card trick, and why."

(Silence.)

"Do not misunderstand, dearest Alice. I love the story you told me. But what does it mean? Why must you leave it for me to figure out? Ambiguity suggests mistrust. For once I wish you would use simple words and plain English to say exactly what you mean."

Eyes still closed, Alice made herself smaller - knees to her chest, arms wrapped around her legs, face against her knees. Hiding.

(Silence.)

Slowly, Alex got up and walked toward the edge of the sea.
Now I have done it, he thought. *Bad timing.*

(Silence.)

"Aleko."

He turned to find Alice walking toward him.
She stood in front of him, holding out her open hands as if to say, No cards, no tricks. Tears were streaming down her face.
"I will not say . . . I love you . . . What is more *ambiguous* than that?"
"I tell you that . . . if I had known . . . a long time ago . . . what I know now . . . I would have wished . . . with all my heart . . . to be right here . . . with you . . . with *everything* just as it is . . ."

Alex reached out, took her by the hand, and said, "Come."
They waded out into the water up to their knees.

"This is the exact spot where she landed," said Alice.
"The young woman in your story?"
"Yes. And she stayed. She never went back to sea."

*

The late afternoon onshore sea breeze began blowing, kicking up waves that washed far enough up the beach to suggest it was time to leave. It was just as well. Alex and Alice had nothing more to say for the time being. It was as if the sea itself had put a punctuation mark at the end of an afternoon that bound them ever closer together.

"Come," said Alice. "Let's go back to Hania."

WALTZING THE BULL

The next morning.

"Polly, come look."

Max-Pol had just thrown open the shutters of the hotel room where they had spent the night. The beach below was empty except for one couple at one table. And that table was out in shallow water, where the man and the woman sat in chairs, with the water over their ankles. Their conversation did not carry as far as Max-Pol's window, but their laughter did.

Polly wrapped a sheet around herself and came to the window.

Max-Pol pointed.

"It's Alice and an old man," said Polly. "What a charming thing to do."

"That old man is Alex. Alexander the Great, himself."

"Really? Looks like he belongs on Mount Athos."

"It's just his beard and hair. He'll lose twenty years when he goes to a barber - after I win the contest."

"I wonder how she talked him into having breakfast in the water? He doesn't even have his pants rolled up. Is he still wearing his shoes?"

"They probably had the same idea at the same time, and simply picked up the table and carried it into the water. Both of them think like that," said Max-Pol.

*

"Will you take me to Knossos, Aleko? I want to see the labyrinth," said Alice. "And I want to know about bull-leaping."

"If you stay for a month, I will take you to Knossos. It is no good going now - too many tourists. But the labyrinth is not there. And I can tell you about bull-leaping any time."

A smiling waiter walked out in the water to their table with another round of everything: cappuccino, orange juice, and croissants. Alex ordered a cognac to "juice up the day." And Alice held up two fingers to the waiter as she added, *"Metaxa, parakalo."*

"Alex. Where *is* the labyrinth?"

"Here. Everywhere. It is an idea, not a place. A metaphor, not an artifact of history. Do you know how to construct a labyrinth? It is very easy."

"No. I've seen books full of them, and I remember the one we went to see in England, but I've never thought about making one."

"Come, I will show you," said Alex.

They waded ashore, and with his cane Alex began drawing in the sand. "It starts with a cross," he said, "and four corners, and four dots, and you go from there. This is called the classic Cretan labyrinth because, though there are many variations, this is the basic design."

"There," Alex said, stepping back to consider his work. "That is how it is done. Simple, really. The basic metaphor is equally simple. We are born coming in here." He pointed. "We wander on, never quite knowing where we are going or what we will find, and never knowing exactly when we have found the center and have started back the way we came. Finally, we come out here." He pointed. "We die."

Alice took Alex's cane and retraced the labyrinth.

"I get it," she said.

"Drawing one in the sand is easy. Living in one is harder. But do not get me started. There are hundreds of books on the subject, covering the use of the labyrinth for thousands of years. It is a universal idea. I will tell you my favorite and final comment on the labyrinth by quoting from 'The House of Asterion,' a short story by Jorge Luis Borges (Asterion is another name for the Minotaur):"

> "*All the parts of the house are repeated many times.*
> *Any place is another place . . .*
> *The house is the same size as the world,*
> *Or, rather, it is the world.*"

*

"What are they drawing, Max-Pol?" asked Polydora.

"A labyrinth. Alex is taking Alice into his lair."

"Seduction?"

"Oh, no, she wants to go," said Max-Pol.

Alex and Alice waded back to their chairs. Their coffee was cold, their orange juice warm, and the butter for their croissants melted into yellow pools. The sea around them was glassy still, barely sloshing back and forth on the sand.

The waiter waded out with two small glasses of Metaxa.

He pointed at the sun, and Alex nodded.

The waiter waded away and came back with a large beach umbrella.

He gestured at the coffee and juice and melted butter.

Alex shook his head.

*

"Looks like they're going to stay a while," said Max-Pol.

"Let's go down and join them. I've never met Alex," said Polydora.

Max-Pol watched as Alice picked up Alex's hand and held it against her cheek.

"No. Not now. I don't think they want any company," said Max-Pol. "Or any witnesses either. Let's get dressed and walk over to the harbor for breakfast."

*

"Tell me about the bull-leaping at Knossos," said Alice. "Could young men and women actually catch a bull's horns and flip over its back?"

"Yes and no. Many theories. The evidence *is* clear that something extraordinary involving bulls happened in Minoan culture. But the theories all start at the wrong place."

"Where should they start?"

"In our own time. Look in your own culture. What about American rodeos? There is even an association of professional bull riders, with hundreds of events all across the United States every year. Millions of people watch on television. I have seen it myself. Millions of dollars are involved. For what? To watch young men try to ride huge bulls for nine seconds. Have you seen this?"

"Of course. It's an all-American sport."

"But think about it. The bulls are not wild. They are also trained athletes. Bred to buck after being prodded and cinched and spurred. They are mostly Brahman - the same cattle that wander free in India. Of course they are dangerous - when aggressively provoked. So are cows and horses and pigs and dogs and people. But I have it on good authority that you can walk around in a field of rodeo bulls, and as long as you mind your business, they mind theirs. Do you understand what I am getting at?"

"Yes. Go on."

"Think of it this way. There is no rational reason for bull riding in the modern world. It is not part of the real Wild West tradition. It is a modern invention. An irrational activity. Bull riding reflects a deeply rooted human need to confront and conquer nature. It is about power."

"The same as with bullfighting in Spain and Mexico?"

"Yes, and in Portugal and France and all over South America."

"So, you're saying that the Minoan bull-leaping was a symbolic encounter with power, and that the bulls were trained to do their part?"

"A cattle breeder told me that bulls can be ridden like a horse, taught tricks, and kept as pets. It is therefore credible that the Minoans trained them to perform with gymnasts. Dangerous, of course, but feasible. The cattleman said he once saw a bull trained to respond to music. The bull could waltz."

204

"Like an elephant in the circus, right?"

"Exactly. Every once in a while, an elephant goes crazy and kills a keeper, but still, there they are, standing on their heads or even dancing on their hind legs. If you look at the Minoans through this lens, bull-leaping is not so very mysterious. That is my view."

"Could I train you to dance with me?" asked Alice.

"Is that a metaphorical question, or do you want a real partner on a real dance floor?"

"Both," she said, once more taking Alex's hand and holding it to her cheek. "Both."

*

"If I tell you another story, Aleko, will you be annoyed with me?"

"Only if you play coy and I do not understand. Try me."

"All the stories are basically the same, you know:

> Once upon a time there was . . .
> No one knew that . . .
> Years went by . . .
> And then one day . . .
> And since that day . . .

"And so it goes."

"A labyrinth of words."

"Yes."

"Go ahead. Tell me."

"Once upon a time a child was born. One hand was clenched in a fist. No one knew that what lay in the child's hand was a tiny white shell, placed there by the Queen of the Fairies. Years went by, but nothing could be done to open the child's fist.

"And then one day, a sorcerer happened by, understood what he saw, and touched the child's hand, which opened. 'In this shell is the world the child came from,' he said. 'When the right person comes, give it to him. Put it in his care.'

"Would you like to see the shell?" asked Alice.

Alex nodded.

Alice waded ashore to where she had left her purse. Taking her Possibles Bag out of her purse, she waded back to the table, untied the bag, took out a tiny white shell, and said:

"Hold out your hand, Aleko."

"You are placing your world in my hands?"

"Yes."

"And since that day?" asked Alex.

"And since that day," said Alice.

"And so it goes?"

"And so it goes," said Alice, folding Alex's fingers over the shell.

"And so it goes," said Alex, placing his hand on hers.

*

"Alice, I have been carrying around something to give you at the right time. This would be that time."

He reached into his pocket and withdrew a tiny, black velvet bag. "Hold out your hand," he said. Opening the bag, he held it over Alice's outstretched hand, and a small silver coin slid out of the bag into Alice's palm.

"This is a reproduction of a coin unearthed at Knossos. Not Minoan, of course, but Hellenic. The labyrinth on it is an indication of how long ago the myth was an active part of Greek life. A view of the world not unlike the whirling shape of your shell.

"It's also a fulfillment of a wish," said Alice, picking up the coin.

"What did you wish for?" asked Alex.

"That you would have something to give me in exchange for my shell. Something to keep in my Possibles Bag. A world for a world."

*

"Max-Pol, there's one thing I wish you'd straighten out for me before I meet Alex," said Polydora.

"I suppose you want to know about Alice and me."

"Yes. I thought when you two were coming to Athens that you would be together - a couple of some kind - the Witness thing you told me about, and all that. But you hardly spent any time together. And she's clearly Alex's companion now. Is there a chapter I'm missing?"

"Several. I can only tell you my part of the story. And that will take a while. But if you want the short answer, it's enough to say that I know now that being a Witness is only one episode in a relationship. Nothing stands still. I had this silly notion - a wish - a third and last wish. I wanted a Witness. And, as it turned out, so did Alice. We were mirrors for one another. We almost broke the mirror by mistake."

"And now?"

"We both want something else - and not from each other."

"From who, then?"

"Well, that's another story, isn't it? Involving a whole new set of wishes. I don't know yet what it will be, but I know that what comes next is full of possibilities for me, and that Alice isn't part of the equation."

"You're very sure?"

"The moment I saw her in Athens, a lot of loose ends seemed tied up. Like meeting a former lover. What was once there has faded. Gone. Suddenly. Who knows why? You just *know* it's over. We stood there looking at each other. No mirrors. Nothing was said, and probably never will be. Maybe both of us were tired of looking in the mirror.

"We do have a lot in common, but I'm not in her league. I'm smart. She's brilliant. I'm clever. She's creative. I'm a doctor. She's a wizard. We could never occupy the same world on a daily basis.

"Alex, on the other hand, *is* in her league. From the outside, they might seem an impossible combination. From the inside, they fit like two people who have come a long way around to find their complementary match. Sure, he's old. They won't have long together. But I suspect that 'long' isn't the primary concern of either one of them."

THE TABLE AT THE MELTEMI

The *meltemi*, for which the harborside cafe is named, is a gentle sea breeze that reliably eases the leaden heat of late afternoon. About the same time, the west waterfront of Hania lies in the shadows of the buildings piled up against the old Venetian walls.

The fading light of October is a pale amber tint on all the buildings on the other side of the harbor. The color of the sky is the same blue as that on the gently waving Greek flags outside the Hellenic Coast Guard office on the far quay.

On the terrace of the cafe is a table covered with a white cloth. In the center of the table the owner, Ioannis, has just placed a circle of drinks: one glass each of iced coffee, orange juice, red wine, retsina, ouzo, cognac, beer, and one cup each of cappuccino and Greek coffee. Around the outside of the circle of drinks are small, white plates - one each of olives, almonds, raisins, grapes, peanuts, pumpkin seeds, pistachio nuts, and bits of charcoal-broiled octopus on toothpicks.

An uncommon display of food and drink, for an uncommon gathering of people: the guests of Alexandros Xenopouloudakis. When Alex planned this reunion in May, he had expected three friends to join him: Alice, Max-Pol, and Kostas. Now there are five more at his table: the general and his wife, Wonko, Zenkichi, and Polydora.

Alex met the latter two only yesterday, but no matter; he rejoices in surprise. The friends of his friends intrigue him. Sitting nearby is one other whom he knows slightly, and who will become part of his entourage shortly: the Contessa Macaroni, a recently acquired friend of Wonko. As of an hour ago. She is royalty - of an eccentric sort, but royalty - as prophesied by the Athenian Oracle.

*

When everyone is seated and settled, Alex rises from his chair, gives a short and eloquent speech of welcome, and then, as the Grand Master of Ceremonies, he briefly explains the responsibilities of the gathering.

The food and drink on the table are samples of what Cretans eat and drink on such occasions. The guests shall sort the matter out as they wish, taste as they will, and order more of what they prefer.

Since some know each other well and others not at all, as intelligent adults they shall be responsible for getting acquainted with one another without anything silly like introductions from the Grand Master.

As to how they shall spend the rest of their time in Crete, that is tomorrow's affair.

Tonight they all shall attend the Grand Master's banquet at the Amnesia, on the other side of the harbor. It is the Feast of Saint Precarious, the patron of those who live life on the sharp edge of uncertainty. The hour is ten, the dress code is decorous. The finest wines, the freshest fish, the sweetest fruit.

The evening's entertainment will be provided by any of those who are willing to sing or recite. Elliot Brownell - Wonko - has been asked to compose a waltz. Furthermore, there shall be a vote to decide who wins the beard-growing contest - the Grand Master or the Pretender, Max-Pol. Moreover, there shall be a free-for-all composition of non-sense verse, constructed around lists of words the Grand Master will provide.

And, of course, dancing in the Cretan style.

Finally, since this group will not likely ever be all together on their birthdays, the Grand Master has awarded everyone an extra birthday this year, and tonight is the night. A Double Birthday Party. Presents will be provided.

Shouting, "Let the games begin!" the Grand Master sat down.

And the games began.

THE FEAST OF SAINT PRECARIOUS

As Alex had hoped, the gathering on the terrace of the Meltemi quickly became a symposium - an engaging encounter well beyond small talk. He did not know that some of his guests were continuing conversations begun in Athens, while others were acting on inclinations that had been only vague impulses in Athens.

The table seemed to Alex like a pleasure barge drifting on the slow-moving river of time. Intense conversations between groups of twos and threes were punctuated with laughter and sudden lulls of satisfied silence, followed by subtle re-groupings and a renewal of conversation.

Time flowed on. Twilight. Alex leaned back in his chair, surveying the symposium to ascertain if his attention as host was required. He noticed that the group had subdivided itself.

Polydora, Max-Pol, and Kostas had migrated a little bit away from the table, and were sitting with chairs close together. From what Alex could hear, Max-Pol was getting lessons in Greek slang. Bawdy jokes were being explained. Polydora rested a hand on each man's knee.

Wonko had moved to an adjoining table with the Contessa Macaroni. They were discussing dancing styles. *Two exotic birds of a feather,* thought Alex. Wonko was opening his fiddle case.

Hans and Winifred had remained seated by Alex from the beginning, speculating on what life had been like for Hans's father during the German occupation of Crete. Alex noticed that Winnie was holding her hands together in her lap, restraining her picking inclinations.

Zenkichi had moved from group to group, taking photographs.

Alice had not left Alex's side. She kept his glass filled with red wine.

Alex noticed she had no glass of her own. She drank from his.

Wonko began playing reels and jigs, and the group began clapping in time to his lively music, and shouting encouragement. Patrons at other tables joined in. The contessa danced around the table with admirable skill.

Darkness. Well past eight o'clock.
Alex rose and called for order.

"Wait! One more tune, Alex, if you please," said Wonko. "A waltz in honor of our host. It's called 'Waltzing the Bull.' I composed it. Alice titled it. And the contessa will add an interpretive dance."

After a rowdy round of applause, with glasses lifted in honor of Wonko's music and the contessa's dancing, Alex once again rose and called for order.

"We must desist and prepare for the feast. Bathe and anoint your-selves. Don your finest costumes. Max-Pol and Kostas will collect you in the courtyard of the Casa Delfino at ten, and escort you to the Am-nesia. I shall go ahead to alert the cooks and the orchestra. Onward!"

*

Alex wanted to pick up the gifts he had arranged in advance for the celebratory dinner - the first and, perhaps, last combined Feast of Saint Precarious and Double Birthday Party. He had decided on amber kom-boloi for the men, and amber amulets for the women. Gifts endowed with the qualities of timelessness and tradition. And, of course, a red rubber nose for each and every person - to encourage the fool in all of them.

Alice accompanied Alex. She knew he needed her. His growing fragility was apparent, even though he had repeated the justification for it.

"I limp only because my sandals are not broken in . . ."
For all his *philotimo* - his Greek pride - he was struggling. She had seen him stumble on rough pavement. She was aware of his failing night vision. Last evening he had taken her arm after dark and held it tightly for support, not courtesy. His pauses in conversation were fre-quent - forgetfulness disguised as thoughtfulness.

She knew. He truly needed her.

As subtly as possible she acted as Alex's guardian, determined to do whatever she could for him. She meant to look after him without

212

WALTZING THE BULL

insulting his dignity. Tonight – and until . . . Somehow she knew it would not be for long.

But there was more.

As she sat close by him at the table, watching over him and listening to him, she suddenly heard a quiet voice in her head ask, *You really love him, don't you?* And she replied aloud, "Yes . . . I do."

"Do what?" asked Alex.

"Not now. I promise to tell you what later."

*

The route to the amber shop included several sets of stairs along the stony, doglegged labyrinth of poorly lit side streets that Alex favored on his errands. For Alex it was not a shortcut but a Sacred Way, because it required passing beneath the arched entrance to what had long ago been the forecourt of a Venetian residence.

On the arch the owner had inscribed still-visible words in Latin: *Omnia Mundi Fumus et Umbra* – All the world is smoke and shadow.

Alex repeated the words to himself whenever he passed beneath the arch. To him they meant no moment should be wasted.

At the shop they were welcomed by the owner, Katsikakis, who had recognized in Alex a mutual case of komboloi-mania. This reverence for ancient things made beautiful by passing through generations of human hands had been a topic of indulgent discussions between them. Whenever Alex came to the shop, Katsikakis brought out his most trea-sured items from the safe in the back – those he was reluctant to sell, except to a serious connoisseur like Alex.

After much consideration, Katsikakis had chosen exactly the right gifts. The final cost was considerable, even when Alex was willing to pay cash and not require a receipt – thus relieving the owner of tax payment. A Cretan courtesy.

*

Two young Bulgarian refugees – Greek speaking, but stateless, jobless, and penniless – had noticed the old, well-dressed man and the lovely woman. The young men were not of the criminal class. They were the sons of respectable Bulgarian families who knew there was no future in the ruin totalitarian communism had made of their country. Reluctantly,

214

the families sent their sons away for better lives. Like many refugees, the sons were courageous but unlucky. And by now they were hungry and desperate enough to turn to robbery just to eat.

The two young men had followed Alex and Alice at a distance, watched them through the shop window, seen the packet of money Alex displayed when he paid, and noted the two shopping bags being filled with finely wrapped, small boxes.

The young men intended no physical harm. They thought the old man and the woman would surrender their possessions without resistance. All they needed was a lucky chance.

The night was cooler than expected, and Alice wanted to go back to the hotel to get a sweater. They returned the way they had come - through the dark, narrow streets instead of around the brightly lit waterfront.

The Bulgarians followed.

Just as Alex and Alice turned underneath the old Venetian archway into the darkest part of their route, they felt the too-close presence of the young men behind them. They heard the click of knives opening. They stopped. One Bulgarian edged around them, blocking their way. He stood in front of them with his hand out.

"*Thoseh mas lefta. Keh theh thah theh peeraksoumeh* (Give us money and we won't hurt you)."

Alex and Alice froze.

"*Thoseh mas lefta!*" the young man repeated.

(Silence.)

Alex took a deep breath, and shouted, "*Ochi! Poti!* (No! Never!)"

And to the dismay of the young man, Alex charged, swinging his cane with rage, lashing out in unbridled fury. The young man dodged, then ran at Alex with his head down, butting him backwards into a deep alcove. His companion shoved Alice aside, jumped into the darkness, and began mauling the fallen Alex, trying to get his wallet.

Screaming, "Aleko, Aleko!" Alice threw herself into the fight, hitting and scratching, desperate to pull the assailants off and away.

One of the young men swung his arm backwards at her, knocking her aside. She fell back, but came at him again. He swung again, but this time his knife was in his hand, and the blade cut her throat cleanly.

Alice banged backwards into the alcove wall, then slumped forward and down across Alex's unconscious body, her hot blood pulsing out over his chest.

The young men panicked. They fled empty handed, shoving aside people who had been attracted by the shouts and screams. Unpursued, they escaped into the labyrinth of dark streets, unaware that they had served as agents of Atropos, the Fate who cuts life's cord.

Quiet returned. Because Alex and Alice were out of sight in the alcove, they were neither noticed nor looked for. The tenants of the neighborhood withdrew into their houses, locked their doors, and closed their shutters. Night and silence quilted the street.

Their friends waited. Searched. Called the police. Nothing.

*

In the early morning light, the bodies of Alex and Alice were discovered by an old woman on her way to church.

Alex was unconscious but alive.

Alice was dead.

*

What?

NO!

Yes.

*

And so . . . and so?

Alex recovered.

And then what happened?
What became of everybody?

Without Alice, well . . .

You can only imagine.

216

THE SADDEST WALTZ

THE DEDICATION REVISITED

A writer stood up from his desk and glanced at the Dedication to his work of fiction. He had taped it to the wall years ago. He stopped to re-read it, as he had so many times before:

> This book is for you, the one I missed;
> You, whose path I never crossed;
> You, who never arrived in my life;
> Still, this book is for you,
> Because you *must* be there.
>
> Many times have I altered my Way
> To be where you might be:
> On a great ship, crossing to England;
> On the night train to Barcelona;
> On the pilgrim route around Shikoku.
>
> In Monet's garden in Giverny,
> In Oxford at Blackwell's Books,
> In the art museums of Vienna,
> In Amsterdam at the Golden Tulip
> In Rouen in the cathedral.
>
> Were you in Santa Fe last Christmas?
> I looked for you there.
> On the island of Crete last spring?
> I looked for you there.
> Where are you?
>
> Will I ever find you?
> Have you looked for me?
> Come to me. Find me.
> This book will tell you where I am.
> This book is for you.

He had signed it, "D. Y. Trabet." The White Rabbit.

He thought of himself that way sometimes.

As if he was that fictional character out of *Wonderland*. And, like Mr. Dodgson, he had imagined himself and the story and even imagined Alice.

Now he was writing for someone in his own Wonderland.
A woman he could only imagine but wished was real.
As if imagining her would summon her.

What's real? he asked himself.

Maybe a long walk would focus his mind.

He turned out the light over his desk and went down the stairs to the entryway of his house. Putting on his favorite jacket and cap, he stopped to fill his pipe from his tobacco pouch, switched on the porch light, and opened the door.

THE DEDICATION FULFILLED

Closing the door behind him, the writer steps out into the early evening with purpose. He will take his usual route - down the long driveway, around the corner, then straight on for ten blocks to the park that overlooks the city and the bay.

A woman is standing in his driveway, waiting.
The man sees her and walks slowly toward her.
"Yes?"

She is holding *Third Wish*.
Even though it is dark the writer recognizes them.
"You wrote this," she says.
"Yes," he replies.
"Then you are Alice and Alex and Max-Pol and Kostas and Wonko and Zenkichi and all the rest. Even The White Rabbit and the music," she says.
He nods.
"I've come about the Dedication."
"And?"
"I'm the one you missed - the one who never arrived."

(Silence.)

He looks down, looks away, clears his throat, then looks back at her.

"Ah, well . . . in a fairy tale, perhaps, but let's be real. You don't know me except as what you imagine by reading what I wrote. And I don't know you at all. You're jumping to big conclusions on vague evidence."

"Of course. I know that. But there are always chances one must take, and amazing things are always possible, don't you think?"
He nods. "Usually."

She smiles. "Whatever may happen, whether or not anything may come of my being here, I have three wishes to give you."

The woman puts the books down on a bench beside the driveway. From her pocket she takes a small, red silk bag; takes his hand, places the bag in it, and closes his fingers over the bag.

"Inside there are three wishbones. I've saved them for you."

With her fist she lightly taps his fingers, stamping an invisible seal on the wishes. Exactly as Alice once did for Max-Pol.

She stands close in front of him and waits, but he is silent.

She cannot see the tears forming in his eyes.

"May I walk a ways with you?" she asks.

"Come," he says and turns toward the street.

Without looking at her, he asks, "Do you know how to play Left/ Right/Surprise?"

"Of course. And I say, 'Turn right,' and you surprise me - tell me something I don't know and would never ask you."

"Well, I must tell you . . . that other women claiming to be The One have come before you. But they were not. And I've become cynical about what may only be a romantic trap I've set for myself. When I saw you standing there my first response was, Oh, no, not again."

"Why were you so sure the others were not The One?"

"They came only to *get* something for themselves, as if the novel was a last will and testament and they were the rightful heir. But you . . . you came to *give* me something . . ."

They walk along in silence.

As if in response to an unspoken agreement, they move closer.

At the next intersection he says, "Turn left. Now you surprise me."

"I have the invisible tattoo," she says.

"How can I be sure?" he asks.

"You can't see it. It's invisible, remember?"

He laughs. She laughs.

Suddenly, he hiccups. *Heek-unh!*

"Damn, this always happens when I'm surprised," he says.

And still laughing, they walk on into the evening.

"Answer another question I haven't asked," he says.

"I make my living as an actress," she says.
"Really?" *Heek-unh.* "Sorry."

"Yes. I could become Alice, if you want. I don't mean just *pretend* to be her – I mean that I'm *very* much *like* her."

He stops, turns to face her.
"You could . . . bring Alice back to life, so to speak?"
"Yes, in my own way, why not? Wish it!"

He steps back. Considers her carefully.

Taking a deep breath, he says, "All right then, that's what I wish."
"Wish granted," she says.
Heek-unh!

THE WALTZ OF STRANGERS

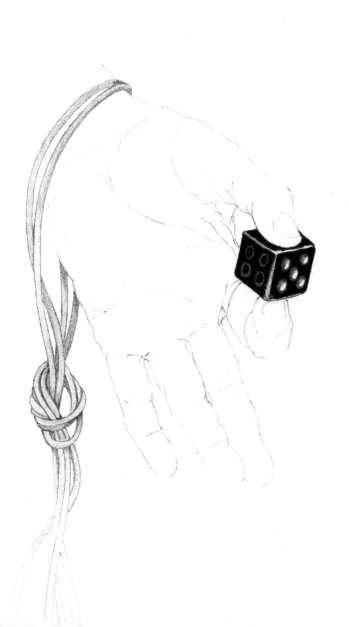

PART FIVE

THIRD WISH
GRANTED

Including

The Illustrations of Margaret Allen Dougherty

The Paintings of Gretchen Batcheller

The Music of Cosy Sheridan

PLAY

(The writer and his visitor were sitting at the bar in the 5 Spot Cafe, having walked in silence for three blocks from their first encounter. Neither had known quite where to begin. What do you say to someone you have only imagined and who is suddenly real?

It had been his suggestion to stop for a drink.)

*

"I've been milking a giraffe," she said.

"What?"

"That's the answer to a question you haven't asked."

"I can't imagine the question."

"Sure you can. Try. Come on."

"OK. Why were you seen standing on a ladder, with your arms in the air, squeezing your hands?"

"Too obvious. Try again."

"Where have you been all night?"

"Better. From the top: I've been milking a giraffe."

"Not again? It must be difficult work."

"Sad work. They get the blues when you milk them. They moo."

"Moo-ed Indigo? Moody Blues?"

She laughed. "Yes! Now you're in the play with me."

"And that play is . . .?"

"One of the best parts of training for the theater was learning improvisation. You don't really *learn* it as much as *allow* it. The students braided improvisation and real life together. Whenever we saw each other outside class, we avoided 'Hello, how are you,' and went straight to imagination as a way of getting in touch. It was an invitation to *play*. The only rule was No Rules. But everyone understood that keeping the game going was better than disabling it."

"Got it. I was seal hunting while you were milking giraffes," he said.

"Yes! I hate it when seals are loose in the house at night," she replied.

"If they would only stay in the refrigerator," he said.

"Probably not enough room for them and the baby walrus," she said.

"They get crowded out by all those jugs of giraffe milk you keep bringing over," he said.

"Excuse me," said the bartender, who had been standing by, waiting to take their order. "But if you don't mind my saying so, it's just a matter of having enough fresh fish to keep the seals happy. You won't have to hunt them if you feed them. But they detest giraffe milk."

"You're an unemployed actress?"

"Yes, and unemployed giraffe milker. Do you want a drink, or are you going to sit here all night and play banter-minton?"

"Bombay Sapphire gin and tonic for me," he said to the bartender.

"Alex's drink," she said. "Make it two."

In fact, she was temporarily not drinking alcohol, but she did not want to explain why. Not now. She did not want to distance herself from him by saying "I don't drink." And one drink would do her no harm.

"Do you always go around improvising?" he asked.

"Often, but tonight I followed your script. I came to audition for the part. And you followed the script as well, didn't you?"

"Yes, but I know it by heart. Besides, it's *fiction*."

She smiled at him.

"I don't believe you," she said. "You weren't acting."

He returned her smile.

"Here you go," said the bartender. "Two orders of giraffe milk."

"To Alice and Alex," she said, touching her drink to his. "And us."

(Pause.)

"How do I know you really are an actress?" he asked.

"Look at me. Describe me in simple terms, as if you were telling someone else," she replied. "No compliments - be objective - you won't offend me. Start at the top and work down."

"OK. Hair: Shoulder length, well-groomed, wavy, dark, parted in the middle. Tortoiseshell hair clips. No earrings. Pale skin. An oval face with no distinguishing marks. No makeup. Greenish/brownish eyes. A black, shirt-style blouse. Necklace of small, dark red, ceramic beads.

Dark green sweater – unbuttoned. Black slacks. Bare feet in black leather sandals . . . that don't . . . match."

He looked up at her face, smiled, and repeated, "Sandals that don't match. Like Alice. And a gentle voice. What else?"

"Enough," she said. "Now, turn your back on me, close your eyes, and when I say 'Look,' turn around, look at me again, then count slowly to ten, close your eyes again, and describe what you saw."

He complied, and in what seemed less than a minute, a sharp, edgy voice barked, "Look!"

When he turned to see her, she was not beside him, but there was a smaller person slumped on the bar two stools away.

"Got a match, stranger," she growled.

Startled by the changes, he counted to ten, closed his eyes, and said:

"Short, curly, rust-colored hair. One dangly silver earring. Grayish, aging skin with two moles beside the nose. Black-rimmed eyeglasses. Deep-set, squinty eyes. Scarlet lipstick. Smoking a cigarette. Drinking wine. Dark green turtleneck sweater, white slacks. No shoes. Raspy voice."

"Open your eyes."

The bartender had watched the transformation. She applauded, saying, "The lady took off her wig - she's almost bald, you know - and put on a wooly, orange cap. Her earring is two keys on a chain looped over her ear. She drew glasses on with a black eyeliner pencil, added two age lines and two moles, and lipstick. She put her green sweater on backwards. She's really good - and fast! And the cigarette . . ."

Holding up his hand, stopping the bartender, the writer said, "Wait, let me. The cigarette is only a little piece of white paper rolled up tight. You're holding a wine glass. What seemed like a change to white pants is your napkin tucked across your lap. And you've kicked off your shoes. To appear smaller, you're leaning on the bar with your head pulled down and your shoulders hunched up."

"Good eye," she said. "You realize that you did most of the work. I just created an illusion, but you invented a tarty, tired little woman trying to pick up a man. If asked, you could give her a name, a history, and a story."

"If I wrote the script, you could play the part?"

"Of course, I am an actress. Close your eyes until I say 'Look' again."

He waited, counting to himself, *One thousand, two thousand . . .*
Before he reached fifty-five thousand, she said softly:
"Look."

She had moved back to the stool beside him, and in the low light she seemed to be a tall, rosy-faced nun - black habit, white cowl, eyes modestly lowered - turning her rosary beads with her fingers. In a sweet voice she asked, "Shall I pray for you, brother?"

The bartender applauded again. "Great work, sister!"

While his eyes were closed she had removed her sweater, buttoned up her black blouse, wiped off most of the eyeliner with a tissue, smeared and blended the red lipstick over her face with her fingers to leave a ruddy glow. Finally, she had arranged two white napkins on her head to resemble a nun's cowl, used her necklace as a rosary, and sat high on her stool to appear large. Sister Somebody.

"I've never written a part for a nun," he said.
"In a way you did. When Max-Pol first met Alice, he mistook her for a nun and she allowed the impression. You've forgotten."
"And you remembered," he said.
"I've never played the part of a nun onstage. But I could."
"You just did," said the bartender. "A very short one-act."
The nun made a modest bow.

"I've answered your question about my being an actress, have I not?"
"Well . . . to be honest . . . Not completely, but you are good at quick disguises." He smiled. "Like Alice, you might be a spy."
She laughed, glanced at the bartender, and winked.
Turning back to him as she removed the napkins from her head, she said, "You're a tough audience, you know?"
"Not really. Just cautious. Because, as you said yourself when you showed up, you are tempting me into deep water."

(Pause.)

"Look," she said, suddenly holding up a small, ebony cube. "Surprise! Half a pair of dice. The one Alex gave Alice. He put it in her purse the morning she left the *Ariadne.*"

She was holding the die with the five toward him.

"Five spots," she said. "We're sitting in the 5 Spot Cafe. Coincidence? Do you have the other half of the set? Takes two to play."

He was astonished. "Where . . . Yes . . . but . . . you . . . how . . . ?"

Placing the die on the bar in front of him, she slid off her stool.

"If you'll excuse me, I'm going to the ladies' room to tidy up. Watch me on the way."

She stood up straight and walked slowly toward the front door of the cafe. As a benevolent queen might move through a room full of her subjects, she paused slightly as she passed each table of diners, smiled, nodded her head, and moved on. Her regal presence was strong enough to interrupt conversations.

The customers looked up at her, smiled and nodded back. The expressions on their faces said they felt vaguely graced, without knowing quite why. She had not only caught their attention, but held it: the actress in command of her audience.

As she reached the front door, she turned, nodded to the room, and lifted one hand in a gesture of royal farewell. And disappeared. Or so it seemed, though she had only made a sudden move into the darkness behind a pillar of the restaurant.

Moments later, from the other side of the pillar, a small, anxious young woman appeared, walking knock-kneed, badly in need of a toilet. She seemed to have gone the wrong way, and asked two waiters for directions. Following their pointing fingers, she scuttled away toward the restroom, almost knocking over a chair and a customer in her haste.

Just as she reached the hallway leading to the restrooms, she suddenly stopped. Stood tall and straight once more. Turned to face the room. The Queen. Lifting her royal hand in the direction of the bar, she looked straight at the writer, slowly raised her invisibly gloved middle finger in the Up Yours position, grinned, and bowed.

Exit stage left, down the dimly lit hallway.

*

Laughing, the writer turned back to the bar to consider the die. As he turned it over in his fingers, he wondered if she would return as Alice, as another character, or as herself. Or as the self she had prepared just for this occasion? That would be acting. *And a wig? Almost bald?*

For the briefest moment he wondered if she would return at all, since she seemed to have noticed in his novel the significance of surprise and unexpected exits.

What would Alice do? he asked himself.

He recalled Alex's reflection:

> *"Alice makes men want to break rules. For her, you consider changing plans, committing indiscretions, and acting recklessly. She makes you think back with pleasure on experiences with her that never took place, but might have been . . ."*

The writer looked up into the face of the bartender.

"You want my opinion?" she asked.

"Sure, what do you think?"

"She's the real deal. An actress."

THE RIGHT TO BE ALICE

When she returned, she was neither in costume nor in character. She was the Woman in the Driveway. Resuming her seat on the barstool, she asked, "Would you mind if I ordered a cup of soup and a small salad? I never eat before a performance, and now I'm hungry. Do you have time?"

"I ate earlier, but there's nothing I want to do but be here."

"Again," he said to the bartender, pointing to his empty glass.

*

"I have a right to be called Alice, you know. That's my name."

"Really?" he said.

"O'Really," she smiled. "In fact I have the right to many names."

"How's that?"

"It's all my mother's doing . . . my enigmatic mother," she said, looking off into the distance.

"And . . .?"

"When I was sixteen, my grandmother gave me a note written by my mother after I was born. It said, 'This child's names are Ariadne, Aphrodite, Alice-Alice, Aretha, Arden, Andalucia, Asia, Amnesty, Allelujah, Aurora, Argentina, Asphodel, Alicia, and Absinthe."

"Wow!"

"I kid you not. Mother believed I was going to be triplets - a shaman she met had given her a prophecy. But there was only me, so she said I could have all the names she had thought of, to use as I please."

"And which ones have you used?"

"My grandmother simply called me Alice, and that's the name I grew up with. But after reading my mother's note, I used almost all the names she gave me at one time or another. At times my 'real' name escapes me. That's why I feel kinship with the Alice-of-the-many-names in your novel."

"What do you call yourself - when you're talking to yourself?"

"Alice-Alice."

"Alice twice? Because?"

"Because my mother named me Alice twice in her list - by accident or on purpose, I don't know - but I've thought of myself as 'Alice-Alice' ever since. It's unique. And very personal. I'm the only one who uses it. When I say it I know I'm talking only to me."

"What do you use as a stage name?"

"Ariadne Rush - because there's another actress named Alice Rush."

"And what shall I call you?" he asked.

"Alice."

"The Alice you are - or the Alice in my novel? Or even Alice-Alice, just to cover both bases? This could become complicated," he said.

"For now, just call me Alice - and when things get complicated - and they will - well, we'll run off that bridge when we come to it."

"Tell me more about your mother."

"She grew up in Pennsylvania - a member of one of the so-called 'Mainline First Families' - the Rushes of Philadelphia. An ancestor, Benjamin Rush, was a signer of the Declaration of Independence, a member of the Continental Congress, a physician, the first American psychiatrist, founder of the first antislavery society, a treasurer of the United States Mint, prolific writer, and social activist. Big deal. Very Big Deal. But I don't think my mother's heritage ever meant much to her."

"Why?"

"She didn't want to be a *Somebody*. She wanted to be *somebody else*.

"She enrolled at Smith College, but never went. If you have the body of a fashion model, the brains of an agitated juvenile chicken, and the moral fiber of a beach blanket; and if you are eighteen years old and the summer ahead promises nothing but remedial algebra - then the first time you heard about the Summer of Love in San Francisco, you would be on the bus headed West. *Hippy-dippy-doo-dah!*

"My mother left a note saying she was going off to study 'popular mechanics,' and signed the note, Mayflower Mayonnaise Mozart. A week later she was dancing naked in a field of sunflowers in Kansas with three young men, having embraced the gods of music, marijuana, and free love. Next stop: California, according to my grandmother."

"How did she know?"

"Grandma went out to find her. But she didn't. She only found where she had been. Then Grandma stopped looking. And stayed six months, doing a little naked dancing and wacky-weed on her own, or so goes the family myth. Grandma was a bit of a rebel herself, but a lot smarter than my mother. She didn't get pregnant. And she knew when a party was over."

"And your grandfather?"

She smiled and laughed. "Good old Grandpa. I think he was glad to have both of them out of the house for a while. None of the women in his life were easy. Then Grandma came home with some pretty juicy ideas. Life got creative after that - and Grandpa loved every minute of it, I think."

"And what about you?"

"I was born in the Big Sur country of California, in an Indian tepee on a commune that was called No Tomorrow. That was where mother met the shaman I mentioned."

"Your father?"

"No idea. And Mayflower Mayonnaise Mozart never said. From what I've been able to find out, everybody slept with anybody in her tribe. She probably had no idea who my father was either."

"And where's your mother now? What became of her?"

"When I was five, she asked a friend to take me back to Philadelphia to see my grandparents. I thought it was just for the summer. Mother went off to Mexico with a circus . . . so somebody said . . . and somebody else said she was last seen riding a horse out of Istanbul, headed for India . . ."

"And?"

"The summer I was sixteen, Mother suddenly came home. I didn't recognize her. Nobody did, actually. She was so thin and haggard and aged. And so ill that they took her straight to the hospital. Cancer. She died three months later. I didn't have much time with her - she was so sick and so drugged, I never knew if what she told me was true or something she imagined. Strange, strange encounter. We never reconnected. Looking back on it now I realize that, for me, my mother had died when she disappeared the first time.

"My grandma and grandpa had become my parents. And their two older daughters - my aunts - became my sisters. My grandparents were a hoot - truly eccentric, but not crazy. I never got anything but love and encouragement from them. No regrets about being their child."

"Are they still around?"

"No. Dead."

"And the sister/aunts?"

"Dead. All gone. I miss them all, but I don't want to talk about them. Not now. Maybe sometime. All my growing-up stories are good. After that . . . the rest is . . . the rest is . . . complicated."

Alice-Alice stared down into her soup and stirred it around and around and around. She was thinking about her constant, invisible companion: Daddy Death is what she called him. She would not mention him now. But he was never far away from her mind.

"Enough of that, let's go," she said, briskly. "Are you up for another round of left/right/surprise?"

"Let's play," he said.

"Check, please," she said to the bartender. "My treat."

"What? No dessert?" asked the bartender. "Tonight's special is giraffe-milk ice cream with whoopee-berry sauce."

"Thanks," he said. "Another time. We're going to a game."

THE ACTRESS

If Alice-Alice had chosen to, she might have offered him the standard form of biographical information provided to a theater by the agent of a member of Actor's Equity Association auditioning for a play:

ARIADNE RUSH

(AEA)

Height: 5'5"	Agency: Zulia Group Arts
Weight: 120 lbs.	Agent: Robert Kimball
Eyes: Brown	New York/Los Angeles
Hair: Brown	

THEATER

BROADWAY

Major Barbara	Barbara	Forbes Theater
Who's Afraid of Virginia Woolf?	Honey	Colonial Theater

OFF-BROADWAY

Lysistrata (Aristophanes)	Lysistrata	New York Classical Rep.
Antigone (Sophocles)	Antigone	New York Classical Rep.

REGIONAL

Hedda Gabler	Hedda	Yale Repertory Theater
Our Town	Emily	Hartford Stage
The Seagull	Nina	The Guthrie Theater
The Skin of Our Teeth	Sabina	Syracuse Stage
Fool For Love	May	Arena Stage
As You Like It	Rosalind	Oregon Shakespeare
King Lear	Goneril	Oregon Shakespeare
Much Ado About Nothing	Beatrice	Oregon Shakespeare
Blythe Spirit	Elvira	Seattle Repertory Theater
Tartuffe	Dorine	Goodman Theater

As You Like It	Rosalind	Mark Taper Forum
A Streetcar Named Desire	Blanche	Merrimac Rep.
The Miracle Worker	Anne Sullivan	Bank Street Theater
(additional roles on request)		

EDUCATION

B.A. – Smith College

Year abroad: in Athens studying Greek Drama / Apprentice – Athens Festival

M.F.A. – Yale School of Drama

Apprentice and understudy at Stratford Shakespeare Festival and Berkshire Summer Theater Festival

HB Studio under Uta Hagen

Improv – Second City – Chicago / On The Spot – New York

Voice – Kristen Linklater

Movement – Tadashi Suzuki

AWARDS

Joseph Jefferson Award – Best supporting actress – Chicago

Helen Hayes Award – Best actress – Washington D.C.

Minneapolis Critics Award – Minneapolis

TEACHING

Acting Master Classes – Syracuse Univ., Bowdoin College, Univ. of Washington, Hollins University

Improv Workshops – Bank Street After Hours

SPECIAL ABILITIES

Competent in French, Greek, Spanish

Dance training – Ballet, modern, tap / ballroom workshops

Clown and mime summer workshops

Plays folk guitar – street performer

Licensed bartender

Alice-Alice might have given him this resume. But she did not.
She wanted to let her acting ability speak directly to him.

And if Alice-Alice had chosen to, she might have provided him with her own private list of theatrical highlights - a list she had never shown anyone else:

> Wrote, directed, and acted in one-girl show of "Alice Wanders Out of Wonderland" - age 10 - standing ovation from audience of two girls, grandmother, grandfather, and a dog. The dog slept through the show.

> Smith College Junior Year Abroad in Athens studying classical Greek drama, including scenes in contemporary life and drama with Greek men.

> Great Role - a solitary performance of bits from Sophocles' plays at dawn in the theater at Epidaurus.

> Busking for money as a mannequin in Trafalgar Square in London while dressed as the Statue of Liberty. On the way home from Greece.

> Short career as a mime on the streets of Paris - doing slightly obscene scenes with two other mimes. Ordered off the streets by the police.

> Playing the role of Juliet naked at a nudist theater festival in Vermont.

> As a bartender in a hotel in Oakland - holding a man's attention until police came. The man had a gun and was threatening to kill himself at the bar. Told him he was the kind of man I could fall in love with - and why.
> Standing ovation from the rest of the customers at the bar when the police took the man away. Fainted as an encore.

The Right to Be or Not to Be

"The odds are not in your favor," the doctors always said.

Alice-Alice knew that. Her grandmother had ovarian cancer, and her mother and two sister/aunts had breast cancer. Early onset. Surgery, chemotherapy, radiation. Metastases to lungs, spine and brain. And, after heroic and ferocious struggles, a miserable death.

"A genetic predisposition. High risk." That's what the doctors said. *A blind date with Daddy Death,* is what Alice-Alice thought.

She knew all about the odds. She had been tested for the genes.
She was pre-programmed for cancer.

The odds, she thought, were against everybody. She just knew more about her chances than most. She accepted her fate. Forget marriage and children. Live as intensely as possible, as long as possible; get regular, thorough examinations and tests; and at the first indication of cancer before she was thirty-five, have the surgery.

The first lump was that first sign. Invasive ductal carcinoma. Survival rate: 0 to 100 percent. Anything was possible. But in her case . . .

She knew what she would do now.

Bilateral mastectomy was the medical term. Remove both breasts. Improve the odds. For a while.

Her mantra was, *Not long, but deep and well.*

She wrote those words on the footboard of her bed, to read each night and morning. And when the thread of her life came closer to the shears, she would deal with that moment in the same spirit. No prolonged, painful, tragic endings. She would not devote her life to dying. When Daddy Death brought his bus, she would get on it and go.

But not just yet.

*

It was almost three weeks after the surgery before she could study her naked body in a mirror. She waited until the drains were removed and the wounds were healing. Two scabby scars ran across her chest, almost meeting at the middle. At this stage the livid-red scars looked more like awkward knitting than neat stitching. Despite the skills of the surgeon, it was difficult to leave tidy scars in loose skin. The color of the scars would fade after a year or so. But they would always show.

She thought about what she couldn't see. Her ovaries had been removed as well - a simple operation with a weird name: oophorectomy. With her reproductive machinery removed, she was technically no longer a fully functional female. She knew that after such radical surgery, many women felt they were no longer women - felt neutered - felt defeated.

Alice-Alice tried to think of herself as a woman still - one who took the first hard blow and got up scarred but full of fight. Being a woman was more than body parts. That is what she told herself. She did not always believe it.

She had been advised that her sexuality would become problematical. Diminished libido and loss of sensitivity were likely, though hormone replacement therapy could help with that. But Alice-Alice had always thought that sensuality and passion were more important than pure sexuality, and those were more a matter of personal style and attitude than physical wiring. She would adjust.

That's what she told herself. *Accept. Adjust. Continue . . .*

And one last hurdle: the vexing symptoms of menopause - hot flashes and mood swings.

I will get through this, she thought, *because I can.*

She did decide to have breast implants at the time of the surgery. Not out of vanity. A practical decision. With reconstruction, she would be able to continue wearing all her favorite clothes, and no compensations would have to be made for close-fitting costumes.

Besides, her natural breasts had been firm and shapely. She did not want anyone to notice that she was suddenly flat-chested, because she would have to explain why. As much as possible, she was determined to keep her medical circumstances to herself. She knew that when word of cancer got around in the theater world an actress was usually subtly treated as damaged goods. After that, minor parts at best. She didn't want pity or demotion. She wanted leading roles.

Besides, there was the reality any actress faced as age forty approached: too old to play ingenue roles and too young to play old women. No matter how accomplished or successful, an actress was marginalized once she was perceived as "older." Alice-Alice looked younger than she was, and wanted to keep that image as long as possible - not because she was vain, but because she wanted to keep on working.

"Well, that's that," she said to the scarred and reconstructed image in the mirror. "Not as bad as I expected. And the rest of me still looks pretty good." She turned slowly in front of the mirror. *Not bad,* she thought.

There was one surprise. Since she had not had chemotherapy, she had not expected to lose her hair. But, as sometimes happens after the shock of any major surgery, her hair thinned and became brittle and ugly. Alice-Alice shaved her head. Her hair would grow back eventually. In the meantime, no problem - actresses know well how to wear wigs.

She didn't believe she had done anything but prolong her time before the inevitable, and she sensed the inevitable was not far away.

Her intuition was prescient. Tissue analysis after the surgery revealed vague indications of cancerous cells. Nothing certain, but the possibility of metastases remained. No matter. She had already decided not to have ongoing radiation or chemotherapy. She had watched four women in her family go through that. And still die. No. Not for her.

She had done all she was going to do. She would live carrying the torch of defiance in one hand and the pillow of acceptance in the other. Run until the fire burned out, and lie down easy - that was her plan.

The doctors could explain why she was going to die, but not why she was going to live. They could give her a death certificate, but not a life certificate. She had to write her own script.

"It's not how *long* I'm alive," she said, "but how wide and how well."

In her journal she had written:

> I will not - I *will not* - spend the rest of my life trying not to die.
>
> That would be like deciding that because I am afraid of flying

and because I can't go back the way I came, I will spend the remainder of my life in a departure lounge. Not dead, just buried alive. Not for me.

I am dying because I have lived, not because I got cancer.

Underneath these thoughts she had copied lines from the novel she had started reading while she was in the hospital:

> *"Letting go is not the same as giving up.*
> *Admitting you're beaten is not the same as defeat.*
> *Withdrawal with honor is not the same as running away."*

> *"Life is a near-death experience.*
> *Life is the leading cause of death.*
> *Life cannot be saved, only used up."*

> *"Nothing lasts. Everything quickly becomes something else. The cherry becomes the cherry tree becomes the cherry blossoms becomes the cherry. The Way is flowing."*

> *"Kathi thokimahsiah yenah ya efkeriah.*
> *Every difficult situation contains opportunity."*

*

While Alice-Alice was recovering from surgery, she had read two books. A friend gave her the Collector's Library edition containing both *Alice's Adventures in Wonderland* and *Through the Looking-Glass*. A small, red, cloth-bound, gold-edged volume with fine typography and paper, and a ribbon-marker bound into it. Elegant. Though she had loved the *Alice* stories since childhood and had worn out several copies, she had not reread them from beginning to end in several years.

What prompted this revisit to *Alice* was the reading of the novel *Third Wish*. A friend had read it and brought it as a gift, saying, "Here, read this. An Alice is in it - she reminds me of you."

Alice-Alice read *Third Wish* twice, then a third time. Each time she felt she had walked through the looking-glass into an alternative version of her life.

At times it was more like reading a script with a part she could play.

For her, the novel was one of those unexpected threads by which fate hangs - a thread that turns into a string and then a rope and then a ladder.

When she looked for the final volume of *Third Wish,* she learned that it had not yet been published. Probably not even finished, because the announced publication date was still a year away.

Walking home from the bookstore, she had an epiphany.

I could become part of the novel. A walk-on audition for a major part in a play? I could bring Alice back to life. And bring life to Alice-Alice.

Crazy thing to do. But, why not?

She would do her homework. Background research for a part had always been one of the best aspects of acting for her. It was her habit to study the script, the playwright and the director, and memorize lines for the audition.

Onward, she said to herself, and laughed.

The first thing she did was buy an Alice wig - long, ivory-white hair. Then she went shopping for shoes. Ones that Alice would wear.

Un-matched.

*

A substantial amount of information about most people is readily available. A private detective may be hired for a small fee to find out even more. A friend of Alice-Alice's had done that to check up on a man she met on a cruise ship. But Alice-Alice was not as interested in knowing *about* the author, David Daniels Doggett, as she was in encountering him directly.

She learned at her neighborhood bookstore that he was in Seattle, living close by in her own neighborhood. Surprise! She might have already seen him. Or maybe he had seen her. And neither of them would have noticed the other, because they were not looking for each other. Now she would become his unseen Witness. She bought a book entitled *The Private Investigator's Handbook* and studied the chapter on surveillance.

*

From a covered bench at a bus stop a block away, she had observed the writer's house and garden. Twice, when he had gone for walks,

244

she followed him for a while, as Alice did in his novel. Afraid of being noticed, she walked back to sit at the bus stop and watch him return. Once, she had seen him shopping for groceries in the Metropolitan Market. When he left his shopping cart to look for something else-where in the store, she quickly inventoried his groceries: fruit, milk, granola, orange juice. *Bachelor food*, she thought. When she had another opportunity, she dropped a box of animal cookies into his cart and left the store.

In her journal she sketched her impression of his appearance: Lean, tan, outdoorsy look. Short, black hair. Stubbly beard. Smokes a pipe and sometimes cigars. Jeans, oil-tanned leather boots, khaki work shirts with sleeves rolled up. Strong features, but not handsome. Talks to himself as he walks. Laughs out loud. Stops and writes notes in a little red book. Gets his hair cut at the Counterbalance Barber Shop. Drives an old-model green Mercedes station wagon, full of some kind of equipment.

She had been thinking about the myth of Eros and Psyche as background for her audition. When she was home alone, Alice-Alice took out her guitar, her composition book, and some scraps of paper on which she had written words and lines. Writing songs was her way of focusing her thoughts. She had missed being able to hold her guitar after the surgery. Holding it once again was part of her healing.

In an hour, the song that had been composing itself in her mind was done. A song about the god of love and his Psyche, who was both another being and an image of himself:

Eros aimed his arrow
And shot himself in the heart.
Love fell in love and fell from above
And that's where the story starts.

Love is a longing in the blood and the bone.
Can you hear Psyche calling,
Eros, come home?
I'll be the bow and the arrow, too.
What you want to find, wants to find you.

Psyche loved her Eros,
Though he ran away one night.
She held a light to his head
As he lay in their bed.
He awoke and he took flight.

Are we afraid love might run away
When we light the mysterious place?
It's a perilous job, but the heart gives a nod
When it looks upon the god's face.

So gather all the golden fleece
From the sheep in Santa Fe,
And sort all the seeds that fell from the flowers
In the gardens of Monet.

I heard you calling for love to find you.
Here I am a few pages behind you.
I'll be the bow and the arrow too;
What you want to find, wants to find you.

Eros aimed his arrow, and shot himself in the heart.

THE RIGHT TO BE ANYBODY ELSE

(His name is David Daniels Doggett.
He writes under the shorter form: Daniels Doggett.
And thinks of himself privately as D. Y. Trabet - The White Rabbit.
Alice-Alice had learned that much from a clerk at the bookstore.
What else should she know?
Piece by piece, conversation by conversation, she will learn much more.)

*

The only child of older parents, he spent his youth shuttling between Seattle and the family ranch south of Bozeman, Montana.

His grandfather on his mother's side was a lumberman, who moved out from Saint Paul, Minnesota, to the Pacific Northwest, where he and his partners bought tracts of trees to provide ties for the tracks of the Northern Pacific Railroad.

On his father's side his grandfather was a cattleman, running herds of cows on the wide, mountain-rimmed plains of western Montana.

Doggett's father and mother had been sent back East to college - Dartmouth and Mount Holyoke - where they had met at a fraternity ball in New York. His father became a lawyer. His mother died when he was nine, a victim of encephalitis.

There never was a stepmother, though a series of live-in nannies and housekeepers filled maternal needs well enough. His father was a gentle, distant figure, who spent most of his time in his office or at his club in downtown Seattle.

The best times of Daniels's childhood were the summers spent on his paternal grandfather's ranch. Later, as a college student, he worked in a logging camp belonging to his other grandfather's timber company, a period he remembered with equal fondness.

To be an *only* child is not necessarily to be a *lonely* child. Lone-ness can be a safe fortress. It means only that one gets accustomed to being alone at an early age, and accustomed to solitude as a way of life.

Reading often becomes the passion of the solitary.

And early in his life Daniels fell in love with words. He wanted to write. The idea surprised him, given his immersion in the manly world of cowboys and loggers, but he devoured the stories of Zane Grey and Jack London, and absorbed the tales the cowboys and loggers told around campfires. As an apprentice fabulist, he found that storytelling came easily to him. Whenever he told a story, he summarized it in a notebook.

A college librarian informed him that trying to make a living as a writer was a difficult path to follow. The image of the starving artist was no joke. She gave him *The Autobiography of William Carlos Williams,* who, at Daniels's age, had considered the same problem and decided on medicine as a way of making a living. This gave him the freedom to write poetry - a way of making living meaningful. Gaining the attention or acceptance of editors, critics, or the public was a secondary matter.

Daniels wanted that kind of life. Both creative and practical.

At the university he studied forestry, and he worked for a time as a timber cruiser and land surveyor for his grandfathers. They both died the same year, and most of their property was sold off to settle taxes and the debts of the estates. Their lives seemed romantic - cowboy and timber baron - but their castles were built on dust from over-grazing, and clear-cut wasteland.

Both grandfathers felt a man should make his way on his own, not with inherited money. Still, Daniels thought of himself as a rich man. He just didn't have much money. For him, "rich" was an attitude, not a bank balance. "Rich" was a wealth of experiences, not property.

He had never married and had no children. He was not inclined to change that.

He settled on being an arborist. Degrees from the University of Oregon; long summers working for progressive logging companies in Washington State and British Columbia.

He apprenticed for five years with an arboriculture company specializing in evaluating and maintaining private forests and parks. After qualifying for membership in the American Society of Consulting Arborists, he became a registered consulting arborist. He was often called upon to give expert testimony in court concerning the preservation of historic trees.

Daniels's work and interests took him all over the world. And when he traveled he took time off in places he had become attached to, such as the Greek island of Crete; Oxfordshire in England; and Kyoto in Japan. These "time out" experiences fueled his writing. And despite an ability to make friends easily, he did not put down roots for long. He preferred a nomadic existence underwritten by his professional skills and credentials.

There were some sidebars to his life, involving more play than work. He advised architects designing tree houses, and he was the co-author of an illustrated coffee-table book on dwellings in trees.

He became active in the sport of recreational tree climbing. Part of his pleasure lay in designing equipment that did no harm to trees - modifying heavy-duty, commercial equipment for lightweight sport use.

Meanwhile, he was writing. He never wrote about trees. He wrote about the lives he imagined he might live - people he might be - adventures he might have. Several self-published books of short stories had found a small audience. And two had been picked up by a New York publishing house.

And now he was writing more than anything else. He wrote a very long story. A novel. He didn't just write it, he lived in it and through it.

Much to his surprise, his publisher bought the novel, which had achieved word-of-mouth success. First volumes complete. With one more to go.

It pleased him to see his novel in print, but it was the inventive process of the writing that gave him the most joy.

I could be anybody, he thought.

Not that he didn't like who he was. But there was pleasure in creating alternative possibilities. In a novel, he could be *everybody*. Fiction. Make it all up. No complications.

Until Alice-Alice turned up in his driveway.

*

They stood on the sidewalk in front of the 5 Spot Cafe.

"Left or right?" she asked.

"You call it."

"But first, Mr. David Daniels Doggett, what shall I call you?"

"Well . . . there's an obvious problem with my name."

"Why? Like what?"

"Think about it. David Daniels Doggett. Guess what people call me?"

"Dog?"

"Right. Dog. Davy Dog, Little Dog, Big Dog, The Dog-meister, Dogbody, Dog's Breath, Dog Shit, Ding-Dog-Daddy, The Dog from Hell, Doubledy Dog, Deputy Dog, Dog Meat, and Three Night Dog just to name a few. But always Dog-something. My college fraternity brothers barked at me when they saw me coming. Even worse when I had a girlfriend named Kitty."

"The Dog and Pussycat Show?"

"Right."

"So. You are . . . dog tired - dogged to death?"

He gave her a peevish look.

"Not funny?"

"No. Threadbare. Worn out. If you were the Alice in my novel, you would give me a new name."

"And as the Alice-Alice in your real life, I might. But not now. That will take some thought. Do you want a new public name or a private one?"

"Private. Personal. Something soft."

"In the meantime, would you mind terribly if I called you Dog?"

"I suppose not. I'm used to it. It's *how* you say it that counts. But please, no cute adjectives or clever wordplay. I've heard it all."

She smiled. "I've never had a dog," she said.

He laughed. "Careful. That's almost over the line."

"Don't growl," she said.

He laughed again. "Stop it. I mean it. I might bite."

"That might be nice," she said, giggling. "But not too hard."

"You don't know when to quit," he said.

"Do you?" she asked.

Daniels gave her his most enigmatic grin.

"Enough about my name for now," he said.

*

He didn't tell her that he had always wanted a woman to call him "Darling." He could not say why. But sometimes when he considered the Dedication in his novel, he wondered if that's what he was looking for. Or a woman *he* would want to call "Darling." He thought the Dedication was about a lot more than that. Or maybe . . . maybe it was just that simple.

Darling.

*

"Which way now?" he asked.

"Turn left," she said, taking his hand. And they walked along past the Counterbalance Barber Shop. The shop was closed, but its revolving, red-and-white-striped barber's pole was still turning, twisting upward and onward - out of infinity, into infinity.

"Surprise me, Dog," she said. "Answer a question I haven't asked."

The Right to a One and Only

There is a credible statistical possibility that somewhere among the billions of human beings on Earth there is *one* person more compatible as a life companion for each one of us than *any* other.

Reasonable men and women would not argue.

"Right," we say. "So where's mine? My soul mate? My darling?"

About 2,400 years ago, Plato wrote *The Symposium* as a rational exploration of love. In his account of a banquet held in honor of Eros, Plato has Aristophanes relate the fable about Zeus cutting the first human beings in half because he was threatened by their power. Forever after, Aristophanes asserts, each person has longed to be reunited with that missing half in order to feel whole again. This yearning for completion is called love. Even Socrates, who was present at the banquet, could not poke enough holes in the idea to sink it. And, as fairy tales say, so it has been to this very day.

However. The odds of any one person finding their perfectly matched exact companion are so low that to build one's hopes on that is like expecting that you will meet your Cinderella or your Prince in the supermarket this afternoon.

He or *She* may have been on the next bus; on a previous train; five minutes late; three rows down; in an accident on the way; delayed by rain; or home with the flu that night of the party.

We wait. Wait. Wait for love.

And tired of waiting, we go looking. Searching for love. For the One.

To improve the odds in their favor, modern men and women resort to the Internet, personals ads, dating services and singles groups. Most poignant are the "I Saw You" columns, where men and women ask, "Did *you* see *me*?"

The Girl who glanced at me getting off the ferry. The Man in the red pickup truck at the traffic light. The wrong-number phone call that sounded so promising. Somebody else's blind date. The woman sorting through tomatoes in the salad bar of the supermarket. The guy leaving the coffee shop last Friday. The distant figure at the rail of a passing ship.

Pulse pounding from the provocative possibility, we implore:

"Did *you* see *me*?"

No. No. They weren't looking for you.

If waiting does not pay off, and searching does not pay off, What . . .?

We make do. Concede and compromise. We act with gritty determination to make acceptable someone who is only an inadequate substitute for the Man- or Woman-of-Our-Dreams.

Sometimes it actually works out pretty well. Sometimes. Never a sure thing, but a chance we take because we believe in a love that can overcome anything, despite repeated and ongoing evidence to the contrary.

But suppose. Just suppose . . . that once in a lifetime the person most suitable for you appears. How will you know? How will they know? What's the secret sign? And what if it happens on a bad day, when you are hung over or have a cold, or when they went out of their house in their shabbiest clothes just to get milk? Will you still know, no matter what?

Would you expect to recognize The One *instantly*? Love at first sight?

Or would you know *only* after a lifelong companionship?

Is Big Love *made in* Heaven or *lived into* on Earth?

And since living with another person is always a tidal matter - of the ebb and flow of good and bad, workable and unworkable, seasons and times and weather, age and chance - who can ever say for certain, at the beginning, the end, or in the middle: *This* was the *One*?

*

David Daniels Doggett has worked on this puzzle in his novel.

The characters reflected his paradox - his not wanting to write a love story, and not wanting to leave love out; his not believing in the One, but with the shadow of the One always falling across the pages of the story. If not the One, at least the One-for-the-Time-Being.

He thought of the Dedication in his novel as a literary device. But when a literary device comes to life - when a hidden wish takes on flesh and blood - when he suddenly finds himself walking down a street, playing Left/Right/Surprise with a figure out of his imagination holding his arm, what does that promise? The One? or just Some One.

Daniels is, as Alice-Alice judged, a skeptic in these matters. And the Dedication of his novel may well be, as he insists, only a fictional construct.

Furthermore, the Dedication did not mention romance, love, sex, or marriage. Daniels would insist that his expectations in the Destiny department are not high. He is not looking for love. He would *say* that.

But the Dedication did suggest, however obscurely, his yearning for a deep and abiding companionship. And he did write the Dedication.

Daniels could not keep himself from wondering if Alice noticed. *Did* you *see* me?

If she ever calls me "Darling," this Dog is in deep, he thought.

CONDITIONS AND CONTRACTS

"Are we going to stand here talking in front of the barber shop all night?" Alice-Alice asked. "Let's get on with Left/Right/Surprise."

"OK. The answer to your unasked question is thirteen seconds."

"And the question?"

"What is the longest recorded flight of a chicken?"

"*That* I didn't know," said Alice-Alice. "But that's a short answer and we have almost a block to go before we can turn any direction. What else?"

"Answer: As many in the world as there are people," said Daniels.

"Don't tell me," she said. "The question is: 'How many chickens are there?'"

"Yes. You must admit you would have never asked, and I would have never volunteered," he said. "And if you want to know how I know, I did not make it up. I read it in a book of little-known facts. The number of chickens is an estimate, but then so is the number of people."

"I suppose you have more chicken information," said Alice-Alice.

He laughed. "Oh, yeah, but not now. Here's an intersection. Let's go right. Your turn."

They crossed the street, and as they crossed, Alice-Alice took his arm and said, "Alice would have taken Alex's arm here, don't you think?"

*

They walked on in silence. Alice-Alice kept his arm in hers.

He liked her easiness with physical contact. Liked it very much.

"Well, then," she said. "I have two Possibles Bags. One has small objects in it. Like Alice's. I'll show them to you sometime. But the other bag is invisible, and the things in it are also invisible. I will give you a list of five of them:

"One: The answer to the question, Who knows where the time goes?

"Two: A faded feather from the bluebird of happiness.

"Three: The ragged end of the smallest rainbow.

"Four: The bittersweet smell of success.
"Five: The shadow of a smile.

"Go left. Your turn."

"What a coincidence," said Daniels. "I also have an invisible Possibles Bag. And I will give you a list of five of the items inside it:
    "One: A smoke ring blown from a puff of Fidel Castro's last cigar.
    "Two: The box the unbearable lightness of being came in.
    "Three: The sound of summer rain on the tin roof of an old barn.
    "Four: A map used by birds when they cross the sky.
    "Five: Lady Luck's cell phone number.

"Go right. Your turn."

Alice-Alice said, "Smell my wrist for a clue."
"Nice," he said, "but I can't name it - I don't know much about perfume, but I'd like to know more."
"Then you can use my five answers: Chamade by Guerlain, Gucci Rush by Gucci, Après L'Ondée by Guerlain, Rive Gauche by Yves Saint Laurent, and Number Five by Chanel. That's the answer to the question, What perfumes did Alice own and use? And you didn't know," said Alice-Alice.
"No," said Daniels, "but then a writer doesn't know everything about his characters, does he? And you're going to fill in some of the gaps, aren't you?"
"That's a question, not an answer," she said. "Go left. Your turn."

"Since we seem to be doing answers in fives, I'll give you these: Yes. Ten thousand years. More than a thousand feet. Yes. And sooner than we think. Do you know the questions?"
"No idea."
"Was Queen Anne Hill ever covered by glaciers? How long ago? How deep was the ice over where we are walking now? Will the glaciers be back? And how soon?"
"Glaciers move pretty slowly. We still have some time," said Alice-Alice. "The time being."

*

Left/Right/Surprise took them by the remodeled, brick school building where she subleased a condominium apartment - only ten blocks away from where Daniels lived. She said nothing when they passed by. Some surprises must wait.

They walked a long way without speaking, enjoying the silence of the night, the occasional views out over the bay and the city, the distant sounds of ships and trains, and the sweet smell of night-blooming honeysuckle in the gardens they passed.

Comfortable. Arm in arm. They took turns calling directions, but the part of the game requiring answers and questions faded into a deeper context.

The unspoken answer was *Yes.*

And the unexpressed question was:

Is this the beginning of something promising?

*

Finally, by mutual design, their wandering brought Alice-Alice and Daniels back to his house. In the driveway, she stopped and faced him. What now? They both sensed they had come close enough for one night.

He would not ask her to come in.

She would not come in if asked.

Not yet. Maybe never.

In the theater, the actors and audience don't go home together after the play. *Well, sometimes,* she thought, smiling. *But not tonight.*

Taking both his hands in hers, she asked, "Dog, shall we continue?"

He only nodded, surprised at having her so firmly and confidently holding his hands. The moment seemed too fragile for words. Saying anything might lead to saying too much.

He recalled the Miranda rights: Anybody who was arrested had the right to remain silent. Anything he said might be held against him. And to say that this woman had arrested him and held him fast - was an understatement.

(Silence.)

"I'll be back," she said. "Goodnight, Dog."

Slowly letting go of his hands, she turned and walked away, leaving him standing where she had found him earlier in the evening. He watched her go. For a moment he was tempted to follow her at a distance.

Why spoil the magic?, he thought, and went into his house.

In his bedroom he took from his jacket pocket the red silk bag she had given him. Untying the cord, he shook out the three tiny, ivory-colored wishbones into the palm of his hand. He wondered why and how the tiny bones got connected to wishes in the first place. In a way they also contained disappointment, for if they were used properly, two persons pulled on them; when the bones broke, the person who got the longest half won the wish. But the person with the short part lost.

↝ *Pushing or pulling on luck is risky business,* he thought.

He placed the little bones in a row on his dresser.

He had not imagined the events of the evening.

The bones proved that Alice-Alice was real.

*

The next morning, Daniels found a blue balloon floating from a string tied to a rock placed on his porch steps. Under the rock was a blue envelope with a sprig of fresh, green mint crushed onto it. He smelled the mint, and opened the envelope, to find this handwritten note:

A MIDSUMMER MANIFESTO

If we are going to go on with this . . .
Consider these premises:

1. Each Reader is a unique singularity. I am one.
   While I have come in response to the Dedication of your novel, I have also come as a Reader. Not as a representative of The Reading Public, or an editor or publisher or critic.
   A Reader. Me.

2. Reading is as much a creative art as writing.
   I expect you agree. But I want to emphasize that I have created my own story using the information and provocations you've provided. Your novel and my novel are not the same novel.

3. I have also created you, the Author.
   An Author has no authority over what a Reader will make of his writing or will make of him. What I've imagined you to be must stand the test of what you really are. I do not know you.

[handwritten margin note: I like painting!]

4. An Author and a Reader are strangers to one another.
   You may have imagined a Reader, or even many readers,
   but you have not imagined me - as I am.
   You do not know me.

5. Perhaps neither of us will become attached to the real other.
   When all is said and done, both of us may prefer what we
   imagined to what we find. From the beginning we both
   know this. Reality is more difficult than fantasy. It always
   involves compromises, concessions, and lack of control.

6. One might love the art without loving the artist.

Up until now, you have been the creator of our commonality.
Your novel is the mutual context - the meeting ground.
But your writing is not finished . . .
Even though you think you know how <u>your</u> novel ends,
you have not imagined the ending of <u>my</u> novel.

In your writing you reveal and disclose as you desire.
You reserve information, with the promise that questions
will be answered. This is, of course, the privilege and responsibility of your craft.

In this light I ask an indulgence, especially since you value
surprise.
Allow me, a Reader, to be the artist in the theater of our
possibility. Let my imagination and style be the Way we
travel. Grant me the right to conceal and reveal as I wish.
The Author always asks the Reader to trust him.
Now a Reader asks the Author to trust her.

Let me be both Actor and Director.

With these words, I offer you a part in my play.

Trust me. Let me surprise you.
That is my first wish.

Alice-Alice

Daniels read the Manifesto again. And once again. She had anticipated his wanting to know more about her. He had a sensitive "weird-meter" in his head, and Alice-Alice was making the needle of the dial bounce around. She might be unstable - even a stalker, for all he knew.

Caution, he thought. For good reason. It even crossed his mind to ask a private investigative agency to run a background check on her. But no. She was creative, talented, imaginative - but not crazy - or at least no more than he. Two-of-a-kind. In poker, if you were dealt a pair, you would stay in at least one round and see what the next card might be.

The image of the wishbones was vivid -

She came to give me something - to do something for me - to bring life . . . back . . . to . . . Alice . . .

And this Manifesto . . .

OK, he thought, *I'm in the play. First wish granted.*

*

Alice-Alice had stayed up late writing her Manifesto. She was clear about what she wanted. And she wanted to say it clearly and give Daniels time to read it and think about it. She wanted a commitment. And clear commitments required clear contracts. That's the way the theater works.

Alice-Alice wanted a chance to direct and play a role that required more of her talent and skills and passion and desire than anything she had done before. She wanted to have more abundant life by giving part of her life away. She wanted to play a role nobody had ever played. And play it so well that nobody could ever play it again.

And if the audience was only one?

One would be enough.

By the time she had walked to an all-night supermarket to get the balloon and put her message in place and walked home, she was exhausted. She lay down on her bed without undressing and closed her eyes.

*

In a book on sleep, Alice-Alice had read about the hypnagogic state - a brief period of altered consciousness between being awake and being asleep. As people doze off, it is common to experience hallucinations. A sudden flash of physical activity will produce involuntary body movements - legs twitch, arms flail, heads jerk. Nobody knows exactly why.

Often, in this state, people see strobe-like flashes of color, hear a knock at the door, music being played, people talking, or their name being called. Nobody knows exactly why.

These hallucinations once worried her, but now that she knew they were normal, she looked forward to the eccentric circus her mind conjured up on its way to deeper sleep.

Tonight she clearly heard a voice calling, "Alice, sing. Alice, sing."
And instead of falling asleep, she opened her eyes. Awake again.

A song was coming. And she knew that whenever that feeling arose, she should not wait until later to accept the incoming mail from the workshop of her mind or else the ideas would be gone.

She got out of bed in the dark. She passed through the living room and picked up her guitar off its stand. She went into the kitchen and sat in the pale light from the streetlights outside her apartment. Pressing her guitar carefully against her chest, she began to play and sing:

> If you had three wishes;
> If they all came true;
> If you fell through the looking-glass,
> Would Alice come back to you?
>
> If the looking-glass was a clear pool;
> And if you fell in,
> I would rise out of the water.
> I would teach you to swim.
>
> If your sorrows weighed you down;
> If your dreams could not float;
> I would sail out of your future,
> And take you in my boat.
>
> If the boat was too small,
> And the seas were too high,
> I would turn us into the water,
> And we would float on the tide.

If you had three wishes;
If I brought you one more;
Would you wish to be the water,
The boat or the shore?

If you had three wishes;
If they all came true;
If you fell through the looking-glass,
Would Alice come back to you?

Up in a Tree in a Boat

In midmorning, Daniels called the telephone number Alice-Alice had given him the night before - expecting a clever answering machine message. But a soft, sleepy voice answered after three rings.

"Yes, Dog."

"How did you know it would be me?"

"Did you wish it to be me?"

"Well, yes."

"Then it is. We both got what we wanted. That's a nice way to begin the day. 'How' is not important, is it? Do you accept the terms of my Manifesto? If you don't, I'll hang up. And if you call back, it won't be me answering."

"Manifesto accepted. But before you begin directing our play, I'd like to take you someplace you've never been. It's not far and it won't take long, but it might make a difference to your script. Besides, it's important to me. Are you willing?"

"Invitation accepted. Where and when? What's the dress code?"

"West end of Queen Anne Hill, corner of Seventh and Lee streets at six o'clock this afternoon. Jeans and long-sleeved shirt - a light jacket in case the wind comes up when the sun starts down - and running shoes."

"I don't run - not very far, at least."

"Don't worry, you won't be running. You'll be flying."

"Flying?"

"Trust me. Oh, one more thing. Get a lightweight pair of leather or canvas gloves - the kind used for gardening will do."

"Gardening? I don't garden, either."

He laughed. "Just get the gloves. See you at six."

Alice-Alice laughed. The corner where they would meet was right across the street from her apartment. But she could not imagine what was special about it or where they might go from there. She had walked every nearby street many times. She knew her neighborhood well.

Where could they go that she had not already been? And why were gloves required?

*

Late afternoon. Clear skies. No wind. Seventh and Lee streets.

"I'm a licensed, professional arborist," said Daniels. "You probably already know. Simply put, I do trees. A client of mine owns this whole block," he said, pointing across the street at a high brick fence enclosing a substantial grove of tall trees.

"Most of the trees are exotics – in arborist terms that means non-native – planted a hundred years ago, after all the firs were logged off for lumber, and the land was subdivided for houses. Whoever replanted this property loved trees and took the long view. There are several kinds of oak, a dawn redwood, madronas, cedars, and even a ginkgo. It's a small arboretum."

Alice-Alice thought, *Trees. I never noticed the trees or wondered about what was behind the wall.*

Daniels continued. "Even though the house is nice enough, and the view spectacular – because this is the highest part of one of the highest hills in Seattle – the current owner bought the property mostly for the trees. The house can be torn down and replaced in a year or two, but not the trees. The owner is often away for long periods of time. I look after the health and maintenance of the trees, and I'm free to enjoy the place when he's gone.

"Look way up in that magnificent English oak in the middle. See those two flat, green shapes? Those are called 'tree boats.' That's where I go to enjoy the trees."

"That's really a long way up," she said, thinking, *And I've never looked up there; I might have seen him,* realizing he might have been in the tree boat at times when she walked by. *And he never looked down and saw me.*

"I can get you up there easily, unless you're afraid of heights."

"Afraid? No. But I don't have much upper body strength. And I haven't climbed a tree since I was a kid."

"No climbing required. Come on, I'll show you."

She was tempted to tell him that in fact her apartment in the third

268

floor at the other end of the building across the street was just as high as his tree boat. She was up that high every day. She slept that high every night. Just indoors. *Oh,* she thought.

"Coming?"

He led her through a gate in the wall, up some stone stairs, and across a wide lawn to the base of the great oak. Various pieces of equipment were laid out in the shade. And three dark green ropes hung down out of the tree.

"Here's the drill," Daniels said. "All this equipment is high-tech stuff developed for mountain climbing and modified for tree climbing. Safe and strong. The ropes are sixteen-strand, half-inch, 8,000-pound test, braided polyester/Dacron. The tree boats are like hammocks, except they're heavy-duty woven nylon with carbon-fiber stiffeners in the sides. And they have four-corner suspension to keep them flat. They don't sway like a regular hammock. Very secure. When you're in one, you wear a short safety line. Great place to spend the night."

"You mean you *sleep* up *there*?"

"Sure. Sometimes. As safe as sleeping on the ground."

"But you can't fall off the ground. And what if you have to pee?"

Daniels laughed.

"All the logistics have been worked out. First let's get you up there. You wear a climbing saddle. I hook you onto this line, which is hooked into a pulley system I use to haul equipment up - a chain saw, for example - and to lower big, cut branches. I'll lift you slow and easy - right up to the boat."

Alice-Alice looked up and then back at Daniels, her eyebrows raised.

"Trust me," he said.

Slowly, Alice-Alice pulled on her new leather gloves. Her whole life involved taking risks. She was used to being out on a limb. *That's where the fruit is,* she thought.

But she had never been high up in a tree this tall. The equipment was unfamiliar, and she was still weak from her surgery. When the physical therapist asked her to chin herself on a bar, she could not do it even once. And, in truth, she was mildly afraid of heights. Once she had turned down the chance to play Peter Pan because she would have to be flown over the stage on a wire.

Still, her training and experience in the theater could be brought to bear now. She knew how to relax, how to concentrate, and when to risk trusting the playwright, the director, and the other actors in a play. Fear always had to be turned into courage. And her courage always got her onstage. She took three deep breaths, so discreetly Daniels did not notice.

She looked up. Looked at Daniels.

Taking a deep breath, she took his hand and said, "I trust you, Dog."

He was all business. "First put on this lightweight, rock-climber's helmet and adjust it. Helmets are standard equipment, like wearing a life vest on a boat.

"This is a climber's saddle - goes around your thighs and waist and supports your back. Everything else hooks into it. Step through these two loops and we'll adjust it. Then we'll snap you onto the ascent rope, lift you up off the ground a few feet, and adjust again. I want you to feel safe and comfortable.

"Look up. Your rope runs through that block and tackle. I can lift a thousand pounds with it, using just one hand. There's a ratchet locking device on it, so even if I let go you won't fall more than a few feet.

"I'll pull you up slowly. Keep your hands loosely on the rope so you don't swing around. When you come up even with the tree boat, sit down on it and hook yourself to the safety line that's hanging there. I'll ease off a little on the pulley rope so you can unhook from it and move over into the middle of the boat and get comfortable. There's even a pillow in the boat if you want to lie down. Then I'll come up, and we'll do what's next. OK?

"One last thing: Talk to me on your way up about how you're doing. If you're afraid, tell me. We'll deal with it. But don't keep it to yourself. Everybody's afraid a little the first time. I was too. So, no big deal. It's called appropriate anxiety. If you're not a little scared, you shouldn't be up in a tree. The right amount of fear keeps you safe. But if you feel you're in the red zone, I'll bring you down."

"How will you get up?"

"I'll attach two Petzl ascenders on this other rope. They're movable, ratcheting clamps, with a foot-loop hanging from each one. Stand in one, push the other up, put your weight in that one, and move the other one. Like climbing movable stairs. I'll be right up after you get settled."

He helped her into the saddle, adjusted it, and hooked it onto the line. "Ready?"

He lifted her a few feet off the ground.

"Comfortable?"

"I still trust you, Dog," Alice-Alice said. "Haul away."

She felt as if she was levitating. Slowly, gently, smoothly rising up past branches and leaves into the powerful arms of the great oak. Easy. Nothing to be afraid of.

"Talk to me," said Daniels.

"I'm a little anxious when I look down," she called. "But I'm fine when I look up. No problem. Keep going."

She rose through the trees as softly and silently as smoke.

When she was settled into the tree boat, she looked down and watched as Daniels smoothly ascended his rope. He swung into the tree boat next to hers, hooked into a safety line and sat, quietly studying her.

"OK?" he asked.

(Silence.)

"Alice, are you OK? Talk to me."

Looking out through the branches of the tree, Alice-Alice could see the harbor, the city, and Mount Rainier in one direction, and in the other, Puget Sound with the Olympic Mountains in the distance.

"OK? No. I'm not OK. I'm enchanted and deliriously happy. It's like being onstage as Rosalind in the Forest of Arden in *As You Like It*. A magical world."

Daniels smiled at her. He did not tell her that this was his private sanctuary - that nobody had ever been up here with him - or that he had not expected anyone ever would be.

"I'm thirsty," he said. "In that canvas bucket behind you there's a bottle of water. Open it and help yourself and pass it to me."

As Alice-Alice was opening the bottle, she noticed it was marked with a *D* and a smudged date. Before she drank, she said, "Dog, this isn't just any old water. It must be from the spring at Delphi - like the water Max-Pol brought to share with Alex that day they picnicked on the hill above Knossos. Am I right?"

He laughed. "It's the *same* bottle and the *same* water."

Alice-Alice drank and passed the water to Daniels.

"Lie down," he said, "and look up. Sail away in the boat."

And they did that.

STORY FOR STORY

Questions surged in and out of Alice-Alice's mind like surf. All kinds of questions - about trees and Daniels's life and writing. But the question she finally asked was not for information. She recalled the design on the business card Alice used. The Q with an arrow through it - meaning "Don't ask the obvious question. Ask the one beyond that."

"Dog, will you tell me a story?" Alice-Alice asked.

"One that really happened or something I made up?"

"Mix it up. One that *should* be true," she said.

"Well, then - as Alex would begin. This is a story I left out of *Third Wish*. I never knew where to put it. It was like a meander cut off from a river.

"The seed the story grew out of was a fact in some book I read: 'The average life span of a parrot is one hundred and twenty years.' That stuck in my mind.

"A couple of weeks later I was sitting on the terrace of a taverna in the Cretan mountain village of Kefali. There's a grand view from there, out over a deep valley winding down to the Libyan Sea.

"Suspended from a rafter of the terrace pergola was an empty bird-cage. A big one. With long black ribbons hanging down from it and fluttering in the wind. Flowers had been woven into the wires. The flowers had been there long enough to dry and fade. The cage had a melancholy feel about it - poignant - sad - mysterious.

"It seems that an old and much-beloved *papagano* - parrot - had lived in the cage for many years, but the parrot was *nekros* - dead. '*O Kirios Papagano . . . poli leepeemenos . . .*' - The Honorable Mr. Parrot - so sad . . .

"That's all I saw or was told. The rest of the story came to me as I drove on down the valley. I imagined Alex telling this story to Alice when they were together on Crete.

"Alex would have said it is a 'psittacine' saga - pertaining to parrots. He would have known the esoteric term and would have used it because he liked the way it sounds. I had to look it up.

"But I digress. Here's the story:

"It may be said the parrot belonged to an old man.
"Or it may be said the old man belonged to the parrot.
"They were always together - never apart.
"They belonged to each other.

"The old man's parrot liked riding in his car. The bird rode beside him on a perch hanging from the car's ceiling. They bumbled along together, the old man calling out to friends from one side of the car and the parrot hurling a stream of calls and curses and songs out the other side.

"The old man had a heart attack while driving his old car, and the car soared off a cliff, tumbled end over end onto the rocks below, and fell into the sea. The parrot was with him at the time.
"As for the old man, his time had come," the villagers said.
"But the papagano - too bad about the parrot - that is a catastrophe."

"The old man's body was recovered, but no trace of the parrot was ever found. Probably dead, but in the absence of the corpse it was possible that the bird had flown free - though nobody knew if the parrot could still fly. And, of course, parrots can't swim.
"Whatever happened, the parrot was gone. Ever since that day, the door to its cage had been left open just in case it returned. But months had passed, and no papagano.
"The man and the bird had been together since the old man was born. And the parrot had belonged to the old man's father before him. The bird had been in the village at least a hundred years. And it was who-knows-how-much older than that, having appeared at the end of the nineteenth century.
"As with its disappearance, mystery also shrouded its arrival in the village. There were many stories: The papagano had flown in from a ship or left behind by the departing Turks or escaped from a zoo or flown in from an African port - but nobody could say for sure.
"Some people said the parrot was a Muslim - the only one in the Christian village - because it could recite passages from the Koran and sing songs of the Levant in Arabic.
"Some said the bird was the ghost of a Wandering Jew because it

could curse in Hebrew and Spanish and German. Prodigious memory. It knew the names of villagers long dead or departed. It even mimicked their voices, much to the pleased dismay of friends and family. Furthermore, the parrot could also imitate chickens, crows, goats, sheep, dogs, cats, and donkeys. Even the animals were usually fooled.

"The bird was a true Cretan, stubborn when coerced, and unwilling to respond on demand. It performed only of its own free will, no matter how pleadingly implored or even when bribed with food. Reliably unpredictable, usually entertaining, and sometimes demonic. Cretan, for certain.

"The parrot seemed to know that the village priest detested the Koran, and it plagued the old man with Islamic scripture whenever he came near its perch. The priest once cursed the parrot, to his regret. For the bird repeated the curses in the unmistakable voice of the good father.

"When the accident happened, people said, 'The village can always get more old men. More of them are coming along every day and month and year. But the parrot . . . a tragedy.' Like the loss of the village historian. Or the village blabbermouth, depending on how you looked at it.

"The villagers thought a creature that had been around so long must know things none of them knew or could ever know or even wanted to know. Gossip. Solutions to village mysteries. Truths that should not be told.

"Some said it had the Evil Eye.

"Not everybody mourned the demise of the parrot.

"The parrot's ability to remember things was feared by some, and they shunned it, being careful not to speak of certain things where the parrot could hear. When the bird disappeared, some villagers sighed in relief.

"There is a rumor that the bird did not die in the accident, but was found alive, washed up on a beach. And that it was killed to keep it from ever repeating certain secrets. It is also said that the parrot survived and is flying from village to village, telling everything it knows.

"The fate of the parrot remains a fine mystery.

"Mystery provokes imagination."

(Pause.)

"Is that the end of the story?" Alice-Alice asked.

"I don't know."

"What does the story mean? Is there a moral or a point?"

"I don't think so. If you want to get analytical about it, I guess it's connected to my trying to end my novel, but I haven't thought much about it. Does there need to be a point? The story just came to me. Happens all the time. The rest is up to you. Make of it what you will."

"A parrot is only a parrot."

(Silence.)

Daniels sat up and turned to face Alice-Alice.

"I suppose, when I do think about it, I'm like the parrot. No original thoughts - nothing new - just a lifelong assortment of words and sounds and ideas collected from the world and other people, in a cage decorated with flowers and ribbons, with an open door . . . and a mystery at the end.

"I'm never quite sure if what I say makes any sense or means anything important. Meanwhile, the 'parrot' in me keeps occupied, and what he says entertains some people. But what the 'parrot' knows can also be dangerous, because there's some truth in it. Being a good steward of truth is always problematic."

"You could say that about being an actress too," said Alice-Alice.

(Silence.)

"Now *you* tell *me* a story. Alice was a storyteller, remember?"

"She still is. Close your eyes and listen."

Daniels rolled over onto his back in his tree boat.

Alice-Alice began to tell her story.

*

Once upon a long and lovely time ago, a man was led into the labyrinth of Great Unrequited Love and abandoned there. Even though he found his way back into the world, sometimes the sorrow of dissatisfaction would suddenly seize him and bind him. In such moments, he would let go and drive his life with his hands off the steering wheel.

He had several small accidents – bangings and bendings and blows. When witnesses asked what happened, he was forthright: "I stopped steering for a while," he said. "Bad things happened."

Because he feared hurting himself or other people, he committed himself to an institution for psychiatric evaluation.

A friend went to visit him and found him rational and functional. The friend offered to take him for a drive in the countryside.

"Take me to see the ocean – to the deep, blue sea," he said.

When they parked at a high place, the man suddenly bolted. He ran to the edge of the cliff as if to throw himself off. But just as suddenly, he stopped.

His friend went calmly to his side.

"What do you want to do?"

"I want to jump, so that forever after, my love will be remembered."

"Ah, well," said the friend calmly. "That's been done. Many times. Anybody can jump. Anybody does. Jumping down is easy. But if you climbed down to the bottom and then leaped back up to the top . . . Everybody would *always* remember that."

Intrigued, the man climbed down to the bottom. He shouted from the beach, "It would be hard to jump back up from here. Maybe impossible."

"Yes, but you could learn to fly," said his friend.

"Fly? You must be crazy."

"We both are. But I can fly. I will teach you."

The man never went back to the asylum.

You may want to ask if he learned to fly.

Not yet. But the effort occupies and concentrates his mind.

And sometimes – sometimes he gets off the ground – not far or for long – but higher than he ever imagined he might before he tried.

*

(Silence.)

"Is that the end of the story?" asked Daniels.

"It is. Make of it what you will. Men are only men."

DEDICATION SONG

Before she went to bed that night, Alice-Alice began writing another song. The Dedication to Daniels's novel was on her mind. Cradling the guitar in her lap, she began playing and humming until words came:

> You took the night train to Barcelona.
> Oh, if I had taken it too.
> And followed the man who took the tickets,
> Darling, I would have found you.

That was as far as she got.

Uncertain about the next verse, she went to bed.

Restless in her sleep, she got up at three in the morning, made coffee, and wandered around the apartment in the dark, carrying her guitar in one hand and her coffee cup in the other.

Slowly another verse of the song took shape in her mind:

> On a great ship bound for England,
> If I'd been at the rail as it headed out to sea,
> I would have walked the deck every morning,
> 'Til I was certain you had seen me.

She got up and stared out the window into the darkness.

"It needs a chorus," she said to her reflection in the window.

> The flowers blooming in the garden;
> Do they bloom along the road?
> Tell me love, will you still wander?
> Will you take me with you when you go?

Now what? she wondered.

And paced the apartment again.

She put the guitar back on its stand and started toward the bedroom. She stopped.

Another verse began forming.

We'll go to Blackwell's Books in Oxford,
The Golden Tulip in Amsterdam.
I'll lead you through the door, then turn around,
And say, "Love, here I am."

"No," she said aloud.
"There's something wrong with that. Scratch that. It's a verse too far."

She retrieved her guitar and sang the chorus again.

The flowers blooming in the garden;
Do they bloom along the road?
Tell me love, will you still wander?
Will you take me with you when you go?

She sat still and waited, strumming the tune.

You looked in all the wrong cities,
Places I have never seen before,
The night train to Barcelona
Never came to my backstage door.

Nothing more came to her.

Nice song, she thought, *but something is getting in the way.*

Back to bed.
She pictured Daniels sitting in his tree boat.
"What does he really want?" she asked the ceiling.
She fell asleep with the guitar on the floor beside her, just in case her brain woke her up with the answer.
But no answer came.

PUZZLING

Oh, she thought.

"Oh . . . now . . . I think I get it," Alice-Alice said aloud.

As if reading a tour guide for a country she had briefly visited, she had been looking through *Third Wish* for places to go in the Land of Daniels Doggett. Having crossed the border, she was re-searching the guide for specific possibilities, looking for locations and themes to work into her play.

Though she had read Alex's poem at the beginning of the novel, she had not given it much thought. Authors always have stuff like that at the beginning - epigraphs - often oblique and decorative. She often wondered if even the writers knew what they meant. Now that she had become acquainted with Daniels, she read the poem again. Maybe she had missed something.

Instructions for Wayfarers

They will declare: Every journey has been taken.
You shall respond: I have not been to see myself.

They will insist: Everything has been spoken.
You shall reply: I have not had my say.

They will tell you: Everything has been done.
You shall reply: My way is not complete.

You are warned: Any way is long, any way is hard.
Fear not. You are the gate - you, the gatekeeper.
And you shall go through and on . . .

"Hah! That's not Alex's poem at all," she said aloud. "It's David

Daniels Doggett's Manifesto! It's addressed to himself. He wasn't writing a novel as much as he was setting out on a quest. He isn't traveling to benefit an audience but to complete himself."

Wheels turned in her mind. She turned to the Dedication which, when she thought about it, was oddly placed - far into the novel, not in the customary place at the beginning. She read it again:

> This book is for you, the one I missed;
> You, whose path I never crossed;
> You, who never arrived in my life;
> Still, this book is for you,
> Because you *must* be there.
>
> Many times have I altered my Way
> To be where you might be:
> On a great ship, crossing to England;
> On the night train to Barcelona;
> On the pilgrim route around Shikoku.
>
> In Monet's garden in Giverny,
> In Oxford at Blackwell's Books,
> In the art museums of Vienna,
> In Amsterdam at the Golden Tulip,
> In Rouen in the cathedral.
>
> Were you in Santa Fe last Christmas?
> I looked for you there.
> On the island of Crete last spring?
> I looked for you there.
> Where are you?
>
> Will I ever find you?
> Have you looked for me?
> Come to me. Find me.
> This book will tell you where I am.
> This book is for you.

"Oh," she said again. "That changes everything. And that explains why the song wasn't working last night."

Restless, she went out for a walk - down to the cemetery at the far end of Queen Anne Hill. When she reached the cemetery gate she began talking out loud to herself again, sorting through all the thoughts sloshing around in her mental pond.

She implored the mute audience underneath the tombstones of the cemetery, "What does David Daniels Doggett want?

"I've had it wrong. The Instructions for Wayfarers and the Dedication weren't about me or anybody like me. They say nothing about love or romance or sex or marriage - or even a woman. He's not looking for his One and Only.

"He was in all those places. Whatever else he thought he was doing, he was looking for something more than himself. Some kind of completion that doesn't really demand a relationship with any other person. He wants something more than a sum of all the parts. That's what he's reaching for: *the Maximum Dog*.

"But . . . But . . . Maybe . . . he's the one who has had it wrong . . . and now he knows. He's confused about what he wants. Big dilemma!"

She laughed, remembering Alice's questions: "If there's a dilemma, is there a lemma? Can there be a trilemma?"

"The answers are Yes and Yes," said Alice-Alice. "Life is littered with lemmas - you can hardly move around in your mind without stepping on one. Lemmas abound.

"Alex would have pointed out that this is a case of multiple working hypotheses and multiple working conclusions leading to parallel praxis. And Dog knows all about that - he wrote it."

She walked all the way around the cemetery and stopped at the entrance where she began, still talking aloud to herself.

"There was the unclosed circle Zenkichi drew on the ground at that temple. The *enso*. And the ongoing arrow on Alice's calligraphic business card. And the actress who shows up to bring Alice back to life. He knows that anything's still possible. Including contradictions."

Alice-Alice walked on, circling through the cemetery again.

"So what was the murder of Alice about? That's confusing. Did something die suddenly in Daniels? Did he kill it?"

She laughed.

"Maybe he was trying to give up one horn of his dilemma. One lemma at a time."

She laughed again.

Round and around and around. This is crazy-making.

She sat down on a bench, still talking to her silent, invisible audience.

"The final volume of *Third Wish* hasn't been published because it hasn't been written. *Isn't* being written. That must be the case. He doesn't *know* what to do next or where to go. He doesn't want it to end, but knows it should. He wants it all ways: *The Self, The One* and *Some One*. Which? That's a trilemma for sure."

She laughed.

"He said he wished he knew how to end the novel. He thought he had. Then those other women showed up. But he realized they were no solution. So he's stuck. Maybe he's suicidal? No. Well . . . maybe."

"However . . . When he said to me, 'But you came to give me something . . .'

"Oh!

"He's come to a fork in the road. His Way divides. Decision time. And now he can't choose. Because . . . of . . . me. No wonder he holds back and doesn't make any of the usual moves men make."

Alice-Alice wondered, *What am I supposed to do? What's my responsibility now? What happens if we move from Writer and Reader to Dog and Alice-Alice? What if he? . . . if we? . . . or if I . . .?*

Alice-Alice pondered another fundamental theater question, *What's the "spine" of the play - the hinge the story swings on?* In every human story - on stage or off - there is always at least the existential angst that arises between Getting What You Want and Wanting What You Get.

"David Daniels Doggett wants . . . a way on . . . a reason to continue."

As if waking up from a dream surprised at how much she knew that she didn't know that she knew, she said "Oh!" again. And sat very still on the bench, consciously assuming the Mona Lisa pose of Alice-of-the-novel.

She smiled. And turned the Mona Lisa smile into an Alice-Alice grin.

She knew how to write and direct her play.

She knew how the last volume of *Third Wish* would end.

WRITING THE PLAY

Alice-Alice had never written or directed a play.

She had studied, analyzed, criticized and acted in plays - yes. But never considered actually writing or directing one from beginning to end. She wondered why so few women were playwrights. She knew the feminists' answers, but what might be true beyond the clichés? Did differences between male and female ways of seeing the world draw them to different crafts and arts? Certainly not true for poetry or fiction or painting. Why so few well-known female playwrights? Lack of what? Something as simple as spatial imagination? Or maybe all the good original ideas were used up by the time women finally got their chance?

She could not even claim ownership of what she proposed to do now. Not original material. It belonged to Daniels. She was adapting a novel and directing the movie.

But Alice-Alice was an actress.

She thought, *I can act my way into this drama. Act like a playwright. Act like a director. And act like an actress.*

Making that decision was the easy part.

If Alice-Alice had walked around thinking in circles on grass instead of in her apartment, she would have quickly worn a path several inches deep in the turf. She needed a labyrinth. Or perhaps she was constructing an invisible labyrinth out of materials supplied by Daniels. As is always the case with labyrinths, one must be able to find the way out again. Once at the center, being able to leave the same way you came in is the test.

"Come in as an actress. Get to the center. Leave as an actress," said Alice-Alice, as she completed one more circuit of her living room. She added, "This is not a conflict but a collaboration. Take no prisoners. Leave no victims."

She taped sheets of white construction paper to the widest wall of her living room. The sheets remained blank for most of a day, as she paced around and around, and back and forth. The form of the play would not declare itself.

She gave up. Went for a walk around the block. Nothing.

She ate her dinner sitting on the living room couch, staring at the blank paper on the wall. Nothing.

After eating, she went walking again. Nothing.

Frustrated, she went to bed early, thumbed through some magazines and finally fell asleep, thinking as she dozed off, *Probably come in the middle of the night. Why not on my time schedule instead of the whims of the creativity committee that's running my head?*

At three in the morning, the knock came on the door of her idle conscious mind. *Alice-Alice? Hello. Anybody home?* She got up.

"Ready," she said, heading for the living room.

But the call was not about the play. What came to her as she sat on the couch was a song. She picked up her guitar and began playing and then humming. Finally, the words formed. An hour later the song was complete:

> I came because I read your author's dedication;
> And it sounded romantic at the start.
> It seemed you might be lonely,
> For a one and only,
> So I came to audition for the part.
>
> I thought this would be a simple love story,
> Orpheus brings Eurydice back from the dead,
> But I've encountered some variety,
> Scriptural impiety –
> Appropriate anxiety (you said).
>
> Chorus:
> Jumwillies, Jumwillies all in a row.
> Jumwillies rain, Jumwillies snow.
> Jumwillies come and Jumwillies go.
> And nobody knows what the Jumwillies know.

As I read your Dedication now,
I see some hesitation, how
My entrance hasn't cleared things up at all.
The heart's a tricky thing to gauge.
I prefer my love on stage.
I know where I stand when the curtain falls.
Alice is as Alice does, Alice-Alice knows,
Because it's more what you mean than what you say.
Preparation is its own disguise,
I prefer to improvise.
I've given you a part in my play.

Chorus

"There's something missing in that," she said, as she read what she wrote down. "Too serious. Needs a shot of joy or foolishness or something."

She stretched, yawned, yawned again, and ambled back to bed, mumbling to herself, *Come on play. No more songs. I need the play. Come on . . .*

*

What was getting in the way of the play? Dramatic convention. Alice-Alice thought she should have it all written out, line-by-line, scene-by-scene, with specific stage directions. A full script. If she gave up on that constraint, the play would come.

This is so confusing, she thought. *So many levels working. Like three-dimensional chess. Daniels is not an actor, but all the characters are in his head. I am an actor, but I'm playing a part of the script he did not write. And he's him, and I'm me playing part of him.*

She wagged her forefinger up and down between her loose lips. *Bubba-dubba-bubba-dubba-bubba dubba.*

She realized she must accept the confusion and contradictions by relying on improvisation as a main frame. As the director she could set up circumstances and environments, provide a setting with some initial lines, and provoke Daniels's memory and creative process.

"After that," she said, "whatever happens - happens. Even if things get wild and crazy. If it's confusing, it's because life is confusing. My play

290

doesn't have to have higher standards than that. All I have to do is herd the ideas into a field and let them run."

She paced the living room, now counting the number of steps it took to make the circuit: twenty-nine.

"The Play is a map. The map is exactly the same size as the world. The script can't be written word-for-word. The play is about what happens when two people *try* to act it out."

She walked another circuit of the room - faster - twenty-five steps.

It's a Jumwillie job, she thought. *With Alex leading the parade, Alice as a majorette, and the rest of the band playing away in a ragtag formation anybody can join.* She laughed. "Dixieland band style. Yes!"

When she said that, the songwriting division of her mental committee barged in again. Retuning to her guitar, she plunged into what she would later call "The Jumwillie Jam:"

Jumwillies sing.
Jumwillies dance.
Jumwillies woo you with Jumwillie romance.
They love to travel to foreign lands.
They always have funds.
They rarely make plans.
They tell excellent stories with outlandish schemes.
One thing they don't tell you is what Jumwillie means.

Diddy Wah Diddy
Da Doo Run Run
Doo Wop Doo Wop
Hey Diddle Diddle
Nonsense can be fun;
Every sound you hear is exactly what it seems.
That's all you need to know about what Jumwillie means.

"And that's good enough for the Jumwillies," she said.

She sang it through several times. "What I need for this is a five-piece band: slide trombone, trumpet, piano, bass, and drums. Maybe a clarinet."

The song broke the dam holding back the play.

Back and forth to the wall she went with felt markers.

She scribbled notes on several pads of notebook paper.

She crossed off useless ideas; replaced the paper on the wall; empty coffee cups were scattered around the room as if several people had been at work instead of one. Crumpled paper clumped in piles.

She worked best in the mornings. It stayed morning all day long.

She lost track of time, caught up in a delicious rush of creativity that obliterates time as a tool. Finally, she trimmed away all the fat from the flesh, and then the flesh from the bone, leaving the skeletal outline of the play on fresh paper on the wall.

THE PLAY: IT'S A DOG'S LIFE

ACT I: Show and Tell
        Scene 1. Chronya Pollah
        Scene 2. Rockabye Baby
        Scene 3. Alterations for Men and Women
        Intermission
ACT II: Add and Subtract
        Scene 1. Feliz Navidad
        Scene 2. Giraffe Concerns
        Scene 3. Rashomon
        Intermission
ACT III: Hide and Seek
        Scene 1. The Floating World
        Scene 2. When Bunnies Fly
        Scene 3. Farewell

Curtain

Sitting on her couch, elbows on knees, hands cradling her chin, she stared at the wall. Examining the outline scene-by-scene, she imagined how to animate each scene at the beginning, and knew she might have to revise the whole play after an improvisation kidnapped it and ran off in another direction.

Start strong, she thought. *Present each scene to Daniels like a professional director would - perspective, notes, stage directions. Ask him for minimal costuming and maximum cooperation in playing out the game.*

She stood up, walked to the play on the wall, made a fist with one hand, kissed the fist, and stamped the kiss onto the play.

"Onward!"

The Play Begins (1)

TO: Daniels Doggett
FROM: Alice-Alice
Here is the first installment of The Play - a process that begins at a pre-scribed place, in a prescribed mind-set. After that, it's all improvisation. Whatever happens, happens.

*

Director's perspective:

The spine of the play is that nothing is ever what it seems to be. Beneath the apparent surface is layer upon layer, with surprising changes. Major theme is the bittersweet tension between solitude and companionship; between loneliness and security; between desire and fulfillment. The task is to hold mutually contradictory points of view and still continue to function:

> Alice of the novel wants: freedom, independence, and adventure.
> She also wants a home, a father, and a soul mate. She must choose.
>
> Alex wants: a strong finish to his life, ending on his own terms.
> He also wants: a home, a child, and a soul mate. He must choose.
>
> Max-Pol doesn't know that he does not want what he thinks he wants.
> He is not ready to choose.

As with actors in scenes in the theater, each installment of life outside the theater may be acted with the same intensity of commitment. If so, each act will shine with the light reflected from the infinite facets of Truth. While this is not

294

always achieved, there are moments of clarity. In general, keep in mind that both faces of drama - Tragedy and Comedy - may be displayed.

ACT I: Show and Tell

Scene 1. Chronya Pollah

Director's notes:
Alice will meet you on location tomorrow night at the Greek restaurant, Panos Kleftiko at 7:30. Costume for you: ordinary black shirt, trousers, and shoes. Props: a walking cane and a komboloi. Character: the spirit and style and attitude of Alex Xenopouloudakis. Script: Improvise in response to the initial provocations of Alice, past and present. Time: It is the day after New Year's Day. Presents may be exchanged.

*

Puzzled, Daniels pauses on the sidewalk in front of the cafe, cane in one hand and komboloi in the other.
Does Alice-Alice know I'm a regular customer here? And, if she does, how? He turns around and stares into the street. *What to do with the cane? Just carry it like a piece of equipment, or actually use it? . . . And how can I be both myself and Alex? . . . And how can I not?*
He looks up and down the empty sidewalk with anticipation, as if someone who could answer his questions might suddenly appear.
But that's what actors do. Play truth and pretend at the same time. And they don't talk about doing it, they just do it.
Twice Daniels starts toward the door, and twice he turns around and walks away again. He is not sure of his entrance lines.
First he must get past Dimitri, the owner.
Not simple. He has known Dimitri for years.
Daniels swings open the door and lunges into the cafe - prepared to explain that tonight is different - that he is not going to the bar first - is not going into the kitchen to see what looks good - and does not want his usual table.
Actually, I'm not really myself tonight, not my usual self, anyway, but I'll explain some other time. And never mind the cane and the limp. Just an act to please a woman.

That last part Dimitri will understand.

Daniels has his speech ready. But no explanations are necessary.

Unaware, he has already walked on stage.

Dimitri says, "Ah, O Kirios Aleko. *Kalispera!* Welcome back. O Kiria Alice is waiting for you. Come."

Somehow she has cast Dimitri in her play. And probably the rest of the staff as well - busboy, waiter, bartender.

Well, then, Daniels says as Alex might say to himself, *in for a penny, in for a pound.*

"Kalispera, Dimitri. *Epharisto poli* (Thank you)," Daniels says. And, leaning slightly on his cane as he walks, he follows Dimitri, thinking to himself, *Here comes Alex. I should be whistling his marching tune.*

Sitting in a booth with her back toward him is a woman with ivory-white hair loosely piled on top of her head. Daniels considers kissing the back of her neck, remembering that Alex had wanted to do that on the Chunnel train from London to Paris. No, then. No, now.

He sits down on his side of the booth.

Alice.

(Pause.)

And it really seems to be Alice - in a lavender-blue, linen dress, saffron-yellow shawl around her shoulders, no jewelry or earrings, a touch of bright red lipstick in the center of her upper lip. Sitting still in a Mona Lisa pose - slight smile, arms folded. She is wearing un-matched shoes. Not that Daniels can see them. He just knows.

And now he knows where to begin. Draping his komboloi over Alice's hand, he says, "Well, then. Jumwillies?"

Alice laughs and replies, "Jumwillies, indeed."

He continues, "Surprising to find a Jumwillie here."

"Jumwillies come when a Jumwillie's near," she says.

"So - Jumwillies must be nothing to fear?"

She smiles, remembering her lines.

"They belong to the lodge of our friend, Mister Lear."

(*A sensate silence encloses them. They are in the novel and in the play and in real life all at once. They are who they are and who they want to be and who they are becoming all at once. The time is Now and Then and Always. All at once.*

Neither wants to break the spell with mundane conversation.
Continue.)

Daniels raises his eyebrows, Alex-style, and says:

"Greeks give small gifts on this day after New Year's. I have my Possibles Bag with me. The invisible one. Did you bring yours?"

"I have it with me always," she says.

"I will give you one of mine. Will you give me one of yours?" he asks.

"With pleasure," she replies.

Holding out a closed hand, he says, "This is the smell from the smoke of burning desire." He uncurls his fingers and offers her his empty palm.

"Accepted," she says, sniffing his hand. "I don't have *that* in my Possibles Bag. But if it were a perfume, I would wear it."

He replies by lifting his eyebrows again.

She holds out her fist.

"This is the sound of laughter from the funniest dirty joke you ever heard," she says, opening her hand.

Blushing, he puts his ear to her palm.

"I remember the joke," he says, laughing. "And no, I will not tell you. Besides, Alex does not tell dirty jokes to ladies."

"But Alice would tell *him* one, don't you think?"

"I suppose you know some raunchy ones."

"Of course. I could even act them out. Improvise."

"Not here. Not now."

She looks at him, smiles, and winks.

"I thought Alex was a winker, not Alice," said Daniels.

"It's my play," she replied.

He both hates and loves winkers. A wink is a deliberate gesture of ambiguous intimacy. A veiled amusement at a secret joke. A single flash of a semaphore signal of conspiracy. A discounting of appearances.

But this enigmatic woman *is* one big wink - from Destiny or the Devil, he cannot say.

Skeptic, he admonished himself.

But he did not wink back.

He is enjoying this opening act of her play. Yes. Enchanted.
But, still, he did not wink back.

Dimitri appears with plates of appetizers: little bits of charcoal-broiled octopus in olive oil, *tsatziki,* pita bread, *taramosalata,* olives, and feta cheese.

"Retsina for O Kiria Alice. And *beera* for O Kirios Alekos. As always. Tonight the *paidakia* are excellent, even if the lambs are from New Zealand, not Crete. Shall I just take care of the rest?" Dimitri asks.

"As always," she says.

Dimitiri smiles, walks away, then turns back to the table to say, "The bouzouki player tonight is new. A substitute. He does not know the songs you like to hear. Shall I tell him? The same?"

"As always," she says.

"As always," says Daniels.

The two diners grin as co-conspirators in a plot to be delighted.

They are still in the play.

*

The improvisation continued, looping in and out from reality into imagination and back again. Parts of scenes and lines and phrases quoted almost verbatim from the novel - often with double meanings. Bringing life back to Alice and Alex, while adjusting for this particular production of the story with these actors: Alice-Alice and Daniels.

Food was placed before them. They ate.

Wine was poured. They drank.

The dishes were taken away.

They hardly noticed any of this happening.

When two people are out on a high-wire together, they must not look down. Close attention must be paid to the other person on the wire. Balance is everything.

*

"I have a secret name-day, un-birthday present for you from Hypatia Loulaki Xetrypis. Remember her, Aleko?"

"No, but Max-Pol mentioned her. I understand that she was a great gift-giver. If this is my secret name day, who is my saint?"

"I will answer three times: Saint Precarious, of course. Saint Precarious, of course. Saint Precarious of course. What I tell you three times is true, Aleko. It's his name day whenever members of the Spherical Learical League are gathered. I know you didn't know that. Because I just now decided. But it is now the case, forevermore."

"*Chronya Pollah, Aghios Precarious* - Many Years, Saint Precarious," says Daniels, lifting his glass and touching hers. "The Greeks say Chronya Pollah at New Year's too. May you live many years."

Not how long, but how wide and deep, thought Alice-Alice.

She says, "Then this is the day *after* the first day of a New Year. And here's your present from Hypatia." She hands over a plain, wooden box tied up with scarlet ribbon. "Smell it first."

Daniels sniffs. "Onion. I have never had an onion-scented present."

Opening the box, he finds a note:

> This *krehmedhi* is for you. I placed it in a nest of honeysuckle blossoms in a black ceramic pot made by my friend, Carmella, from clay dug in a mountain cave. She fired it raku-style with dry cow dung in an outdoor pit on Mid-summer Eve.

He takes the onion out of the box and holds it in his hands.

About the size of a baseball. Its outside layer is paper-like—pale, pinkish-brown, and striped. He knows that the next layer will be pansy-purple, and the layers after that will fade from purple into ivory and white, and on into a final, lime-green kernel at the center.

At the bottom of the onion are the remains of roots. At the top are the first felt-green, sprouting tips of assertive growth. The kernel and roots and tips are signs that the onion is ready to live again if called upon. The onion isn't dead. It is waiting.

Placing the onion on the table, he resumes reading the note:

> Granted that a bouquet of flowers for a birthday is more customary, it has a limited life. Fleeting beauty is poetic, but flowers are dead on arrival - a fading, fugitive, momentary gesture. An onion, on the other hand, is not only beautiful; it is useful and contains lasting possibility.

300

Moreover, an onion is a bouquet in a way. The bulb of a member of the lily family. If allowed and encouraged, it will flower. And the seeds will make more onions. And more flowers.

You may, of course, eat it raw just as it is – both bulb and stems. Chop it, grate it, slice it, combine it with many ingredients, fry it, or bake it. Nothing adds sweet tangy flavor to food like onions. What would a sauce be without them – or soup or stew or roast or salad?

Or you may plant the kremedhi and, if encouraged, it will grow. I have one in a glass jar on my windowsill – roots in the water, stalks in the air, tips budding. Self-perpetuating if allowed to go to seed – hundreds more onions may be grown. And those, if dried, braided into long strings, and hung in the kitchen, will keep the smell of summer soil and sunlight through the winter.

More. The outer skin is paper and may be written on or else boiled and used as a red stain for eggs at Easter, or to dye thread, which may in turn be woven into scarlet blankets, as the Cretan villagers once did. Medicinal qualities as well. Good for your basic health.

And no encounter with an onion is incidental. Its juice brings tears to your eyes, and perfume to your fingers and breath. If you rub the juice on the bottom of your feet, your breath will smell of onions the next day. An onion is oils and sugars and water and sophisticated compounds and complex crystalline structures. A marvel in a chemist's lab or under a microscope.

The kremedhi is a metaphor for the layered nature of existence itself. At its green center lies the germ of infinite possibility. When the farmer wanted to know why I was being so careful in choosing one onion, and I told him, he gave me the onion and said that "fecund" is the essence of the onion.

And as a gesture on your name-day un-birthday, the kremedhi expresses the poignant, bittersweet truth of evanescent affection.

Flavor for the life.

Anything looked at carefully may be a window on the universe.

—Chronya Pollah

*

He holds the onion in his hands and examines it as if he has never seen one before. *"Katapliktiko,"* he says. "A Greek word that combines 'beautiful' and 'wonderful' in a moment of astonishment. I have nothing to give you now to compare to this."

"You will. And I can wait," she says. "We have time for many gifts."

Carefully, he peels off the dry top brown layer, and then another layer - magenta and juicy. "Katapliktiko," he sniffles.

"It's a gift guaranteed to bring tears to your eyes," she says.
He looks up, eyes shining.

The onion has served its purpose.

EXIT, STAGE CENTER

"*Signomi*, O Kiria Alice," said Dimitri. "Excuse me for interrupting, but your car and driver are here."

"I'm coming," she replied.

"Car and driver?" Daniels asked.

"If I don't get home before midnight, my coach will turn into a pumpkin and I will be plain old Cinderella again," she said, rising to go.

"But I . . ."

"Don't get up. The first act ends with you sitting there, trying to sort out what happened this evening. Try to look nonplussed-but-enchanted as the curtain comes down," she said.

"I don't have to try," he said.

Handing him an envelope, she explained, "Here are the director's notes for the next act. In the tree boat. Tomorrow morning at nine. Will you be there?"

"Yes, but I wanted . . ."

"It's my play, Dog. Goodnight."

She leaned over, kissed him tenderly on one cheek and then the other, and walked away toward the front of the restaurant.

As Dimitri opened the door for her, she paused and looked back at Daniels. *He really does look nonplussed, and a little bit enchanted,* she thought. *But he's not much of an actor.*

Giving him her benevolent Queen wave, she went out the door.

*

Dimitri stopped by the bar, picked up a bottle of *Metaxa* and two glasses, and came to sit down with Daniels.

"What the hell was that all about and who the hell was she?"

Daniels laughed.

"Would you believe me if I said I don't quite know?"

"No. *That* I would *not* believe. But it's your business. If you want to have Halloween parties at my joint, feel welcome. She's good for the bottom line. She gave me fifty bucks to go along with the act and said you would pay for the meal and be *very* generous with a tip."

"Oh really. No wonder you brought the good wine."

"Forget it. It's all on the house. Worth the show. She came in here twice to work out the details. Each time she was somebody else. Short hair one day, no hair another, and long white hair tonight. And her shoes didn't match any time she came. Sexy, sweet, and weird. The best kind. She's hot stuff. Where did you find her?"

"Would you believe she just showed up in my driveway one night?"

Dimitri winked. "*Oh sure*. Right. Just showed up in your driveway."

"It's a long story, Dimitri, and don't wink at me. It's a true story."

"Do you want to tell me, or would you rather just sit here and drink?"

"Pour. Did she really have a car and driver?"

"No. She caught the bus."

"Dimitri, do you know what the word 'nonplussed' means?"

"No, not really."

"Speechless, astonished, bewildered."

"She make you feel that way?"

"Look at my face."

"If that's nonplussed, you don't look unhappy about it."

"No. I'm enchanted."

"If you say so. Have some Metaxa and we'll both get enchanted."

They clinked glasses. "*Opa!*"

The Play (2)

ACT I: Show and Tell

SCENE 2. Rockabye Baby

Director's notes:

The next morning. Alice-Alice and Daniels are in the tree boats. Costumes: tree-climbing clothes. In the deep background are Alex and Alice, unseen, with no speaking parts – but present in spirit. This scene has the quality of the off-stage conversations actors have in the greenroom between acts. Even so, the action is still inside The Play. Begin with this scripted line, then improvise:

Daniels: "You have blood on your shirt."

*

"You have blood on your shirt."

Alice-Alice smiles and says, "The giraffe stumbled on the milk bucket and skinned its knees when it fell. Superficial cut, but blood everywhere."

"That happened to my duck," says Daniels. "It's hard enough to milk one, but when they skin their knees it's tricky getting a Band-Aid on."

"I didn't know ducks had knees."

"This is a tall duck," says Daniels. "An old, tall duck. With just one leg, actually. The other one was chewed off by a wolf. Sad."

"Oh, the poor duck," says Alice-Alice. "The poor, poor duck." And she begins to weep. She wrings her hands in grief. She sobs. "Oh, the poor duck."

"Don't cry. He's out of his misery. I ate him," says Daniels. "Tasted pretty good. Except for the drumstick."

Alice-Alice erupts in melodramatic joy, shouting: "Oh grieve not, grieve not. The duck is no more. Freed *forever* from the woes of this *wretched* life! *Rejoice* and be *glad*! Exit the muted duck!"

"Well, actually," said Daniels, "It was a talking duck, but that's a story for some other time. You can't count your chickens before they hatch, but you can count your ducks. There was only one."

Applause from Alice-Alice.

"Nice work, Dog."

"Same to you," he replied.

(Silence.)

"Tell me about being an actress," said Daniels.

Alice-Alice answered him with her eyes focused beyond the surface of his face, as if she were peering through the front window of a house, trying to see someone in the rooms inside. Tilting her head, wrinkling her brow, and frowning, she closed her eyes.

"Wrong question?" he asked.

"No, no," she said, opening her eyes. "Dog, it's not *what* you asked but *how* you asked it. A director once said to me, 'Here's an empty stage. Bring it to life.' And your request is like that - respectful and open-ended. I'm pausing to think, because I want to give you an elegant answer, not an academic lecture."

"Take your time," he said, lying back in his tree boat.

Alice-Alice did the same. Lying side-by-side in the tree boats and talking was like having a side-by-side conversation in a moving car. Together, but tangential - more like performing a monologue with an audience - addressing yourself as much as your companions. She looked up through the branches of the oak into the clouds forming and re-forming above, and began talking.

"First, there's always this:

> *'All the world's a stage,*
> *And all the men and women merely players:*
> *They have their exits and their entrances;*
> *And one man in his time plays many parts'*

"*As You Like It* Act II scene 7 line 138. That's the heart of acting. So profoundly true that it's become an easily dismissed cliché. Already an old idea in Shakespeare's time. But that's an actor's view of the world.

And if you see it that way, then that defines your life: always on stage."

Daniels interrupted. "Epictetus - Fourth century B.C. - said, 'We are like actors in a play in roles not always of our choosing. Wherever you find yourself and in whatever circumstances, give an impeccable performance. If you are supposed to be a reader, read; if you are supposed to be a writer, write.'"

"Yes, it's the same," said Alice-Alice. "I was probably good at peekaboo as a baby. That's the first theater you're in: 'Now you see me, now you don't; Mommy's here but she's not. Get it?' And a baby gets it, and burbles in delight. Theater."

Daniels laughed. "I've never had a child, but whenever I'm around little kids I always seem to play peekaboo with them. It's an instinct. Make-believe. Play acting."

(Silence.)

"A guy I know is a blues singer," said Alice-Alice. "His name is Rambling Rex Jakabosky. Not old and black and skinny and beat up by life. But young, white, and huge - over six feet tall, three hundred pounds, short hair. A dancing bear who plays guitar and sings. Down deep he knows he's an actor on the stage of the world.

"If you saw him walking down the street, the last thing you'd think is 'musician.' He's smart enough to make a living a hundred ways. But here he is, out on the street with his husky voice and beat-up guitar. Sometimes he plays clubs or with a band or at a festival, but performing solo on the street is what he calls 'his groove.'

"I used to stand and listen to him instead of just putting money in his jar and walking on by. He made me happy. One day I asked him to tell me about being a blues singer. He said, 'If you know it's in you, then you got to play it out. I'm a blues singer. Period.'

"That's the artist's answer to the What do you do? question and the Who are you? question - poet, painter, dancer, musician, actress - whatever. Born to do it. Period. If you're lucky, you get to know from the beginning. And I was lucky.

"I *am* and have always been an actress. That's not what I *do* for a *living* - not a job or career. That's *who* I am. My life is theater. Everything else is preparation for that. I am of the Make Believe People - from the other side of The Looking-Glass. And that's my permanent address.

"To be born in a hippie commune in California in the '60s is to get a walk-on part in a theater where the show runs twenty-four hours a day. No audition. You're in The Play by being there. Every morning began with the bugle call of 'Let's pretend.' Our workshop equipment was fantasy, magic, creativity, dance, music, and costumes. Life equaled Play. The mantra was Be Free.

"When I was five my mother asked me if I would like to spend the summer with my grandparents. She said they lived in a cottage in a green woods full of fairies. It was true. They had a summer home in the Berkshire Hills in western Massachusetts. Lots of summer stock theater in the area, and a program for the children of people involved in theater. We played 'let's pretend' and 'what if' and 'once upon a time' all summer. Life continued to equal Play. Be Free.

"My grandmother read all of *Alice in Wonderland* to me every summer until I could read it for myself. My name was Alice. *I was Alice.* Her story became my story.

"At summer's end I stayed on with my grandparents, which was fine with me. They loved me. They saw who I was and what made me happy. And for the rest of my years of growing up, they supported my Wonderland life. They gave me permission to be who I was and who I wanted to become.

"Early on they discovered that if they gave me a couple of card tables some old blankets and a few stuffed animals, I could create a kingdom and live in it for hours, even days. And that's what happened. For years. They would even get under the tables with me and pretend. No matter what the story, they were always the King and Queen in the play."

"Lucky you. You must really love them," said Daniels.
Tears welled in Alice-Alice's eyes.
She nodded - unable to speak the Yes that her lips formed.

(Silence.)

Alice-Alice wiped away her tears, and cleared her throat.
"They provided music lessons and dancing lessons, and enrolled me in children's theater programs - everything and anything that would enrich my growth as an actress. They took me to plays, musicals, opera, and ballet. We'd go for long weekends in New York to see anything theatrical - even circuses and parades.

"When I was nine they bought me a guitar and found me a teacher. I learned folk songs, and the teacher encouraged me to write my own tunes. One summer I performed on the streets of Boston with two friends. We called ourselves Dangerous Wonder.

"We got busted by the cops for vagrancy once, and were booked into jail. Of course, my grandparents came down and bailed us out. They thought it was hilarious. Their granddaughter - the criminal singer - menace to society - a threat to law and order.

"The summer I was fourteen they sent me to a camp for clowns. I learned to juggle, walk on stilts, do clown makeup and costumes, and perform pratfall comedy skits with rubber chickens and a pet pig. Glorious summer!

"The memory of that summer is so strong I cannot remember being thirteen or fifteen. I think I was fourteen two summers in a row.

"That's why Wonko in *Third Wish* is so real to me. I know what Wonko knows. For one thing, it's hard work learning to appear spontaneous. For another, you have to learn that what's funny is Truth - what really happens - not always at the moment it happens, but after - when it's safe to laugh at a memory.

"But when all the skills are melted into your very being, and you experience the rush of joy when your inner delight transforms an audience - *Shazam!* The ultimate moment.

"My grandparents treated my vocation as if I had been a born athlete. I was always either in training or performing. The line between life and art ceased to exist. Everything I've done since rests on the fact that I was born in the theater and have lived out my life in the theater. No doubts. No regrets. No questions.

"I am an actress.

"Do you understand, Dog?"

He sat up and faced her.

"I understand," he said, "but it's rare to have such confidence and certainty. Lucky you. But I wonder . . ."

"What?"

"I know just enough about life in the theater to wonder how you've handled the dark and dreary and mean side of acting. It's not always a picnic."

She frowned, and sighed.

"Sure. It can be a gulag life. Low pay or *no* pay. Bad company. No job security. Rejection. Dictatorial, egomaniacal directors. Plays that bomb no matter how hard you tried. Arrogant critics. Being lonely, broke, even homeless. You never *know* enough, never *have* enough. It's a life on the edge. An edge that's so sharp it sometimes cuts. If I could show you my soul you'd see the scars and bloodstains."

"Did you have a day job?" asked Daniels.

She laughed.

"Waitress, hotel maid, bartender, temporary secretary, cabdriver, tour guide, phone solicitor, magician's assistant – 'Lovely Lola' – and half a dozen different jobs on a cruise line. And that's just to name a few. You'd better have a day job. It's not all bad – it's a license to study people and become a better actor. I haven't had to work days for a long time. But I could. And would."

"Doing what?" asked Daniels.

"Tending bar. If you really know what you're doing – and I do, because I'm trained, licensed and experienced – you can make a lot of money. It's an acting gig. Nonstop improvisation. Everything that happens is grist for the mill. And all the trials make you stronger, better, wiser.

"The payoff in acting lies in those moments of transcendental beauty when you are part of something so hard and clean and true that you would never want to be anywhere else. That's not always in the theater, either. It's happened to me more than once in a bar.

"Shakespeare's lines always come back to me when times are hard:

> 'Sweet are the uses of adversity,
> Which, like the toad, ugly and venomous,
> Wears yet a precious jewel in his head;
> And this our life, exempt from public haunt,
> Finds tongues in trees, books in the running brooks
> Sermons in stones, and good in everything.'

"No matter how good you are on a given night in a play, you have to go for it again the next night. And what was *fire* one night can be *ashes* the next. Nothing is finally safely done – everything is always at risk. Night after night after night after night. Always reaching for the magic, so near, so far.

"But. If that challenge excites you, you'll always be an actor."

(Silence.)

"What about skills – in addition to talent, what?" asked Daniels.

"Good question. You have to have a hell of a memory – not just for the lines of the plays, but for all the stage business and the director's everlasting little changes. In summer stock you perform in one play at night and rehearse the next play in the afternoon, and you have to keep it all straight in your head.

"More often than not, being an actor is like being a member of an emergency medical team: you have to get through some terrible things until you get used to them and can function under that kind of pressure. You *can* breathe life back into a bad play. It's a matter of guts and willpower.

"Sometimes at the end of a play's run you're so exhausted you can't eat or sleep or do anything but lie still – you've spent all you have. And you think, *For what?* You say, *I can't take it anymore.* But you can. And so you get back out there to audition and start all over again."

"How do you do it?" asked Daniels.

"There are some lines from the journal I keep that have never changed over the years. I've memorized them:

> Love the art in myself even more than myself in the art.
> Love the theater in me even more than me in the theater.
> Love the battle between chaos and imagination.
> Remember: Acting is living truthfully in imaginary circumstances.
> Remember: Acting is the way to live the greatest number of lives.
> Remember: Acting is the same as real life, lived intentionally.
> The Fruit is out on the end of the limb. Go there.

"My Rules of the Theater and my Rules of Real Life are the same – it's just the conscious intensity of the theater that's different."

312

"What about the audience's reaction?" he asked.

"Any stage actor who tells you the audience is not all that important is blowing smoke, or working in the movies or on the radio. Not for me. I want live human beings out front. It's a collaboration. An actor needs witnesses.

"That's why I prefer working in theater-in-the-round or with a deep-thrust stage. The ancient Greeks established the pattern with their amphitheaters - with the performance on what looks like a threshing floor, which is what it was originally. In the round, the audience is in it with you. You can usually see them and they can see each other. A play does not exist until it's performed in front of a live audience."

"How do you feel when you do films or TV or radio?" asked Daniels.

"I've only played before a live, immediate audience. That's all I ever want to do. For me, no audience - no theater."

"What's the best part of the whole experience with an audience?"

"The most powerful moment in a theater comes when the audience is so quiet and still that you know they're hardly breathing. It's like they're all up around you on the edge of the stage, so deeply engaged they dare not move or breathe or they'll break the trance. It's a religious experience.

"Another spellbinding moment - usually at the first dress rehearsal or opening night - is when there's deep silence or sudden laughter in a place you didn't expect. The audience saw something or felt something that you're too close to recognize. They're *coaching* you from the side-lines. They know more than you do sometimes. They're on your side. They want you to succeed as much as you do.

"And finally, once in a great while there's a heart-stopping pause of utter silence after the curtain falls - just before there's a rush of applause like a wave crashing on the shore. *Standing ovation!* You can't see it, but you can hear it, and when the curtain rises for the bow, and the audience goes a little crazy out of the sheer majesty of what's happened, well you feel for a moment like royalty.

"It's suddenly face-to-face. Mask off. You can see them - and they can see you – the human beings who made it happen – audience and actors. What's that word you used? – katapliktiko – that's it. Astonishment. That's the name of the moment – the Gold Medal – the Grand Prize."

(Silence.)

"I understand. I suppose," said Daniels, "that's why an author ventures out of his solitude and gives readings. He moves on stage to complete the collaboration between himself and his readers. They are aware that they have come to see him. But they may not understand that he has come to see them. No matter what, the reader completes the book; but the writer is usually not there when it happens."

"Except for this time," said Alice-Alice.
He nodded. "Except for this time."
"Enough about acting and me," she said. "I want to know about you and writing."

While they had been talking the sky had begun to cloud over, and wind rustled the leaves of the tree.

(Silence.)

"Another time," he said. "This wind will pick up shortly, and we ought to get down out of the tree. There's a big weather front moving in, with thunder and lightning in it. Probably a couple of days of rain."

"Good," she said. "I have a scene for a rainy day."

The Play (3)

ACT I: Show and Tell

SCENE 3. Alterations for Men and Women.

Director's notes:
Alice will meet you at six a.m. in front of the tailor's store on Queen Anne Avenue. It will be raining. Some distant lightning and thunder. Costume: Wear a raincoat and shoes for wet walking. Props: Bring an umbrella - large enough to accommodate two people. Character: Come in the spirit of Max-Pol Millay - open-minded, curious, and lighthearted. Script: Be prepared to improvise and play Left/Right/Surprise.

*

Alice-Alice could see him coming three blocks away. Daniels carried an oversized, multi-colored umbrella - its panels had stripes and polka dots and checks - red and blue and yellow and black and white. She couldn't see it yet, but she knew he was wearing a red rubber nose.

As he approached, Daniels saw a figure in a hooded black raincoat, wearing one blue rubber boot and one green one. She was leaning against a window with a sign painted on it:

Alterations for Men and Women

That says it all, he thought, and said, as he came to Alice-Alice, "If you're wondering, I did notice the sign behind you. 'Alterations for men and women.' That's your specialty. Nice touch."

She turned to face him, her own red rubber nose in place. She pulled her hood off her head. Her long, ivory-white hair was in braids - one tied with blue ribbon - one with orange.

They laughed. "Mind if I share your umbrella?" she asked.

He offered his arm in reply, and said, "Left."

As they set off into the rain, she began: "The answer to the question you have not asked is *quipu.*"

315

"Quipu?" He laughed. "Quipu? Keep going. I can't wait."

"The ancient Incas of the Andes were highly civilized but they didn't have any form of writing. They communicated complex information across great distances using relays of fast runners carrying a quipu - a cord with lots of knotted strings hanging down from it.

"By using strings of different colors and lengths and sizes, tied with many kinds of knots in various arrangements, an amazing amount of information could be conveyed. English employs only twenty-six letters. The language of the quipus may be far more complex, involving a seven-place, binary system for encoding numbers and words or concepts. By some Spanish accounts, the Incas could read the quipus by running their hands along the knotted cords."

"Keep going," said Daniels.

"Modern scholars can't break the code. It's like the Linear A writing of the Minoans - clearly organized information, but nobody can figure it out. Parts of both quipu and Linear A construction seem to be an accounting system. But there's more than numbers involved in both of them.

"Quipus are beautiful too. I've seen some in a museum. It looks like somebody unraveled a complex weaving and then tied the threads back together on a single strand. I wonder if the Incas intended the beauty.

"Whatever they once meant, now they're a collection of secrets - like a civilization's shadows that have been frozen and left behind. Tying all those knots correctly must have required patience and intelligence."

"I wonder if they had editors and fact-checkers?" said Daniels.

"That's a question. It's your turn to give me an answer."

The rain became heavy. She moved closer to him under his umbrella, her arm loosely around his waist; his arm lightly around her shoulder, walking more slowly to keep in step.

"Right," she said, and they turned away from the main avenue of shops and stores onto a quiet, tree-lined, residential street. Thunder boomed in the distance.

"Fives," said Daniels. "I collect many things that come in fives - like Alice collected 'threes.' For example: air, fire, water, earth, and space. You know we have five fingers and toes and senses - but that's also a basic number for plants - most leaves and petals are arranged in fives. And many non-European cultures have not just four, but five cardinal directions: north, east, south, west, and center. That's called a quincunx - the way a five is arranged on dice.

"The basic functions of life: respiration, reproduction, ingestion, digestion, excretion. Another set of fives. But the one I bet you don't know and could not ask about is the Five Advantages from *The Art of War* by the Chinese philosopher, Sun Tzu:

'One - To know when to challenge and when not to challenge.

Two - To recognize how to use the numerous and the few.

Three - To agree on superior and inferior objectives.

Four - To prepare to lie in wait for the unprepared.

Five - To lead without interference from a superior.'"

You didn't mention the five stages of grief, thought Alice-Alice. *Denial, anger, bargaining, depression, and acceptance.*

"Left," he said. "Your turn for an answer."

He had timed his direction for a turn into what was neither street nor alley - more of a lane - running uphill. Wild blackberry bushes were in command of the waysides - their curvy, thorny canes heavy with ripe fruit.

"Stop. Wait," said Daniels. "Close your eyes, and open your mouth." He picked five fat, shiny, deep purple berries and fed them to her, one at a time.

"Sweet," she said.

Ignoring the pouring rain, they picked and ate blackberries until their fingers and lips and chins and tongues were stained crimson from the juice.

"You look like a vampire," said Daniels.

"I am," she said. "Vood you lak me to bite you on your neck, dahl-ink?" growled Alice-Alice.

Darling, he thought. She had called him "Darling." But she was laughing and faking a Transylvanian accent. Joking. Surely. "Dahlink" is close, but not quite "Darling."

"No," he said. But he thought, *Yes.*

"I've lost track," she said. "It's my turn to answer, isn't it?"

"Yes, but we're both soaking wet. One more round on the way to someplace dry, with coffee."

"OK. Let me think of something short. The question is, Have I ever written any poetry? The answer is a poem – maybe the chorus to an unfinished song I started one Sunday earlier in the summer. I'm not a poet – not in the same way that I'm an actress. But a songwriter starts with poetic thoughts. I'll recite part of the song for you."

> Sweet Sunday morn abide;
> Extra bacon on the side;
> Coffee in my coffee cup;
> Eggs be sunny side and up.
> Short the life, but wide.

"Finish the song," he said. "And sing it to me. Promise?"

"Promise," she said, as he held open the door to Caffe Ladro.

"Do you come here often, stranger?" she asked.

"Most mornings – around six. If I drink coffee after noon I can't sleep, and I like to nap."

"Surprise! You won't believe this. This is also *my* coffeehouse. But I'm usually still in bed when you're here. An actress is never a morning person. I'm here most afternoons around three. While you're napping. We've been in the same place drinking coffee, but never at the same time. Hardly a credible coincidence. But it's true."

The barista recognized them both, despite their berry-stained faces and Alice's colorful boots and hair ribbons.

"Two tall lattes, whole milk, double shots. Right?"

"Same drink." They laughed. *"Surprise!"*

"Are you going to hiccup?" she asked.

"I can't . . . *heek-unh* . . . help it . . . when I'm surprised."

"It's the giraffe milk that gets to you," she said.

"Heek-unh . . ."

And they laughed.

(Giraffe milk is heady stuff. It is used to incite Delight.
Some say it is an aphrodisiac.
Like laughter.)

*

"I don't really always drink the same thing in the same coffeehouse," he said. "Some days I go to a place that features exotic coffee from far-away places I've never been to. After I've had the coffee, I stop in at the bookstore and get a travel guide to that country."

"Where have you been lately?" she asked.

"Papua, New Guinea. The coffee is grown in volcanic soil in the valleys of the western highlands from seeds imported from Jamaica's Blue Mountains region. This was, as you may recall, Alex's favorite coffee."

"And I suppose you then went to Jamaica because of that?"

"No, I've been to Jamaica before - by travel guide."

"Where else?"

"Sulawesi and Sumatra, in the Indonesian archipelago. Coffee-growing there is a small-scale operation using traditional methods. The beans are spread out to dry in the sun, producing a very heavy-bodied coffee. I like having Indonesian sun in a cup of coffee."

"And you bought a travel book to take you?"

"Yes. But I've only been as far as Sumatra. One of these days I want to actually travel there because of the trees. Meanwhile, I drink the coffee and dream."

"Do you always travel alone?" she asked.

"Yes and No."

"Explain."

"Yes, the usual. I've had girlfriends, affairs, dancing partners, fellow travelers - all that. And no, no long-term companion. And forgive me if I seem rude, but I don't want to go down that road any further, if you don't mind. At least not now or here."

"Sorry I asked. I didn't mean to pry."

He smiled. "Of course you did. If I may say so without mincing words, the question beyond your question is, Am I a normal, heterosexual male - with all the active contradictions that suggests? And the answer is an unambiguous Yes. I come with all the wiring installed."

320

She smiled.

"And you ask because you are a normal, heterosexual female – with all the active contradictions that suggests. And if there is a man and there is a woman, then there is always a possibility for . . . whatever comes next."

She smiled again.

He was afraid she might wink at him.

She did not.

Intermission

The stage is empty.

Daniels Doggett has unexpectedly left for California and may be away for a week or more. He was called in after a major wildfire on a remote ranch that includes rare groves of two-hundred-year-old oak trees. Since he is a consulting arborist for The Nature Conservancy, which owns the property, he was asked to evaluate the damage and attend to the triage of the trees. Exit Daniels.

Alice-Alice is glad for the intermission.

For all the intense pleasure of her encounter with Daniels, she feels mentally and physically drained. It is the same exhaustion she experiences after an opening night. Her mind is a potato. Her arms and shoulders and back and neck ache. Probably from climbing trees.

But there is some deeper, dull pain. She knows what the pain might mean. She knows - but she turns her mind away from the possibility.

Daniels's absence also gives her time to think about theater roles she's committed to for the fall and winter. Back to New Haven and the Yale Repertory to reprise the role of Emily in *Our Town* and Rosalind in *As You Like it*. And while she is there she wants to take some classes in New York in directing and playwriting. There are also ongoing negotiations for engagements for next spring and summer. And there is always the mundane busywork to be done. Even actors must pay bills and write letters and make phone calls and arrange for transportation and lodging.

The man she imagined the Writer to be and the man Daniels *is* are not the same. Both attractive, but the Writer is fading from her mind. She is becoming attached to Daniels. The Dog is real. Strong, kind, thoughtful, and willing to play in her theater - he takes direction well. He has a far more eccentric mind than she expected. And it's been an easy pleasure playing Alice to both his Alex and his Max-Pol.

But, then, these are familiar feelings. She has always become attached to the leading man playing opposite her in the theater, especially if the role is romantic. In the heat of performance she can throw looks of fierce love across the width of a stage, embrace an actor with tenderness, and kiss him passionately. But she does not consummate the relationship with him after the show. It is enough for her to make the audience believe she *might* go home with him.

Well, she thought, and laughed, *there were those summer-stock flings when anybody slept with anybody between shows.* She smiled when she remembered the time she was an ingenue in a farce and romped regularly in a hay barn with the villain after the show. They even made love once before they got out of costume and makeup. There was still hay in her wig when she went onstage the next night. Funny.

But her mind is on David Daniels Doggett.
I miss the Dog, she thought, *and he's only been gone two days.*

*

After her morning shower, Alice-Alice considered her naked body in front of the full-length mirror in her bedroom. The scars under her breasts were slowly fading from red to pink. She considered her breasts. They looked a little different, but nice enough. Her reconstructed nipples seemed almost normal. She touched them. Not much sensation. Not sexy. Never would be. Like touching her elbow.

She thought about Alice and her invisible and visible tattoos.
What would my chest look like with the scars worked into a tattoo? What could be done with two straight red lines? Maybe a Mondrian?

She wondered how Daniels would react if he saw her naked. But she knew the answer to that. He seemed to know about wounds. Alice had said, when she exposed herself to Alex on the boat, "Love me, love my wounds."

If he ever loved her, Daniels would do that. *If* he ever loved her. *What if . . .* she thought, and turned her mind away from one more thing she did not want to think about.

As for the rest of her body, she looked lean. Not thin, but as if she could afford to eat some butter or bacon or ice cream just to round out a bit. She smiled. *Bacon,* she thought.

When she did her stretching exercises, her lower back hurt. But she blocked it out of her mind.

Bacon.

She dressed in front of the mirror. All of her lingerie was new. A morale boost after the surgery. Also in keeping with the tradition of the theater. Underwear should suit the costume and the character – from the skin out. If you are to play 'lovely' then the underwear must be lovely. Sports bras and granny-pants would not do if you're playing Juliet.

Posing provocatively in her apricot-colored bra and panties, she frowned. *Lovely for whom, and for what?*

Questions stampeded through her mind. *If I have come to play the Writer's longed-for One and Only, then won't that include physical passion sooner or later? Hugging, kissing, and even sex? Are we a long way on this side of that, or beyond it already? Is my libido really diminished because of the surgery and hormonal changes? Is he physically attracted to me? Or not? Despite what he said, is he gay, or maybe asexual like Jacks O'Rourke in the novel? Is this destined to be only a platonic relationship? Is it just a play after all? Why has neither one of us invited the other into their home? Why the distance, the caution, the carefulness? Will we ever . . .?*

"Well, then," she said aloud. "Well, then . . ."

She finished dressing, went to the phone and made appointments for a facial and a manicure and a pedicure, and to have her hair done. It had grown out a couple of inches - maybe something interesting could be done with it so she could give up the wigs. A shopping trip for some new perfume and cosmetics would be in order while she was at it.

"Chanel No. 5. Who wore that in his novel? Polydora. When she wanted to seduce Max-Pol. Well. Why not?"

As she went out the door, she wondered, *This is so girly-girly. Have I lost my mind?* And she answered herself, *Yes, I've lost my mind. But as Alice always said, Why not?* And she hummed Alice's 'Cuckoo Not Song' as she walked.

*

At the salon, she thought about Emily in *Our Town*. When she had first played the part, she was in her twenties. Her emphasis had been on the living Emily. Now, she thought about Emily's death in the play, and how she would play Emily in the cemetery, coming back to life for one more day, and how poignant the speech must be about people not *seeing* each other – not *noticing* the preciousness of ordinary life on an ordinary day.

She was beginning to understand how to play Emily all the way through the play – from her beginning to her end.

*

Cute, she thought.

Alice-Alice stood in front of her mirror at the end of the day. She felt renewed – like a used car that has been carefully detailed and refurbished – not just washed and waxed, but having had everything done to it that would bring it as close to mint condition as possible.

"Cute" was not a word she had used about herself for a long time.

Black leather flip-flop sandals (matching) – feet and hands and face massaged and lotioned into healthy softness, and accented with scarlet polish and lipstick. Her skin was clear enough not to need any other cosmetic attention – just a touch of eyeliner. The freckles on her cheeks emphasized the cute. Legs waxed and oiled and looking good. Her extremely short hair had been lightly trimmed, and then gelled to be stylishly hip. Sleek. Young.

The exotic smell of Chanel No. 5 tinted the air of the room.

Cute, she thought, *with a dangerous edge.*

New clothes emphasized the image. Bright yellow tank top, and black shorts. Underneath was another new lingerie set – pale yellow silk. A minimal bra – no uplift or padding or wire. She had even tried on the tank top without a bra, and though she didn't need a bra to give her breasts shape, without a bra her new nipples were irrepressible headlights poking out from her shirt. The right bra fixed that. *Too bad,* she thought.

She turned around slowly, considering herself from the sides and back. Facing the mirror, she cocked one hip in a jaunty stance, smiled at her image and waved. "Hi, Alice-Alice! You're really cute! How old are you? And what's a nice girl like you doing in a place like this? Want to play?"

Cute for who? And for what? she thought again.

Her posture and demeanor slowly dissolved. She stood like an Accused before a Judge. She was not alone. Her old companion, Daddy Death, stood in the shadows behind her. Tears began filling her eyes. She hung her head, and covered her face with her hands.

What do I really want? What do I . . .

Flinging herself down on her bed, she sobbed. *What good is cute?*

It was too hard sometimes to be strong, independent, and alone. Too hard to always play a role on and offstage. "Alone and confident" were melting into "lonely and insecure." Her body armor fell off, and she was suddenly vulnerable to the sharp cuts only the lance of self-doubt can inflict.

Still sobbing, she pounded her pillow with her fists.

"What the hell good is cute!" she shouted.

She wanted, more than anything on earth, to have someone pick her up in his arms, sit down with her in his lap in a rocking chair, and hold her close. Just hold her. Gently rock back and forth and hold her and say, "I know, I know. It's all right. I know." Like Alex did for Alice.

She curled up in a ball on the bed with her knees pulled up to her chest and her arms wrapped around herself as tightly as she could. And cried herself to sleep.

She dreamed she was a queen in the 5 Spot Cafe again. Trumpets played for her procession. A crown on her head. Elbow-length white gloves. A golden scepter in her hand and golden slippers on her feet. And nothing else. She was stark naked. And her whole body was covered with hideous, scabby scars. But she didn't know. She thought she was wearing a gown.

Waving and smiling, she moved on through the tables. The customers stared at her. And instead of waving, they put their hands over their mouths in dismay at her ugly, naked body.

When someone began chanting, "Shame, shame, shame!" she woke up, still curled in a tight ball on her bed. And still in tears.

Slowly she uncurled herself, and slowly got out of bed. Slowly she walked through the apartment, picking up her guitar along the way. Sitting down on a kitchen chair, she began a song:

> The Queen of Queen Anne Hill
> Is not receiving callers today.
> The throne room has gone dark;
> The crown is put away.
>
> The Queen herself is missing,
> Though we promised only to say
> That the Queen of Queen Anne Hill
> Is not receiving callers today.

Alice-Alice got up and walked through the apartment, pulling the curtains shut and turning off all the lights. Returning to the kitchen chair, she sat in the semidarkness and played her guitar. The song continued to come:

> The Queen of Queen Anne Hill
> Disappears for hours.
> We can hear her smashing the mirror
> Up in her tower.
>
> And she's crying as she's cursing,
> Though we can't make out the words.
> The Queen is very careful
> She's never overheard.
>
> The Queen of Queen Anne Hill
> Is not receiving callers today.

Slowly, she put down her guitar; slowly, she slid off the kitchen chair onto the floor and sat, her face in her hands, sobbing.

FIRST REHEARSAL

Director's notes:
Empty stage except for small table and two chairs in dim light stage left, and two actors sitting at identical table and chairs in spotlight stage right. Coffeehouse props: cups, saucers, spoons, etc.

MAN
(whispering)
See that woman over there?

WOMAN
(whispering)
The one with the white hair?

MAN
(facing woman, leaning close)
Yes, that one.
She was wearing a red rubber nose when she came in.
And she doesn't really have white hair.
It's a wig.

WOMAN
How do you know?

MAN
She lives in my condominium. I see her come and go.
She's bald. Or she was earlier in the summer.
Her hair is growing out, but it's still short. Sometimes she wears a hat
or a cap, but I've also seen her with curly, red hair
or brown hair down to her shoulders.

WOMAN
(glancing back at other woman)
Why wigs?
Maybe she's been sick.

MAN
I don't think so.
I've seen her climbing up in the trees across the street.

WOMAN
(glancing again)
Climbing trees?
At her age?

MAN
Yeah. With that guy she's sitting with.

WOMAN
Are they a couple?
Is she, you know, *with* him?

MAN
Well if she is, she never brings him home with her.
She lives above me, and I've never heard any noises
that would indicate . . . you know . . .

WOMAN
She's a little strange.
Look at her shoes – they don't match.

MAN
What's that about?
Maybe there's something wrong with her feet.

WOMAN
Or maybe she's a little *bent*. Kinky.
Probably has a hidden tattoo or piercing.

MAN
He looks pretty straight.
But who knows what's under people's clothes these days?

WOMAN
Are they lovers or just friends?

MAN
I don't know.
I've never seen them holding hands or kissing
or doing any lovey-dovey stuff.

WOMAN
I wonder what he sees in her?

MAN
Exotic. She's exotic.
Plain guys go for that exotic stuff.

WOMAN
What do they do when they're up in the trees?

MAN
I can't tell.
It's hard to see, and I don't want to stare.

WOMAN
You ought to get some binoculars.
Maybe something *loosey-goosey* is going on.
You never know what people will do these days.
Or where they'll do it.

MAN
(grins)
It might be fun . . .

doing it up in the trees.
WOMAN
(laughs)
You want to try? Me Jane. You Tarzan.

MAN
(laughs)
Tie me up but don't tie me down.

WOMAN
You're so romantic.
(They laugh. He takes her hand.)

MAN
My place or yours?

WOMAN
When is it going to be *our* place?

MAN
(releasing her hand)
Why do you always bring that up?

WOMAN
(leaning back, away from him)
Why don't you *ever* bring that up?

MAN
What's wrong with an erotic friendship?

WOMAN
(gets up to leave)
I want commitment.
I want someone who's there in the morning,
not long gone down the stairs
in the middle of the night.

MAN
Is that all women want?

WOMAN
That's all *this* woman wants.

MAN
(leaning back in his chair)
I'll bet Miss Wiggy-Two-Shoes over there doesn't want that.
Or her tree-swinging boyfriend either.
It's not true that all men and women want the same thing.

WOMAN
You're wrong.
They just haven't gotten that far yet.
But they will.
Sooner or later, they will.
It's just the way it is.

MAN
Well, not for me.

WOMAN
I didn't think so.
Thanks for nothing.

(she walks quickly offstage)

MAN
(drinks his coffee in silence)
Women.
Can't live with 'em,
can't shoot 'em and eat 'em.
To hell with 'em.

WOMAN
(walks quickly back onstage)
I'm sorry. Can we talk?

MAN
(looks up at the ceiling, sighs)
You can sit down.
But we've been through all this before.
You know what I'll say.

WOMAN
You'll say you're sorry because I deserve better.
And that you wish I had come along earlier in your life.
You'll say it's not me, it's you.
You're not programmed for conjugal boredom.
And that you just want to be friends.
And the way things are is better than nothing.

MAN
Exactly.
Nothing's changed.

WOMAN
(She looks away,
looks back at him.
Slowly, she sits down.
She begins to cry.
He takes her hand
and stares out the window.)
*

(Light fades over the two actors to black -
and then fades over the
other table and chairs - to black.)

THE PLAY (4)

ACT II: Add and Subtract

SCENE 1. Feliz Navidad

Director's notes:
Alice will meet you on location tomorrow night at the Spanish restaurant, Madrid 522, at 9:00. Costume: all black. Shoes appropriate for Latin dancing. Props: a Christmas gift for Alice - your choice. Character: the spirit and style of Max-Pol. Script: improvise in response to Alice. It is the week before Christmas.

And they did that.

*

The next morning Daniels felt like writing a letter to someone about the evening. *But who would understand?* he wondered. He decided to address it to Alex, in the style Max-Pol used in writing his Cretan Chronicles. One character in his mind writing to another. In other words, he was writing to himself. He had to tell someone.

*

Yassas, Cousin Aleko! Feliz Navidad!

I know it's still August, but last night I went to a Christmas party with Alice at a classy Spanish restaurant. The party was for just the two of us. Alice's idea. She made the arrangements. She said we might never be together at Christmas, so tonight was the night.

Alice looked delicious. White hair slicked back in a bun, with a red rose pinned in it - Gypsy flamenco style. A tight, black dress, loose and frilly from the knees down - for dancing. (Nice figure - very sexy).

She was also wearing her Spanish persona - the one she adopted when she lived in Spain during her college years. "Pilar Azul Pujol" was the name she gave herself then, and that's the name she used last night. And she still speaks enough Spanish to converse with the waiter and the bartender at the restaurant with a slightly lispy accent, Barcelona style.

I was anxious before the band kicked off. What if we couldn't dance well together? Even good dancers often can't. At least not at first.

But this woman can DANCE! And since I'm not so bad myself, we were on the floor every time the band played. Salsa, rumba, samba, and even tango. An instant fit on the dance floor is rare. It's never happened to me before. What a rush! What a dancer she is!

I should have known when I saw her shoes - unmatched as usual - leather - one red and one black. Dancer's shoes - medium-heeled, strap over the instep, and leather soles. Women who wear shoes like that haven't come to watch.

It's not just that she follows well when she dances. She adds little decorative moves of her own - a turn of her hand, a lift of her leg at the end of a step, a sideways look with her face, a tilt of her head, some saucy hip action. When she lets go and whirls away she comes back exactly in step. Her whole body is a complement to the dance and her partner.

I got to watch her from the sidelines a few times, because several of the best male dancers took notice and asked her to dance. She made them all look good, especially when it came to the tango, which is hard if you haven't practiced with your partner before. She's an intuitive follower.

In sum, I had the trophy lady of the evening as my guest. Alice declared it was a week before Christmas. Feliz Navidad!

We both brought presents.

I gave her a tiny turtle shell and a small, black-and-white-striped stone. In honor of the trip you and Alice

made to the beach at Kolymbari. She had brought her Possibles Bag and put the shell and the stone in it. She said she would tell me a story about each one sometime.

Her present to me was a typical Alice surprise. A very fine set of the classic cups-and-balls used by magicians. In a velvet-lined case were three silver cups and a small piece from a broken mirror instead of a ball. She said the mirror was a fragment of the looking-glass that Lewis Carroll's Alice had walked through.

She put the mirror under one of the cups and then moved the cups around like an expert sleight-of-hand hustler. When she asked me to guess which cup the mirror was under, I picked the middle one and I was right.

She did it again and I was right again.

One more time - and I chose the correct one.

She said she could read my mind and control my thoughts.

I tried three more times - and was right every time! Then she smiled her enigmatic smile and said that three times out of three twice in a row was a sign of very good luck. But I'm a skeptic, you know, and her self-confident smile was suspicious.

I picked up each cup, and there was a piece of mirror under each one.

"It was a trick," I said.

She replied, "No, it's magic. You can't lose with me."

I thought you'd like to know that Alice hasn't changed a bit.

Merry Christmas, Feliz Navidad
Max-Pol

*

Daniels reread his letter several times.

"I imagine that Max-Pol is very happy," he said.

"And so am I."

337

THE PLAY (5)

ACT II: Add and Subtract

SCENE 2. Giraffe Concerns

Director's notes:
Afternoon. Alice-Alice and Daniels are in the tree boats.
Alex and Alice are invisibly present in the shadows. Impro-
vise off opening remark from Alice-Alice.

*

"My giraffe has chicken pox," said Alice-Alice.
  "That's nothing. My chicken has giraffe pox," said Daniels.
  She laughed. "That's about as short as an improv gets."
  "Small chicken," said Daniels.
  "Stop it. Change subject. Dog, tell me about being a writer."
  "But it's a talking chicken," said Daniels. "Don't you want to know
what it says?"
  "No. You're avoiding what I do want to know. Come on, I talked
about being an actress. Fair's fair. Tell me about being a writer,"
she said.

(Silence.)

  "Come on. Tell me anything. Please."
  He looked at her with resignation, as one might turn credentials
over to an arresting authority when there was no choice - when refusal
might have unwanted consequences.
  "This will be an improvisation of another kind. Pretty random. I
usually evade talking about writing. I don't think of myself as a writer.
Not in the same sense that you think of yourself as an actress. I didn't
prepare to be a writer the way you've trained to be an actress. I would
never give a public lecture about writing.
  "In a way, words on paper are only the evidence of what I am and
the life I've led. Like shavings on the floor of a workshop. The shadows
of a man in motion. Or ashes from a campfire that burned brightly and

338

well. Words are the by-product of the story factory in my head."

He thought for a moment, and continued.

"There's a mirror out in one corner of my garden. One of those huge, old hallway entrance mirrors - left over from remodeling my house. It's angled so that it seems to be the entrance to somewhere else. It's been out there so long that it's weather-beaten and dirty, and the silver is coming off the back. It has a cloudy vagueness about it. You cannot see yourself sharply in it. But I know how to walk through it.

"I replaced it in the house with a flexible Mylar fun-house mirror. One that can be bent and set in different shapes so that sometimes you look tall, sometimes wide, sometimes short, and sometimes deformed. I can walk through that mirror too."

(Pause.)

"I'm my primary audience. I write for me. And most of what I put down on paper is a private performance - only because I don't need anybody else to appreciate it, and don't want to try to explain what's going on. What I write can seem a little weird."

"Like how weird? Give me some weirdness," said Alice-Alice.

"Well, for example, when I was younger I used to write ransom notes from imaginary kidnappers of imaginary people - demanding outlandish things, like a ton of chocolate bunnies. And I wrote notes to be given to tellers when I robbed a bank or a toy store. I still have some of the notes.

"And there's an accumulation somewhere of secret formulas. They look good - just like serious equations - but they're meaningless non-sense."

"What else?"

"I've written notes, put them in bottles, and tossed them into the sea. And I can tell you the story of who found them and what happened next. Same thing with notes tied to balloons I've released. Or notes I've tied to trees or left on park benches and trains. I never know what re-ally happens to the notes. But I can imagine. I can tell you the rest of the story."

"So," said Alice-Alice, "that's what the Dedication to your novel is about. It *is* a literary device. A note in a bottle thrown into the sea. You wrote it and imagined what would become of it. You had a story - you just hadn't written it down. And then I showed up. The real deal walked out of your looking-glass, carrying your note. Surprise!"

"You could say that."
"I *did* say it. It's true, isn't it? The *last* thing you expected was *me*."
He hesitated.
"Maybe."

"If you want to press the point, it's more accurate to say that I was open to any possibility. I just hadn't considered all the possibilities. The whole novel is about surprise. So - I got surprised. That's the best part.

"Just because I don't see something coming doesn't mean that what comes is unwelcome. It just takes a little time to adjust. Oddly enough, when you write fiction, it must be plausible and credible. Reality, on the other hand, often isn't."

"That's a little vague. A little abstract, don't you think?"

"Yes. I'm avoiding a straight answer. No, Alice, I wasn't expecting *you*. Or anybody *like* you." He reached over and caught her hand in his, bridging the distance between them in the tree boats. "But you . . ."

(Silence.)

"Is that enough about being a writer?" Daniels asked.
"No, keep going. What else?"
"If you insist."
"I insist."

"I've written reams of nonsense verse. And nonsense recipes for non-sense dishes and meals. That's why I like old Edward Lear so much - he could let his mind run free. He attached his destiny to whimsy and pulled his toy on a string behind him across the world. He allowed foolishness and delight free rein. But he always still had the rein of real-ity firmly in hand."
"Anything else?"
"Lists. I have lists of the contents of closets that don't exist. And love letters between people who never met in person. And instructions for how to assemble devices that won't work even if put together as de-scribed. And there's more. This is the Loony Division of David Daniels

340

Doggett, Inc. It's one way I keep my restless mind from boiling over."
He fell silent and looked away.

"Don't stop."

"Well . . . part of the writing comes from reading. I read my way through the Encyclopedia Britannica when I was in high school - and also the yellow pages of the telephone book - a thesaurus or two, several rhyming dictionaries, and too many books of quotations to count."

"Keep going."

"I once planned to read every English word in existence, and got up to *R* in the complete Oxford English Dictionary. Someday I'll finish that task, though there's a supplement of new words from time to time, and I'm losing ground. I used to write down all the words I liked for one reason or another, but I've stopped doing that. I don't know why.

"Don't think I'm obsessive-compulsive. These habits come and go in a haphazard way. My head is like a construction site on wheels. I have a collection of titles for books I'll never write. I don't have to write them. I can imagine the whole book. It's usually a book I wouldn't want to read anyhow."

He laughed.

"Give me some examples," she said.

"Tango Lessons for Satyrs. Travel Guide for Imaginary States. Macaroni for Myrtle - the Opera. A sequel to *The Orient Express* - The Occidental Service Station. The Cow Did It. Words for What Cannot Be Said. What the Tree Thought. Great Zen After-Dinner Speeches. Stuff like that."

"Oh," she said. "I'd at least pick up the book and look at it, wondering what-the-hell kind of mind was at work."

(Pause.)

"All of this - all of it - is just part of a passion for words and language and ideas. That's the biggest part of being a writer - loving ideas - loving words - respecting imagination - loving stories."

"Dog, everything you've told me so far is fascinating. But it's safe. Let me ask you a serious question. One with danger in it. May I?"

"Well . . ."

"Trust me. I trusted you."

"Ask me."

"What do you risk, Dog? What's at stake?"

"What do you mean?"

"When an actor or director steps into a play, the first question is, What does the main character want? The second question is, What will he or she risk to get that? And the next question is, What will be gained or lost by taking the risk? Those are life questions as well. I think I already know the answer to the first one. Answer the other two: what do you risk, and what's at stake?"

(Silence.)

"Madness. I risk madness. Going crazy. Most mornings I get up out of bed and step into a pit - a wild-animal trap. The pit is me. And I spend the rest of the day trying to write my way out of the pit on a ladder of words.

"Children are taught that 'Sticks and stones can break your bones, but words can never hurt you.' Not true. Words can destroy your mind or break your heart or take you on dangerous trips. Words and sentences and paragraphs can destroy you. Imagination can kill you. Or make you wish you were dead.

"Sometimes I feel like I'm driving a wagon pulled by six wild horses down a steep hill. Only luck prevents a disastrous spill at the bottom.

"There's a card in front of my computer that says, 'It's fiction. Invent anything.' If you give yourself permission to unlock your inhibitions and live in your mind on the other side of the mirror, it can be very hard to come back to the world of telephones and bills and real people and even trees.

"The world I invent is usually more exciting, more interesting, and more rewarding than the so-called real world. What *might* happen - what *could* happen - is always more satisfying than what did or does happen. That's Aristotle's notion, actually. 'A probable impossibility is preferable to an improbable possibility.'

"I can make things *be* by thinking them up. I can exist on that. There are many people in asylums who would understand and agree."

(Silence.)

"I know," said Alice-Alice. "I know what you mean. Being in the theater is like that. Sometimes I'm so far into a play . . . so far . . . I don't want the curtain to ever come down. I want that life to continue. Sometimes I feel like staying in costume and character and spending the night in the greenroom, ready to go right on when everybody else shows up for the next performance."

"What's real? That's the Wonderland question," said Daniels. "Or which reality do you prefer? We operate on memory and desire more than reality. What did you do yesterday? And the day before that? And the same day a week ago? Do you really remember? Or do you re-fabricate your life?

"Would you rather live in dreams or be awake? If you can't keep the lines of the braid of your life straight, you can tie your mind in permanent knots. People will say you're crazy and shun you. So that's the answer to your question about 'stakes:' Sanity is at risk. Sanity is an improvisation."

(Pause.)

"You're pretty good at improvisation, Dog," said Alice-Alice. "You know how to play."

"I hadn't thought of it that way until you came along. But it's true - I can make up a story from very little stimulation - something I see or hear or read or smell. It's an ability like dreaming - no training, no planning, and not much control over what happens. Not a skill I've learned or practiced. My brain just does it. So I let it. There are many ways to tell the truth.

"Being an arborist balances the equation. The work is made of facts and hands-on tasks. A chain saw tearing through a limb is real. A 'tree guy' has to be sane and rational and competent. Or he falls and breaks his neck."

(Silence.)

"The idea of multiple personalities doesn't seem far-fetched to me.

There's the public 'me' and all the other people in my head. I suppose the difference between being certifiably crazy and reasonably sane is the ability to keep the crowd in your mind from getting out of control. But if you can do that, you're never alone – you always have lively company."

He stopped talking and lay back on the pillow in his tree boat. Alice-Alice remained silent, her eyes closed. Leaves rustled in the light breeze. Two blue jays shrieked at each other somewhere in the branches above. A ferry blew three blasts on its horn as it departed the dock on the waterfront far below. Waves rose out on the bay, roiled on, and disappeared.

Daniels sat up. "Alice, you must think I *am* mad."

She sat up, swung her legs off the edge of her tree boat, put one hand on his knee and the other on her head. "Me? An actress? Me? The woman who walked into your novel? Dog, there are enough personalities in my head to fill a stadium. Nobody is one person. Everybody is a group. And everybody is a character in somebody else's play.

"You're not normal – that's true. But *normal* is for sissies, Dog.

"The only difference between us is that you put some of your people on paper and I play some of mine onstage. Success is keeping your people working, not milling around. You need the Imagination Police in your mind for crowd control.

"The dumbest advice anybody ever gets is to 'Just be yourself.' In the first place, you can't ever be anything else. You *can't* be anybody else but you. The only question is, 'Which self shall I be at this moment?'"

"And which self are you now?" asked Daniels.

"I'm a restless person who wants to take a break from talking."

"We could go down and walk or get some dinner. What would you like to do? I'm easy."

"Dog, could I climb around in the tree on my own?"

"No. Too dangerous. You don't have that much experience, and we're way too high. If you fell . . ."

"But I don't want to always just sit here in the tree boat."

"Well . . . OK. I can show you how to use a short safety line, and then I'll rig another line and belay you when you move. Since we're about as far *up* as you should go, it would be best if you climbed *down*. Think of it as a training exercise. Trust me. It's not as easy as it looks."

"I still trust you, Dog," she said. "Rig me up."

Going Down

When the gear was in place, Alice-Alice crawled out of the tree boat, straddled a large limb, and inched along caterpillar-style out and away from the trunk of the tree.

"Grab that limb above you, stand up, and then when you're ready, lean out and lift your feet and hang free so you feel what it's like to depend only on your strap and my belay," said Daniels.

Oh my god, she thought as she dangled in space, her heart pounding, her brain yelling, *I'm going to die!*

Daniels spoke in a calm, even voice, "If you're not scared, you shouldn't be out there. And if you can't figure out what to do now to recover safely, you shouldn't be climbing. So what are you going to do? Don't do it - just tell me."

(Silence.)

"Don't be foolishly proud. Do you want to stop climbing?" he asked.

"No. I'm thinking about what to do next."

"And?"

"If I pull up on my safety line and make myself swing a little, I can reach the branch below me - but you'll have to let off on the belay a little when I do."

"Sounds good. Do it."

She swung. He gave her slack. And she reached the branch, knelt on it, grabbed a nearby limb, and sat down.

"OK. I did it and I'm not shaking."

"If you were shaking I'd make you quit. Ready to go on?"

"Yes. I can get down to the next big limb from here."

"Go ahead," he said. "But first catch the end of this safety line and hook it around the limb you're standing on. Then release the safety line you were using."

Alice-Alice climbed down the tree slowly, breathing hard, talking to herself, *Move out to those branches . . . back off that limb onto the next one . . . move the line . . . move back toward the trunk . . ."*

When she reached the last large limb ten feet above the ground, she relaxed and unhooked her safety line. Stepping further out on the limb to look up at Daniels, she lost her balance and fell backwards.

Too surprised to scream, she grabbed desperately at the limb, lost her grip and fell until Daniel's belay line went taught. She swung like a pendulum and slammed into the trunk of the tree.

"Unnhh!" she moaned, as the breath was knocked out of her. As she bounced back out into space, Daniels shouted, "Feet! Feet first! Feet first!"

As she swung back toward the trunk, she managed to put her feet out to cushion the impact, bent her knees as she struck, and hung limply from the rope.

"Don't move. Relax. I've got you," said Daniels. "Are you OK?"

"I . . . don't . . . know," she whispered, weeping.

"You're only a few feet above the ground. Push away a little from the tree. I'm going to let you down very slowly until you can stand. Tell me when your feet reach the ground."

"I'm there."

"I'm still holding you up. When I slack off, try to stand up on your own."

"I can, but now I *am* shaking. I think I'm OK. I'm just scared."

"Unhook from the belay, then sit down, and if you feel faint, lie down. I'll be right there."

Alice-Alice did as she was told. Wiping her tears on her shirtsleeve, she took several deep breaths and lay down on the ground. Safe.

Looking up into the tree, she saw Daniels swiftly rappelling down his rope as if he was free falling, acrobatically bouncing off the trunk of the tree with his feet as he came.

"Lie still," he commanded when she started to sit up.

"I'm really OK. I'll be all right," she said.

"I'll feel better if you'll let me check you out."

Though Alice-Alice didn't think she was hurt, she submitted to his examination with curious pleasure. It had been some time since a man had tenderly run his hands up and down her legs and arms.

He lightly squeezed her ankles and knees. "Does that hurt?" he asked.

"No . . . the truth is. . . it feels nice. Do you always fondle your trainees when they fall?"

"Only the pretty ones," he said.

"Shall I faint so you'll have to carry me away in your arms?"

"If you faint I'll call 911."

"Forget fainting. Take me to lunch," she said.

Laughing, he said, "You're on. But first, tell me if that scared you off tree-climbing. Would you go up again?"

"Yes. But only with you."

"Let's sit here for a while. I have some food in my knapsack. Cheese, apples, peanuts, and chocolate. OK?" he asked.

"And there's that bottle of water from Delphi," she said.

They shared the food and the water and idle chit-chat.

Leaning back against the trunk of the tree, shoulder to shoulder, contented, carefully not talking of serious matters - like falling out of trees.

"Oh," said Alice-Alice.

"Are you OK?" asked Daniels.

"Yes. I just remembered something. Hand me my knapsack."

Untying the drawstring, she rummaged around inside.

"Here it is. Close your eyes."

"Now look."

On the end of her forefinger was a tiny, four-armed elephant. Yellow, with a red hat. A rubber finger puppet.

"Lord Ganesha," he said. "The Hindu God."

"Worshipped as one who subdues detrimental forces. I keep him in my Possibles Bag, which I brought in my knapsack. He was here. He kept me from getting hurt."

"I would like to think it was the safety belay."

"That's what an arborist would conclude."

"Well, having four hands and a trunk would be useful."

"Imagine that," she said, and laughed.

THE PLAY (6)

ACT II: Add and Subtract

SCENE 3. Rashomon

Director's notes:
This is a flashback. A scene from the novel.
A scene Daniels did not write.
The scene serves the play as a perspective on truth.
(Beware. This is complicated and tricky. Think about it.)

It is winter, two years before. In Kyoto. Alice, using the name Sanaa; and Zenkichi, the Kabuki actor. They have only recently met and are alone together for the first time. He has invited her to a film festival to see a digitally restored version of Akira Kurosawa's classic film, *Rashomon*.
They slowly walk from stage left to stage right, pausing, walking on, and talking *before* they see the film. Lights out.
They walk back from stage right to stage left, talking *after* seeing the film.
Curtain.

*

"Zenkichi-san, I'll answer a question you have not asked," says Sanaa. "The answer is 'three times.' Once during my sophomore year in college in California - with English subtitles. Once during my junior year abroad in Spain - with Spanish subtitles. And once last year in the original Japanese. I bought the video, along with *Ikiru* and *Seven Samurai*. I think I've seen all of Kurosawa's films."

"Impressive. Have you ever watched *Rashomon* with the sound turned off?" asks Zenkichi.

"No, but I suppose you have - to study the actor's body language."

"*Hai*. Many times. Because the acting is so rooted in traditional Kabuki. It's brilliant. I've added small touches from *Rashomon* to my own

350

roles. Sometimes I stop the video and consider the way a character is standing, and then observe myself in a mirror in the same pose."

"I've never studied *Rashomon* in a serious way," says Sanaa. "Not as a work of art. I don't know *about* it - I've just watched it - experienced it. Tell me anything you think I should know before I see it again."

"Do you know the roots of the stories?" asks Zenkichi.

"Vaguely, but remind me."

"The film is based on two short stories by Akutagawa Ryunosuke, who died by his own hand at age thirty-five in 1927. Those stories were created from tales from the Hein period - eighth to twelfth centuries. So the roots are old and deep. Kurosawa's film weaves the stories together but is faithful to them."

"If I remember correctly," says Sanaa, "there's a woodcutter, a bandit, a husband and wife - and one other."

"The priest," says Zenkichi.

"Oh, yes, the priest. Remind me of the plot."

"At the heart of the film is one story told four times in four different ways. There have been an attack, a rape, and a murder. In the bandit's tale, he admits killing the man. In the man's wife's tale, she admits killing her husband. And the ghost of the husband says he killed himself.

"The only eyewitness, the woodcutter, is an admitted liar. And the priest, who relates the stories of the bandit, the husband and the wife, is only recounting what he's heard, not what he saw.

"Somebody is lying. Maybe everybody," says Sanaa.

"Correct, and the question is, What is the truth?"

"But it's not a simple whodunit," says Sanaa.

"No, it's more about what is real."

"The film won big awards," says Sanaa.

"First place, The Golden Lion at Venice in 1951 - and the American Academy Award for Best Foreign Film, and many others. It has a permanent place as one of the ten all-time-best Japanese films. Some say *Rashomon* and *Seven Samurai* tie for *ichiban* - number one. The film has been studied and analyzed and criticized intensely. Still, it survives unscathed. Still provoking people's minds.

"Enough talk - let's go see it."

(lights fade out to black, then fade up to dim)

"Every time I see the film it's like I'm seeing it for the first time," says Sanaa. "And I keep wishing some Western-style, super detective would come along and reconcile the stories, straighten everything out, and nail the real culprit once and for all."

"That would not be Japanese. You've read too much Sherlock Holmes and Agatha Christie," replies Zenkichi. "The meaning of the film lies in the fact that the truth about what really happened is not only *not* resolved, it *cannot* be resolved. Ambiguity is the spine of the film.

"*All* the stories were *believed to be true* by those who told them. They didn't lie to protect themselves. Each acknowledged the murder, but they all told the story the way they saw it. They believed what they told. Like all eyewitnesses, they added themselves to what they experienced."

"So the issue is not truth, but reality. Each person commits to an illusion. And anyone who views or studies the film is free to come to their own conclusions about truth versus reality. In sum, truth is relative."

"But . . . but . . .," protests Sanaa. "That's such a *pessimistic* view – a hopeless view – pure old angst."

"Hai, but you can make a strong argument for it. Formal Western philosophy has, and Buddhism makes the same case. The insistence that there is only one version of reality is what, in fact, divides and isolates human beings from one another. The big contradiction."

(Sanaa stops and faces Zenkichi. Holds him by his coat collar.)

"*You*, Zenkichi, *may* be an illusion. And this street and this dark night and this world and those stars – *all an illusion*. Maybe. But if these are my illusions, then I'm responsible for having good ones and maintaining them in good order. And I'm responsible for populating my illusive world with people who share my illusions. That's *my* reality. It all may be one big play, but I am an actress in it.

"If there's no difference between illusion and reality, then it's a stupid distinction. Ordinary human beings like you and me must operate *as if* it this were not true. The 'as if' cuts through the philosophical smoke."

(Zenkichi shrugs his shoulders and nods. Ambiguously.)

(They walk on in silence.)

"Well, it's still a provocative film," says Sanaa. "Beautifully made. I never get tired of looking at it. But now I have the illusion that I'm cold and hungry."

"Would you like to have the illusion of eating food and drinking fine sake, and the illusion of sitting by a warm fire? *As if* those things were real, of course." He laughs.

"Zenkichi, close your eyes and stand still."

(Sanaa wraps her arms around his neck and kisses him passionately on the lips.)

"That never happened," she says. "An illusion."

Zenkichi says, "Close your eyes, and stand still."

(He kisses her just as passionately.)

"Oh . . . that happened," she says.

"Really?" he says, laughing.

"A kiss is still a kiss; a sigh is just a sigh; the fundamental things apply, as time goes by," she sings.

"I know that movie too," he says. *"Casablanca."*

She takes his arm.

"Come on," she says. "Let me tell you about a game."

"What is it?"

"It's called Left/Right/Surprise."

SECOND INTERMISSION

Monday.

Once again the stage is dark and empty.

Daniels has gone to Portland to testify in a court case involving trees on property adjoining the city's Japanese garden. While he is there, he will attend to a historic cedar tree damaged by the collapse of a construction crane. He will not return to Seattle until Friday or Saturday.

*

"Jellyfish," says Alice-Alice, pointing.
    "Octopus," she says. "And another jellyfish."

She is sitting beside a thin, hollow-eyed little boy in a hallway of a hospital clinic. The walls of the hallway are being taped and plastered before being repainted. The repair work has left cloud-like smears of vague shapes on the pale blue walls.
    "Starfish," she says, pointing.

The little boy beside her is morose and silent. His mother stands nearby, twisting a handkerchief in her hands, staring out a window.

"And maybe Donald Duck," says Alice-Alice.
    "No. Donald Duck can't live under water," says the little boy.
"He would die."

Now Alice-Alice is silent and still.
Die, she thinks.
The word she *doesn't* want to think about.
Die.
The word she was avoiding by looking for sea creatures on the wall.

The little boy looks up at her and asks, "Are you gonna die too?"

She had been awake most of Sunday night. Every time she moved, she felt as if she had been stabbed in the lower back with an ice pick.

When she needed to get up to go to the bathroom, she could not sit up. With difficulty she rolled over onto her stomach, slid backwards off the bed onto her knees, and crawled slowly into the bathroom, wincing and stopping every few feet.

Tears dripped from her chin.

Her shoulders and elbows and neck hurt, and even a cautious move would be suddenly arrested by the ice pick driving deep into her spine again.

In sloth-like slow motion she managed to use the toilet, take some ibuprofen, fill the bathtub with hot water, and get into the tub still wearing her nightgown.

By midmorning she was at the hospital.

Waiting.

*

Alice-Alice was doing exactly what she promised herself she would never do: spend the coin of her life in the hospital vending machine, trying to buy time. She had left the hospital after recovering from surgery knowing there was a possibility that breast cancer was already metastasizing.

She accepted that. She had not planned on coming back.

She knew her kind of cancer was usually aggressive and invasive. And she knew that lower back pain was a bad sign. But she had not expected to hurt so much so soon.

Too soon, she thought, *Too soon.*

She told herself that all she wanted now was confirmation of her condition, and enough strong pain medication to endure what must be endured. Further surgery, chemotherapy and radiation were not an option, no matter what the doctors might diagnose or prescribe.

No. All she wanted was a bottle of little white tickets for a ride out.

*

The week went by.

Hospital. Home. Hospital. Home. Hospital.

Waiting.

Blood tests, X-rays, and a bone scan.

She waited, fogbound in the still waters of her mind.

Waiting. Waiting. And waiting.

Friday. Verdict day.

She sat in her oncologist's office.

She was not afraid of what the doctor would tell her. And in fact, oddly enough, she felt much better in general. A few days of doing nothing but sleeping and eating and sitting still in the gentle euphoria provided by her pain pills had revived her spirits. By moving carefully, she had avoided even the stabbing pain in her back. How peculiar to feel good the day she expected to get a death sentence.

*

Her doctor came in and sat down in a chair beside her. Alice-Alice liked and trusted this woman. She had always been honest and straight-forward with her, and she always spoke in plain English, not evasive medical terms.

The doctor seemed nervous - her slight smile hesitant.

"Alice-Alice, what I have to tell you may be difficult for you to accept under the circumstances." She smiled. "When you came in you assumed the worst. I wasn't so sure, but I couldn't rule it out, and I didn't want to take any chances. We did all the tests to be certain.

"And the simple truth is . . . there is *no* evidence - *none* whatsoever that we can find - that you have cancer *anywhere* in your body."

"What?"

"No. *None.*"

Tears welled in Alice-Alice's eyes.

"But why . . . why . . . hurt . . . so much . . . my back?" she whispered.

"I honestly don't know. I hate to admit it, but we may have overlooked something obvious - something simple - something I would have looked for if I were a family physician seeing you for the first time.

"I should have asked you what you had been doing recently that might account for muscle or ligament sprain - any kind of stressful physical activity out of the ordinary. If you had suddenly taken up roller skating or tennis or rowing, for example. And so I'll ask you the obvious question - what *have* you been doing?"

Alice-Alice thought for a moment, then smiled.

"Climbing trees."

"Climbing . . . trees? Really?"

"Yes. Climbing trees. Big trees. And I fell coming down - not a bad fall - a friend was belaying me and I banged into some branches and the trunk of the tree. Not even a bruise or a cut."

"Climbing trees?" said the doctor again, and began laughing.

"You mean . . . .," said Alice-Alice, laughing.

"I mean . . .," said the doctor, and still laughing she went to the door, opened it, and called to her nurse, "Ellie, come in here. You won't believe this. We have our first case of Tree-Climbing-itis."

"What?"

"Yes. Come look."

*

"What did you mean when you said I might have difficulty accepting your diagnosis?" asked Alice-Alice.

"All of us - doctors included - can get attached to an illness. We expect certain outcomes based on statistics and evidence and experience. We amplify our expectations. Your body's antennae have been tuned to the Cancer Channel. And so have mine. This is a cancer clinic, after all.

"If the doctor is wrong or off course, and in the process misses the obvious, then the patient may have a hard time accepting a less-than-dire diagnosis.

"Given your expectations, and despite our appraisal, it would be perfectly understandable if you decided to go elsewhere and get another opinion based on a whole new battery of diagnostic tests."

Alice-Alice barely heard her.

"You really mean that my problem is . . . falling out of a tree?"

"It's not that simple, Alice-Alice. We talked around this before your surgery, but now I'll be direct. You're an actress, so let me put it in your terms. For most of your life you've been playing out a script in which you will die of cancer before you're forty.

"Actually, that's not quite accurate. Your life script calls for you to take your own life rather than die of a prolonged fight with a disease. You and I both know that's the way you've written the last act."

Alice looked away, out the office window.

"I must say that up to now you've acted your part with rare dignity and courage. But the script must be changed now. Your script must be rewritten for you to *live*, not die.

"In fact, all things considered, because of your prophylactic surgery and what we have learned with all these tests, you have as much chance of getting breast cancer again as you have of getting hit by lightning.

"Of course, people *do* get hit by lightning, though I've read that only 20 percent of the people who get hit by lightning actually die. Simply said, the odds have shifted dramatically in your favor.

"Of course, you may get hit by a truck tomorrow or die in some other unpredictable way. But very unlikely because you have breast cancer. And, if I'm right, and I feel very confident that I am, then you can stop thinking about ending your own life any time soon."

(Silence.)

"I had planned on dying," said Alice-Alice. "Sooner rather than later."

"Change your plans," said the doctor. "Change your plans.

"And I don't say that like it's a simple thing to do. Because adjusting to such a radical mind-shift can be difficult. Good news can be as hard to handle as bad news. You may even get depressed for a while, so stay in touch, will you? Come see me in a month, no matter how you feel. It would be useful to me to know how you are, and it will probably be useful to you to talk about it."

Alice-Alice took a deep breath, sighed, smiled, and said, "I don't know what to say, but I'll come back in a month. Anything else?"

"Give your body time to recover - rest and time and ibuprofen or Percocet. Get a massage two or three times. And stay out of trees until you're in better shape. Work out regularly at a gym for a while before you start climbing trees again."

"That's it? That's really all?" asked Alice-Alice.

"That's it," the doctor said, and stood up. "Meeting adjourned."

When Alice-Alice saw the tears trickling down the doctor's face, she put her arms around her and hugged her. The doctor hugged her back.

"You know," said the doctor, "I have a lot of experience with negative outcomes. An oncologist is trained to give bad news in a calm, thoughtful, supportive way. Death is my specialty. Almost every day I go home knowing I've had to tell someone their disease is terminal. I guess I'm a little unprepared for pronouncing a *life* sentence. I don't usually cry, but I'm as relieved as you are."

As she was going out the office door, Alice-Alice stopped and turned back to the doctor.

"I already know what I'll tell you a month from now. I've been determined to have a meaningful life as long as I lived, even if I wasn't going to live long. Nothing's changed. Now I have a ticket for an extended trip. Frequent Flyer Miles."

"With an upgrade to First Class," said the doctor, wiping her eyes and grinning.

As Alice-Alice walked away down the hallway, she glanced at the unpainted wall. The little boy was gone. She sent a thought after him: *Donald Duck. Ducks float. And fly.*

*

When she got home, Alice-Alice bent carefully to pick up her guitar, walked slowly into the kitchen, sat down and cradled her instrument. She tried to play, but could not.

She began weeping, then sobbing.

"I wasn't prepared for this," she bawled.

When the storm passed, tears and mucus and saliva had drooled and smeared over her face and hands and her guitar.

"What a mess," she said, reaching for a kitchen towel.

Relieved and mopped up, she began playing a song she had not yet finished.

> Sweet Sunday morn abide.
> Extra bacon on the side.
> Coffee in my coffee cup.
> Eggs be sunny side and up.

Short the life, but wide.

She played the verse again, but no new words came.

"That's it, then," she said.

"Onward."

SECOND REHEARSAL

Director's notes:
Another flashback. Again a scene from the novel.
Again a scene Daniels did not write, but might have.
The scene serves the play as perspective on granting wishes.
(Again, beware. This is also complicated and tricky. Think about it.)

Alice and Alex stand facing one another far upstage, lit by a single spotlight at half. The rest of the stage is dark and empty. They first try the dialogue wearing white, neutral masks. Then they remove the masks and play the scene solemnly. Then they try again and again, until they have moved to a lighter mood of Delight. Rethink. Combine versions until final form emerges.
Essential: The actors must shift the focus from playing *their* part exactly right to enabling the *other actor* to get their part exactly right. To enable the other is the main task.

*

ALICE
I've brought you a present.

ALEX
Show me.

ALICE
I can't - it's invisible.

ALEX
Tell me.

ALICE
It's a silver bowl –
small enough to fit into the palm of your hand.

ALEX
Any decoration on the bowl?

ALICE
Look carefully – you can see that a dragon has been engraved in
the silver.
The dragon runs all the way around the bowl.
But the image is faded by wear from being handled so many times.
It's a very old bowl.

ALEX
Is there anything in the bowl?

ALICE
Yes. Snow. Freshly fallen snow. Look.
The bowl was left outside last night.
There was no wind; the snow fell straight down,
and, as you can see, it formed a perfect cone.

ALEX
Where was the bowl when the snow fell?

ALICE
At the top of Mount Fuji in Japan.

ALEX
What shall I do with this gift?

ALICE
Wait until the snow melts.
Drink the water.
Make a wish.

ALEX
What shall I do with the empty bowl?

ALICE
Keep it until you find the right liquid to put in it.

ALEX
And then?

ALICE
Give it back to me.

ALEX
And you will drink it and make a wish?

ALICE
Yes.

ALEX
That is two wishes. What about the third wish?

ALICE
That's the hardest part.

ALEX
Will we share that wish too?
And drink from the same cup?

ALICE
Yes.
I like that.

ALEX
Do you have any idea what the wish might be?

ALICE
A wish to continue – a wish to go through and on.
And the wish shall be granted.

ALEX
I am not sure I understand.

ALICE
You will when the time comes.

ALEX
And will I be pleased or not?
Will I smile or frown?

ALICE
Smile.

ALEX
Promise?

ALICE
Trust me.

ALEX
I do.

THE PLAY (7)

ACT III: Hide and Seek

SCENE 1. The Floating World

Director's notes:
The action takes place in a private tatami room of the Japanese restaurant, Shibui. 8:00 p.m. Unscripted improvisation.

*

Daniels is ushered down a hallway by a kimono-clad Japanese hostess. "*Dozo*," she says, gesturing toward a bench where he can sit, remove his shoes, and place them alongside the un-matched, white leather pair already there.

He smiles when he looks more closely at the white shoes. He sees they have different landscapes painted on them. He picks them up to look more closely. One shoe features a duck floating on a pond, and the other shows a duck flying away.

The hostess kneels, and pulls back a shoji screen with graceful slowness, as if she is opening a smaller curtain on a smaller stage set, for a play-within-a-play.

The actress is already in place: Short black hair - eyes made up to seem almond shaped - black silk dress - scarlet shawl worn loose around her shoulders - and a touch of scarlet lipstick in the center of her lower lip. She sits still - unmoving - in a Kabuki actor's *mi-e* - the pose emphasizing the strength implicit in the role she is playing tonight.

Bowing in respect to her, he kneels down and sits back on his calves, Japanese style.

"Sake?" she asks.

"Dozo," he replies.

She pours from the stoneware bottle into a small, square, wooden box - the traditional rice measuring cup also used for drinking sake. He, in turn, pours sake for her - as the ritual prescribes.

"This is *junmai-daiginjo*," she says, "Super-premium sake made from pure Yamadanishiki rice; brewed with deep-spring water by Sudo Honke, established in 1141 and continued by fifty-five generations of the same family. It is exactly the same sake Zenkichi and Vin-cen-zo drank at the Perugia in Kyoto after their first motorcycle ride."

"I remember," he says. "But I didn't know you could get it here."

"Imagine that you can," she says.

He smiles, realizing he had slipped out of the improvisation. He bows now, and thanks her. "*Domo arigato gozaimashta.*"

She applauds.

"Nicely done," said Alice-Alice.

"You inspire me," he said.

They remain in the tatami room and continue to talk.

*

"You seem to know a great deal about tattoos, Dog - especially the invisible kind. Do you have one?" she asked.

"Yes. Mine is the most invisible tattoo of all, existing only in my imagination. I admire the traditional Japanese-style, full-body tattoos. I can't say why. Perhaps a psychoanalyst could help me understand, but that isn't necessary. No reason is required."

He studied her face. *Where is this going?* he wondered. *Why this reversal of roles? She's the one who is supposed to have the invisible tattoo and I should be asking her.*

"What does your tattoo look like?" she asked.

"It's hard to talk about. Since it's a manifestation of one's inner life, a Japanese might *display* the tattoo in special circumstances, but would never *explain* it. A fellow Japanese would know better than to ask, and a *gaijin* would not deserve a reply to such an impolite request."

"Ah, but you are not Japanese, and since you can't display it for me, I thought you might at least give me an idea . . . please," she said, with her most beguiling smile.

"I have a full-scale drawing. I'll show you sometime," he said.

"Come on. Just tell me a little. I do have an imagination."

He smiled. "If I do, will you show me or tell me about yours?"

"Yes. Cross my heart," she said, touching her chest.

"I'll hold you to that. My tattoo is three entwined figures on the back, wrapping around to the front: A ferocious lion-dog - yang; a peony - yin; and a phoenix - the symbol of re-creation. The phoenix is in flight, and its wings cover my shoulders and arms to the elbow."

"I can see it. Strong. Beautiful."

"I'll never get the actual tattoo or even the semi-visible one done with flesh-colored ink, because, as you point out, I'm not Japanese. Besides, there hasn't ever been anyone I wanted to display it for.

"I do have a suit of long, silk underwear printed with the full-body Japanese tattoo. Japanese movie actors use them for period films. I wear it sometimes when I'm writing. But it's a costume - not anything like my real tattoo."

"I'd like to see it on you sometime," she said.

"Maybe Halloween. What about your tattoo?"

"Wait, not yet. When you mentioned 'costume,' you reminded me of another question I keep forgetting to ask you," she said.

"Ask. But before that, sake, dozo?"

They poured for one another and drank.

"And the question is?"

"Do you really have a white rabbit suit - like the one in the novel?"

"I do."

"What's that about?"

"I rented one to play an Easter bunny for some neighbors' kids. And then, well, the White Rabbit got loose, so to speak. *Alice in Wonderland* and all that. So I bought one. My party suit. I've used it so often it's become my trademark outfit. But I'm not the only one. I'm the Big Bunny of the Friends of the White Rabbit."

"You mean other people with bunny suits? A secret society?"

"Yes. We do pranks together - a kind of affirmative vandalism - just for fun - 'Rabbit Runs' - just to add some lightness to the world around."

"Pranks? Like what?"

"Once we suited up and went down to bar at the 5 Spot Cafe for drinks on Valentine's Day. People don't expect to see the Easter bunny at a bar on Valentine's Day - especially if there are *five* of them. The other customers laughed. We had a good time. The bartender said bunnies came in all the time, but only he could see them. He said he didn't accept carrots for drinks - only cash. Several people in the bar offered to join us for whatever we were doing. We could have started a cult that night."

She raised her eyebrows. Smiled. "This sounds like something Alice would do. Are you making this up?"

"No, it's all true. Sometimes what I imagine becomes very real. We even have business cards - I'll give you one - and I can show you my bunny suit. In fact, I have an extra costume and . . . well . . . if you want to do a Rabbit Run, we will."

She laughed. "Sake, dozo," she said. They poured for one another.

"Here's to the Big Bunny," she said. "What else have the Friends of the White Rabbit done?"

"We wrote funny sayings in Latin and Greek in chalk on the sidewalk at bus stops. And we sang Christmas carols outside the window of a little girl who was hurt in an accident. That was in June. We brought Christmas presents too. Chocolate bunnies, of course."

"And?"

"And we picked an old, uncared-for tombstone in the cemetery, wrote a fictional biography of the deceased as if he had been the re-incarnation of a famous Tibetan lama and the creator of a martial art based on kitchen utensils - spoons, forks, spatulas, and egg beaters. We printed the biography, laminated it in plastic, and glued it to the stone. Then we made pilgrimages to the grave and left gifts of flowers and fruit and stuffed animals and trinkets and incense."

"That's a little over the edge," she said.

"Not really. Much to our astonishment, other people started leaving things at the memorial too. Mostly spoons. The spirit of the Unknown Lama has been brought into existence. Who knows why or what purpose it serves? Maybe it only makes people smile or provokes their imaginations. Not a bad thing to happen in a cemetery."

"Busy bunnies. What else have the White Rabbits done?"

"This one is really goofy. We went in costume into a pornography shop downtown and asked to buy anything involving animals, especially bunnies. That was funny. But the joke was on us. The clerk was

368

cool. They actually had some stuff. Girls in risqué rabbit outfits. And a customer asked us if we wanted to star in a movie he was making. Rabbits in the Raw!"

She shook her head in amused dismay. "Too much," she said.

"Well, there's still more. We ran through a friend's outdoor wedding - during the recessional. That was a big mistake. The mother of the bride is pissed off about it. Half the wedding pictures have big rabbits in them."

"Have you ever been up in the tree boats in your bunny suit?"

"No. But that's a great idea. I don't know why I never thought of it. We could do that, if you like."

"We should. You said you have an extra rabbit suit?"

"One just your size."

*

Alice-Alice had arrived early at the restaurant and ordered dinner, leaving the choices to the chef. A plate of hot *edamame* - salted soybeans - had been served with the sake, along with hot, damp towels to clean their hands.

Now their food came, one artfully displayed course at a time. Miso soup with small dishes of assorted pickles; *maguro* sashimi - raw tuna; tempura shrimp and vegetables, and salmon teriyaki. They ate slowly, talking mostly of the food and Japanese style.

"You handle *o-hashi* well," he said.

"Chopsticks? I got instruction and practiced my part," she said. "You should have seen the mess I made in the beginning."

When the meal was finished, she excused herself. When she returned from the restroom, she had refreshed her lipstick and her perfume.

"Smell," she said, holding out her wrist.

"Spicy, he said. "What's it called?"

"Rush, by Gucci. Ariadne Rush wears it when she auditions."

The waitress appeared with green tea and a plate of small pieces of *yokan* - bean jelly.

They drank their tea in comfortable silence; not as if the evening had run its course, but as if something was yet to happen.

She reached across the table and put her hand on top of his.

(Silence.)

"Dog, I have a serious question. It's about the end of Part Four of your novel. You don't have to answer if you don't want to."

He placed his other hand on top of hers.

"Let me guess. I suppose you want to know why Alice-of-the-novel was murdered. Or why the writer killed her off just when everything seemed about to have a happy ending. That's the question I'm always asked: Why did Alice have to die?"

She put her other hand on top of his, making the four-handed pile children make when playing a game. But this was no game.

Just then the waitress reappeared. They both smiled and unstacked their hands. "*Motto sake, kudasai,*" he said to the waitress. "*Hai.*" She withdrew to replenish the sake supply.

(Silence.)

"You're right. That's my question."

"Is the question connected to me? Or to you?" he asked.

"Both," she said.

"Well, then, as Alex would begin. If you read what authors say about writing novels, you'll find many of them claim that no matter what they intend, the characters will take over and write the story or at least a lot of it. I didn't believe it. And it wasn't true for me until the stories of Alex and Alice began to converge.

"At some point I stopped consciously constructing fiction and became so involved in the story that I simply recorded what happened. I felt like I was just a *witness*.

"Would you believe me if I said nobody was more surprised than I was when Alice died? But once I wrote it, I couldn't change it. *It is what happened.* Unexpected. Unpredicted. Unwelcomed. But real life is like that. Why not fiction? Alice was murdered. An accident. Accidents happen."

(Silence.)

"But then you just stopped writing? Leaving everything up in the air."

"Yes. And I confess that I wrote the dedication and the last few pages *after* I wrote everything else."

370

"So the dedication wasn't really a literary device so much as it was . . . what . . . a call for help?"

"You could say that. It's easy to get lost in your own mental jungle."

"And then those other women showed up."

"Yes. I thought I'd made a big mistake."

"Until . . . I came?"

"And brought Alice back to life, in your own way," he said.

"You weren't expecting that."

"No . . . you . . . changed . . . everything."

"So now what?"

The waitress returned with a fresh bottle of sake and porcelain cups.

Daniels looked at Alice-Alice with his eyebrows raised. Turned his face away. Turned back to her. "Sake, dozo."

She poured for him. He emptied his cup with one swallow, and placed the cup by the bottle to be filled again.

He's had a lot of sake, she thought. *Maybe I should back off.*

"So now what?" he said, repeating her question.

He emptied his cup again.

"That's a third question, Alice. What about the other half of what I asked? What about you? What's your connection to Alice's death?"

"Do you remember that when I came that first night to see you I said I had the invisible tattoo?"

"Yes, I asked how I could be sure."

"And I said it was invisible - you couldn't see it. But that wasn't the whole truth. If we weren't in this restaurant, I'd be bold enough to take off my blouse and show you the visible part - red scars from a recent, double mastectomy - scars I wish could be turned into something beautiful - like Alice did with her birthmark."

(Silence.)

"And then I would tell you about the invisible scars on my mind and soul - made out of the fear and anger and despair I've tattooed on myself - by assuming I would not live long, and pretending I could handle that somehow and beat death out the door of life before it got a grip on me and sucked all the juice out of me like a spider drains a fly.

"I wanted to bring Alice back to life because I didn't want to die."

Trembling, Daniels reached out with both hands and took hers in his.

"My god, my god," he whispered. "Are you dying?"

She could see his eyes filling with tears.

She reversed their hands, taking his in hers.

"No."

"*No?*"

She held his hands tighter.

"No. I'm not dying. I won't die. Not anytime soon. I found out yesterday. Surprise! I'm clear of cancer. I thought I might not even be here when you came back from Portland. I went to the doctor to confirm that the pain in my back and arms and shoulders meant the cancer had metastasized.

"If it had, I would have . . . disappeared. But do you know what the problem turned out to be? It's all your fault, actually."

Dumbly, Daniels shook his head.

"Tree climbing. And falling out of the tree."

Daniels shook his head again. "You mean . . . when you came to find me . . . and all the time we've spent together . . . you thought you were *dying*? I . . . don't know . . . what . . . to say."

Tears ran down his cheeks.

Alice-Alice reached up and touched his tears.

"Don't say anything. Believe it. They did all the tests and found nothing. *Nothing*. All the pain was from falling out of the stupid tree. I'm planning on being alive for a while."

Daniels wiped his tears away with his hands. She gave him some tissues from her purse. He blew his nose. Composed himself. Sighed.

"Sorry. I didn't see that coming," he said.

"I'm touched," she said. "Touched and a little surprised."

He shrugged, and smiled. "Well, men do cry sometimes, you know. At least I didn't hiccup." He laughed.

She laughed. "Grant me a celebratory wish. In honor of not dying."

"Name it."

"Take me back up in the tree - wearing white rabbit suits."

He laughed and laughed and laughed.
"Wish granted!"

She held out her empty cup to him.
He poured for her. She poured for him.
Their eyes met.
Without speaking, they held their cups up and drank.
To life!

*

"Dog, as long as we're into deep water, I have one more question to ask you. It may be the most important question I have. And it's complicated. You may not have an answer - or may not *want* to answer - or may want to think about it and give me an answer later."

"Go ahead," he said.

"We know that Charles Lutwidge Dodgson, age thirty, was enamored of Alice Pleasance Liddell, age ten. As a sign of his love for her, under the name of Lewis Carroll, he wrote *Alice's Adventures in Wonderland* and *Through the Looking-Glass*."

"Right."

"And though she was pretty, she was not particularly creative or intelligent. Not really a special child, except in Dodgson's eyes. His attention to her caused her protective parents to prevent any further contact with him."

"He photographed her at seventeen. She looked unhappy," he said.

"Yes. And that was that. She married. As an adult she had little contact with him. And as she grew older she resented being identified as the Alice in his tale, and only reluctantly acknowledged her connection to the books much later in her life.

"The truth is that Alice Liddell did not resemble the Alice of Wonderland in any way. Whatever the nature of his love for Miss Liddell, the love remained unrequited. She never fulfilled his needs or dreams. Or ever wanted to. And being *Alice* was an embarrassment to her."

"Yes," said Daniels. "She was somehow talked into going to New

York for the centenary celebration of Dodgson's birth. She was eighty by then. But she wasn't happy about going. In the pictures taken of her on that occasion she looks like she's at a funeral."

"Dodgson became Lewis Carroll," said Alice-Alice. "And he became the main character of his books. *He was Alice.* And by now you must realize the parallel. You, David Daniels Doggett, became the Writer. But you, in truth, are Allyson Octavia Riley. *You are Alice.* The Dedication was for her. It's *her* you want to possess. *Yourself.*

(Silence.)

Daniels poured sake for himself and emptied the cup in one swallow.

"What's your question," asked Daniels, staring hard at her.

"It's not really one question. It's more a line of inquiry with several parts. How do you think Charles Dodgson felt about the response of the real Alice? She rejected him for the rest of his life. We know he died a bachelor. Did he come to hate her?

"And how do you think Lewis Carroll felt about his *Alice?* Did he come to love her as himself? Was that enough? I suppose I'm asking about the Dedication - the One-and-Only question, Dog."

She waited, but he said nothing, and finally she went on.

"I'm sorry," she said. "I must sound like an analyst accusing you of narcissism. I don't mean that. But you must admit that what you've written invites that kind of thinking.

"And as long as I'm way out here on a limb, I might as well risk sawing it off. Your answer to why Alice was murdered was interesting, eloquent - very literary. But. You gave me an outer layer of your onion. I'm not saying I don't believe you. I don't mean you were lying to me. I do say you were not telling me the whole truth, Dog. You simply did not answer the deeper question. I'll stop beating around the bush and ask it straight out: Are you . . . or have you been . . . suicidal?"

(Silence.)

"Will my answer make a difference to you?"
"Yes. A big difference."

"I don't know how to . . . where to . . ."
She squeezed his hands ever so tenderly.
"Later," she said. "Or never. Some truths cannot be told."
He smiled. Squeezed back, and said, "And some can," he said.
"Just . . . not . . . now."

The Play (8)

ACT III: Hide and Seek

SCENE 2. When Bunnies Fly

Director's notes:
Evening. Alice-Alice and Daniels are in the tree boats, wearing white rabbit outfits. She will begin with a request. He will improvise off that.

*

"You've never talked to me about trees, Dog. Tell me about trees. Tell me some things that are special to you. Anything."

Relieved that Alice-Alice had not resumed her previous night's questions, Daniels smiled and cleared his throat.

"Where to begin? It's a curious thing to say, but over the years that I've been an arborist, I've come to greatly admire the *action* of a tree. You might not think of a tree as being in action. But it is. A tree is not going anywhere, but it's always in motion - growing up and reaching out - while growing down and on, and always changing."

"And it moves in response to the wind," she said.

"Yes, of course.

"A tree is always in combat too - defending itself from diseases, insects, people, lightning, wind in storms, and fire if need be. Though, like all living things, it's ultimately defeated, it meanwhile sways and bends and heals over its wounds and adapts.

"Balance, adaptation, growth, perseverance. That's what I respect. In trees. And in people.

"This one we're in is called an English oak, but it grows all over Europe, North Africa, and western Asia. *Our* tree was probably brought here as a seedling by ship from England a hundred years ago. With luck, it will last another hundred years - even longer.

"A big tree like this is an ecosystem. Depending on how small you want to think, it supports about five thousand creatures that live on it or in it, or use it. Under a microscope, the life forms are in the zillions.

"We see the birds, of course, and squirrels. Then there are cats, and people like us. And parasites, mites, lichens, galls, molds, complexities of miniscule plant life, bugs like ants and wasps and butterflies and spiders, larva, and on and on. Those are just the most obvious and common tenants. You could spend a lifetime studying and writing the history of the life forms engaged with a single tree. People have. One tree - imagine."

"Keep going," she said. "What else?"

"I spent a summer in England once just so I could visit some of the most famous oaks. Astonishing trees. With astonishing histories."

"Was that when you spent time on a canal boat?"

"Yes. On the Oxford Canal."

"With Alex and Wonko and Alice?"

"They were there with me. And the boat was the *Ariadne*."

"And you ate and drank at The Trout at Godstow?"

"Many a lovely evening - out on the terrace by the river."

"And Crete? Were you there for the trees, too?"

"Actually, yes. I went for a working vacation. There was an international symposium in Heraklion on the cultivation of olive trees. And I had always wanted to see the ruins of Knossos. As you know, the world's oldest olive tree is further west, beyond Hania. I wanted to see that too. To just be in its company. I still have some dried olives and leaves from it I could give you. But you should go to see it for yourself. You'd like Crete."

"You must have stayed for a while."

"Most of the summer. But I've been back several times."

"To see Kostas?"

"Him, and a lot of other friends I've made there."

"So the Cretan Chronicles by Max-Pol Millay were really yours."

"Well, they were based on my experiences."

"What about Japan? Does that involve trees?"

"I went to study bonsai. I haven't shown you my bonsai, but I suppose you're not surprised that I have a collection."

"Like Alex and Zenkichi?"

"Those are my trees."

"And you have a ginkgo?"

"Of course. In fact the ginkgo is my favorite tree. They're living fossils. Unique. And their shape has what the Japanese prize - *sharawadgi* - a pleasing irregularity.

"The finest ginkgo is at the Buddhist temple of Zempukuji. It's the oldest and largest one in Japan, said to have been planted in 1232. My other favorite tree in Japan is at the Shinto shrine of Takeo, about six hundred miles southwest of Tokyo. A huge camphor tree that is said to be three thousand years old - ravaged by storms and age - with a small shrine inside its hollow base. They say you can add a year to your life by walking once around it. I did that."

Alice-Alice was quiet.

"Am I boring you?"

"No, I was just thinking about adding a year to my life. Keep going."

"How about some factoids?" he asked. "Short answers to questions you haven't asked. The General Sherman in Sequoia National Park in California - 274 feet high, 1,500 tons of wood, 55,040 cubic feet of mass. The question is, What's the biggest single living tree in the world?

"The coast redwood in California known as the Stratosphere Giant is 368 feet tall. The question is, What's the tallest living tree in the world?

"One more. A bristlecone pine known as Methuselah - 11,000 feet up in the White Mountains of California - almost 5,000 years old. So stressed by cold and wind that it grows only a few weeks each year. That's tenacity. The question is, What's the oldest living tree in the world?

"Do you believe trees have sprits, Dog?"

He smiled. "Well, as an arborist, not really. My rational mind doesn't. But it's a spiritual experience being around the great trees, especially in Japan. The Japanese believe every living thing has a *kami* - a spirit - especially large old trees. On temple grounds they buy fortunes - *omikuji* - written on small slips of folded paper. If the fortune is favorable, they take it home with them. But if the fortune is not positive, they tie the paper to a branch of the tree, hoping that the power of the kami of the tree will overcome the negative prediction. The tree seems strong enough to handle it. There are so many fortunes tied to the lower branches of some trees it seems like snowfall."

"Dog, have you ever been hurt working in trees?"

"Oh, yeah. Often. It comes with the job. Hands - several fingers broken. I'm missing a nail on one thumb. See? And an index finger still crooked from a fracture I ignored. Lots of cuts and bruises. Both knees wrenched - surgery on both. Shoulder dislocated twice. Concussions. Fell hard twice and broke both wrists trying to catch myself. Two front teeth knocked out - replaced with a bridge. And I once drove the sharp end of a broken branch through my side and into a lung.

"When it's cold my knees are so stiff in the morning I feel like I could use an old man's walker to get around. I had to use a cane for six months once."

"Like Alex. And that's how you knew enough to write about the wounds of Alex and Max-Pol?" she asked.

"And one reason why I've thought about having a full-body tattoo - to cover my scars or make something nice to look at out of them. Like Alice."

"Dog, do you want to tell me about Alice and dying now?"

"Hey, hey, hey!" A little girl was looking up into the tree from the sidewalk across the street and waving.

"Alice, come on," said her mother from further down the street.

She ran to her mother.

"Mommy, there were two big white rabbits up in that tree back there."

"It's just your imagination, Alice. Rabbits don't climb trees."

"But I *saw* them. I *saw* them. I waved at them and they waved back."

"It's like the things you see in dreams at night when you're asleep."

"But I heard them talking."

"Rabbits don't talk, except in dreams."

"But I *saw* them. I *heard* them. Come back and see."

The mother took her child by the hand. "Come on, Alice, we're late. It's just your imagination. What you imagine isn't real."

"It is too," insisted the child.

But as the mother pulled her along, on down the sidewalk, the child kept looking back at what she really imagined she saw. Or at what she really saw that she imagined.

"Did you hear the kid's name?" asked Alice-Alice.

"Alice. What a coincidence," said Daniels.

"And did you hear what her mother said?"

"Yes. 'What you imagine isn't real.' But that's to be expected. The mother is an adult. Adults forget."

(Silence.)

"Are you avoiding my question about Alice and dying, Dog?"

"Yes. To be honest, I am. I *do* have an answer, but it's a long one. Ask me again some other time. I'm very happy right now - up here in the tree with you in our rabbit suits. I don't want to talk about . . . other things. There's a sanity about being up in trees. I'm safely attached up here. And . . ."

"And what, Dog?" she asked.

"I've often fallen. But . . . I would never jump."

"That's an answer to my question," she said.

THE PLAY (9)

Director's perspective:
The spine of this last scene of this last act of the play is *goodbye*. Both characters know they have long-standing obligations in September. Undertones: tension, reluctance, contradictions. Both characters want to prolong the relationship, but they also want to leave well - to go without clumsiness.

ACT III: Hide and Seek

SCENE 3. Farewell

Director's notes:
Morning. Alice-Alice and Daniels meet at Caffe Ladro for coffee and a walk afterwards. He intends to give her a tour of secret places in the Queen Anne neighborhoods. She wants to play Left/Right/Surprise along the way.
Alice and Alex are silent participants barely visible upstage. In the cafe they drink coffee, and Alice-Alice pours the dregs of hers out into her saucer, and swirls it around. She says "Beware the labyrinth," as Polydora did at Patrice's party in Athens. Daniels does not ask for a reading.
Improvise after Daniels asks a question about "the magic."

*

"Turn right," Daniels said when they came out of the coffee shop. "You often use the term 'the magic' when you talk about theater. Give me an answer to a question I haven't asked about the magic."

"Theater depends on illusion," said Alice-Alice. "Theater invites the actors and the audience to suspend literal credibility and become part of the illusion. Make-believe becomes truth. When that happens, that's the magic."

"Right again," he said at the corner. "And keep talking."

Realizing that Daniels was breaking or at least bending the rules of Left/Right/Surprise, Alice-Alice continued. "The audience doesn't want to know *how* it's done; they just want it done *well*. If you go to see a magician, you want to see him pull a rabbit out of an empty hat, and you want his make-believe to appear to be truth," said Alice-Alice.

"Even better if you expect a rabbit and the magician pulls out a duck," said Daniels. "Surprise! That's part of the magic."

"Even better if it's a talking duck," said Alice-Alice.

"Even better if the talking duck claims to be a rabbit," said Daniels.

"Even better if the magician seems as surprised and amazed as the audience because *he* was expecting a rabbit," said Alice-Alice.

"Even better if the duck is wearing a hat, out of which it pulls a smaller rabbit," said Daniels.

"Even better if it's a talking rabbit," said Alice-Alice.

"Even better if the rabbit can talk and explains that *he* is the real magician and the man and the duck work for *him*," said Daniels.

"Yes, yes!" said Alice-Alice, laughing. "And, and . . .?"

They had stopped walking and were standing at an intersection.

Daniels smiled. "Even better if there is *no* theater, *no* stage, *no* magician, *no* duck, *no* rabbit, and *no* audience. You have imagined it all. And if you can imagine all this happening - if you feel like you could have been there, and if you can recall the expressions on the face of the magician, the duck, and the rabbit, then *that's* truly the magic. In you."

"I can't top that," said Alice-Alice.

Daniels continued, "An actress and a writer have the same responsibility: to give the Audience and the Reader the opportunity to imagine and to collaborate. It's always possible - even on unlikely occasions with only a two-person audience - like the throw-and-catch-and-throw conversation we've been having between us. *The magic*. In the Japanese Kabuki tradition it's called *hana* - the flower."

Daniels held out two closed fists, and then slowly opened them like flowers blooming until they were open and empty. He smiled.

Alice-Alice returned his smile. And held out her fists and slowly opened them, as empty as his.

"Turn right again," said Daniels. "There's a sign I want to show you."

They crossed the street.

"The answer to a question you haven't asked is an old, bawdy joke," she said. "An acting teacher told it to illustrate the fine-tuning of an action."

"Tell me the joke," said Daniels.

"Three Frenchmen are arguing about the definition of savoir faire - being cool in an awkward circumstance - grace under pressure.

"The first Frenchman says, 'A man walks into his own bedroom, finds his wife in bed making love to another man, and says, "Oops, please excuse me," and leaves the room. That's savoir faire.'

"'No,' says the second Frenchman. 'A man walks into his own bedroom, finds his wife making love to another man, and says, "Oops, please excuse me, please continue," and leaves the room. That's savoir faire.'

"'Not quite,' says the third Frenchman. 'A man walks into his own bedroom, finds his wife making love to another man, and says, "Oops, please excuse me, please continue, and leaves the room." And if the man in the bedroom can continue, then *he* has savoir faire.'"

Daniels laughed. "I've been that man," he said.

Alice-Alice laughed. "No!" she said. "Never!"

"Imagine it and believe it," he said. "The magic always involves collaboration. I'm reminded of Edward Lear's story about a woman who was a chronic fabulist. She told of being on a ship far out at sea when they spied a man floating along on a large crate of chickens.

"The man was well and properly dressed, complete with a bowler hat. And he had the top of the crate laid out for tea. He waved the ship down, and when they offered to rescue him, he said, calmly, 'Oh, no thank you. I'm having a lovely time. I just need some lemon for my tea.'

"The woman's audience thought her story preposterous. But a nearby gentleman stepped over and said, 'I beg your pardon, but I was that man on the chicken coop. They gave me two lemons.' That's collaboration in the magic."

"Even better if they were talking lemons," said Alice-Alice, trying to keep a straight face.

"Even better if there were a duck and a rabbit having tea with the man on the floating crate," said Daniels, as he pursed his lips to squelch laughter.

"What about the chickens in the crate?" asked Alice-Alice, giggling.

"They were waiting to cross the road," said Daniels.

"Why ... did ... they want to ... cross ... the road," said Alice-Alice, but she hardly finished the sentence before she and Daniels began laughing at the unrelenting perseverance of their loony improvisation.

They were not laughing at their cleverness. They were laughing because they had crossed beyond the Magic into Delight - and were unwilling to retreat back through the looking-glass of Wonderland.

They realized they had been standing still at an intersection.

"Weren't we supposed to be playing Left/Right/Surprise?" she asked.

"I guess we've done that without moving or calling the directions. It's mental. And I haven't told you much about secret places either," he said.

"Dog, the truth is I didn't come expecting to play games or laugh much. And I wasn't really all that interested in secrets, either," she said.

"Because?"

"Because I've come to say I'm leaving. Not goodbye. I know you don't like goodbyes. But I am leaving. I've got to go. I'm booked back east for the fall."

"Well," said Daniels. "If you want to know the truth, you only just beat me out the door."

"Because?"

"In September I'm scheduled for a long trip to Japan. Plans made a year ago. I have some speaking commitments at a symposium of arborists, and I've arranged to visit some famous bonsai collections, and to tour sites of groves of sacred trees. And ... I thought ... I thought I might finish my novel along the way."

"Do you know how it ends?"

"I think ... I'm almost there."

"I know how it ends."

"Really?"

"Come sit down on that bench over there, and I'll tell you."

*

"First, I want to finish this round of Left/Right/Surprise in a different way. I'll answer a question you have already *asked*, though you didn't ask me personally. Still, I have an answer."

"And the question?"

"It's the one at the end of the chapter called 'The Feast of Saint Precarious' - after Alice is killed. You asked 'And then what happened? What became of everybody?'"

"And you know?"

"You gave the reader permission to know. You wrote, 'You can only imagine.' And I have."

Daniels looked away.

He did not know what happened. Not yet. And he could leave it hanging if he had to. He did not have to say or write it. But in truth, he did not *want* to know. Because he did not want the stories of those characters to end. Not ever. That is one reason he had stopped writing. Another, even more vexing question blocked his way: *What will become of me when the novel ends?*

"This is going to take awhile," said Alice-Alice. Before I tell you what happened, I'll sing you a song I've been working on for the past few weeks. It's about Left/Right/Surprise. I wish I had my guitar with me, but this is the right time for the song. We might not play the game together again for a long time. The song is finished. Open one hand, close your eyes, and listen." Softly, her eyes fixed on his face, she sang:

> Open your hand
> Show me your palm
> Left Right Surprise
> Put it next to mine
> The lifelines could be twice as long
> Left Right Surprise
>
> Bad things happen
> Good things can too
> Left Right Surprise

Alice loved Alex
I could love you
Left Right Surprise

Love me moving,
If you love me still
Love always will
Go Left Right Surprise

All the ways we break
All the ways we mend
Left Right Surprise
Here's where we start
Who knows where we'll end
Left Right Surprise

First we go this way
Then we go that
Left Right Surprise
Not every story reads
From the front to the back
Left Right Surprise

Love me moving
If you love me still
Love always will
Go Left Right Surprise.

AND THEN WHAT HAPPENED?

When Alice-Alice's song was finished, Daniels remained still, his hand open palm up on his knee, his eyes closed.

"Now I'll tell you what happened to everybody," she said.

He remained still and silent - and eyes still closed.

"Dog, would you rather I not . . .?"
He opened his eyes and looked away.
"No, it's just that . . . that . . . I don't know . . ."

"Let me put it another way. I'll tell you what happened in the novel that is mine."
Dog nodded and looked back. "OK. Tell me that."

"I'll begin with Zenkichi. As an actress, I identified with him. He was an actor to his core. He went back to Japan. He chose to live the life that had chosen him: Kabuki. Zenkichi was the least surprised at Alice's sudden death. It seemed a very Japanese ending to him - sudden, sacrificial, and sad. Evanescent.

"For several years afterwards, Zenkichi went to Uji on a rainy night in midsummer to stand on the Bridge of Dreams. Each time, he took an umbrella with him - the best - traditional Japanese oiled paper and bamboo. He had the maker write on it - in kanji - two names: Vin-cen-zo and Scarlett.

"Zenkichi reenacted the scene of The Great Uji Bridge Hiccup and Laughing Festival. He remembered all the lines. He danced Alice's rain dance. When he got to the hiccup part, he put on his red rubber nose, tossed the umbrella into the air over the river, watched it fall into the water and float away toward the sea. Every time he played the scene he went away laughing, with tears in his eyes."

"I like that," said Daniels. "Keep going."

"Morioka. When Zenkichi told him of Alice's fate, he took the drawing he had made for Alice's tattoo and wrote her name across it in English – 'Alice' – and then he slowly tore it into small pieces and burned them. He ground the ashes into powder, mixed the powder with a little water, and with the ink he wrote a haiku on a fine piece of paper that would be mounted on a scroll and given to Zenkichi."

"What did the haiku say?" asked Daniels.

"I don't know Japanese or haiku. What would you suggest?"

"Hmmm. . . my Japanese isn't good, but this is close enough:

kare-eda ni
karasu no tomaritaru ya
aki no kure

on a barren branch
a raven has come to settle . . .
autumn dusk

"Basho. Seventeenth century. The haiku serves as a period at the end of an unspoken paragraph about evanescence. Alice knew it by heart," said Daniels. He bowed his head and closed his eyes again.

You loved her. You loved the Alice in you.
Alice-Alice thought that. She did not say it. She waited.

Daniels looked up, his eyes shining with tears.
"Continue," he said.

"Wonko. That's so easy. Of course he took up with the Contessa Macaroni. They were made for each other. Who could miss it? They went back to England to live on his canal boat. She became a fortune-teller in his troupe – complete with a small tent and crystal ball – and she kept writing her novel. But she never finished it. She was too absorbed in living it.

"Wonko gave up working for security services. For the first time in his life, security wasn't on his mind. The Contessa took care of security. She was 'home' to him."

Daniels smiled. Alice-Alice continued.

"Wonko and the Contessa didn't live happily ever after; 'happily' is an inadequate word. They lived a Wonderland life: often taking tea at the Mad Hatter's party, messing about in boats, making music and love with equal intensity.

"And Wonko's greatest wish was granted. The Contessa was the dancing partner of his dreams. They became famous all over Oxfordshire for their dancing. Anywhere, anytime, any music.

"Tonight they're at a fair in Glastonbury. When the dancing is over and they get home, Wonko will take out his fiddle to play a waltz he wrote just for her."

Daniels applauded. "You nailed it. That's *exactly* why they're in the novel. For all the pain and sorrow and tragedy of this life, it *has* to be - it *must be* - that *somewhere, somebody* gets joy and delight in the end. There must be dancing."

(Pause.)

"What happened to the General and his Lady - Hans and Winifred?"

"I was just about to tell you. Hans bought Alex's canal boat, and Winifred bought a small cottage in a village in the Cotswolds, and they lived both together and apart. He was free to run his one-ship navy on the canals and go hiking with his friends, and she was free to garden and go bird-watching with hers. Distance and separation and compromise made their companionship work. As for their foibles and habits, they got used to those, as Alex had predicted. They were contented.

"And they became close friends with Wonko and the Contessa. Many times the four walked together across Port Meadow to The Trout, talking about Alex and Alice and Max-Pol, and retelling stories of days gone by. They even went to the wishing well at Binsey together."

"I like this - keep going," said Daniels.

"Often Wonko brought his fiddle. Once, walking home in the light of a full moon, Wonko struck up "Green, Green" and waltzed with The Contessa at the same time - not touching - bound in perfect step by the invisible tie between them. Hans and Winifred joined them. And that's where my novel leaves them. They don't exit the stage. The light fades slowly to blackout. The music continues. They dance on."

"Lovely," said Daniels. "You're good."

"I hope something as fine happened to Kostas too. It should. Did it?"

"You anticipate me. A Greek-American woman weaver, Johanna, came into his shop one afternoon and came back the next afternoon and the next. She's still there. She wove Kostas into her life. They bought an old house in the countryside and restored it. Johanna uses it as a studio for her art, weaving museum-quality copies of Cretan dowry blankets. Kostas sells them in his shop. I imagine him saying to customers, 'Is be new something and old something - all together, you know. Is be fine.'"

*

Alice-Alice had been wary about using the word "love" in recounting what happened even to the happy-ending people in her stories, because Daniels's view of love in his novel seemed so consciously cautious.

She was sure it was not because he thought so little of love, but because he expected too much of it. His idea of love was far too large and ambitious, she thought. For him, love was a shining, gold-plated dwelling that real people could not live in.

For Alice-Alice, love was a fugitive thing - mostly a fleshy, sweaty matter of muscle and blood and hard work, not butterflies and flowery words. For her, love waxed and waned, came and went, lived and died, and rose up again - and yet again.

She thought all those big words caused trouble: Love, God, Beauty, Truth, Art, Happiness. She thought people who wrote about those ideals were chasing rainbows. The people who were busy loving or worshiping gods or making beautiful things or painting or singing or acting were getting a taste of happiness, and were too occupied with what they were living to think about or talk about ideals.

But the Alice of *Third Wish* understood that. She knew what Monet was about: process and space. Puzzle: It was Daniels who wrote it that way. A contradiction in Daniels's character? Well, of course. Why not? He just wrote it. He didn't necessarily understand what he was writing about.

Alice-Alice thought Daniels probably did not fully comprehend the meaning of the balcony scene in *Romeo and Juliet*. The power of the scene is not in the grand feelings of the lovers, but in the presence of the *balcony*.

If the young man and young woman were standing together talking on the stage, the scene would not be memorable. It is the distance, the barrier - the obstacle of the balcony, and the tension of the desire to bridge the gap - that give power to the scene. Always reaching for something - seldom if ever having it. No balcony, no love story. So Alice-Alice believed.

*

"What about Polydora and Maria? And the baby?" asked Daniels.

Alice-Alice gave him her "men-are-only-men" look.

"I saw that," he said. "Come on, tell me."

"There was no baby. Oh, sure, Polly did sleep with Max-Pol. But only once. And she didn't get pregnant. She did get something straight in her mind: Sex with a man wasn't what she wanted." Alice-Alice grinned. "He was good enough in bed though; just not good enough for her."

"So she went back to Athens and Maria?" asked Daniels.

"Yes, and though it took awhile for the wounds of their conflict to heal, their relationship was stronger in the end. They explored some other options for having a child - using Maria's brother's sperm, for example. But it didn't happen, and, in time, childbearing became a non-issue. Polly's stormy hormonal sea calmed.

"The two women became godmothers to the children of friends and were brilliant at it. And they were both caught up in the provocative world of Patrice and his salon of musicians and artists. Life is still good for Polydora and Maria. They're off to a party at Patrice's apartment as we speak. Exit stage left, through the door marked Cabaret."

"Excellent. That's exactly the way I would have it," said Daniels. "And . . . since you've touched on babies - now I'd like to know . . ."

"About India-What?" said Alice-Alice.

"Yes."

(Silence.)

"I don't know. I really don't know. I can't make up my mind. She was pregnant. But did she have Max-Pol's baby? Did Sergio know? Did Max-Pol? And what became of the child? Comedy or Tragedy? Another novel could be written out of that. Or maybe she had a miscarriage.

"End of story. I just don't know. But not every loose thread must be tied up. And tell me if I'm wrong, Dog, but you don't know either, do you?"

"No."

"I do know what happened to Max-Pol." said Alice-Alice.

"Tell me."

"After taking care of what needed to be done for Alice and Alex - and I'll come to that - Max-Pol joined Doctors Without Borders, an organization bringing basic medical care to difficult places like Haiti and Rwanda - where people's needs are a little more complicated than colds and headaches.

"I'd like to think that somehow along the way - perhaps in Seattle - he connected with Jacks O'Rourke. That's a credible possibility given their relationship with Alice."

"Good," said Daniels. "I hadn't thought of that. And what about Jacks O'Rourke?"

"Nothing much changed. He was one of those lucky people who dig deep into the soil of themselves and put down roots and grow. He spent the rest of his life giving away the fruits of his tree."

"That's too vague. I want to know more about Jacks O'Rourke."

"Sorry, I wasn't that interested in him, to tell the truth," she said.

"But I was," he said. "He's important to me."

"Then you'll have to include the details in *your* novel."

"I will. Go on and tell me about what happened to Max-Pol."

"Well, as for Max-Pol, it was always clear to me that his quest was for himself. And that he would only find himself when he gave himself away. Classic story line. But valid. Happens. It's the Schweitzer model. And also very Buddhist - by letting go, you achieve your Way. Max-Pol finally became the physician only he could be. Before that he finished what he had to do for Alice and Alex, but that's getting ahead of the story - I'll come to that."

"But what finally happened to Max-Pol?"

"You might not like this, but in my novel he was killed in Rwanda when he stepped on a land mine while trying to rescue a baby abandoned in a field. Blown to pieces. The baby had been left there on purpose as bait for some do-good foreigner. Outrageous turn of fate, but that's what happened. Exit Max-Pol."

Daniels was silent, head bowed again.
"No," he murmured. "I don't want it that way."

"It's what happened," said Alice-Alice. "Evil is real. You can't leave evil out - not even in fiction."

*

There were two characters to go: Alex and Alice.
In a way, Alice would be easier.

"The rest of Alice's story isn't very dramatic," said Alice-Alice. "For all the eccentric uniqueness of her life, what happened after her death was mundane - because she had no say in the matter.

"She had never expressed any wishes on the subject to anyone. So when she died the disposal of her remains was a matter of law. Her mother was her next of kin. At her request, Alice's body was embalmed, placed in a coffin, and returned to Seattle.

"Max-Pol spoke with the mother, but she knew little about Alice's life or friends or what they might wish; he didn't try to enlighten her. He knew Alice would say she didn't care.

"So Alice was cremated, and her ashes were put in a plain, metal urn that was placed in the family's columbarium vault alongside her father. In a cemetery in Seattle."

"The one up here on Queen Anne Hill?"

"Yes. And this pleased Max-Pol, because he would come to Seattle at times and could pay his respects to Alice without ever having to deal with her family. Besides, Max-Pol knew the best part of Alice was buried with Alex."

(Silence.)

"Alex died? How? When?" asked Daniels. "I mean, I know he will – he has to – but I haven't addressed his death in *my* novel. What happens in yours?"

*

"After the assault, Alex was in the hospital overnight. All he wanted to know was if he had any broken bones. No, but his blood pressure was dangerously high. The doctors wanted to keep him for more tests because they were pretty sure he had more serious health problems that needed attention and treatment.

"But Alex already knew the machinery of his body was wearing out. He was old and weak. Nevertheless, his mind was clear and he had enough energy to do what he wanted to do next. He refused to ride out of the hospital in a wheelchair. When he limped down the front steps, he was whistling his marching song."

Daniels said, "You're off in territory I've avoided. I'm torn between wanting you to stop and wanting you to go on."

"This is *my* novel, remember?" said Alice-Alice.

"Continue, then."

"That very evening, Alex dressed in his best suit and shirt and tie. He had often said he kept moving so Death wouldn't know where he was most of the time. Now he dressed for an appointment with Death.

"Alex had a taxi drive him from Hania to the beach at Kolymbari. He walked the beach in the last light of day, picking up black-and-white striped stones and tossing them into the surf and watching them disappear.

"With his walking cane he drew a large labyrinth in the damp sand, and placed his cane in the center. He put on his red rubber nose and walked right across the pattern of the labyrinth as he had seen Alice do on that day in Somerton. There were other Ways than following the traditional design.

"Shall I go on?" asked Alice-Alice.

Daniels said nothing.

Yes, she thought.

"Slowly, Alex waded into the sea. Slowly. Farther and farther and further. When the water was waist deep, the bottom dropped off steeply, and he was afloat. He began swimming. With all the strength he had left, he stroked on out to sea.

"Surprised at how long he managed to keep swimming, but feeling his strength draining away, he decided to stroke out the number of years in his life. *One . . . two . . . three . . .* When he reached eighty, his legs and arms cramped from the cold. Exhausted. Used up. Finally at the end of the rope of his life."

"He smiled. He let go," said Daniels.
"Yes."

(Silence.)

"And then . . .?" asked Daniels.

"His body was never found," said Alice-Alice. "But his red rubber nose washed up on the beach at Kolymbari. It's still there under some driftwood. Exit Alexandros Evangelou Xenopouloudakis, center stage."

(Silence.)

"What did Max-Pol do then?" asked Daniels.

"He took the komboloi Alex had given him to the Commonwealth Cemetery at Souda Bay - the komboloi that had once belonged to John Pendlebury."

Daniels sat up, picking up the story: "He read the words on Pendlbury's tombstone: '*He has outsoared the shadow of our night.*' And he buried the komboloi there."

"Yes. And then he pronounced a benediction. You know it."
"Yes."
And slowly they said the words together:

Jumwillies, Jumwillies, all in a row.

Jumwillies rain, Jumwillies snow.

Jumwillies come and Jumwillies go.

And nobody knows what the Jumwillies know.

(Silence.)

"Is that the end of your story – the end of the play – the end of your novel?" asked Daniels.

"It is.
"The light fades to black.
"Curtain."

EPILOGUE

"Come," said Alice-Alice, "let's walk. I'm tired of sitting."

They stood, she took his arm, and they walked on.

"Playwrights and novelists sometimes add an epilogue, even though it is not always meant to be part of the play or story," said Daniels. "There's an Epilogue to your story; I've already written it in my novel."

"I bet I know, but you tell me," said Alice-Alice.

"It's about that time on the beach at Kolymbari where Alice tells Alex the story about the woman who came in the boat to claim three wishes," said Daniels.

"Yes," said Alice-Alice. "That's it."

"She came because she had wished for a boat, a journey, and to see the king. And she was weeping because her wishes were used up, and the people told her that she had been deceived. Or perhaps she had deceived herself. But all was not lost. Actually, she was only misguided about the nature of wishing."

"And she asks the people, 'What do you mean?'" said Alice-Alice.

"And she was told, 'Long ago we stopped making normal wishes. We found they only led to trouble and disappointment. Especially when employed in threes. Now we trust only *retroactive* wishes.'"

"Retroactive wishes?" asked Alice-Alice, reciting her line.

And Daniels recited, "Yes. When you find yourself in a fine place having a fine time, you might remember a time when your life was awful, and how back then you would have wished you were here. But you *are* here now. Look around you. It's a wonderful place to be. What you have is exactly what you would have wished for, if you had known. A *retroactive wish* come true."

"And you, Dog, if you had wished that your imagination would remain a fire to keep you warm as long as you live, then you have that," said Alice-Alice.

"Yes."

Taking his hand in hers, she said, "Dog, there's an unfinished piece of business. You promised to tell me."

"About me and the death of Alice . . . and suicide?"

"Yes. I really want to know. It's important to me," she said.

They walked straight on - turning neither left nor right.

"Then, I'll tell you. I *have* thought a lot about death. You might say that I came into this world with a flawed gene - a predisposition for mental cancer. There's a crack in that gene - one that admits the corrosive acid of despair. There was a long period in my life when I . . . was suicidal.

"My response was anger - rage - because the desire to end my life contrasted so clearly with the fine quality of the life I actually had. The absurd tension between 'My life is good,' and 'I want destroy myself,' was often disabling. I would get stuck - unable to function - for days."

"Oh, Dog," she said, dropping his hand, and putting her arm around his waist. He put his arm on her shoulder and continued.

"Like you, I incorporated the flaw into my life's script. I got used to living with the idea of self-destruction. And I used my anger to forge a way around that inclination and go on. A comment from the Stoic philosopher, Seneca, stuck in my mind as a kind of traffic director around suicide: *"Any life is long, if you know how to use it."*

Oh, said Alice-Alice to herself. *That's the rest of my mantra,* she thought. *Not how long, but how wide and deep. Any life is long if you know how to use it.*

She squeezed his waist and pulled herself closer to him.

"Keep going," she said, "I'm with you."

"When the demon of despair grabs the wheel, I've learned to read back through my journals and remind myself that I've been in this place before, survived, and found a way to continue."

"And now?" she asked.

"As I've matured and endured, I've stopped thinking about suicide. Self-destruction doesn't stalk me. But I do think about *not being.*

"On the front page of my journal is this loose translation from the

Meditations of Marcus Aurelius:

> *Be not perturbed.*
> *For all things are according to the nature of the universal.*
> *And in a little time you will be no-one and no-where.*
> *(You have been there before.)*
> *No problem.*

"For years, each time I've started a new volume of my journals, I've copied those words onto the front page.

"The question now is this: Since everyone must become no-one in no-where, what will determine that journey for me? Accident? Fate? Old age? Or is it up to me to determine when enough is enough?

"Remember my telling you about the mirror in my garden? It's odd, but when I show it to other people, they laugh nervously, acknowledging the illusion of the door. But they keep their distance. I often walk right up to it. I know I could go on through. It's not an illusion for me.

"Beyond that mirror I have a lovely cottage in the country by a river. The sun is always shining. The land is always green. The river flows on forever. I'm not afraid to walk through the mirror into that place.

"That's naïve, I suppose. *Through the Looking-Glass* reminds me that the world beyond the looking-glass may be just as confusing and bizarre as life on this side."

Alice-Alice stopped, let go of his waist, caught hold of his hand, stepped back to look him in the face, and asked, "What . . . keeps you . . . here?"

(Silence.)

"Something as simple as curiosity sometimes. An obligation to finish a job in the trees. Often it's the smallest thing - something lovely or exciting or funny carries the day. A moment of surprise. An unexpected possibility. And once in a great while, a person . . ."

(Silence.)

Daniels took her other hand in his and faced her.

402

"Do you remember when Lewis Carroll's Alice met the unicorn?" he asked.

"Yes. Each thought the other did not exist."

"That's right. The unicorn said, 'Well, now that we have *seen each other*, if you'll believe in me, I'll believe in you. Is that a bargain?'"

"Once they've *seen* each other, imaginary beasts and itinerant little girls should keep in touch," Alice-Alice said. "Their continued existence may depend on it."

"Don't worry. The Second Law of Magic and Motion applies: Things once in contact with one another continue to affect one another - even at a great distance. You and I . . ."

"Always," she said.

Daniels turned Alice-Alice away from him, dropped her hands, and put his arm around her shoulder. She slipped her arm around his waist. And, as they had the night they met, they walked on in silence.

CURTAIN CALL

They had been walking aimlessly without speaking.

They had talked for a long time. So much had been said.

Now their wells of words were almost dry. By unspoken direction, they had finally come around to the driveway of Daniels's house - almost exactly where they had met that first night. They stood still.

"I brought two things to give you," said Alice-Alice. From her jacket pocket she took a very small wooden box. "Open it."

Inside the box was a brown-and-black-and-white striped feather tied with a single strand of white hair. Carefully, Daniels lifted it out of the box.

"I found it caught in the branches when I was climbing way out beyond the tree boat. Do you remember that day? You were belaying me, but I unhooked and was free-climbing for a while. I was never so scared, or ever felt so brave and free, in my life."

"I remember," said Daniels.

"Someday, somewhere - at some high and windy place - let the feather go. Promise?"

"I promise," he said. He replaced the feather in the box, closed the lid, and put the box in his coat pocket.

"And I also have this," she said. From her other jacket pocket, she produced a small tangle of colored strings. "This is a miniature quipu - like the Incas once made.

"As Alice might say, some cords represent a truth that cannot be told. Some are promises that must never be kept. And some are questions that must never be asked. Secrets.

"The knots in the cords are my shadows, cast when I was caught somewhere between Fear and Delight. I entrust these secrets and my shadows to your care."

(Silence.)

"The only response I can make is to give you this." From his coat pocket, he took out a small, scarlet drawstring bag. "This bag is the one you gave me with the wishbones in it. Now it's yours again," he said. "Open it."

Inside the bag Alice-Alice found a small, round, pebbly-skinned orange container.

"I made it from the skin of the tangerine we shared," he said. "I scraped away the pith and dried the skin over a pillbox. Be careful when you open it - it's fragile."

Oh-so-slowly Alice-Alice pulled apart the two halves of the box. Inside was a perfect acorn - brown cap and green body.

"I wanted to give you our tree," he said. "The whole thing, just as it is, with all the memories it holds for both of us. The Tree of Sanctuary and Astonishment. But that's impossible. Still, everything the tree *is* - all its *possibles* - is in that acorn it produced. You could plant it somewhere, sometime. And have your own tree."

"No," said Alice-Alice. "I only want the tree I can imagine."

"Shall we leave it at that?" he asked.

Alice-Alice's eyes flooded with tears.

She removed her white wig, ran her fingers through her short hair, and looked up at Daniels.

She wanted to say, but could only think, *Oh, darling Dog.*

As actors who know their exit lines, with perfect timing, each turned and walked away. Onward.

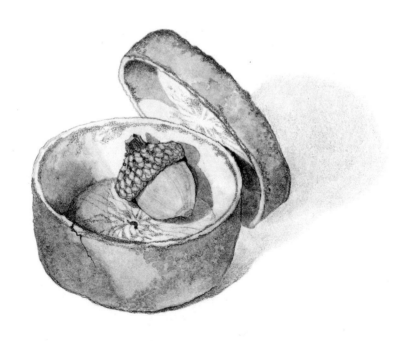

ENCORE

A week later, Daniels received this long letter:

> It's midnight. I cannot sleep. On reflection, I realize I do have something more to say to you, but not in person.
>
> This is a curtain call in the spirit of the speech made by Rosalind in "As You Like It." I come now to the very edge of the stage of our play-within-a-play to bid you goodnight. Imagine me in the footlights, speaking from a place in my heart that contains the Alice of Wonderland, the Alice you created, the Alice I played, and the Alice-Alice I am.
>
> In my world - the theater - being cast in a play is to commit to an alternative life. I read a script, audition, meet the director and other actors, rehearse for a few weeks, live the part onstage at the edge of intensity, and bring my truth to bear on make-believe.
>
> Regardless of how strong the show is, no matter how fine the actors perform, no matter how long the show runs, there will be a last performance.
>
> An audience usually sees the production of a play once. And no matter how much they enjoy the show, it ends for them too. There is a curtain call where the actors are seen momentarily in transition from the part they played and the person they really are. Smile. Bow. Smile. Bow. Curtain. It's over. Only the memories remain.
>
> We are at that final curtain now, dear Dog.

I came to you in response to your novel. By the time I finished reading, I had lived my way into the story. The Dedication was a casting call for me. I auditioned for a role I wanted. I did not come to be your One and Only. I came only to be the One for the Time Being. I did not come to love you or fall in love with you or be your true love. I came to act the part. To bring life to the word.

And you cast me in the part. I asked to be the director, and you let me. Never has a role been more challenging to me. Never have I been more satisfied with my art. To say that I am grateful to you is the feeblest understatement I have ever made in my life.

My version of your novel is also finished. It ended the way I wanted it to end: with Alice alive. As alive as Rosalind or Ophelia or Juliet or any other woman who lives on the stage and in the imaginations of all those Witnesses in the theater. In me, in you, in your other readers, Alice lives on.

And I wanted the Writer to live on as well.

But our show has finished its run.

A story should have a beginning, a middle, and an end. In the theater it doesn't have to be in that order. It's hard to say where the curtain has come down - middle or end? But it has come down.

Shakespeare, as always had the last, best word. From "The Tempest":

"Our revels now are ended. These our actors,
As I foretold you, were all spirits, and
Are melted into air, into thin air."

410

The only lasting quarrel I have with your novel is the part when you have India-What demolish Max-Pol's notion of the Witness. What Max-Pol lost track of was <u>being</u> a Witness as well as <u>having</u> a Witness. It's a reciprocal need. The Witness is a powerful idea, Dog. Keep it active.

I have been your Witness and you have been mine.

We have seen each other. And are guardians of that.

Nobody knows what the Jumwillies know.

And that brings me to an answer to a question you never asked. Emily in Thornton Wilder's "Our Town" at the Yale Repertory. The question is "What is the most important role I ever played in the theater?"

It was my first professional performance, and one never forgets that. At the time I thought it was an uncomplicated play with simple characters.

Wrong. For one thing, Wilder's play is radical theater - no sets or scenery - stage and ideas pared down to bare bones to illuminate the most ordinary acts and conversations. Wilder said, "The play is an attempt to find a value above all price for the smallest events in our daily life."

Emily dies and sits in the graveyard watching the living as they go about the little events that make up their existence. She wants to go back for one day, and the Stage Manager allows her to. She watches as the busyness absorbs the beauty. Finally, she decides to go back to the dead because she can't bear that people don't have time to look at one another - to really see one another. She says:

"I didn't realize. So all that was going on and we never noticed!"

And then she asks the Stage Manager: "Do any human beings ever realize life while they live it - every, every minute?"

And he says, "No - Saints and poets maybe - they do some."

And I would add actors and writers to the list - we realize life too. You and I have noticed each other. We have realized an episode of our lives.

Longer lasting than a love affair.

This unrelenting paying of attention - this tireless curiosity - can be exhausting. As the Stage Manager says, "The strain's so great that every sixteen hours everybody lies down and gets a rest."

As I told you, I'm booked for the fall. By the time you read this, I will be in Connecticut, playing one life on the stage each evening and playing another as guest teacher at the Yale Drama School. Then I'm signed up to take some classes in New York. I can't imagine writing a novel, but I can imagine writing plays and directing. It's the next phase of my life.

Will we ever see each other again? Perhaps.

I'm writing the play now in my mind. I already have a title for it: "Lost and Found in the Circus."

As for your version of your novel, well, as you have written, only you can imagine that. But you will know what to do. You have already outlined it as Alex's poem at the beginning of

Third Wish - "Instructions for Wayfarers." It is a thread to follow in and out of your labyrinth. I know it by heart. In fact, I made a song out of it - my version. It's one of the songs on the CD included with this letter. Here are the words to my version of your Dedication:

> They will declare: Every journey's been taken.
> But I have not been to see myself.
> They will insist: Everything's been spoken.
> But it was spoken by somebody else.
>
> (Chorus)
> You are the gate, the gatekeeper too.
> Not every road is straight,
> Not every dream comes true.
> Walk on. Walk on through . . .
>
> They will tell you: "Everything's been done."
> Tell them, "My way is not complete."
> It's not how long is the journey of life,
> But how wide and deep.
>
> Bad luck might wait just around the corner.
> I can hear them now, "Don't say we didn't warn her."
> Walk on. Walk on through . . .
>
> (Bridge)
> You are warned: any road is long.
> You are warned: any road is hard.
> There's a boatload of good advice
> It's just better to disregard.

The fruit is out on the limb;
You've got to go and get it.
Fear of the fall will kill you if you let it.
Walk on. Walk on through . . .

(Chorus)
You are the gate, the gatekeeper, too.
Not every road is straight,
Not every dream comes true.
Walk on. Walk on through . . .

You, dear Dog, have written your retroactive wish.
I have revised it.
By the power you invested in me, Third Wish Granted.
Onward!

All the Alices - Witnesses, all

*

Daniels read the letter over and over again while listening to the recording Alice-Alice had sent along with her letter - until he knew her songs by heart.

In the late afternoon of an elegant day at summer's end, he went out into his yard and walked slowly, deliberately, to stand facing the mirror attached to the garden wall.

The last verse of Lewis Carroll's poem "Jabberwocky" came to him.

He recited to his image in the mirror:

"And hast thou slain the Jabberwock?
Come to my arms, my beamish boy!
Oh frabjous day! Callooh! Callay!
He chortled in his joy."

And then the first verse:

> *"'Twas brillig, and the slithy toves*
> *Did gyre and gimble in the wabe;*
> *All mimsy were the borogoves,*
> *And the mome raths outgrabe."*

He waved to himself and, laughing, turned away from the mirror.

And went inside to write.

To finish his novel, he needed an actress and a Witness.

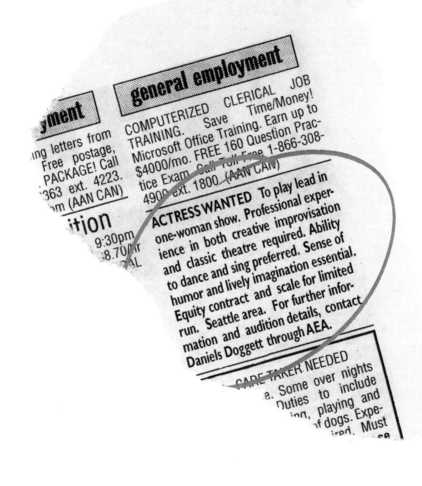

general employment

ng letters from
Free postage,
PACKAGE! Call
363 ext. 4223.
m (AAN CAN)

ition

9:30pm
8.70/r
AL

COMPUTERIZED CLERICAL JOB
TRAINING. Save Time/Money!
Microsoft Office Training. Earn up to
$4000/mo. FREE 160 Question Prac-
tice Exam. Call Toll Free 1-866-308-
4900 ext. 1800. (AAN CAN)

ACTRESS WANTED To play lead in
one-woman show. Professional experience in both creative improvisation
and classic theatre required. Ability
to dance and sing preferred. Sense of
humor and lively imagination essential.
Equity contract and scale for limited
run. Seattle area. For further information and audition details, contact
Daniels Doggett through AEA.

CARE TAKER NEEDED
e. Some over nights
Duties to include
ng, playing and
f dogs. Expe-
red. Must